The Hundredth Queen Series
Book Three

EMILY R. KING

This is a work of fiction. Names, characters, organizations, places, events, and incidents are either products of the author's imagination or are used fictitiously. Any resemblance to actual persons, living or dead, or actual events is purely coincidental.

Published by Skyscape, New York

www.apub.com

Amazon, the Amazon logo, and Skyscape are trademarks of Amazon.com, Inc., or its affiliates.

ISBN-13: 9781542048347
ISBN-10: 1542048346

Cover design by Jason Blackburn

Printed in the United States of America

For Joseph, Julian, Danielle, and Ryan.
Your names are in my book, front and center.
Happy now?
Love, Mom

AUTHOR'S NOTE

The religion of the Tarachand Empire, the Parijana faith, is a fictional variation derived from Sumerian deities. However, the Parijana faith and the Tarachand Empire and other empires do not directly represent any specific historical time period, creed, or union. Any other religious or governmental similarities are coincidental and do not depict actual people or events.

1

Kalinda

The burial starts at daybreak, before the heat of the jungle evaporates the dew and suffocates the morning breeze. Our solemn group congregates in the stern of the riverboat and watches Deven and Yatin finish tying heavy stones to the body's ankles and wrists. Indah has already washed the deceased in almond oil, a ritual in her homeland, the Southern Isles. Pons, her beloved guard, helped her wrap the departed with white bedsheets.

Natesa slips her arm around my waist. I hold on to her, shifting my weight off my sore leg. Prince Ashwin stands to the side, his head down, but I can still see his red eyes and nose.

Deven straightens slowly, as though every part of him aches. I recognize that feeling, that sinking heaviness like quicksand. Everyone aboard moves with the same cumbersome slowness, as though we are all tied down by millstones.

The rush of the River Ninsar fills the silence. If only life could be as constant as a river. Although I believe death is not the end and our spirits live on, I am never fully prepared for life to dry up.

Deven bows his head and offers our traditional Prayer of Rest. "Gods, bless Brother Shaan's soul so that he may find the gate that leads to peace and everlasting light."

Yesterday afternoon, I found Brother Shaan slumped over in his chair outside the wheelhouse. For the past fortnight, since we fled the city of Iresh, he prayed diligently for the gods to preserve us in this dire time. Indah said his heart merely failed, as aged hearts do. But I think his fear put him in an early grave.

Deven finishes by adding his thoughts. "Brother Shaan was a dedicated, loyal, and loving member of the Brotherhood. He exemplified the five godly virtues in every way and served Anu with his whole heart." His ragged voice catches. "He will be missed."

Yatin, his brother-in-arms, squeezes Deven's shoulder. The soldiers slide the body to the edge of the skiff. Pons helps them push the remains overboard, and the water splashes in finality.

Tears sting my eyes. The body floats for a heart-wrenching beat, and then the stones drag Brother Shaan below the surface of the murky river.

"Enki," Indah says, praying to the water-goddess. "Send your sea dragons to ferry Brother Shaan's soul to the Beyond and wash away any memory of pain or anguish from this mortal life."

Her burial prayer is unusual to us Tarachandians, who worship the sky-god Anu. Indah's people believe sacred creatures of the deep, sea dragons, ferry their souls to the Beyond or the Void when they die. In this moment, when we cannot stop to dig a grave for Brother Shaan, as is our custom, her words are a much-needed comfort.

Pons is the first to leave, going to oversee our navigators, the pole pushers. I should rest my injured leg, but I linger near Deven. The river leads us along, and the place where Brother Shaan sank drifts away in our shallow wake. A mangrove forest crowds the riverbanks, thriving in the brackish wetlands between the rain forest and the Sea of Souls. The tree roots, partially submerged in the muddy waters, ascend from the surface like knobby stilts. We are nearly to the river delta. Brother Shaan was so close to viewing the sea . . .

Yatin steps to Natesa's other side. "Are you all right, little lotus?"

She runs her hand down his chest. "Yes." Her burly soldier with a thick beard came aboard the skiff very ill. Indah, the most experienced Aquifier aboard, cured Yatin's ailment, and Natesa has finished nursing him back to health. Yatin slimmed down while he was unwell, though he is still the biggest man on board. We were so concerned about his recovery and my tournament injuries, we neglected to care for Brother Shaan.

We all bear the weight of that guilt.

Natesa and Yatin take the walkway around the side of the boat. Ashwin has left, having snuck off when no one was watching. He and I have not spoken since Iresh. I spend my time with Deven—and Ashwin avoids us. This was the closest the three of us have been in days.

Indah comes to my side. "Kalinda, it's time."

Given the solemnness of the morning, I consider canceling our session, but Indah's healing powers are the only reason I can stand right now.

Deven has yet to look away from the river. I consoled him the best I could last night, but Brother Shaan was his mentor. Some losses leave behind holes that cannot be filled.

Accepting Indah's arm, we let Deven mourn in peace.

Lying on a cot in the wheelhouse, I feel Indah's powers flow over me like tepid streams of water. She lets go of my temples, her expression tight. My hour-long session has not gone as expected.

She cleans her hands in the washbasin. The fresh scents from her healing waters, coconut and white sandalwood, waft off my skin.

"Well?" I ask.

"The bone in your leg has knit back together, and the sword wound on your side has closed to a faint scar."

Both injuries were sustained during my duel in the trial tournament, but they are not what concerns us. Before our escape from Iresh, the Voider, a corporeal demon set free from his prison in the evernight, breathed his poisonous fire down my throat. Despite Indah's efforts to cleanse me, his powers still slink icily through my veins. Not even a pain blocker, Indah's rare ability to suppress hurt for a short time, allays the cold.

I close my eyes and search inside myself for the single perfect star in my vision. The ever-burning light is the source of my Burner powers—my soul-fire. No mortal or bhuta exists without this inner radiance. I locate the star but its vivid light is hazy. "I see a greenness behind my eyelids."

"That's from the demon's powers."

"Can you get rid of them?"

"I don't know how," Indah replies, helping me sit up. "In a sense, your soul is frostbitten. If the injured parts were an extremity, I would recommend amputation, but as the damage is internal . . ."

"You cannot amputate my soul." I finish with a strained laugh, though I find nothing humorous about my memory of writhing on the ground in agony, tormented by the slow, torturous burn of the demon's cold-fire. The initial anguish has abated, but it left dark stains inside me, like tarnished silver. The Voider's powers would have destroyed me if I were not one quarter demon. All Burners descend from Enlil, a bastard son of the land-goddess Ki and the demon Kur. I suppose I should appreciate my ancestry. But I am not grateful. Not at all.

Indah's golden eyes reflect her worry. "I'll find you a more experienced healer in Lestari. In the meantime, save your strength and powers."

I have had no need to call upon my Burner abilities since I battled the Voider. But what will happen when I need them? I suspend my concerns. We are nearly to Lestari, the imperial city of the Southern Isles. I can hang on until we arrive tonight.

Pushing to my feet, I test my weight on my bad leg; no pain hisses at me. Indah offers me her arm, but I pick up my cane. "I'll be all right on my own."

I shuffle out the door, mindful of the gentle sway of the ship. Several steps later, I rest in a sunny patch of deck. The brightness warms my skin, but the inner hoarfrost will not yield.

"Does Indah know you're out here alone?"

I swivel toward Natesa and link my arm through hers. "I'm not alone. You're here."

"Let's walk." She tugs me from the banister, and we stroll around the outer deck. Her hips swish, swinging her braid like a pendulum, though not on purpose. Natesa cannot suppress her curves any more than I can change my skinniness.

As former rivals in my rank tournament among the rajah's wives and courtesans, for a time we could not stand each other. Natesa and my other competitors fought to gain a better life in this world of men. Only I won the rank tournament. My second victory in Iresh's trial tournament secured my throne as rani of the Tarachand Empire. I competed against four female bhutas in a series of contests designed to test our powers. My prize is to wed Prince Ashwin as his first wife, his kindred. I respect Ashwin, but marriage to him hardly feels like a reward.

"The prince left rather quickly after the burial," Natesa notes.

"He's avoiding me."

"He's avoiding Deven. Did he tell you about their altercation?"

"No . . ."

Natesa's lips twist wryly. "Right after we left Iresh, Deven struck Ashwin and nearly threw him overboard."

Gods help me. As captain of the guard, Deven's duty is to protect the prince, but he blames Ashwin for unleashing the Voider. The demon came disguised in the physical form of Ashwin's father and my deceased husband, Rajah Tarek. For releasing him, the Voider must grant Ashwin his heart's wish—to unseat the bhuta warlord from the Turquoise Palace in our imperial city of Vanhi.

The demon rajah has set out to do just that. He delivered our people from the awful encampments in Iresh, earning their devotion while preying on their suffering. Our army intends to march with the Voider to far-off Vanhi. The rest of Tarek's wives and his courtesans are trapped there; my friends and fellow sister warriors, held captive by the warlord and his band of rebels. I want to see the ranis released, but the demon rajah cannot be allowed to overthrow the warlord. If he succeeds, he will be free to inflict terror on our world.

"I've tried to explain," I say, "but Deven won't listen."

"Maybe he's right to be angry." Natesa's gaze wanders to the river. "Even Brother Shaan feared our fate."

Unfortunately the loss of Brother Shaan is another tragedy for Deven to blame on the prince. "Ashwin couldn't have known that the demon would disguise himself as Tarek and convince our people he's their rajah."

We round the stern of the boat and nearly bump into the prince. He holds an open book, appearing as he did when we first met. Only, this time, I do not mistake him for his father. Ashwin may possess Tarek's compelling good looks, but he is kindhearted. From his wounded expression, he overheard our conversation.

"Your Majesty," Natesa says, bowing. "We didn't see you there."

"Clearly." He snaps his book shut. "I'll go around."

He starts to pass, but I loop my arm through his. "Walk with me?"

Ashwin slowly pivots and rubs the side of his head as though massaging a headache. I tug him forward, and Natesa gladly goes, leaving the other direction.

"How have you been?" I ask the prince.

"Well, thank you." His perfunctory answer quiets me. The clack of my cane on the wooden deck is the only noise between us. I have nearly given up on a conversation when he asks, "How are you feeling?"

"Better. Indah said I should be walking on my own soon."

He nods but says no more. I long for the easiness we once had between us. In Iresh, while Deven was imprisoned in the military encampment, Ashwin and I learned to trust each other. I still wear the brass wrist cuff he lent me for good luck before my final trial. Ashwin is my second cousin and only living family. Dissolving his friendship is a loss I cannot sustain.

I stop, halting him. "What can I do to fix this? The awkwardness between us is unbearable."

"You know what I want." He looks everywhere but at me. "I can repeat my wishes if you'd like, but I will keep my word. You won the trial tournament and have no further obligation to me or your throne."

"Do you really think I'd abandon you?"

His brow creases. "I thought now that Captain Naik has returned—"

"The Tarachand Empire is my home too. *Our* people have been deceived by the demon rajah. He's marching upon *our* palace with *our* army, where *my* fellow ranis are held captive by the warlord. I'm with you, Ashwin. Perhaps not the way you hoped, but we'll confront the demon rajah together."

His lips twitch, withholding a smile. "Understood, Kindred."

I pull him forward, and he keeps up, relaxing into my side. "Where did you find your book?" I ask of the text under his other arm.

"I stuffed it under my shirt before I left Iresh."

My gaze flies to his. "You did not."

"I did. I saw it on the ground and grabbed it."

Ashwin has read more books than anyone I have met. "Is it any good?"

"Dull as a cow's nose. On the upside, I learned how to sew a turban." He shows me the title. *A Seamstress's Guide to Men's Attire*. A laugh erupts out of me. He chuckles quietly, his shoulders shaking.

I sober some, questioning the appropriateness of our humor just hours after Brother Shaan was laid to rest. But Brother Shaan believed all children of Anu, bhutas and mortals, should dwell in harmony. He would like for Ashwin and me to make amends.

We reach the unoccupied bow. Past it, blue sky yawns above the water and mangroves. A breeze tousles Ashwin's short ebony hair. I rest on the wide ridge near the rail, winded from my short jaunt.

"Can I escort you back to the wheelhouse?" he asks.

"I'll stay here awhile." Ashwin does not sit, nor does he leave. His indecision about our closeness exasperates me. I have missed him, but the sentiment clings to my tongue. He may interpret my feelings differently than I intend. "Thank you for the stroll."

He hesitates, all seriousness. "I'm going to regain the empire, Kalinda."

Ashwin bears the bulk of his transgressions alone. I have seen him pacing the deck at night, kneading away headaches and raking his fingers through his hair. Brother Shaan's death only adds to his remorse. Ashwin loves the empire and his people. He will not rest until he wins them back. I consider his bloodshot eyes. "I know you will."

He smiles a little and bends down to kiss my cheek. I turn into him; he smells of coconut shaving oil. We both misjudge how close we are, and his lips land on the corner of my mouth.

His look of surprise fills my sight. He pauses and then presses his lips to my cheek properly. His tender mouth lights a fire across my skin. Warmth pierces inside me, straight to my core. I lean into him to prolong our connection. For the first time in days, my inner chill thaws, and my soul-fire burns true.

Ashwin pulls back. Cold rushes inside me again. I gape up at him, speechless. He beams, delighted by my reaction, and saunters away.

What has just happened between us? I . . . I let him kiss me. *Twice.*

Watching my reflection on the water, I try not to think of Ashwin, but my head keeps reeling. As soon as I reunited with Deven, I set aside my romantic feelings for Ashwin. Yet the prince's kiss could have lasted longer without any protest from me. Is it possible that I still care for him as more than a friend? I cannot ignore those soothing seconds when the winter inside me melted . . .

"There you are," Deven says.

He tugs down his scarlet uniform jacket and sits beside me. Since this morning, he has shaved his thick beard and trimmed his hair short beneath his turban. He is prepared to meet the Lestarians, looking every bit a handsome officer of the imperial army.

I rest against him, nestling into his side, and wait for him to inquire about Ashwin and me. But either Deven did not see us together or he does not wish to speak of the prince. I do not raise the subject either. Ashwin's kiss was innocent, a gesture between friends, but admitting to one such gesture could lead to questions. Sometimes the truth is more harmful than an omission. And I am not the only one who has kept secrets.

"Natesa mentioned you tried to throw Ashwin overboard," I say.

"It was more of a shove," Deven replies, taking my statement in stride.

I give in to a sigh. "You shouldn't have done that."

He bristles. "It's my responsibility to defend the empire. The prince had just unleashed the Voider. By all appearances, he was a threat."

I thread my fingers through his. "The prince is your ruler. As soon as he takes a wife, he'll be rajah." I have unintentionally led us into a topic of conversation I have dodged for days. Deven has not asked me to walk away from my throne. He understands my rank as rani is my godly purpose—and my choice. Or more accurately, an accepted obligation. But neither of us knows where that leaves us or our dream of a peaceful life in the mountains. "You have to put aside your hard feelings. We have enough division plaguing us."

He tenses, his voice strained. "I'm trying, Kali. I have a lot on my mind."

More than Brother Shaan's passing wears on him. His mother and brother, Mathura and Brac, were stranded at the border between the empire and the sultanate. Two Galers were sent to find them but have yet to return. Each day we wait increases Deven's angst.

I cup his smooth cheek. "I know you are."

He leans into my touch. His features are an appealing mishmash of hard planes and pliable smoothness, like his two main roles: soldier and dedicated worshiper of the Parijana faith. I bring my lips to his. He tugs me closer, and his sandalwood scent fills me up. His body heat skims mine but does not soak in or alleviate the cold inside me. I disregard whatever that may imply and trail my fingers up his neck. Hot need builds at the base of my throat, yet the frost within me perseveres. I pull away, breathless and shivering.

Deven's soft brown eyes study me. "What's wrong?"

"I . . ." *I don't know*. "I should lie down."

I use my cane to stand, but Deven sweeps me into his arms. My feet flail out, and my hands fly up to his neck. "Put me down!"

"All right," he says evenly and then starts for the wheelhouse.

I pull the skirt of my petticoat and sari close beneath me. "You said you'd put me down."

"I will . . . on your cot."

"But I can walk!"

Deven calls ahead. "Coming through!"

A chair blocks our path. Indah and Pons dine on a late breakfast of mashed fruit and currants. Pons's hair hangs down his back; the top and sides of his head are shaved. He grabs Indah's seat and slides her out of our way. I blush at their open stares. The Aquifier and the Galer are in love, yet they do not show it with public demonstrations. I sense Pons would if Indah were willing, but she is private about her affections.

Deven carries me through the open wheelhouse door and lies down with me, our bodies filling the cot. "See? That wasn't so awful."

I sink against him. "I could burn your nose off for that."

"You like my nose."

"I do," I say, kissing the tip.

He slides his rough palm under my blouse and across my bare back. His touch warms me in places Ashwin's kiss could never reach. I press my lips to Deven's again, indulging in the sensation of his body tight against mine. My fingers creep across his muscled shoulders, but his jacket prevents them from meeting skin, constricting my touch. Deven does not stop kissing me while he undoes his front buttons, preparing to take off his jacket.

The door swings open, and Natesa pulls up short. "I'm sorry to interrupt." Her eyes sparkle at finding us entwined. "We've reached the river mouth. A Lestarian ship is waiting."

Deven nuzzles my ear. "Someday I'll have you to myself," he says in a husky rumble.

A warm chill courses down my neck. "I'll hold you to that." I kiss him once more and sit up. Dizziness whams me from rising too fast, and I sag forward.

"You should lie down," Deven says, rebuttoning his jacket.

"I'm fine. Just give me a moment." After a few more breaths, my vision clears.

Deven places his hand on my shoulder. "Kali, you really should stay here."

"I said I'm fine," I snap. I know I am weaker than usual. He need not constantly remind me. "Natesa, please hand me my cane."

Deven grabs the cane and thrusts it at me. Natesa shrinks away and tiptoes out. Deven is worried about my health, but I have greater concerns.

"I have to greet the Lestarians," I explain. "Our first impression must reflect well on the empire."

Indah assured Ashwin and me that we can rely on Datu Bulan, the ruler of the Southern Isles, for aid, but we are placing a lot of faith in a stranger. The Voider is positioned at the head of the most powerful army in the land. We can only hope the datu will recognize the threat he poses and join us to stop him.

I stand and temper my frustration. "I need to go, Deven."

"You also need to take care of yourself." He reaches for a stray hair against my cheek. I swipe it away before he can, and he draws back, hurt.

"I'm sorry," I whisper. Embracing my throne means accepting my responsibility to assist Ashwin. "We need to keep our distance now that—"

"No need to explain." Deven adjusts the cuffs of his jacket with short, irritated jerks. "It would reflect poorly on the empire for the kindred to favor her guard."

"It's only for a little while." I seek out his understanding, but his expression remains defensive.

Ashwin appears at the door. "Kalinda," he says tentatively, gauging Deven's scowl and oppositional posture. "Indah is asking for us."

"I'm coming," I say, leaning into my cane. Even though Deven is upset with me, he hovers close, as though expecting me to topple.

Anu, please don't let my legs give out or I'll never hear the end of it.

By gods' virtue, I cross the wheelhouse on my own, and Ashwin leads the way.

2

Deven

I grab my sword from behind the wheelhouse door and follow the click-clack of Kali's cane. Since sustaining her injuries, her already tall, lean frame has thinned to frailty. She stoops over like a crane, her healing leg quaking from exertion.

Skies, she's stubborn.

Helping her would be easier if she would quit interpreting my aid as her failing. She is not weak; she is in need. Before the Voider blasted her with his cold-fire, Kali shone bright as the sun and enchanted nature-fire into a huge, fiery dragon. It hurts to see her struggling.

Indah and two more Lestarian Aquifiers use their powers to guide our skiff across the choppy delta waters. I managed to avoid seasickness on the smooth-flowing river, but my stomach is less enthused about the open water. On either side of the inlet, the coastline stretches into the distance, dotted with palm trees along alabaster beaches. The rest of my party line up at the rail, staring at the waiting ship.

The larger watercraft is more suitable for open seas, with a flat bottom, high bow, and lower stern. I estimate its length at three hundred cubits and width about half that size. The exterior has been painted a true blue, and the prow is shaped into the head of a sea dragon. The military vessel has a single mast but no sails or steering oar. Aquifier sailors stationed on the starboard and port sides power the vessel. Hollow barrels are mounted at the stern—water cannons. The Lestarian Navy protects merchant and passenger vessels from the raiders that troll these waters. A serpentine sea dragon, mirroring the prow, decorates the amethyst flag snapping in the wind atop the mast.

We reach the navy vessel and stop before the teak hull inscribed with the name *Enki's Heart*. Pons throws the line up to the sailors. They fasten it and drop a rope ladder. I climb the ladder first. Two older official-looking men wait to greet us on the pristine deck. The crew consists of men and women, all in baggy knee-length trousers and tunics.

One of the older men with a long white beard holds a trident as I would a staff. He is chewing a wad of something green—mint? I heard mint chewing is a popular pastime among sailors. The Lestarians watch me with their golden eyes. I leave my sword sheathed and return their scrutiny.

Prince Ashwin arrives next and then helps Kali off the ladder. I do not react, pretending her accepting his help does not bother me, but I want to pitch him overboard. I barely restrained myself earlier when I saw him kiss her cheek. A seemingly harmless act, except that he holds the power to force her to wed him. She believes he will not, but I am slow to trust anyone dense enough to release a demon.

Yatin and Natesa come aboard next. Natesa leaves her hand free for the dagger at her waist, mistrustful of the strangers. Yatin's daunting size and ropy beard cause the strangers to shift nervously, even if he is mild unless provoked.

Pons arrives next, his blowgun wedged in his belt. He is a trained soldier, though his main duty is guarding Indah. He assists her on deck, and the white-bearded man with the trident grabs her up in a hug.

"This is my father," Indah says proudly, "Admiral Rimba, head of the Lestarian Navy. Father, this is Prince Ashwin and Kindred Kalinda."

The admiral bows. "Welcome aboard. This is Ambassador Chitt," he says of the nondescript dressed man beside him. "He's the standing bhuta emissary."

"Please, call me Chitt," the ambassador says. Gray streaks mix into his otherwise coppery hair. He is tall, about my height, but rangier in build. Cords of lean muscle run up his forearms and disappear under his thin tunic. He may be a diplomat, but his hands and arms belong to a man acquainted with labor. Something about his rugged features is . . . familiar.

"Kindred, for a time I was your father's delegate," he says. "I accompanied him on several mediation missions."

"His delegate?" Kali asks.

"Kishan was the previous bhuta emissary," the ambassador replies. The breast of Chitt's tunic bears the fire-god's symbol, a single flame. Admiral Rimba wears the water-goddess's emblem, a wave, on his collar. Both marks identify them as bhutas.

I exchange a glance with Yatin. The sultan employed bhutas in his military as well. They did not treat us well.

"I'd like to hear more about my father sometime," Kali says.

Ambassador Chitt's presence niggles at my memory as he answers, "It would be my pleasure."

Indah picks up where she left off with introductions, continuing until she ends with me. "And this is Captain Deven Naik."

"General Naik," Prince Ashwin corrects.

I flinch at my new title of command. After I accosted the prince, I did not think he would honor his word in promoting me to general. And just who am I the general of? We have no army. The only soldier under my command is Yatin, and my friend would follow me anywhere, regardless of my title. If the prince thinks he can persuade me into liking him, he is dimmer than I thought. My father was the army's previous general. Under the rajah's direction, he massacred hundreds of innocent bhutas. Inheriting his seat of command is neither a prize nor honor.

"Good to meet you, General Naik," Chitt says, examining me as well. "We were told you have another passenger, a member of the Brotherhood?"

"He passed away." I cut a glare at the prince. Brother Shaan worried himself to death because of him. The thought of the Voider let loose in our world was too much for his old heart to handle. I already miss him.

"Has anyone arrived ahead of us?" Kali asks. Pons has been listening to the wind for messages from my family, but none have arrived. "Deven was separated from his brother and mother. They and two Galers, more of our guards, are supposed to meet us in Lestari."

I pray they are already there.

"We haven't seen or heard from them," replies Admiral Rimba, squashing my hopes. He continues, speaking around his mint chewing. "But they could have arrived after we left this morning. We'll soon find out. We must leave now to reach the isles by sunset."

He and Indah direct us to a cabin at the center of the deck. Pons falls in line behind them, his expression sterner than usual. It is strange not seeing him beside Indah. Prince Ashwin and Kali follow next with Chitt, who chats politely about the humid weather.

Ahead of me, Natesa whispers to Yatin, "Does the ambassador look familiar to you?"

So it isn't just me.

I step inside a half second after them and miss Yatin's answer. Benches with pillows line the rectangular cabin, and the doors slide closed to circumvent the wind. Everyone finds a secure place for travel. Of course Ashwin occupies the seat beside Kali. I sit near the exit, splitting my attention between the foreign navy and my rani.

Sailors shut the sliding doors, leaving the door facing the stern open. The Aquifiers manning the deck lift *Enki's Heart* on a mountainous swell and fly us forward on a continuous wave. My fingers curl around edge of the bench. In no time, the ship rocks Kali to sleep. I keep alert, less trusting of our hosts than the others, but my attention wavers as nausea dangles in my belly.

Everyone else watches the passing scenery, unbothered by our bumpy speed. Natesa and Yatin point out seabirds and jumping fish to each other. I scan Natesa's hands for the lotus ring Yatin saved for her. When he was ill, he asked me to give it to her on his behalf. I told him to hold on to it. Now that he is well, I thought he would propose, but Natesa is not wearing the ring.

Yatin notices my ashen pallor. "Do you need a bucket?" he asks in his gentle burr.

"No, just fresh air."

I compose myself and leave the cabin. When I am out of the others' view, I stagger to the rail and retch overboard. Spray shoots up, cooling my cheeks. I empty my stomach and slump over. Past the bow, the sea rolls on with no end in sight. I have never seen anything more empty or dreary.

Chitt steps on deck and joins me. "General, do you know Mathura Naik?"

I gulp down more nausea. "She's my mother. How do you know her?"

"We met years ago at the palace. She had a little boy with solemn eyes about this tall." Chitt measures the height of a small child. "He wouldn't fall asleep without his wooden sword."

"You spent time in the courtesan's wing," I say flatly. They only could have met there. My mother was one of Rajah Tarek's courtesans.

"Mathura was sent to my chamber." At Chitt's use of my mother's first name, I grip the hilt of my sword. "We talked all night long about my travels. Her curiosity for the world was infectious."

Tarek forced my mother to entertain his men of court and visiting dignitaries. "You never touched her?" I press.

Chitt's golden eyes flash. Antagonizing a powerful Burner may not be my brightest idea. "General Naik, I do believe that's a question for your mother."

"I'll be certain to ask her."

"I hope you do." He considers me closer. "I heard Mathura has another son."

"My half brother, Brac."

"You mentioned you were separated from your family. Are they in danger?"

"I don't know."

A frown marks Chitt's brow. "When we reach Lestari, I'll do what I can to find them."

"Why?"

"That's another question for Mathura." The ambassador pats my upper back in an overfamiliar gesture. "You had the same grave stare when you were a boy . . . and the same affinity for weapons." He eyes my sword with a side smile that sends a jolt through me.

I gawk after Chitt as he returns inside. I have seen that smirk a thousand times from someone else . . .

Holy gods, I just met Brac's father.

3

Kalinda

I wake to find I am alone in the cabin. Out the open doors, our party congregates along the bow. Deven braces against the portside rail, wearing a dazed expression. I meet him on deck, achy but rejuvenated.

"Are you all right?" I ask.

"It's been an odd day." When no one else is looking, I stroke his hand. His distracted mood peels away, and he smiles. I want to wrap my arms around him, but propriety must be upheld. Deven points past the bow. "We're here."

The afternoon sun lights up a far-off wall. The towering pile of stones shoots up from the sea, many times higher than our vessel's mast. While squinting, I make out a passageway in the barrier. A low, arched bridge, like a strand of a spider's web, spans the gap.

"What is it?" I ask.

"A breaker. Indah said it encircles the whole island. It fortifies against intruders and errant waves." Deven sounds impressed, as am I. This wall in the middle of the sea is remarkable.

A dark line on the northern horizon draws my attention. Admiral Rimba stands on the lookout deck on top of the cabin. I call up to him. "What's that behind us?"

The admiral swivels around and stares past our stern. The line comes into focus—a tremendous wave advances toward us at an alarming pace. He shouts from above, "Sailors, full ahead! Passengers to the cabin!"

"Good Anu," Deven breathes.

We grip the rail, and *Enki's Heart* races for the island. Seawater mists our faces, and the wind blasts my hair behind me. The crew scrambles to the water cannons. The other members of our party and Ambassador Chitt make their way down the rail from up deck, hand over hand. Deven and I try to let go of the rail and cross the deck into the cabin, but the ship dips and soars over every roller, and the prow splashes up more surf. Despite our increased haste, the tidal wave continues to gain on us.

Natesa gapes at the towering wave. "Where in the skies did it come from?"

Indah pushes her forward. "Everyone inside!"

Deven and I stagger across the deck and into the cabin with them. Out the front window, the protective breaker grows higher and taller. Past the guard bridge, I glimpse the safety of a cove.

A shadow falls over the ship. I look out the open door—and the wall of water crashes into us. The cabin's structure holds, but waves rush in and knock us down. I slide across the floor, soaked through in an instant.

The water recedes, violent streams of cold that slap and drag at me. Deven crawls to my side, his turban missing. Ashwin lies on his belly, coughing up water but otherwise unharmed. Natesa and Yatin hold each other in a puddle, while Indah and Pons brace themselves in the corner.

At our stern, a ship barrels for us. The three-mast vessel is painted an incongruously cheerful yellow. A dark cloud hangs ominously above the ship, punctuated by lightning. Thunder rumbles, an imminent warning of the vessel's pursuit.

"Water cannons portside!" shouts Admiral Rimba.

The ship careens alongside us, its size filling the sky and its water cannons aimed to shoot. I wipe water from my eyes and peer up at the vessel's black flag with its white symbol—a large shark with jagged teeth.

The sea raiders' emblem.

Our pursuers employ their cannons. Saltwater jets in through the doors of the cabin, blasting one off its hinges. Deven crouches over me and absorbs the spray. The targeted streams of water force two of our cannons into the sea and crush another. Several of the crew are swept off deck into the rough waves. The terrible winds bellow, and the ship creaks and groans.

The raiders lower their biggest cannon at our cabin and blast more water at us. Deven is pushed off me, and he slides to the door. Pons grabs his wrist, and they are both swept out on deck and dragged to the rail. Pons latches onto a crate, stopping them from falling overboard, but Deven's legs dangle over the edge.

I lurch out of the cabin, onto the open deck. Harnessing my soul-fire, I send a heatwave into the storm. "Enough!"

My flames evaporate the water on my hands, fizzling the drops to steam. A man high up on the opposing deck comes to the rail to see who cast the heatwave. Ambassador Chitt flanks me, his hands also glowing.

"What do you want, Captain Loc?" Chitt calls to the man on the other ship.

"We have no interest in you or the navy, Ambassador." Captain Loc points at me. "We've come for the kindred and prince. Rajah Tarek has offered a reward for their return."

"Prince Ashwin and Kindred Kalinda are under our protection," Admiral Rimba answers, calling across the watery divide. Though the sea between our ships has started to calm, tension churns in the thundery sky. "I suggest you go before our fleet arrives." He points to vessels speeding out of the breaker from the island.

"Give us the prince and kindred, and we'll leave," Captain Loc replies.

Behind me, Ashwin is stony, but I read him as well as he does one of his books. I turn to Captain Loc. "The prince and I stay."

Captain Loc goes on, unruffled. "Kindred, your husband requires your presence."

I throw a warning heatwave at his ship. The Voider is *not* my husband. My fire glances along their bow, scorching a line across the hull. Men dive away from the path of my fury. Captain Loc ducks behind the rail and rises again.

An exquisite chill, akin to delight, empowers me. The raiders fear my abilities.

And well they should.

But Captain Loc does not direct his crew to retreat. My impatience surges. *Go away.*

Flames fly from my hands, high across the water, their centers white and their edges a strange pale green. My heatwave hits the vessel's mast and burns its flag. Captain Loc summons a pillar of water to extinguish the fire and then raises snakelike streams from the sea and aims them at me.

I stand ready, bolder with Chitt at my side than I would be alone. The navy vessels race closer, moments away. Should the raiders engage us, they will have to engage their entire fleet.

Captain Loc throws his streams of water at the hull. Waves splash the deck, hitting my sandals. "Another day, Kindred." He signals to his crew, and they maneuver their ship farther out in the open water.

I hobble across the deck. Deven sits away from the rail near Pons, catching his breath. "Those dolts," I say, helping Deven stand. "Rajah Tarek is *dead*."

Deven squeezes water from his tunic and soaked turban. "I never thought anyone could be more dangerous than Tarek, and then I met the demon impersonating him."

Pons summons a breeze that rushes over us, wicking away the immediate wetness of our clothes. After the wind passes, he says, "The reward for bringing you back must be generous. Captain Loc wouldn't risk attacking a navy vessel this close to Lestari without incentive."

Deven and I swap a look. Our decision to meet up with the Lestarians has already proven beneficial. I just hope our meeting with the datu goes well.

The other navy ships arrive and surround us. Admiral Rimba shouts for his crew to retrieve the sailors who were cast overboard. A crewman cleans up the deck, tossing aside debris so the others may more easily work.

Deven groans and leans against me, but his complaint is of exhaustion, not of injury. "I'll help so we can be underway," he says. "The sooner we're on land, the better."

I hold on to him longer than necessary . . . and then another breath or two after that. He finally pulls back, and I reluctantly return to the cabin to check on the others.

Chitt intercepts me at the broken sliding door. "I'd like a quick word, Kindred." Since he is blocking my way, I wait for him to go on. "Have your powers always been that greenish hue?"

"They're usually the color of a star, but I've been unwell lately."

"Perhaps it's of no concern," Chitt answers, though his tone implies otherwise. "Each Burner's powers have a unique color. Mine is a deep currant, and your father's was a vibrant tangerine. But I have never seen a Burner's fire any shade of green."

I had not thought to compare my fire to another's. Burners are too few for such an opportunity to easily arise. The only other Burner I have met and fought alongside is Brac. I wish he was here so I could ask him if the color of my powers is abnormal.

Ashwin squeezes past Chitt and hooks his arm through mine. "Kalinda should rest, Ambassador."

"Of course. Thank you for your time, Kindred." Chitt bows, his expression no less troubled.

Ashwin and I stroll down the deck and rest on an overturned crate. When no sailors are near, he speaks. "The attack was our fault." His small voice is packed with regret.

"No one was hurt."

"Thank the gods. Do you think we'll be safe in Lestari?"

I look to the stone breaker in the distance. "Let's pray so."

Ashwin scoots closer to move out of the path of a working sailor. I should put another gap between us, but the prince's touch tames the chill prowling inside me.

Since the Voider tainted me, I carry his malevolent powers like an invisible brand mark. I told him I am nothing like him. I am a bhuta, a half-god, so I must be *good.* Whatever sickness he put inside me cannot change my heritage. But something is amiss. My powers are different, and not just their color. I feel . . . less in control.

Leaning into Ashwin, I watch the sea and try not to think about what lies beneath the surface of my skin.

We sail up to the monstrous breaker in a long line of vessels. Seabirds screech above our procession, some of them nested along the craggy cliff. The crew slows our approach, and we wait our turn to slide under the bridge on the low tide. Water cannons are mounted on the span, aimed at the open water. *They're larger than the raiders' cannons,* I think. They should keep the raiders out.

Enki's Heart glides up to the opening, next in the fleet to pass through. Soldiers watch us from the guardhouse on the bridge, and then we coast beneath them into the shade. Through the shadows, I make out runes etched into the underside of the arch.

"What do they say?" I ask Ashwin beside me.

"Water in our blood," he answers, reading the ancient script. I saw that line once in a book about bhutas. *All mankind was created in the likeness of the gods—sky in our lungs, land beneath our feet, fire in our souls, and water in our blood.* Ashwin grimaces at the etchings. The last time he read runes, he released the Voider.

"I'm sorry," I say. "I didn't think."

Before he can reply, we emerge into a sparkling blue cove. A verdant island awaits across the water. The city of Lestari rises from the sea with dignified refinement. A labyrinth of waterways weaves beneath picturesque houses built on platforms and secured to stilts erected upon the beach. Thick columns, endless windows, and wide-open terrace balconies line every level of the staggered structures. Palm trees thrive on patches of white sand. Arching bridges span the azure inlets, connecting the city without disturbing the ebb and flow of the tides.

The Pearl Palace, the grand centerpiece of the Southern Isles, extends into the sunset sky with spindly spires glossy as the inside of an oyster. As I watch, residents light torches to illuminate the roads and homes darkening in the failing daylight.

Our vessel slips down a main channel toward the heart of the city and past water mills that power textile, paper, and flour mills. The Lestarians use the tides resourcefully, though I suspect they have ongoing Aquifier aid. A woman guides one of the water wheels, pushing a stream through the wheel's slats.

An outdoor market runs alongside the opposite bank. The sea breeze flutters orange-and-lime-colored sunshades stretched between lean-tos. Merchants present a spread of enticing goods, from painted pottery to ripe bananas. Fish hang from rafters, drying in the late-day sun as buyers purchase their wares before nightfall. Everyone's clothes and faces are clean. Everything about Lestari is immaculate, like a perfectly round pearl.

The waterway pushes us through the open gates of the Pearl Palace, where *Enki's Heart* bumps against a dock. A medium-height old man dressed in all white waits there. Several guards, also in white, flank him. The man's gray hair hangs past his shoulders, and a strand of pink shells rings his neck. His deeply tanned brown skin is sun worn, like cracked leather.

Our party disembarks, and Admiral Rimba leads Ashwin and me to the gray-haired man in white. My bad leg aches. I left my cane on the riverboat to avoid the impression that the kindred of the Tarachand Empire and two-time tournament champion cannot walk without assistance.

Admiral Rimba bends into an impressively low bow. "Datu Bulan, we bring you Prince Ashwin and Kindred Kalinda."

"I have eyes, Admiral," the datu answers, quirking a bushy brow at my slouch. He is not a big man. Even stooping, I tower over him. "Welcome to Lestari, Jewel of the Southern Isles."

My posture aggravates my sore leg. I speak to hide my discomfort. "Thank you for your hospitality. Have any members of our party arrived before us?"

"So far, only you," replies the datu, revealing a gap between his top front teeth.

Ashwin stands taller, as he often does when I am at his side. "We're eager to discuss the happenings in Iresh."

The datu's eyes cool on the young prince. I have only seen Deven look at Ashwin with that much distaste. "We are preparing supper for you and your viraji. First, let us direct you to your chambers."

I startle at the datu's formal endearment for me, and, at the fringe of my sight, Deven stiffens. No one has called me viraji—intended queen—since Tarek claimed me as his final rani.

"Datu Bulan," I say, "there's been a mistake. I'm not—"

"Kalinda isn't well enough to stand here any longer," Indah finishes. "She suffered an ordeal while securing her throne in the trial tournament. I must insist she rest."

Datu Bulan dons a paternal friendliness. "Then let's move along."

Ashwin pulls back. "Datu, may I have use of your library?" He intends to research the Voider. Bhuta powers cannot injure the demon, so we have to find another way to stop him.

The datu does not balk at the prince's request, nor does his glower lessen. "As you wish."

Admiral Rimba steps forward. "Pons can escort the prince."

Deven does not object to leaving Ashwin in Pons's care, but Indah raises her voice.

"Must it be Pons, Father? We only just arrived."

"The ambassador and I have matters to attend to," Admiral Rimba clips out. "Have you any grievance, Pons?"

Pons tucks his arms in, his chin high. "No, sir." He speaks to Ashwin. "Your Majesty, if you'll follow me, I'll show you the way to the library."

Ashwin begins to go with him, and the newness of this place lands on me all at once.

"Will I see you soon?" My question arises as a demand. Distance between Ashwin and I has not troubled me before, but the pressure on my chest will not abate.

"I'll find your chamber later," Ashwin promises, and he sets off with Pons.

My anxiety dissolves . . . until I catch Deven's sidelong look. I cannot say what came over me, except that I am not as comfortable in the company of our allies as I thought.

Admiral Rimba leaves with Chitt, and Datu Bulan shuffles up the main walkway in sandals that are too big for him. An amethyst banner with a sea dragon hangs above the arched entry. Through the main doors, pastel shells encrust the ivory walls and lanterns. Additional banners drape from the vaulted ceilings, splashes of majesty that offset the neutral décor.

In the center of the entry hall, a fountain cascades down from the second level between the double staircase. The datu slows before the fountain's base so we can view the lifelike sculpture of Enki riding astride a sea dragon. The creature's sleek, serpentine body is half submerged in the miniature rapids. The goddess holds a trident in one hand, her arms open to the archipelago of the Southern Isles.

I recognize the depiction of the legend from my history lessons with the Sisterhood. "This scene portrays the creation of the isles."

Datu Bulan smiles, revealing his toothy gap. "Very apt, Kindred. We tell our creation story every spring at the highest tide."

"Will you tell us?" Natesa asks him. "I didn't listen as closely in class as Kalinda." Yatin releases a deep chuckle, and Natesa elbows him to be quiet. She was more studious in the sparring ring than the classroom.

Datu Bulan gazes up at the water-goddess sculpture. "Our island is nearly as ancient as Enki herself. Our ancestors dwelled contentedly by the sea until the gods left the mortal realm for the Beyond. As soon as Enki departed, the sea rebelled. Tides flooded the villages and farmlands."

I listen closely. His brogue is somewhat hard to follow, his *k*'s and *r*'s rushed or not enunciated. Indah and Pons have accents as well, but theirs are less noticeable.

"The islanders feared for their lives, but they loved their home and would not flee for the mainland. They congregated along the shoreline and confronted the roiling waves. The sea waited for them to turn their backs on the surf so it could ambush them and sweep them away, but the islanders stood firm and prayed for Enki to save them. When she saw they would not be moved, she bridled the sea and dragged the high tide away from the villagers. In the absence of her waters, more fertile islands rose up from the seafloor for them to build and plant upon." The datu dips his fingertips in the fountain. "We still offer daily sacrifices to Enki. In return, she preserves us from the tides."

I memorize Enki's beautiful yet fierce stance, her open arms beckoning for me to believe.

Datu Bulan motions for us to move along. We trail him up the grand staircase and down a wide corridor. Etchings above the doorways draw my notice. The godly virtues—obedience, service, brotherhood, humility, and tolerance—decorate every threshold. The temple sisters emphasized sisterhood instead of brotherhood, but otherwise the virtues are the same ones we strive to emulate in Tarachand.

Natesa sees them too. "Why are the godly virtues over every doorway?"

The datu stops. "To remind us of our divine path." He passes through a door and we follow.

The spacious chamber is open to a terrace and balcony, letting in the briny scent of the sea. A fountain flows down the wall into a low basin. The running water continually cools the room. The furniture is crafted from durable grasses and driftwood, and thin white linens cover the bed. Deven prowls around, checking the chamber's security. I can already tell he does not like the terrace; it is too easy for someone to slip in unseen.

"This is lovely," I say.

Datu Bulan lifts the back of my hand to his lips. "Anything for a two-time tournament champion. I would trade all my pearls to have hair like yours in my collection."

"Ah . . . thank you?"

"It's a compliment, Viraji. I collect rare and valuable treasures." Bulan lifts his shell necklace for me to see. "I traded a bucketful of black diamond sand for these. They can only be found in the Northern Sea."

I touch a smooth pink shell. "They're exquisite."

"Not as exquisite as your hair." Datu Bulan delivers his flattery with utmost sincerity, as though very few things in the world awe him more than his strand of shells. Then he sweeps his hands behind his back, nods farewell, and shuffles out, his too-large sandals slapping the floor.

What a curious man.

"Yatin and I will sleep here," Deven says of the lounges on the terrace.

"The kindred is safe," Indah assures him. "We're a peaceful people."

"So were our people once." Deven strides to the balcony and scans the city beneath the twilight.

"Let's find my room." Natesa grabs Yatin by the hand and tows him to an antechamber.

I sit at the driftwood table and wrap a blanket around my shoulders to ease my inner chill. Indah kicks off her sandals and puts her feet up. The damp air adds dewiness to her brown skin and fullness to her wavy dark hair.

"Why does the datu think I'm Ashwin's viraji?" I ask quietly.

"He assumes you'll wed the prince because you won the trial tournament." Indah glances past me to Deven and speaks lower. "Bulan is different than Rajah Tarek. He has only been married once, and it was for love. His wife died years ago. Their only child, the princess, will inherit his throne."

A female heir? Tarek would have never endowed his throne to one of his daughters. He saw women as accessories, servants, *things*.

"Princess Gemi is a Trembler like her mother was. She will be the Southern Isles' first female ruler and our first bhuta ruler in a long while. Bulan believes bhutas and women should be in power to diversify our leadership."

His coolness toward the prince becomes clear. "He doesn't like Ashwin because he's a mortal man?"

"No, Bulan doesn't know him as well as you. Ashwin was harbored by the brethren until Tarek's death forced him from hiding. Our informants have been watching you since you left Samiya. The datu will help your people, but only if *you* are part of the new empire."

Bulan will only aid us if I plan to marry the prince. I do not have to tell Indah a union with Ashwin is not in my future. She has seen how close I am to Deven. I glance his direction. He tarries at the balcony, out of earshot. "I will be part of the new empire, but not as Ashwin's wife."

"You don't have to wed him," Indah explains. "Just let the datu think he's your intended."

I consider what I must do to maintain the illusion that I am Ashwin's viraji, and my insides scramble. I do not wish to lie to Bulan, but perhaps I can leave his assumption uncorrected . . . "What about you and Pons?" I ask, eager to veer the topic of conversation to her. "Will you and he wed?"

Indah's gold eyes darken. "My father disapproves of our closeness."

"Then why is Pons your guard?"

"He isn't my guard. He's the datu's Galer Virtue Guard. Bulan likes how we work together, so we often receive the same assignment."

Virtue Guards are bhutas who counsel and protect the physical and spiritual well-being of mankind. I assumed Pons was Indah's guard because he always hovers near her, but it makes sense that he serves the Southern Isles as a Virtue Guard. Indah has always treated him as her equal.

She slips on her sandals and rises. I did not mean for my prying to shoo her away. "I'll send for the healer I told you about. He lives on an outer island and should arrive by boat tomorrow. My mother is off island as well, on assignment for the datu. My father said she's unable to return to meet you and the prince."

Indah told me her mother serves as the datu's Burner Virtue Guard. All four divisions of bhutas work together here. "Will you see her soon?"

"I spent time with her before I left for Iresh. We'll meet again before long."

Indah starts to go, but I call to her. "Is Lestari really so safe?" The breaker is high and thick, but the palace and city are less guarded than any other I have visited.

"You're just as safe as the rest of us." Her frown overshadows her reassurance. Only after she leaves do I work out her meaning.

No one is safe so long as the Voider is in our world.

I hobble to Deven on the balcony, bringing my unease with me. I have difficulty believing the raiders could not find a way onto the island. The Voider certainly gave them the proper motivation to try.

Deven watches the city intensely, dissecting every weakness of this stronghold. Lestari is lusher than the desert surrounding Vanhi but as isolated as the Alpana Mountains where I was raised. I still miss home, usually when I think of my best friend, Jaya. But remembering her requires that I also think of her death, and that hurts too much to dwell on.

Deven's temples bounce, his jaw is so rigid. He must be thinking of his family. I slip my hand closer to his on the banister. His pinkie finger reaches for me. I do not glance at our tiny link, but his jaw loosens and my knotted stomach relaxes.

Natesa romps back into my chamber. "My antechamber is huge!" Yatin strolls in after her, his hair and shirt mussed as though they had been kissing. "The vanity has makeup, and I found silks in the wardrobe. I'll help fix up your appearance, Kalinda. We cannot let the Lestarians think our ranis are slovenly." Only Natesa can volunteer to be of assistance while criticizing someone at the same time. "What time is supper?"

"Soon, I hope," Yatin answers, patting his slimmed-down girth.

Natesa grabs him and Deven by the arm and drags them to the door. "You both need to leave." Yatin goes willingly, but Deven digs in his heels.

"We can wait on the terrace—"

Natesa shoves him out, shuts the door, and whirls around. Her critical gaze sweeps over me. "Let's hope supper is running late."

I bottle a retort—I know better than to back talk when she is preparing to beautify me.

While Natesa searches the wardrobe for a garment I can wear to supper, I sit at the vanity before the mirror glass. My cheekbones are sharper than usual and my skin is a sallow yellow. She was right. I do need her to fix me up.

For a second, my pupils flash with a sapphire flame. I blink and peer closer at my reflection. My eyes have returned to their normal deep brown, stark against my pallid complexion, yet the memory persists.

You're just as safe as the rest of us.

Am I really? The Voider is far away, but a piece of him is right here. Planted inside me.

I drop my face in my hands. Before the Voider poured his cold-fire into me, my powers were improving and expanding. I had mastered soul-fire and nature-fire. Wildfires heeded my command. Flames bowed to embers at my feet. I even summoned a dragon of fire and rode upon its back. I should not fear a flash of blue in a mirror glass. And if it were only my imagination, I would easily overlook it. But agony has a long memory, and the cold inside me will not let go.

4

Deven

Yatin is stationed on the opposite side of Kali's door. We stare forward, arms tucked close, and stand guard. The hushed corridors allow my thoughts to wander back to Indah and Kali's earlier conversation. They assumed they talked quietly, but I overheard enough. The datu trusts Kali—a wise decision. But Kali is not the prince's intended, and the datu should not pressure her to commit to him or compel her to choose between us. That is the very reason I have not imposed my will on her. I will not offer her my future just to outpace another man or from fear of losing her. When I ask Kali to spend her life with me, my proposal will originate from love, and love only.

Thinking of proposals reminds me . . . I look askance at Yatin. "What happened to your lotus ring? Did you lose it?"

"No."

I wait, but he does not go on. "Did you change your mind about giving it to Natesa?"

"No."

His one-syllable replies rub me the wrong way. Yatin and Natesa can be together. They have nothing standing in their way. I pray every day for Kali and me to gain that level of freedom. Why is he squandering it?

Indah comes down the hall wearing all-white robes, the preferred state of dress in the Pearl Palace. I have not known her long, but she looks more tired than usual. I knock on the door, wait a moment, and then open it for her. Within the chamber, Natesa arranges the low neckline of Kali's white-and-gold robes. Her hair has been brushed to a shine, and she has color, albeit from the rouge on her cheeks. I step in, staggered by her loveliness.

"You look stunning, Kalinda," Indah says.

"As do you," Kali returns.

"What do you think, *General*?" Natesa asks, her smile impish. She is a quick study at ways to boil my blood.

I clear my throat. "Um, yes. Stunning."

Kali lowers her kohl-lined lashes, her dark hair forming silky waves around her lean shoulders. "Any word from Iresh, Indah?"

"I've spoken with the datu," she answers. "Deven, would you please close the door?" My insides grind as I shut Yatin outside and give Indah my focus . . . barring the part of me that wishes to run my lips across Kali's cheek. "It's been too dangerous to send scouts into Iresh, so Galers have been listening from the coastline. From what they can tell, the refugees have taken over the city under the Voider's direction. He and his soldiers are gathering resources to march."

This was my fear. The demon rajah is pillaging Iresh to feed, clothe, and arm his troops. Once he finishes picking the city clean of everything valuable, they will march on Vanhi.

"The Voider has declared Kalinda and Prince Ashwin traitors. He offered the sea raiders ten thousand coin each for their return. Should Kalinda and the prince return to Tarachand, imperial soldiers are ordered to seize them on sight."

"I know at least two soldiers who won't obey that command," I say, referring to Yatin and me.

"It's all right, Deven," Kali says, more weary than outraged. "The people already despise my bhuta heritage. *That* I anticipated. But Ashwin is their ruler. They need him. We all do."

Her loyalty to him jabs at me. Does Kali need Ashwin any more than any other citizen of the Tarachand Empire?

Prince Ashwin enters and strolls directly to Kali. He changed his attire to the local cultural favorite for men: baggy trousers and a lightweight tunic with a low-cut collar. Pons is not with him, nor did I see him in the corridor.

"The palace library is larger than the sultan's," Ashwin tells Kali. I've already found several texts to comb through while we're here."

She grasps his hand in hers. I force my jaw to unclench. *They're friends, family, co-rulers. Nothing more.*

"We have news from Iresh," she says. "The demon rajah has declared us traitors."

Ashwin sways back on his heels, but she maintains her hold on him. Why is this a surprise? We came to Lestari to plot against the demon rajah. Even the real Rajah Tarek would denounce his son for this. The boy prince is an idealist, and a stupid one at that. If he does not start acting like the leader we need, Brother Shaan will not be our only casualty.

"He won't catch us," Kali promises. "We'll stop him first."

From the corner of my eye, I see a shadow move outside. I sidestep to the terrace to investigate.

"How? We cannot kill a demon." Prince Ashwin clutches the hair at the sides of his head. "Maybe we should turn ourselves in and spare our people more harm."

"No," Kali counters firmly, "we'll find a way to send him back to the Void."

A small figure hides around the corner, pressed against the wall. Reaching back as though to scratch my side, I grab my sword and draw on our intruder.

A young woman leaps into the open, wielding no weapon except for her fists. She stomps her foot, and a vibration carries up from the ground. I stumble backward. She tries to leap over the banister, but I grab her by the tunic and spin her around.

She cannot be more than twenty. In a black tunic over trousers—a man's attire—her unintimidating frame is lean but scrappy. Her bare feet are decorated with henna patterns, the moon phases, and her toenails are painted pomegranate.

"Princess Gemi?" Indah questions.

I let the princess go and lower my blade. "Did your father send you?"

She snorts. "No. He thinks I'm preparing for supper."

"Your Highness," Ashwin says, "I'm Prince Ashwin from Tarachand."

The princess juts out her pointy chin, her wide-set eyes flat. "Aren't you the rajah by now?"

"Formally, I cannot hold that title until I take a wife."

"You aren't marrying me," the princess retorts, a hair away from a threat. "I don't care how badly my father wants to reopen trade with the empire."

"We've come for another matter." Kali steps to Ashwin's side, a slight movement of protection that I both admire and abhor. "I'm Kalinda."

Princess Gemi sniffs. "*You're* the two-time tournament champion? You're thinner than a twig."

"So I've been told. Do you spy on all of your visitors?"

"Only the ones I deem too dimwitted to catch me." Princess Gemi's attention roams to me. She has the same heavy accent as her father, dropping her *r* and *k* sounds. "I was told imperial soldiers are two tides shy of a full moon. You are . . . ?"

"Deven Naik." I omit my military title to annoy the prince. He rewards my efforts with a scowl.

The princess swings her leg over the banister. "I'll reserve you a seat by me at supper, Deven." Her grin reminds me of Brac's. And like Brac, beneath her arrogance lies steely independence. I find myself wanting to return her grin, but Princess Gemi drops into the garden and dashes off.

"She's . . ." Kali sifts for the right word, "dynamic."

I sheathe my khanda. "Indeed. A spirited one."

Kali sticks me with a perturbed look. I send one back at her. The princess was abrupt, even rude, but by all appearances, harmless. I can stand bad manners over idealism. Ashwin could take a lesson in authority from the princess of the Southern Isles.

A low horn calls us to supper. Indah says the blare came from a conch shell, but it sounded like an elephant with a bad cold.

We gather on a terrace overlooking the cove. Moonlight silvers the water, and a breeze rustles the canopy. Star-shaped yellow flowers grow along the path, their bright petals splashes of light outside the glow of the chandelier lamp. The datu waves for us to occupy the table. Kali and Prince Ashwin take chairs near him, and I sit between the princess and Ambassador Chitt.

"Gemi," the datu says, "you didn't have time to change before our meal with our guests?"

She still wears a black tunic and trousers. I have never seen a woman wear a man's clothes before. My mother would be beside herself to put the princess in a skirt.

"My apologies, Father." Her response is exceptionally uncontrite, but he lets her alone.

Explosions sound behind me. I swivel around to look at seawater bursting up from the cove, geysers lit by flames of deep red and vibrant yellow. The plumes fan out in rows, and the fire follows, illuminating the streams.

"How did you . . . ?" Kali trails off in amazement.

"Aquifiers enchant the water to shoot into the sky, and Burners throw their fire behind the fountains for light," the datu replies. "We perform this exhibit for honored guests and hope you will enjoy it."

The jets of water dance in practiced patterns and varying heights, gradually building to a finale. Countless fountains gush to the sky, lit by a rainbow of fire. Then all at once, it is done.

Prince Ashwin is the first to applaud. "Spectacular."

I join in, impressed, if not also confused. Anu gave bhutas their abilities to guide mankind onto a path of virtue. Is entertaining supper guests the best use of their powers? Kali holds herself close, chilled by the night, and frowns.

Servants bring plates of spiced fish. I sample a bite and wrinkle my nose, then chase the food away with a drink of coconut water. Down the table, Kali watches me, her own plate untouched. Her eyes shine with humor. Neither of us likes the briny flavor.

"Prince Ashwin, I must know, why did you release the Voider?" The datu's direct question draws our attention to the prince. Indah and Admiral Rimba dine across the way. Natesa and Yatin are eating in their chamber. "Indah told me what happened, but I'd like to hear your explanation."

Kali responds for Ashwin. "The sultan's vizier began the incantation. He intended to use the Voider's power to enslave bhutas and overthrow the empire."

"And yet the demon has still come to reap revenge on the world." The datu relaxes into his high-backed chair, his attention sharpening on Ashwin. "Tell me why I shouldn't tie a millstone to your neck and drown you in the depths of the sea?"

Finally, someone who sides with me! Prince Ashwin's panicky gaze seeks me out to defend him. I scoop another bite of food. Fishy flavor aside, this is the most amusing supper I have had in a long while.

Ashwin grimaces. "My heart's wish is to regain my imperial city and palace. I didn't know the Voider would come disguised as Rajah Tarek."

Datu Bulan drums his fingertips against the table. "Agency is not only what we do but why. What else did your heart's wish entail?"

After a strained pause, Prince Ashwin replies, "I wished to return to my palace."

"And wed the kindred?"

Kali chokes on her drink and turns to the side to cough.

"We aren't officially betrothed," Ashwin replies.

My brows shoot up to my hairline. What in the gods' names does that mean? The answer is either yes or no. Kali continues to clear her throat. The prince does not clarify, leaving the datu to presume what he will about him and Kali.

"How do you intend to win back your palace?" Bulan challenges. "Voider aside, the bhuta warlord will not withdraw."

Kali jumps back into the conversation. "Once we regain our army, we'll unseat Hastin. But we cannot do that without your aid."

The datu slips his hand down the front of his tunic, over his heart. While he thinks, he scrutinizes Kali and Ashwin. Does he also notice how close they are sitting together? At last, he voices his verdict. "You have use of my navy."

"How will your fleet reach Vanhi?" Prince Ashwin asks.

Princess Gemi adds her thoughts to the mix. "We could reach out to the Paljorians."

Datu Bulan shakes his head. "Chief Naresh is a pacifist. In all his years ruling the Northern Peaks, he has never deployed his army for or against a regime."

"If I may," I say, drawing all eyes to me, "we shouldn't need the Paljorians. So long as your navy can utilize the waterways for travel, we can confront the demon rajah in Iresh before he leaves for Tarachand."

The prince slumps, as if he should have thought of that himself. My proposal is simple, but our success hinges on us reaching Iresh before the demon rajah leaves. He is taking longer than I anticipated to rally his men and resources. Maybe he is waiting for the raiders to bring him Ashwin and Kali . . .

"Wisely strategized, General Naik," says Datu Bulan. "The admiral and our fleet will depart in the morning." Tomorrow? Deploying the navy should take days. They must have begun preparations before our arrival. "I presume your party intends to go with them."

"We do." Kali's tone turns guarded. "What do you require from us in return?"

"My requests will be reasonable, Viraji." The datu smiles broadly. I understand where Gemi gets her charm, but must he refer to Kali as Ashwin's intended? "Prince Ashwin, have you ever seen an arctic tiger? Their coats are ivory with charcoal stripes. I traded three barrels of shark fins for one pelt. It's mounted in my study. You and I will retire there to discuss our terms."

Ashwin does not refuse. He has little leeway for the terms of our alliance, and the datu knows it. Bulan will walk away from the negotiations table with more than a fair trade.

The datu and Ashwin excuse themselves. Kali watches them leave, her focus so severe I question her ability to drag Ashwin back by sheer will.

Princess Gemi tilts her head nearer to me. "Come walk with me along the shore."

I search Kali out across the table, eager to leave, but Indah and the admiral have engaged her in conversation. "Thank you, but I'm obligated to stay here."

"Is your pining stare for the kindred an *obligation*?"

Gemi is too perceptive. "You aren't told no often, are you?"

"You'd be the first," she says, and I exhale a laugh.

"General Naik," Ambassador Chitt says from my right, "may I have a word? It's about your family."

"Go on, Deven," Princess Gemi says, her mouth upturned. "I'll watch over the kindred."

Kali overhears the princess and narrows her eyes at us. I lift a finger to her as I rise, indicating I will return momentarily. Chitt and I stroll down a pebble pathway toward the inlet.

"On my order, Pons has flown to Tarachand to find your family," Chitt says.

As a Galer, Pons can ride the skies on a wing flyer, the fastest form of travel. We have not had access to the flying contraptions since leaving Iresh. I appreciate Pons's and the ambassador's assistance. "Thank you."

"We'll keep looking until we find them," Chitt says. Although we just met, I am inclined to trust his word. He stops at the inlet, the palace lights shining onto the still water. "My friend from Janardan contacted me. A platoon of elephant warriors and bhuta soldiers escaped the demon rajah and are hiding. I may be able to convince them to join the battle in Iresh."

Manpower from the Janardanian army would be advantageous. "Do you think they could meet us in time?"

"They should. Their troops travel by land barge," Chitt explains. Tremblers power the stone-wheeled barges that are big enough to carry a herd of elephants. I have never seen one myself, though I have heard they are a sight to behold. "I'd leave in the morning to reach them."

He sounds uncertain about going. I question why and then realize two things: I am the general of the imperial army and he is offering me his assistance, and he does not want to leave in case my mother and brother arrive. "You should go. We need all the troops we can gather."

"Do you need to consult with Prince Ashwin?"

"No."

"Then I'll leave tomorrow." Chitt's gaze skitters to the cove and breaker, then back to me. "One more thing. The sea raiders were spotted offshore west of here. We have increased our lookout guards, but I thought you should be aware."

I, too, examine the breaker from afar. "Can they get through?"

"There are ways," Chitt admits, "but Captain Loc doesn't wish to engage our entire navy. The admiral is aware and has put precautions in place for the voyage. You'll be safe. I hope and pray that you—" He halts and bows, a swift change to formality. "May the gods be with you."

"And you, Ambassador." I watch Chitt go, curious what he stopped himself from saying. I never had a proper father—mine wanted nothing to do with his bastard son. Brac and I have always had that in common. I am not sure how I feel about that changing.

When I return to the terrace, a platter of fruit and yogurt dip have been set out, and Kali, Indah, and the admiral have gone. Princess Gemi is the only one left.

"You just missed them," she says. "They took the kindred on a tour of the palace." I start to leave to find Kali, but Gemi grabs my forearm and brushes a finger across my skin. "Stay and have dessert. You hardly touched your supper. You must be hungry."

I am, in fact, starved. The threat of seasickness prevented me from eating much on the riverboat, and tomorrow, I will be back on the water.

Gemi wears a sly smile as she tops off my wine chalice. "Nush," she cheers.

In Tarachand, it is rude to refuse a host's offer of food or drink. Besides, Kali is safe with Indah and the admiral, and I have an unobstructed view of the breaker from here to keep an eye out for the raiders, should they try anything. Picking up my chalice, I return to the table and eat.

5

Kalinda

Shadows swathe my bedchamber. Natesa and Yatin are shut in her antechamber, their supper scraps left on the terrace, deserted beside a lit lamp. I envy their freedom to shut out the world and lose themselves in one another.

Deven has not yet returned. I did not want to leave him behind, but Indah and the admiral suggested they show me more of the palace, and I could not stand Princess Gemi a moment longer. She sat so close to Deven during supper she was nearly in his lap.

A warm gust grazes my ear, but a blizzard rages inside me. I gravitate to the lamp and lean over nature's flame. My soul's reflection takes form—a fire dragon. I study the small, serpentine figure for changes since the Voider poured his cold-fire inside me, but it gazes up as usual and awaits my command.

You're a lovely sight. I reach for the fire dragon, seeking its warmth. I am not afraid of a burn or any other reprisal. Both of us are born of fire, though only one of us is the master.

My hand touches the flame, and the dragon recoils. *Shh. I am fire, and fire is me.* The dragon bares its fangs and then flies down into the center of the flame and vanishes.

The lamplight flickers in the breeze. My soul's reflection has never retreated from me before. I suppress a shudder, the cold inside me seeming to snicker at my failed effort to elude it. What are my powers good for? Tarachandians believe I should be stoned or locked up. The sultan believed bhutas should be slaves. And the datu treats our gifts like sideshow displays. I did not master nature-fire or learn how to scorch and parch soul-fire to entertain people.

But I have always flouted convention. My fevers made me an outcast at the temple, and my disgust for Tarek made me an outcast at the palace. My uncommon Burner powers make me unusual even among bhutas. I was born a rogue. I am the daughter of a Burner and a rani. Two people that by all rights should never have fallen in love. I came into this world with a purpose, to finish what my parents began. The Voider can steal Tarek's identity, our army, and our people, but he cannot take away my birthright.

I wave my hand, and the flame puffs out.

Darkness rushes in, and a heavy, burdensome premonition prickles at me. *Someone is here.* I draw one of the twin daggers strapped to my thighs and peer into my shadowy room. Out of the darkness steps a man not of flesh and bone. He consists of the vile parts that are left after a body decays. I throw out a heatwave and illuminate him.

"Tarek?" I whisper.

He shields his eyes. "Put out the light." Tarek's voice wrenches me out of my shock. I push more soul-fire into my fingers. He shies from the radiance. "I've come to warn you."

"You're *dead*."

"Kalinda, I will not see my empire fall. Tarachand is my legacy."

Every pain he caused me fires off inside my head and heart. I want to let the past go, put all this ugliness behind me, but my memories shackle me.

"Your *legacy* is of fear and hatred." My hands burn brighter. Tarek cringes, and his indistinct form begins to fade. "Go away. You'll find no mercy here."

He peeks out from behind his blurry fingers. His haunting voice roughens. "Kalinda, I still love you—"

I hurl a heatwave at him. His hazy shape shatters into a thousand oblivions that shower down, hit the floor, and disappear.

Light. I need light. Shaking all over, I rush around, lighting every lamp until the chamber is aglow. I slump down onto the bed.

I still love you.

I rap my fists against my head to bang out his voice. "Leave me alone. Just leave me alone." In the abrupt silence that follows, my clarity sharpens to an unbearable point. "I hate you," I whisper to him, wherever he may be. But my abhorrence is irrelevant. To the gods, our marital bond ties my soul to his. I will be Tarek's wife for eternity.

Someone touches my shoulder. I whirl around with my dagger, and Ashwin lurches out of striking distance. "It's me."

I drop my blade. "You snuck up on me."

"I knocked before I came in. Are you all right? You're shivering."

"I . . ." Not knowing where to begin, I start to cry. Ashwin enfolds me in his arms. I clutch him close and rest my cheek against the hollow of his neck. A steady current of heat flows off him and into me. "You're so warm," I push out from between chattering teeth.

"What happened?"

"Tarek was here." My tears flow faster. "Why couldn't Jaya have visited me? My soul should be tied to hers, not his."

"Kali, you're making no sense. You saw Tarek?"

"He was a shadow, but it was him. He said—he said—" My voice hitches, and I press my cheek hard against Ashwin's collarbone. He rubs my back, his heart drumming near my ear. "Do you think I'm bound to him forever?"

"No one can rule your heart, not even the gods."

"But our matrimony vows—"

"Marital bonds cannot last past death; otherwise every marriage in every life would be honored. Think of the tangle of nuptials." He runs his hand down my hair. "As I understand it, souls aren't bound by wedding vows but by love."

I swipe my forearm across my damp nose. "Tarek repulses me. Don't you despise him?"

"He angered me sometimes . . . but mostly he made me sad." Ashwin pauses and then whispers, "We were both a disappointment to each other."

I do not share his rationale. "I hope Tarek suffers an eternity of darkness for taking Jaya from me."

Ashwin leans back until we are eye level. "Tarek hasn't taken Jaya away forever. Have you heard the tale of *Inanna's Descent*?"

"Once." Non-deity myths were not part of my studies. I am in no mood to listen to childish stories, but Ashwin wants to cheer me up, so I oblige him. "Inanna went into the Void to search for her lost intended."

"Her intended was not lost. A demon seduced him. Demons have corporeal bodies like you and me, though they're monstrous. This particular demon had the power to assume a mortal form."

Much like the power Ashwin gave the Voider when he released him to fulfill his heart's wish, but he brushes over this similarity.

"The night before their wedding, the demon took the form of Inanna and entered her intended's bedchamber. Trusting the demon *was* Inanna, he went off with her into the evernight." I settle closer to Ashwin, his voice a mild rumble. "The next morning, Inanna donned her wedding robes and set off to be married. She waited at the altar all day for her intended, but he did not come. Jilted, she returned home and locked herself away. She refused to see anyone and could not find the strength to change out of her bridal attire. Many nights later, she woke to find her intended at her bedside. He could not step out of the dark, nor could she light a lamp without him fading. He had traveled by shadow to tell her he was trapped in the Void."

Traveled by shadow. Ashwin once told me that when the day was made, so was the night. When man was made, so was his shadow. The

Void dwells in darkness, and life dwells in light. Can spirits in the Void, both living and dead, travel into the mortal realm so long as they stay in the dark? Is that how Tarek came to me? "I never understood how Inanna's intended visited her."

"Numerous sources cite that mortals trapped in the Void are confined to the dark. They can visit our world at night, but they must return to the realm below during the day. Inanna spent every night with her intended. But she could not bear to leave him in the dark for eternity, so she descended below to find him and came upon the first of seven gates. Each guardian required a toll for her passage and to point her in the right direction. Inanna paid with the clothing and adornments of her wedding attire. After the final gate, her torchlight went out. Inanna feared she would be lost in the dark forever, but she sensed her intended was close by. Following the promptings of her heart, she found him near death. She had to get him out, but she could not see the way. Inanna cried up to the gods, but none would listen except the fire-god Enlil, who had a weakness for mortal women. He took pity on Inanna and sent her an ever-burning ember to light their path back to the mortal realm."

Ashwin skims his finger under my chin. His voice gentles between us, a silky caress. "Love bound Inanna and her intended together and gave them direction in the dark. If their love can overcome the Void, so can yours bind you to Jaya in this life and the next."

Tears blur my sight. I did not think a tale could lessen my sorrow, but Ashwin's storytelling and assurances soothe me.

The mood between us shifts. The intent of his touches changes from comfort to one of need. His hug becomes more for him than me, and his heart beats faster.

I should pull back. Push him away. But his nearness calms the blizzard inside me. I am not parching his soul-fire. He is bequeathing it to me.

Ashwin settles his forehead against mine, his gaze trained on my mouth. His thumb brushes over my bottom lip, and my stomach bubbles like hot springs. His breath smells of cinnamon. A craving for more of him ripples out in a wave. How much warmer would I feel with his lips on me? I tip up my chin and wait for more of his light.

"Kali," Deven says.

He stands in the doorway, his emotions progressing from disbelief to hurt. Ashwin's arms fall from around me, and my teeth clack together, snapping me back into focus.

Deven crosses the chamber and throws Ashwin to the floor. "You have no honor! You're taking advantage of her loyalty!"

His fury shocks me. He rarely reacts without forethought or context. "Deven! I was upset and—and Ashwin found me." I reach for him, but he brushes me aside.

Natesa and Yatin run in from the other room in their nightclothes and draw up straight.

Ashwin shuffles back from Deven on his elbows. "Kalinda is aware of her actions. I'm not forcing her to stay with me. This is her choice."

Deven leans over Ashwin and grabs the front of his tunic. "Keep your hands off her."

Ashwin yanks himself from Deven's grasp. "Touch me again, General, and I'll have you imprisoned."

"Both of you stop it!" I say.

"I'm not your general," Deven grits out. "I won't serve a man I don't respect."

"Deven," I breathe. "You don't mean that."

He retreats from Ashwin, his arms and fists bunched. "I serve *you*. But if you continue to align yourself with this boy . . ."

"You'll denounce me too?" The challenge slips out of me testier than I intended. But the thought of him coming between Ashwin and me . . . I *need* Ashwin's warmth.

Deven draws up to his full height. "My apologies, my queen. You're free to do as you wish."

He revolves and marches out.

"Deven, wait!" I hurry after him, but he whisks ahead. In my effort to keep up, my limp worsens. We venture down corridor after corridor, and I quickly lose my bearings. I ignore the pain in my leg for as long as possible, but when he is nearly out of sight, I double over. "Deven, please."

He pauses and stares over his shoulder at me, his flinty expression split by shadows. "How long have you and the prince . . . ?"

"We became friends in Iresh," I say. "What was said at supper about us was for the datu. He'll aid the empire so long as he thinks Ashwin and I are committed."

"Then what was that just now? Were you practicing your commitment?"

"That was . . ." *A mistake.* But my excuses will only serve to bruise him more deeply. Telling him Ashwin's closeness acts as a balm for my wounds is ridiculous. I cannot understand the oddity of our connection myself.

"Are you in love with him?" Deven questions, eerily calm.

I hug my torso, trying to strangle the cold inside me. My need for heat is paramount, unquenchable. For whatever reason, Ashwin answers that necessity. I cannot deny he has some hold over me. "No, but we . . . we need each other."

Deven drops his chin, his jaw twitching. "I told you once that I won't stand by while you spend every meal, every public showing, at another man's side. I told you I want you by *my* side, and I still do."

"And I still want to be there."

He lifts his gaze and searches me for sincerity. I meant what I said. He must see that. But bleakness enters his voice. "I won't interfere again. When you decide what you want, I'll be waiting."

Deven charges off without a second glance. I lunge after him, but pain shoots through my knee. Backing up, I rest against the wall and push my palm over my heart. Maybe I can wring out whatever nonsense has come over me. I care for Ashwin, but I *love* Deven.

My body trembles from indecision. Even after recognizing the distinction of my feelings, hunger rises in me to return to the prince's pacifying arms . . .

Gods, I'm incorrigible.

I lower myself to the cool floor and rest my leg. The Voider's icy breath rages within me, freezing me to my spot. The corridors all look identical. I chased Deven so far, I cannot recall the path back to my chamber. Not that it matters. I have little strength to do anything except huddle into myself and try to regain some warmth.

A nudge rouses me awake. "Were you here all night?" Indah asks, standing over me.

Morning's first rays lighten the corridor. I push up from the floor, astonished I slept here. I understand why neither Deven nor Ashwin searched for me, but I am surprised Natesa or Yatin did not come looking. They must have assumed I was with Deven. "What time is it?"

"Dawn." Indah joins me on the floor, our backs leaning against the wall. "The navy is finishing preparations for the voyage. We'll leave for Iresh soon."

"Did Ashwin and the datu come to an agreement last night?" I was so upset when Ashwin found me, I forgot to ask.

"I don't know about the prince, but Bulan is pleased. Ashwin offered up lumber, grain, and livestock in exchange for our help. Our food stores have been low for some time, and we don't have enough land to cultivate the agriculture necessary for our population." Indah presses a hand to her stomach.

"You still aren't feeling well?"

"I'm a bit run down from traveling, but I'm fine," she says. "I'm glad I found you. I didn't get a chance to ask you last night: Do you and Ashwin intend to marry?"

"You know we don't. Why?"

Her lips mash together. "At supper, when Ashwin said you weren't officially set to wed . . . he wasn't telling the truth."

Indah can sense the blood flowing through another's body, specifically when someone's pulse speeds up, such as when they are lying. Her prowess for sensing people's dishonesty is a valued asset, but it can be disconcerting when someone I know is her target.

"Are you certain?" I ask. Ashwin would not go against his promise to relinquish his first rights to me.

"I don't know what it means," Indah says, quick to qualify her inkling. "I only know what I sensed."

"But I'm not his intended."

"Does *he* know that?"

"Yes . . ." After Indah's persistent silence, I add, "I—I think so."

My actions may have confused more than just me. In all fairness to Ashwin, I have acted erratically lately. I must dissolve this strange bond between us. Yet even as I resolve to speak with him, like a rabbit scurrying into a cozy burrow to escape winter, I want to bundle myself in his arms.

Datu Bulan strolls down the corridor, sporting a knee-length night tunic and oversized sandals. He carries a water cup, sipping from it every so often. "Blessed be Enki's sea, ladies." He does not let on if he finds it peculiar that we are seated in his corridor. Staring down into his cup, he says, "I once traded ten coconuts for an icicle frozen by a northern Aquifier. It melted by the time I brought it home, but that water was the freshest drink I ever had."

I cast an inquisitive glance at Indah. Northern Aquifiers dwell in the arctic tundra and are rumored to manipulate ice and snow. How the datu came upon one or why he thought an icicle would last in the Southern Isles is beyond me.

He strides away, his sandals slapping against the floor, and then halts. "Indah, I do believe Pons is looking for you."

She shifts to a kneeling position. "He's returned?"

"He and the others."

"What others?" I ask.

"Come on." Indah stands and hoists me up. I hurry down the corridor with her.

"He's in the prince's chamber," Datu Bulan calls after us.

Indah pulls ahead of me and reaches Ashwin's open door first. Pons stands outside the threshold. They saw each other just yesterday, yet Indah clutches him close. Pons's arms come around her slowly; he is taken aback by her open affection.

"You didn't tell me you were leaving," she says.

Rarely have I seen Indah fret over Pons. They are usually together, but they were not always. Pons was born in the sultanate, while Indah is a native Lestarian.

"I didn't want to worry you," Pons says, then sees me from over Indah's shoulder, and they shuffle out of the doorway.

Within the chamber, Ashwin is seated at a desk with piles of books before him. His hair and tunic are rumpled from a sleepless night. I am within his sight, but he pays me no heed. I lock my knees to stop myself from rushing to him and alleviating my inner cold at his side. He must be hurt that I ran after Deven last night instead of staying. Offending those I care about has become a terrible habit of mine. How will I make this right?

I am so preoccupied with Ashwin, I overlook the other people in the room.

A middle-aged woman drags me into her arms. "You're even skinnier than I recall."

"Mathura!" I hug her back, inhaling her jasmine scent. Her dark-brown hair is tied back in a braid, the customary style for an imperial courtesan. Her sari is travel worn, but she still appears stately.

Rohan sits off to the side on the terrace. Dishes of food are set before the young Galer, who is known for his big appetite, but Rohan slumps in his chair and touches none of it. His older sister, Opal, is not here. I do not see Brac either . . .

Deven races into the room, halts abruptly while surveying the chamber, and then flies at his mother. They embrace as tight as they can.

"You're thinner too." Mathura pats her son's cheek. "And you need a shave."

He chuckles—one of my favorite sounds. "I've missed you too, Mother." His scarlet uniform jacket hangs open, and a day's worth of facial hair covers his jawline. I love him this way best, when he is in between a smooth face and a full beard, neither done up nor undone.

Ambassador Chitt barges into the chamber, his chest heaving as though he has run the length of the island. He walks to Mathura, never taking his sight off her. "I was preparing to embark when I heard of your arrival."

Mathura extends her hand, and he cups it in his. "It's been a long time," she says.

They know each other? I watch Deven for an explanation, but he is unreadable.

"You're even more beautiful than I remember," Chitt murmurs, and Mathura's cheeks pinken. I cannot recall if I have ever seen her blush. "Where's your other son?"

Deven snaps his chin sideways and scans the room. His gaze catches mine momentarily and then barrels onward as though I were a stone he kicked out of his way. "Mother, where's Brac?"

Mathura tenses in anticipation of his reaction. "I meant to tell you as soon as you walked in. Brac isn't here."

"Where is he?" Deven's low question slices, an order that must be met.

Rohan answers, his voice abysmal. "Brac and Opal were flying near the Tarachand border when their wing flyer was shot down. We tried to circle back, but the demon rajah's army was upon them. Opal sent a message on the wind for us to go. We lost sight of her, and I haven't heard anything since."

Deven freezes. The same dread locks me in place. I fear for Deven and his family, but even more so for Rohan. He and Opal were orphaned after their Galer mother was executed in a bhuta raid. They have only each other. My chest squeezes in empathy. His dependence on his sister reminds me how much I relied on Jaya.

Ashwin pushes up from his desk. "The imperial army is at the border? We were told the demon rajah is still in Iresh."

"Our informants were misled," Pons replies, coming into the chamber with Indah. "I flew over Iresh. The city has been abandoned. Only the Tarachandian civilians and a few soldiers remain. The imperial army will cross into the empire soon."

"How is that possible?" Ashwin sputters out. "Your scouts said—"

"They were listening at a good distance," Pons explains. "They heard travelers leaving Iresh and assumed they were Janardanians fleeing."

"Was my brother captured by the demon rajah?" Deven asks, still motionless.

Mathura flourishes her hands in chagrin. "We don't know."

The navy is useless now. Their ships cannot reach a landlocked army. "Pons, how long until the army reaches Vanhi?" I ask.

"At the rate they're marching, six days."

Ashwin pounds his fists against the desk and hunches over, startling Rohan. "I need to speak with the general and the kindred alone. Everyone else is dismissed."

Indah and Pons leave without a word. Rohan slogs out after them, his breakfast gone cold.

Deven embraces his mother again. "Brac will be all right."

Mathura lays her cheek against his shoulder. "I lost him once. I cannot lose him again."

Brac was presumed dead until a few moons ago, a cover-up for his real mission of joining the rebels. He worked with Hastin to unseat Rajah Tarek but gave up that life when he reunited with his family.

Deven holds Mathura for a long moment. "I'll find him, Mother. I swear it."

She releases him, and I fight back the urge to take her place in his arms. I do not need his comfort; I want to comfort *him.*

Chitt offers Mathura his elbow, and they go. Only Deven, Ashwin, and I remain. Given our quarrel last night, it is a wonder we are all in the same room together without arguing.

Ashwin waits until the door shuts and extends a letter to us. "Late last night, I received a message from the bhuta warlord. Hastin has requested a meeting with the kindred and me."

Of course Hastin knows where we are. He has informants all over the continent.

Deven demonstrates no inclination to take the letter, so I do and read the warlord's message aloud. "'I would like to propose an accord. Meet me in Samiya to discuss uniting against the demon rajah.'"

My heart yanks hard in my chest. I have not returned home since Tarek claimed me, but I dream of the mountains often. Jaya is always in my dreams, as is Deven. "Why the temple?"

"Samiya is a neutral site," replies Ashwin. "Hastin wouldn't dare attack us on sacred ground."

"You've clearly never met the bhuta warlord," Deven retorts.

I finger the Tarachand seal, a scorpion, at the top of the letter. Hastin stole this parchment from the rajah's personal belongings in the palace. I want to disregard his request just to spite him, but I consider it for the ranis and courtesans he has trapped there. They and their children are caught in the middle of this war. An alliance could set them free.

"We should go," I say.

Deven tugs the letter from my hand. "I cannot believe you're considering this."

"We cannot rightly ignore him. The demon rajah is more powerful than we are, and he has our army. The Lestarian Navy is of no use to us now."

"Not entirely." Deven tosses aside the letter. Ashwin tries to catch the corner, but it drifts out of reach to the floor. "Other waterways lead to Vanhi. The navy could still fight with us."

"Hastin's troops are already *in* Vanhi," counters Ashwin. "With the rebel soldiers on our side, we can surround the imperial army when they reach the city."

"The imperial army may be scattered, but it's the largest in the world," Deven explains. "On his way, the demon rajah will pick up deserters. The closer he gets to Vanhi, the more loyalists he will bring into his fold. Army outposts are stationed all along his route. His troops will rally with him, and his ranks will swell."

"Even more reason why we need the rebels," I counter. "Hastin may have a vendetta against Tarek, but he's no fool. He knows he cannot defeat the demon rajah without help."

"Do you really believe the rebels want to unite?" Deven jabs a finger at me, marking his every point. "Hastin betrayed you. He tried to murder Ashwin by burning down the Brotherhood temples. Hastin will sooner slit the prince's throat than unite with Tarek's heir."

Ashwin swallows loudly, his color paling.

I have not forgotten Hastin's actions. Nor has my guilt lessened over my former naivety. Hastin used me to further his vendetta against Tarek. The result goes beyond the loss of the Turquoise Palace and his imprisonment of the rajah's wives and courtesans, many of whom are my friends. Hastin murdered palace guards and soldiers. To escape him, citizens fled the empire to the sultanate. Many fell ill with swamp sickness in the encampments and died. Our downtrodden people were primed for the return of Rajah Tarek. Without their hardships, I doubt they would have so readily accepted his miraculous resurrection. But thanks to Hastin and the landslide of suffering his insurgence caused, our people and army are now following a demon.

No, I have not forgotten Hastin's part in our misery. But I am not the same woman I was when we first met. Hastin will not deceive me again, nor will he keep what is rightfully mine. He has my father's journal, my only connection to my parents. The last time I saw the warlord, he dangled the journal before me as a bribe, but I refused to align with him over Ashwin. I have been patient long enough. I want what is mine.

"Kali, this is *Hastin*," Deven says. "He's setting a trap."

I nearly crack under the weight of his warning, but the gods have preserved my life to stop the fall of the empire. And I will do just that. "We cannot stand against the demon rajah alone. Partnering with Hastin is our best chance of winning."

"I'll send him a carrier dove right away." Ashwin selects a plain piece of parchment to jot his letter upon. "We'll agree to meet at the Samiya temple, far away from the sea raiders and the imperial army."

"You'll also be far away from help when Hastin stabs you in the back," Deven clips out.

"We have another reason to meet in Samiya." Ashwin picks up an open book. "I spent the night researching demons in hope of discovering the Voider's identity. Many demons serve Kur, but I narrowed them down per their abilities and found one that possesses the icy breath of cold-fire." He shows us the page with a sketch of a demon exhaling a plume of blue flames.

Deven and I shuffle closer to read the caption beneath the drawing, and our sides bump. He steps away and tells Ashwin to summarize.

"The demon's name is Udug, Kur's top commander. Udug has three siblings, who are also eternal soldiers of Kur's: Edimmu, Asag, and Lilu. All four of them possess a version of bhutas' land, fire, sky, and water abilities."

Deven's brows shoot up. "Udug and his siblings have *bhuta* abilities?"

"A perverted form of them, though their powers are rarely seen in our realm. It's a long-held belief that demons are more powerful in the dark."

The Voider—Udug—serves the demon Kur, who holds a grudge that goes back millennia, to the war between the sky-god Anu and his primeval parents. Kur means to avenge the deaths of the primeval gods by wiping out mankind's strongest connection to Anu—bhutas. The First Bhutas vanquished Udug long ago, and their method was recorded in a sacred book. A book Udug destroyed.

I point at the picture of the Voider. "What does any of this have to do with Samiya?"

"The gods' temple was built at the top of the Alpana Mountains," Ashwin answers. Every member of the Parijana faith believes in Ekur, the gods' mountain house, though no mortal has seen it. "This book says the only way to vanquish a demon is to banish it, just like the First Bhutas did. We have to find the gate to the Void and return Udug through it. The gate is rumored to be hidden near Samiya."

The sisters spoke often of Ekur, but they neglected to mention that an entry to the Void was close to our temple sanctuary. That is, assuming they are aware it is there.

Deven blusters out a breath. "Kali, he's only trying to convince you to go with him. The rebels don't want to make peace with us. Hastin will never side with *him*." He motions at Ashwin. "He represents everything the warlord despises."

Ashwin rubs the back of his neck tiredly. "Your concerns are noted, Deven."

But his concerns are no excuse for his lack of compassion. Ashwin has scars running down his back from a lashing Tarek gave him. He suffered his father's wrath as much as anyone. "Ashwin is not his father. You need to stop punishing him for Tarek's actions."

"I'm not punishing him. I'm reminding you who he is and how much Hastin hates him." Deven puts his hands together as if in prayer, begging me to listen. "This will end badly. Please. Go with the navy or stay here. I'll rejoin you after I find Brac."

"Come to Samiya with me." My selfish request is small of me. But I do not care.

Deven stares back, incredulous. The events of last night are too fresh in his mind. The back of my throat aches for his forgiveness. "Kali, I have to find Brac."

"You said yourself he'll be fine. He's too clever to be captured. Come with us."

"You know I cannot."

I know Deven will risk his life to save his brother's, and I cannot bear to lose him. I try one last entreaty. "I cannot imagine returning to Samiya without you."

Deven's eyes go wide, and understanding passes between us. Returning to the Alpanas together is our dream.

Ashwin drops the book on the table with a bang. "I'll go to Samiya alone, then."

"Wait." I grasp at him, desperate for all of us to come to an accord. "Please, don't go."

"Yes, you stay," Deven growls. "I was just leaving."

I let go of Ashwin and reach for Deven. "I didn't mean—" Deven prowls out and slams the door. I think to follow him, but the prince encloses my stiff frame in an embrace.

"Let him go. You won't change his mind."

I try not to melt under Ashwin's touch, but his body heat soaks into me, and the sudden change is irresistible. "Maybe we should listen to him."

"Kalinda, we're acting in the empire's best interest. Together with the rebels, we will stop Udug."

For the first time, Ashwin sounds certain that we can succeed. I drive away my guilt at needing—and appreciating—his touch and remain near him.

We will go to Samiya without Deven, but his refusal to support us leaves a sourness in my mouth. He of all people should appreciate why we need the rebels' help. With Udug closer to Vanhi than we believed, trusting the warlord is a risk we must take.

6

Deven

I lean against the wall outside the prince's door, my fists quaking. *Kali took Ashwin's side*. They should be rerouting the navy to Vanhi, yet all they can think about is the warlord.

Shortsighted fools. The demon rajah's head start could mean the end of the war. I push away from the wall and march down the corridor.

Turn back and tell her you love her. Don't part in anger.

I nearly bow to my apprehension but stay on course. Last night, I slept on a bench in the garden instead of returning to Kali's chamber. I resolved to leave her be, and I will, because the only other option is to compel her to choose between the prince and me *right now*. And that would make me an even bigger fool than they are, for I am not merely competing against a prince. I am up against her throne. She is long past needing me as her guard. Whatever happens on that mountaintop, Kali can defend herself. I am more concerned about them wasting time.

But time is all I can give her. Time to consider her future. Time to remember she never asked to become a rani. Time to realize she can have a peaceful life with me.

Unless I am utterly mistaken, and Kali has chosen her path. She may, in fact, never relinquish her throne. She may be falling in love with Ashwin, and she is sparing me heartache by not saying so . . .

I increase my pace, no longer departing in anger but with another emotion that I do not allow myself to inspect too closely before I shove it down and lock it away.

Yatin and Natesa dine on breakfast in Kali's chamber. Natesa leaps out of the way when I storm in, the swinging door knocking against her chair. Rohan nibbles on pieces of mango. He is just fourteen, two years younger than his sister Opal. *Anu, let our siblings be safe.*

Mother sits out on the balcony, smoking her handheld hookah pipe while she speaks with Ambassador Chitt. Smoke curls rise around them.

"Rohan told us Brac and Opal are missing," Yatin says in his deep burr.

I pace alongside the breakfast table, half expecting Kali to realize her foolishness and join us. But Ashwin was right—this is Kali's choice.

Natesa dishes rice into a bowl in front of Rohan. He ignores it. Yatin tips back in his chair, closer to me. I pause beside him.

"He asked where Brother Shaan was," he whispers.

Grief over the death of my mentor rises anew. Brother Shaan took in Opal and Rohan after their widowed mother was executed and found them safe passage out of Vanhi. Rohan and I feel his loss the most.

I pace again, restless to act. I cannot wait for Kali forever. If she thinks Ashwin's plan of allying with Hastin will save us, then let them have their idealistic idiocy. My brother needs me.

I stop tromping around. Rohan deserves more time to mourn, but I need his help. "Rohan, I need you to fly me to the location where you last saw Opal and Brac."

The Galer unbends from his slouch, buoyed by my request. His eagerness quiets my concern about how he will fare on our mission.

"Deven, don't be rash," Yatin says, direct but always respectful. "Rohan said the army has catapults and more than enough soldiers to fire them. The troops will shoot you from the sky."

"The army will have marched on by now. Brac and Opal could be waiting for us where they landed. I need a Galer to take me."

"And me," Natesa says.

Yatin and I stare at her in joint astonishment. She blushes, squirming under our silent enquiry. *Why is she volunteering?* Natesa takes care of herself. She has extended her self-preservation to include Yatin, and sometimes Kali, but no one else. Especially not Brac. The two of them have never gotten along. He parched her the first time they met, and she has never forgotten.

"We should stay," Yatin counters. "The wing flyer will travel faster without us."

He has a point, but I would appreciate two more people on the lookout for Opal and Brac. Even so, coming along is their decision. I have no illusions about how dangerous this will be.

"I want to go," Natesa insists. "My older sister passed away last year. After our parents died, she was all the family I had left." She speaks more quietly, to steady her voice. "I don't want either of you to lose a sibling as well."

Her concern extends to Rohan, as his circumstance closely mirrors her own. His sister is also the only family member he has left. I should have considered Natesa's decision was personal, but she often acts impervious to heartache, others' and her own. I am beginning to see she is not as immune to compassion as she would like us to believe.

Yatin links hands with her. "We'll both go."

"It's settled then. Eat up, soldier." I slap Rohan on the back. "We need your powers refreshed for our flight."

Rohan perks up even more at "soldier" and shovels in mango as fast as he can chew.

"Should we tell Kalinda and Ashwin?" Natesa asks, eating the last of her breakfast.

"They already know." Despite my effort to sound neutral, rancor burns my tone. Natesa pauses chewing, sensing I am omitting something. I set forth our plan before she can prod at me. "Rohan, can you be ready to depart in an hour?"

"I'll do my best," he says, cramming his mouth with fruit.

"Everyone be ready to leave then." I step nearer to the terrace. My mother and Chitt are still conversing in private. Their bodies are turned toward one another, sealing me out.

I clamp off a sting of envy. I have fretted over my mother's safety for days. Chitt has no right to reenter our lives and take all her attention, particularly after abandoning us. He may not be my father, but he could have filled that role for both Brac and me. Gods know we needed him.

Buttoning up my jacket, I stride out of the chamber. I will keep my word to my mother and find Brac. No other outcome is acceptable.

Less than half an hour later, I weave my way down the dock rife with sailors preparing for departure. A dozen moored navy vessels line the wharf. Most are built like *Enki's Heart*, with one mast and the capacity to hold up to two hundred passengers. The ship on the far end is the biggest, with three masts. I anticipate it can carry twice as many people. On the whole, I estimate the navy is sending up to three thousand men to battle.

Past the sailors loading supplies for their voyage, I locate Admiral Rimba on the largest craft. He waves me aboard. I jump on deck and maneuver through the working sailors.

"General Naik," the admiral says by way of welcome, "I received word that the kindred and prince aren't coming. Are you still joining us?"

"No, sir, but I *am* leaving for the continent. My brother has gone missing. I told my mother I'd find him."

Admiral Rimba frowns at my brusqueness and then enters the cabin. I follow him to his command console, which is covered in maps. He removes mint leaves from a small tin and rolls them into a bundle. "Indah told me Prince Ashwin and Kindred Kalinda are departing for the mainland by another means as well."

"We're not leaving together. They have another destination."

"So I heard. They intend to meet the warlord." Admiral Rimba presses the bundle of mint into the side of his cheek, but it does not impede his speech. "And you'd like for us to alter our destination from Iresh to Vanhi."

"I would," I reply, relieved one person in Lestari understands military strategy.

The admiral waves me over to the map at the other end of the console. "Datu Bulan agrees. He sent orders for me to lead the fleet up the River Ninsar. The river goes around the Bhavya Desert and connects here, to the River Nammu, which flows into Vanhi. The passage narrows, so we must sail single file, but we should fit."

"Should?"

"Our navy has never voyaged that far inland."

The odds continue to stand against us. "How long until you reach Vanhi?"

He weighs my question before replying. "We have enough Aquifiers to propel us there in seven days. The reverse journey is six. Pushing upriver against the current will slow us."

The demon rajah is estimated to arrive in Vanhi within six days, but I do not press the admiral. He and his men realize our urgency and will do their best. I point to the section of the map where the two rivers meet. "My party and I will meet you here. How long do we have?"

"About four days. If you aren't there when we sail by, we will continue on without you."

"We'll be there."

Admiral Rimba pushes a pin into the map at the cross section of rivers. The finality of our arrangement bores into me. I must find Brac and meet the admiral's fleet on time, or we will be on our own.

Natesa and Rohan wait in the garden near the wing flyer. Yatin stands off to the side, frowning up at the sky. One would think airsickness afflicts him instead of me. I am already ill in anticipation of our flight.

Yatin and Natesa have changed into sturdier travel clothes. Natesa traded her skirt for Princess Gemi's favored attire, loose trousers. They also brought supply packs for themselves and Rohan, and one for me. My mother and Ambassador Chitt stand off to the side, come to say good-bye.

Tears shine in Mother's eyes. "Be careful."

"I will." I draw her in close. She smells of hookah smoke and jasmine.

"Love you, Deven," Mother whispers.

Emotions crowd my voice. I manage a nod, and she moves on to bid farewell to the others.

Ambassador Chitt saunters over, his hands clasped solemnly behind him. "I heard about Prince Ashwin's plans. He sent word to the warlord, but he isn't waiting for a reply. He, the kindred, and a small group of guards are flying to Samiya. He asked me to go with them and help negotiate."

Chitt has closer ties to Hastin than we do. The warlord once served with Kishan, Kali's father, as well. "Do you think Hastin will unite with the empire?"

"Difficult to say. Hastin has always been unpredictable."

I scoff under my breath. Unpredictable? The man is volatile.

"I'd like to join your group instead, if you'll have me." Chitt clasps and unclasps his hands in front of himself uncertainly. "Your mother said it was all right to tell you our history. Mathura told me long ago that Brac is my son. I sent dozens of letters to Tarek requesting to acquire her. It felt uncouth to offer him coin, but men like Tarek put a value on everything. I offered a more-than-fair amount for Mathura's freedom, but I didn't consider how much Tarek relished possessing something another man envied." Chitt glances at my mother, who embraces Yatin in farewell. "I should have known he would never let me have her and Brac."

"You asked for them both?" I ask, cocking a brow.

"And you," Chitt amends. My disbelief falters. "I asked to trade for all three of you. I own a sizeable plantation on an outer island, plenty of room for two boys to run around. You're a little older than I thought you'd be when we met again, but perhaps someday you'll visit me there."

"I'd enjoy that." Chitt was not required to justify himself to me, but I am grateful he did. "You should go to the sultanate. Gather the Tarachandian army and stand by for word from me or Admiral Rimba. We may yet need their troops."

Mother rejoins us, slipping her arm through mine. "What did I miss?"

"Ambassador Chitt has some business in Janardan," I answer. "You should go with him."

Mother squints at me. "I don't need you to manage my life, son."

"I know he's Brac's father," I answer without condemnation. Though she prompted Chitt to speak with me, she still blanches. "You need time to discuss how to approach Brac with the news. He'll have questions, but I think he will be open-minded."

My mother gives a closed-lipped nod. I kiss her cheek, and then Chitt draws closer to her. Seeing them side by side, I imagine what it would be like to visit his home together. *May we all live long enough to find out.*

The first stirrings of Rohan's winds whistle through the garden.

"Deven," Yatin calls. "We're ready."

"Shouldn't you wait for Kalinda?" Mother asks.

"Kali would be here if she planned to see us off." I start for the wing flyer. I could seek Kali out and plead with her to change her mind, but the last time I thought I knew what was best for her, I wound up in a prison camp and she sought solace in the boy prince. And truthfully, I am not fully prepared for her ultimate decision.

"Deven!" a voice shouts from behind me. My foot strikes a lump on the ground and I stumble sideways. Princess Gemi hurries to me. "Sorry. I meant to stop you, not trip you." She gestures at the mound of grass she lifted with her powers. "You're leaving?"

"That's right," I reply, setting off again.

She stays at my side. "Admiral Rimba said you're meeting the fleet in a few days. I asked to go with him, but my father won't allow it. May I go with you?"

I halt and take in her white tunic tucked into dark trousers and the machete at her waist. "You don't strike me as the type of woman who asks permission."

"You've never angered my father."

"You aren't instilling much confidence in my letting you come along."

I stride away, but she tugs me back. "Please, General." She rests her hand on my chest and bats her sooty lashes as though a gnat is caught in her eye. "Let me go with you."

"You really aren't told no often."

She runs a finger up my neck to my chin. "I'd never tell *you* no."

A chuckle escapes me. Even if Princess Gemi were to charm me, I cannot give her what she wants. "The prince has more clout with your father than I do. Ask him." She begins to protest, but I rush right over her. "I won't be accused of kidnapping the datu's heir. I suggest you endear yourself to Ashwin or forget about leaving Lestari."

She drops her hand. "The prince is a wet noodle. I knew right away you're the one I could count on." I should be irate that her fawning over me has been a manipulation, but I am tempted to ask her to repeat her wet noodle comment to Kali. "Will you at least put in a good word for me with Ashwin?"

I grin humorlessly at her request. "You're asking the wrong person. Persuade Kalinda to your side, and you'll get what you want."

"That's it? I need only talk to the kindred?"

"Believe me," I call out, winds whipping at my back, "she can be hard to convince."

Everyone waits aboard the lightweight, birdlike flyer. I climb on, lie across the riding platform between Yatin and Rohan, and grip the bamboo navigation bar.

"Could you hold on any tighter?" Rohan asks me.

I purse my lips, a warning for him to stop teasing. He knows how much I dislike flying.

His summoned winds pluck us off the ground into the morning sky. I wave farewell to Mother and Chitt and stretch my gaze to the palace grounds and balconies for a glimpse of Kali. But we whizz away from the glimmering spires that soar over the aquamarine cove, and pass over the breaker.

The Sea of Souls unrolls like a ribbon to the horizon. Down the coast, a ship lurks near the breaker. The sea raiders' yellow two-mast vessel is easily identifiable. The raiders must be lying in wait for the navy's departure. I expect they will assume the prince and Kali are aboard one of their ships and pursue the fleet to the mainland. At the very least, Kali's decision to fly to Samiya will help her evade Captain Loc. Even so, I already regret leaving without bidding her good-bye—and gods' mercy.

7

Kalinda

I limp down the corridor for the open archway that leads to the garden. A breeze flows inside, the tail end of stronger drafts summoned by a Galer. I quicken my step, but my bad leg gives out, forcing me to brace against the doorway.

Gritting my teeth, I hustle outside under the palm trees. Whooshing air momentarily steals my breath. The wing flyer is airborne. Deven, Natesa, and Yatin ride with Rohan. I limp for the garden clearing, calling for Deven. The loud winds thrash the palm fronds and drown out my shouts. The wing flyer streaks over the cove and quickly shrinks into the sky.

I plunk down on a stone bench, rubbing my sore knee. After Deven left Ashwin's chamber, everything moved so fast. Ashwin dispatched a carrier dove with a letter to Hastin, and then we went to the datu. Bulan agreed with our endeavor to ally with the rebels and ordered Indah and Pons to fly us to meet Hastin. Everyone launched into a flurry of preparations for our departure. I returned to my empty bedchamber to collect my belongings when, from the terrace, I saw Deven and my friends leaving. I squeeze my eyes shut on gathering tears. Gods know when we will meet again.

"Kindred?"

I stifle a groan. *Of all the people to see me upset . . .*

Princess Gemi sits beside me. "I realize I haven't made a good first impression," she says, "but nothing happened between Deven and me."

"I didn't assume otherwise." My chilliness should be off-putting, yet the princess loiters.

"He watches you, you know. My father used to look at my mother the same way Deven looks at you." Princess Gemi hugs one knee to her chest, the ease of her trousers allowing the movement while retaining modesty. "The general's party is supposed to meet with the navy in four days where the River Ninsar connects with the River Nammu. I'd like to go with the sailors, but the admiral won't let me on board without the prince's permission. He's a taskmaster about protocol. Can you help a fellow sister warrior?"

Her sweet talk about sister warriors does not motivate me, but Admiral Rimba requiring her to receive authorization from Ashwin is ridiculous. Datu Bulan enlists female Virtue Guards, and women serve in his navy. Clearly he approves. Moreover, Princess Gemi is a grown woman and the next ruler of the Southern Isles. Fighting for her homeland should be her choice.

"Tell Admiral Rimba I've requested your attendance. And let him know my party will also meet with the navy where the rivers connect."

She scrunches her lips to the side. "Will the prince honor your decision?"

I can think of no reason why Ashwin would protest bringing another bhuta into our ranks. We are willing to accept the rebels' assistance, so we can certainly accept hers. "If you'd like to ask him, he's inside. But you should hurry. The fleet looks ready to disembark."

Princess Gemi's attention zips to the docks. The sailors have finished loading the vessels and they file aboard. She hops up. "No need. I'll tell the admiral. We'll meet again in four days!" She takes off downhill with a speed and ease that wring a drop of envy out of me.

Trousers on a woman. Why didn't I think of that?

I step out from behind the dressing screen wearing plain dark clothes that I found in the cabinet. The fitted trousers will take some adapting to, but I already prefer their convenience over the lengthy process of pleating, pinning, and tucking a sari over a blouse and petticoat. I smile to myself as I pack another set of trousers and tunic to bring to Samiya.

"What's so amusing?" Mathura asks, entering my chamber.

"I was imagining Priestess Mita's expression when she sees me in trousers."

Mathura sizes me up. "A skirt is more proper for a rani, but they're flattering on you."

I glimpse my profile in the mirror glass. The trousers define my lower body and hips. Priestess Mita will say my attire is scandalous, but my wardrobe is the least of the changes that have come over me since we last saw each other.

"You just missed Deven," Mathura notes.

"I know." I stuff the last of my belongings into my pack, pushing hard to fit the extra clothes. Between the colder mountain weather and the chill inside me, it will be a battle to stay warm.

Mathura sits on the end of the bed. "Natesa told me you've grown close to Prince Ashwin." Before I can guess what she is insinuating, she finishes. "That's for the best. You're the kindred of the Tarachand Empire, and a good one at that."

I narrow my eyes at her. "What do you want, Mathura?"

"Deven will never interfere with your duties. He'll hold on to the dream of you unless you tell him otherwise."

"I love your son," I say, forcing an even tone.

"Do you love him enough to step away from your throne? Few women have the influence you hold. Natesa says the prince respects you—he says you're equals. Do you understand how rare that is? That's a gift from the gods. You'd be a fool to squander it."

She forgets I am not only the kindred; I am a Burner. My people will never accept me as I am. Even the ranis held captive in the palace were raised to despise my kind. I hid what I am from them, and I doubt I will regain their trust once they learn my true heritage. "When the time is right, I *will* step aside."

Mathura clucks her tongue. "My son is a good man, but that's folly, Kalinda. You're a *rani*. You'll always be beyond his reach."

Gods alive, I hope Deven does not share her opinion.

Maybe he does. Maybe that's why he left without saying good-bye, why he hasn't asked me to relinquish my throne. Maybe he's afraid I won't walk away.

More doubts worm into my mind. I sided with Ashwin about the rebels. But Deven understands loyalty and duty better than anyone else. He will think back on our disagreement and realize that I supported Ashwin for the sake of the empire. I just hope Deven forgives me for the hurt my choice is causing him.

Mathura adjusts her sari pleats. "I'm leaving for Janardan with Ambassador Chitt. I trust when I see you next this will be resolved."

"It will be." By then the war will be over, and Ashwin will have secured his throne and palace. I will be free of my obligations. Free to openly love Deven. And free to tell Mathura to quit meddling.

I will savor that day.

A knock comes at the door, and Indah lets herself in. She is followed by a balding man in a long indigo robe.

"Healer Mego has come for Kalinda," says Indah. "We'll leave you two alone."

Mathura rises, stately in her grace. "Think on my words, Kalinda." She bows to emphasize my standing as kindred and sweeps out of the chamber after Indah.

Healer Mego sets his basket down on the table, rolls up his sleeves, and examines me with pale-gray eyes. "Indah told me you were corrupted by a demon."

I grapple with his verbiage. "Corrupted" sounds as though I have been irrevocably wrecked. "We don't have long before I have to leave. Can you heal me?"

"All in due time." He unpacks his basket and lifts his hands, palms facing me. "I need you to burn me."

"B-burn you?"

"Don't fret, child. Do as I say." Healer Mego presses our hands together, our palms and fingers touching. His old hands are marginally bigger than mine and smooth as the inside of a coconut. His arms are covered in more hair than his head. "Go on."

My fingers glow white-yellow with soul-fire. His flesh must be blistering, yet he does not wince or draw back. He fixates on my fingertips. As I push my powers into them, my fire darkens to greenish yellow, then a sickly jade, and then . . . sapphire sparks fly out.

I douse my powers and shrink away from the vanishing blue fire. The healer lowers his unburned hands.

"How . . . how did you do that?" I ask.

"Years of practice." Healer Mego unrolls his sleeves, his gaze resisting mine. "I'm sorry, Kindred. The Voider's toxins are beyond healing. Only he can remove his poison from you."

"What?" My hope to extract the cold-fire within me wastes away. "But what if he doesn't?"

"Then I'm afraid his toxic cold will smother your soul-fire until it's gone."

"I'll *die*?" No mortal can live without soul-fire. It is our essence.

"Your mortal half is already dying." At my expression of horror, he adds, "You can try Razing, but I do not recommend you do so. The poisons would be quelled for a short while, but they would return twofold."

My belly flips and dives. I have razed once before. An Aquifier cut me several times to bleed out a poison that hid my abilities. I will not relive that excruciating ritual for a temporary reprieve. "Can you do anything?" I plead.

"No," he replies, his tone gentle. "I'm sorry."

I sink onto the chair, knocking my pack to the floor. The temptation to lie down and let the cold consume me nearly pushes me to tears. The healer repacks his basket. Why did he even come if he cannot help me? I want to tell him to go away, but I withhold my bitterness. Lashing out at him would be wrong, and I cannot abide the thought of Udug winning in any small way. He will not compel me to cry or give into my endless shivers. He would have me believe I cannot survive. But we have the Lestarian Navy on our side, and soon the rebels will stand with us. Both are mercies from the gods.

I harvest a kernel of courage and push out my voice. "How long do I have until . . . ?"

"The full effect of the poisons takes a moon to manifest."

"Udug poisoned me a fortnight ago." I have about that much time left to find a remedy the healer is unaware of or persuade Udug to cure me. Any chance is better than the healer's predicted outcome. "Are you certain no one can ward off the Voider's powers?" I ask, thinking of Ashwin. "What if someone's soul-fire can lessen the cold within me?"

"I would caution against relying on another's soul-fire to supplement your own. Such practices are unpredictable and will worsen your side effects." My fear returns, as does his kindly voice. "If you stay in Lestari, I will make your final hours comfortable."

I scoop up my bag. "I must go."

"Kindred, I pray you'll reconsider. The damage the Voider's powers are wreaking—"

"Is less than what he plans to do the world." I pause at the door. "Thank you. I trust you'll keep this between us." I wait for the healer to grasp my expectation and then go.

Ashwin rushes down the corridor, dressed in his travel clothes. "There you are. We're ready to depart." He slows to a halt, his eyes growing. "What are you wearing?"

"Trousers. Mathura said they flatter me."

His color reddens. "I—she—" He fumbles for words that do not come.

Healer Mego exits my chamber and leaves in the opposite direction.

"Who's that?" Ashwin asks.

"A healer Indah sent to see me. Should we go?"

"Wait." Ashwin holds me in place. "What did he say?"

I am dying, not dead. Right now the difference, thank Anu, is tremendous. I muster a wobbly half smile. "I'll be fine."

"Thank the skies." Ashwin's arms come around me. "You're my strength, Kalinda. I cannot do this without you." I should move away, but his nearness drizzles over me like warmed honey.

Healer Mego must be incorrect. Ashwin's touch serves as an antidote to the Voider's poison. Embracing his nearness for the good of my health cannot be harmful or I would feel something besides this blissful absence of cold.

He releases me, and the hoarfrost inside me shakes loose again. My body's reaction makes up my mind. I cannot do this without him either. Ashwin will be my protection against the Voider's poison in the days to come.

Outside the main palace entrance, a wing flyer fills the crushed shell courtyard. Ashwin and I join Pons and Indah, who secure our packs to the passenger platform with rope. Datu Bulan speaks to a palace guard off to the side. In the distance, the last navy vessel disappears through the breaker passageway, out to sea.

"I didn't know the datu kept wing flyers," I say.

"He traded the Paljorians for them a few years back," Pons replies.

"Prince Ashwin," asks Bulan, striding over, "have you seen my daughter? Gemi was supposed to meet us here."

"She's gone with Admiral Rimba," I answer. "Gemi volunteered to enlist, and I accepted."

The datu's mouth drops open, and his color rises.

Ashwin mutters a curse and scrubs at his forehead. "Kalinda, you didn't."

"Gemi said the admiral wouldn't allow her to go without our authorization." I lob my gaze back and forth between them, uncertain why they are angry. "I saw no sense in turning down a capable Trembler."

Datu Bulan blusters out a string of indecipherable syllables and then shouts at his guard. "Signal the bridge! Tell them to bring back my daughter!"

"They're gone, sir," replies the guard. "The navy has passed through the breaker."

"Then send a boat after her!"

"Princess Gemi said she wanted to go," I explain, trying to pacify him.

The datu marches up to me, his white robes stark against ruddy cheeks. "The admiral was under orders to leave my daughter here. Prince Ashwin and I determined Gemi wouldn't go to the war front. The prince suggested we exclude her, a bhuta ruler. All command was to fall to her should you fail. Now the demon rajah could wipe out my people's future!"

"My apologies," Ashwin says. "The kindred was unaware of our agreement."

"Gemi didn't tell me either," I add. "I'm sorry."

Bulan jabs his finger at my nose. "If anything happens to her, I will find you." He swings around in a cloud of white and trudges off.

Indah calls out from the wing flyer, "Gemi will be fine. Bulan still thinks of her as his little girl, but I wouldn't engage her in battle."

Ashwin speaks under his breath. "That may be so, Kalinda, but you should have discussed this with me first. We should make these decisions together."

"You didn't tell me to leave Gemi behind," I whisper in return.

"I suggested she stay to appease Bulan. Did you not wonder why he sent Indah to Iresh to participate in the trial tournament instead of Gemi? He values his daughter above all else. Ensuring her protection was my best leverage. Even with that, our trade agreement was too generous." Ashwin is irritated with me, but also with himself for negotiating poorly.

"Excluding Gemi from battle wasn't our choice to make," I say.

Ashwin rubs at his headache. "In this case, it was."

I cut off my next retort. Naturally, the datu wants to shelter his daughter, but had Gemi been a man, I have no doubt she would have been sent off to war. Had Gemi been a man, who would Ashwin have suggested we leave behind? Another woman? Would he have excluded *me* from battle?

"What's done is done," he says. "From now on, we consult each other about everything."

"Fine." I revolve away and hastily tie my hair back for the flight.

He climbs onto the wing flyer with Indah and Pons. I ride beside Ashwin, careful not to touch him or his healing warmth. After all I have done to secure and retain my throne, I deserve his trust to make decisions by myself.

Pons's winds elevate us. Indah releases a squeal of distress, her grip a stranglehold on the navigation bar. *She's afraid of flying?* Come to think of it, I have never ridden on a wing flyer with her.

A hearty gust propels us over the palatial city. Indah buries her face against Pons's back, hiding from the lofty view. I drink in the sight of the turquoise cove and ivory beaches. Lestari truly is a haven. I wish I had relaxed and enjoyed our reprieve in paradise. Our stay was too short and fraught with strife, but Princess Gemi's willingness to dive into battle boosts my confidence that we—the Southern Isles, Tarachand Empire, and rebels—can unite to defeat the foe that threatens us.

8

Deven

The ripe scent of drying manure wafts from the field. Beneath my boots, the grass is trampled with wagon and horse tracks. After nearly two days of flying, stopping intermittently along the way, I am thankful my feet are on the ground.

I crouch and finger the grass; it is still damp from the rainstorm that passed through this afternoon. Although the traces left by the demon rajah's slow-moving army are three days old, the troops' absence does not put me at ease.

Yatin and Natesa search for signs of Brac and Opal nearer to the tree line. Dense foliage dissuades wanderers from venturing into the Morass. The jungle dominates Janardan's territory between the sea and the empire. Brac and Opal would not duck into that tangle of trees unless they wished never to come out.

Rohan scours the grasslands behind me, sending whistling gusts through low bushes to expose any place our siblings could have hidden. Where in the gods' names did they go? Brac left no discernible footprints or scorched vegetation to hint at his direction.

The army's tracks tell another story. Indents in the drying mud came from heavy artillery, catapults that fire heavy bolts and large rocks.

Other wagons were weighted down with rams and siege ramps to scale or pound through thick, high brick walls. All of this I can discern. These defenses are standard among the imperial army. But still no sign of Brac.

"Rohan, where did you last see them?" I ask, my attention split between him and the jungle to the east. The Morass forced even the demon rajah to go around it.

He strolls to a knoll. "They crashed here. We couldn't circle back because the archers started shooting." His voice cracks, as is common for boys his age, and he clears his croaky throat. "Opal was lying right here, last I saw her."

Arrows stick out of the ground. I inspect the flattened grass and find splinters of the wreckage. The troops must have disassembled the wing flyer and hauled the parts along as firewood. At least we know Opal and Brac did not fly away from here.

"What's nearby?" I ask Yatin, the experienced navigator in our group.

He studies the position of the sun. "The closest village is due south, a day or so on foot."

The army is trekking northwest into Tarachand. The border is not too far ahead. South would be Brac and Opal's wisest direction. Yatin and I would select that route, but we searched the end of the clearing and found no tracks heading to the village. Any other tracks they left were beaten into obscurity by the hundreds of men who came through.

"There's another possibility," Yatin says lowly.

Rohan kicks at the end of an arrow protruding from the ground. Neither of us wants to consider that our siblings were taken. I would like to think Brac would not have been captured without setting this field alight to stand as a memorial to his indignation, but circumstances could have stopped him.

"It's likely they've been captured." I put off the prospect that anything worse has happened. We will explore one possibility at a time.

"The rest of you stay here and guard the wing flyer. I should return the day after tomorrow, in time for us to fly to the meeting point."

"I'm going with you." Rohan holds his thin body tense, anticipating my refusal, but I respect his grit. "You'll need me to listen for my sister."

"We should all stay together," Natesa says, pinning me with a fierce stare to wither me into compliance. She forgets I grew up in the palace surrounded by sister warriors. They could sober a drunkard with a single glare.

Yatin stays locked in worry. He is a friend to Brac and me, but he came along only after Natesa committed to the task. I should not have agreed to let them join us.

"We cannot take the wing flyer or they'll see us," I explain to dissuade her. "My guess is the main body of troops are a day, maybe a day and a half, away. We'll have to run through the night to catch up to them."

Natesa stretches her arms over her head. "I won't let you slow me down."

She's as stubborn as a ratel with a viper in its teeth. I look to Yatin to make her see reason.

"We'll keep up, General," he says.

I hate that title of command and what it meant to my father. If he were here, he would order Yatin, Natesa, and Rohan to follow him with no thought for their safety. I will not force them either way. "Your choice, but if you come along, I'm not your commander."

"Understood," Rohan replies, mustering a brave front. Still, his disappointment in not finding his sister drags his mouth down.

I asked him along. I put it in his head that we could find Opal and Brac, so I distract him from his concerns by asking him to help me drag the wing flyer into the trees for cover. Yatin and I also drop our swords there. Their size and weight will slow our pace. Yatin sulks back into the field, brooding about leaving his khanda behind.

Natesa offers him her haladie, a double-sided knife. "I still have daggers."

"Thank you, little lotus." Yatin bends his huge frame over her and kisses her nose.

Kali kissed my nose just two days ago. The memory pulverizes me. *She made her choice, and it wasn't me. I may need to get used to this feeling.*

Our group takes turns whittling down our packs to necessities. Rohan is the smallest of us, even slighter than Natesa. As Yatin helps him tighten his straps, I slip goods from Rohan's pack into mine and then regard the path left by the army. The flatland lies open ahead, beckoning us homeward.

I set off at a jog, and three sets of footfalls follow. My friends match my assertive pace, and we trek onward to our beloved empire of unforgiving deserts and unreachable mountains.

9

Kalinda

Freezing weather has come early to the Alpana Mountains. We fly in a steep climb over the powdery hills, the higher peaks obscured by soupy clouds. Snowflakes pinwheel around us. The white flecks land on Ashwin's dark eyebrows and pale cheeks. We huddle together on the passenger plank, our teeth chattering out of sync with our shivering.

Pons guides us up, up, up, into thinner air. Indah burrows under a wool blanket, her eyes shut; she's awake but barely tolerating our ascent. Our two-day flight has felt endless. I have never known a wintry depth this dreary. I cannot distinguish where the poisonous cold inside me ends and the bracing weather starts. Each pull of air drives icy spikes into my chest. A growing numbness dulls my focus and drags my eyelids closed.

"She must stay awake," Indah calls to Ashwin over the wind. "Warm her!"

Ashwin wraps his arm around me, and I curl into his side. His body heat combats my chills and helps me withstand the pressing cold.

He lays his cheek against mine, and his voice rouses my senses. "You smell like moonlight."

I lift my chin, and our noses bump. His soul-fire glows deep in his eyes, a well of captivating warmth.

Pull away. Don't be enticed—

His lips graze my cheek. Heat blazes through me, starting as a spark and igniting to a blessed burn. The ice inside me melts, dripping away. *I'm so close to feeling whole again . . .* I press against him more snugly and slide my hands around his bare back, the bitter winds a distant force. His lips grasp at mine and bore past the last of my restraint. My return kiss writhes with need as Ashwin's soul-fire blinds all else.

The wing flyer banks sharply, wrenching us apart, and I see the beacon atop the temple's north tower. *Home*. The last time I saw this light, Deven led me into the forest to show me what I thought would be my final glimpse of Samiya.

The reminder of Deven sobers me. I pull away from Ashwin, sick to my stomach. I do not know how to stop wanting or needing him. Even now, while shivering once again, I crave a reprieve. But I have to fight the cold, if only to outlast the war.

Our wing flyer soars over the stone temple that clings to the great cliff. The courtyard is empty and the meditation pond frozen over, but the sparring circle has been cleared away of snow and ice for training. My last skill trial here was the first time I spilled blood. More memories of my childhood bombard me: the outer gate that locked us temple wards in and the rest of the world out; the meditation pond that I soaked my feet in on a warm summer's day; the chip in the temple wall I fired stones at with my slingshot.

We descend to the courtyard and land in the sparring ring. I breathe in the trees and clouds, the crisp air filling me up. I have missed the wholesome scent of the mountains. Indah jumps down from the wing flyer and staggers for the corner of the courtyard. Halfway there, she bends over and retches. Our landing must have unsettled her stomach. I climb off after Ashwin and Pons and make a move to follow her.

Pons waves me back. "I'll check on her." He goes to Indah's side and holds her hair up. An ache digs into my breastbone. No matter what Admiral Rimba has against them being together, they deserve whatever happiness they wish.

A petite, hunched old woman occupies the open temple doorway. An oil lamp illuminates Priestess Mita's wizened face and gray hair. I can feel the weight of her glower from here. She does not know why we have come; she simply has never liked me. She favored Jaya. I should have known my returning as a rani still would not win her over. Ashwin starts for the priestess, and after a weary sigh, I go too.

"Rajah Tarek?" Priestess Mita whispers.

Ashwin flinches, as he does every time someone mistakes him for his father.

"This is Prince Ashwin," I correct.

Priestess Mita dips into a bow. "Pardon my error, Your Majesty. Where is Rajah Tarek?"

"He was killed," Ashwin answers levelly. He bore no affection for his father in life and is not hypocritical in his death. His aloofness is in part to shield me, for I ended Tarek's reign. Ashwin is one of the few people I entrusted with the truth of his father's demise.

"My condolences." Priestess Mita ends on an awkward pause while examining my trousers. "We're honored you've come home, Kindred Kalinda. Who are your companions?"

I glance across the courtyard. Indah has finished retching, and Pons is walking her slowly over to us. "Indah and Pons are visiting from the Southern Isles."

The priestess straightens from her hunch. "Foreigners?"

"Friends," Ashwin amends. "They're welcome in the empire."

We leave off that they are bhutas. Priestess Mita still believes Tarek's warped fallacy that bhutas are soulless demons of the Void. She does not know I am a bhuta, or a Burner, the rarest and most feared of my kind.

"As you wish, Your Majesty." Priestess Mita recognizes her rudeness at leaving us out in the cold. "If you would please, I'll escort your party inside. We reserve the lower floor of the temple for honored benefactors. Our wards live separately on the upper floor. You understand that we must protect our daughters' innocence."

I seal off a flare of anger. Protect them for what? To stand naked and blindfolded in the Claiming chamber before a strange man—an *honored benefactor*—and let him look them over like prized sheep?

Seeing my grinding jaw, Ashwin takes my hand. "We understand," he says. *But does he?* "Thank you, Priestess."

She sniffs, dismissing my show of temper, and leads us down the stairway alongside the cliff to the lower entrance. Indah and Pons catch up as the priestess ushers us inside. I scarcely viewed the benefactors' chambers the day I was claimed, but they are not as lavish as I recall. At the time, the gold-leaf furniture, silk draperies, and brass lamps were extravagance beyond my imagination. My own quarters were cramped and plain, the colors drab as the stone walls encasing them. Now that I have experienced true affluence and luxury, I notice the patched holes in the draperies, the flaking leafing on the dinged furniture, and the faded bedspread and stringy tassels. These accommodations are far below the prince's privilege.

Ashwin smiles at the priestess. "This will do nicely."

"Do you have a room for us?" Pons asks. Indah leans against him. I was wrong about her being queasy from the flight. She must have fallen ill.

Priestess Mita scowls at them. "Though we've never allowed outsiders to stay here, we'll make an exception for the prince's companions."

I step forward to defend my friends, but Pons answers. "Your hospitality is appreciated."

The priestess snubs him with nary a glance. "Kindred, your companions must remain out of sight from our temple wards." She means Pons and Indah. She cannot keep me locked down here. "As should you,

Your Majesty. You'll find everything you need in your chamber. One of our sisters will bring your meals. When would you like the recipients of age shown to you?"

"Shown?" Ashwin questions.

"He hasn't come for a Claiming," I snap. On the temple floor above us, girls of all ages, from infants to eighteen-year-olds, train to become whatever their benefactor claims them for. The girls of age are shown to the benefactor so he may select those he desires.

Priestess Mita's confused gaze bounces to me. "Then why have you come?"

"The prince wanted to survey our temples," I say. "I offered to accompany him."

"But you didn't bring our supplies."

"No," I start hesitantly. "We weren't aware you're expecting a delivery."

"We haven't received goods or necessities in over three moons. Surely the brethren must know of our shortage. I've sent them several letters."

The Brotherhood temples send a supply caravan every other new moon. They must have stopped once the rebels infiltrated the imperial city. With the empire in disarray, the Sisterhood temples have been forgotten. The Samiya temple is the farthest away from Vanhi and the most secluded. They must be running dangerously low on reserves. Except for a garden that is now snowed over, the sisters and wards are dependent upon the generosity of benefactors, who provide food and clothing in exchange for the privilege to come and claim wards.

"We were unaware of your circumstance," Ashwin says. "I'll remedy your shortage of supplies in haste."

I cannot puzzle out how he intends to fulfill his pledge, but his swift assurance appeases Priestess Mita.

"Will you please show us to our chamber?" Pons asks the priestess. Indah has not spoken since we landed. She sways some on her feet, her pallor worsening by the second.

"Right this way." Priestess Mita bustles to the door that leads to the corridor.

Pons lags back. "Can we trust her, Kalinda?"

"She may be rude, but she won't harm you." I rub Indah's arm. "Go rest."

They follow the priestess out, and a thought strikes me. *I need another room as well.* This chamber has only one bed. Priestess Mita must assume Ashwin retained me as his kindred. Sleeping in the same chamber with him would be disastrous. I need only catch a chill during the night and seek out his comfort . . .

My throat heats to an itch. "I'll ask Priestess Mita for quarters of my own."

"No need for that." Ashwin runs his finger over the mantle and comes away with a clump of dust. "You can have the bed. I'll sleep on the floor." He lowers to his haunches and stocks the hearth with kindling. "Did my father board in this room when he last visited?" His simple question carries a strained undertone.

"He did." I met Deven in the corridor outside this chamber. How different my life would be if he had been a benefactor and claimed me instead. Or had I never been claimed at all.

"Kalinda, would you please?" Ashwin motions to the kindling piled in the hearth.

I go to his side and press my finger to the firewood, coaxing in heat. My powers shine but are still tinged green. Just as the kindling ignites, sapphire sparks fly from my fingers. I quell my powers and sneak a glance at Ashwin. He was preoccupied with the wood pile and did not see. I imagine the blue sparks I saw moments ago evolving into cold sapphire flames and shiver.

Ashwin throws a log onto the growing blaze. "Does the temple have a library?"

"Yes, on the upper floor."

"I may find a text about the gate to the Void."

Ashwin has an aptitude for research. If the gate's location is written in one of the library books, he will find it. "Wait until tonight when everyone's asleep. How will you solve the temple's supply shortage?"

"I don't know yet." Crouched near the fire, he prods the logs with the fire iron. "Can you find out how dire it is?"

"Yes. I'm going upstairs now."

Ashwin pushes a tired hand through his hair, which is still damp from the melted snow. "Will you tell the priestess the real reason why we've come? She should be made aware about our meeting with Hastin."

I owe Priestess Mita no such explanation. She lost my esteem as a sister in the faith when she allowed the rajah's monstrous general to claim Jaya. The priestess should have protected her. She should have protected us both. Instead she still preaches that men are our betters, our gods. My time in the world of men has taught me that any man worthy of my admiration would never force me to worship him.

Moreover, Priestess Mita will be livid to discover the bhuta warlord is meeting us. Her concern will be for the wards; she is not entirely hard-hearted. But informing her of our plans will feel akin to asking permission, which, as her rani, I am no longer inclined to do.

Ashwin watches moodiness come over me—my stiffening features and pressed lips—and rises. "I can speak to her if that would be easier."

He detects the furious storm brewing inside me, but he cannot identify the origin. I cannot settle upon the right words to explain my upbringing. How it feels to be raised for the sole use of another, to exist to fulfill another's whims and desires and taught to never think of my own wants or needs. I never had to enlighten Deven. He saw firsthand the damaging effects of his mother's service as a courtesan. But Ashwin was too sheltered in his youth to grasp the destructive, selfish nature of the supremacy his birthright entitles him to wield. With a flick of his finger, he may claim any girl in this temple or in the whole of the empire.

Still.

Even after I have ended Rajah Tarek's tyranny.

Even though I am a two-time tournament champion and the kindred.

Even with Ashwin striving to improve upon his father's legacy.

The unjust division of rights still reigns.

"I'll take care of it," I say, picking up a lamp. I go into the corridor and start for the stairway. My injured knee aches, and I could use a long nap, but I cannot wait to see the only person left at the temple who I consider my friend.

I take the long route to the infirmary to bypass Jaya's and my former bedchamber. I cannot bear to view our place of happiness or confront those memories. By now, two different wards are dwelling in our haven, replacing us as though our friendship never was. But the ghost of Jaya entwines with the sandalwood incense burning in the halls. She is everywhere: in the walls, in the floors, in my heart. Running from her is pointless, so I allow the loss of stolen wishes to fester. My longing for her is deeper than any other ache or pain I carry.

The door to the infirmary stands open. I enter and survey the vacant cots. The strong aroma of medicinal chamomile unburies a landslide of memories. Most of my childhood was spent in this chamber, endless days lying in a sickbed with raging fevers.

Healer Baka jots in her patient log at her desk. Her spectacles have slid down her nose, perched on the end. When she lifts her quill to dab on more ink, my shadow pulls her attention upward. She inclines back in her chair on a whispered prayer. "Thank Anu."

Old, held-in anger charges out of me. "Did you ask Anu to send you a Burner?" Healer Baka concealed the truth of my bhuta heritage to protect me from Tarek's hatred for my kind. Though her justifications were well founded, I have yet to recover from her deception.

"Brother Shaan wrote me to say you're full into your powers." Her voice brims with pride. "Let me have a look at you." She comes and turns me into the light.

"I haven't changed much. I'm still thin as bamboo."

"Haven't changed? You're a rani!" She skims her palm up my cheek, her eyes shining. "You've become the woman the gods intended."

I tug her hand away. "Jaya—" My voice shreds to a rasp, and before I can stop them, tears pour down my cheeks. "Jaya's dead."

Healer Baka enfolds me in her arms. No one else knew Jaya as well as I did, except for Baka. When Jaya died, I had no one to mourn her with, no one who fathomed my bereavement. "She's well, Kali. Jaya was good and pure. She'll have a new life in her new form, and her loving spirit will continue to bless others. You may miss her, but do not mourn her. You will meet her again."

I hold Baka tighter, clinging to her sentiments. "You truly think so?"

"Time is relative in the Beyond. Jaya will be born again, and you will reunite with her in another life." My crying lessens to quiet hiccups. Healer Baka goes to close the door most of the way for privacy. Passersby would find it suspicious to find the infirmary sealed off. "Brother Shaan hasn't written since your wedding. I began to worry."

"A lot has changed since I left." I set aside my grief to deliver the news. "Brother Shaan passed away."

Healer Baka draws into herself. She and Shaan had a long-distance friendship that began in Vanhi years ago. They trusted each other implicitly. "I've missed more than I realized," she says.

"Why don't I tell you everything over a hot drink?" I am cold, and Healer Baka keeps the most delicious herbal tea mixes.

While she prepares the tea, I relay all that has happened. Unloading the burden of my loss for Jaya opens a floodgate of confessions: falling in love with Deven, murdering Tarek, my expansion of Burner powers, and Ashwin unleashing the Voider. The only part I omit is Healer Mego's prognosis of my condition. Baka listens, interrupting only once for clarification about the Voider returning in the physical form of Tarek. Long after we sip the last of our tea, I finish my summary and await her reaction.

"I'm . . . I'm at a loss," she says. "You and Natesa are *friends*?"

"Out of everything I told you, that surprises you most?"

"You forget that I helped raise you. I've seen stray cats get along better than you two."

I chirp a laugh. "Well, it wasn't without effort."

"Kali, I'm so glad to see you again, but . . . you shouldn't have returned." My chin ticks sideways at her reprimand. "Your health is poor. I can tell you're hurting more than you let on."

"I'm fine," I say, fiddling with my teacup.

Her expression does not change. "Even if that were true, you shouldn't have agreed to meet Hastin here. He's too dangerous."

"*He* picked Samiya for our meeting place. I wouldn't have considered accommodating him, but the demon rajah is marching on Vanhi as we speak."

Healer Baka pulls back slightly. "Your intentions for coming here aside, you've brought more mouths to feed. We're living off our fall harvest."

"The prince is aware and has promised to arrange for aid." I leave out that he has no idea how he will do so, and Healer Baka notices. She pushes her spectacles up her nose in a quick jerk, still troubled. "I won't let anything happen," I say, a guarantee that even to me sounds more convincing.

She holds my solemn gaze. "I have to tell Priestess Mita. For the good of our daughters, she needs to know."

I lock my jaw. "The priestess sent me to die in Rajah Tarek's rank tournament."

"You lived."

"But Jaya didn't!"

Healer Baka lays her hand over mine. “Priestess Mita’s strongest virtue is obedience. She submitted completely to the rajah, perhaps to a fault. But you know as well as I do that she couldn’t have stood up to him.”

I uncross my legs and rub my sore knee. I can no sooner rid myself of its ache than I can set aside my resentment for the priestess or my longing for a future with Jaya.

“Let me give you something for your leg.” Healer Baka rummages through her herb cabinet and takes out a jar. “I’ll mix a salve for the pain.”

“An Aquifier has been healing me. She’s very gifted.”

Healer Baka lowers her chin and peers over her spectacles at me. “Not all gifted healers are Aquifiers.” She hands me parchment and a piece of charcoal and then waves at the cot in the corner, the one that was once mine. Jaya used to sit beside me and watch me sketch for hours. “This won’t take long. Have a seat and draw while you wait.”

I should return to the lower floor, but I do not trust myself alone with Ashwin. And I have not sketched in so very long. This opportunity to create is too precious to squander.

I settle into the lumpy straw mattress while Healer Baka crushes herbs at her workbench. The fragrance of brewed tea and chamomile strokes my nose. Although Jaya’s place remains empty beside me, I press the charcoal stick to the parchment and draw as though she is watching.

10

Deven

My lungs and legs burn. Night left long ago, but the day has been in less of a hurry to end. All day long we have jogged over fields and marshes, side-footed down deep gullies, and marched up slippery hills, yet the imperial army is still in front of us. In the past hour, their tracks have led us into an autumn forest. The sunset streams through the trees that are thick with auburn leaves and the scent of inbound rain. The leaves' redness, illuminated by the light, reminds me of Kali's fire dragon in Iresh: fierce and bold, awe-inspiring. Just like the woman who summoned it.

My comrades' pace slows to a grinding walk. I am tired, but not as tired as they. My urgency to find Brac fuels my strength, but I cannot run forever.

The farther we trek, the more certain I am that my brother was captured and the less I can deny that this is my fault. A moon ago, I let Brac and Mother stay behind in Tarachand. Before leaving Janardan, I sent Opal and Rohan—two young Galers, hardly old enough to live on their own—to find them instead of going after them myself. Both decisions led to this plight.

Rohan falls back, nearly out of view. Yatin and Natesa tread closer, shuffling through the fallen leaves. Trails and trails of broken branches lie before us, trodden down by heavy wagons and soldiers. Somewhere far ahead, leading the troops, is the demon rajah.

"Deven," Yatin says, panting, "how much longer?"

Natesa lags behind, clutching her side. Rohan stumbles after her, even farther in the rear. None of us wants to risk not returning to the wing flyer in time to meet with the navy, but we cannot continue through the night.

I stop with Yatin. My knees wobble, close to giving out. "Stay here with the others. I'll pull ahead and then circle back."

Yatin bends over to catch his breath. "You'll be of no use to Brac exhausted."

"Exhausted is better than absent." I swipe at perspiration dripping in my eyes and mumble an explanation. "This is my comeuppance."

"The gods aren't punishing you, Deven. You're punishing yourself."

I rest on a raised tree root. Finding Brac is paramount, but so are the welfare and condition of my friends. "I should never have separated from my family."

Yatin sits, his bearded face sweaty and flushed. "As I recall, Brac offered to stay behind. Seems to me you're angry about something else."

My friend may be big, but he has never been slow. "Kali and the prince arranged to meet the warlord in Samiya. I tried to talk her out of it, but her mind was set." I have had plenty of time to mull over why she sided against me, and I will relent on one point: Prince Ashwin and Kali must do all within their power to protect the empire. But depending on the warlord is still a bad idea. "Kali supports the prince's efforts."

"Kalinda has a will of her own, and a strong one at that."

He did not walk in on her cozied up to Ashwin; otherwise he would not try to reassure me by touting her strong will.

Yatin pats his trouser pocket and then pats it again. He switches to his other pocket and takes out the lotus ring. "Gods' mercy, I thought I'd lost it."

I start to ask why he has not yet given Natesa the ring, but I hold my question when she staggers up to us.

"Praise the skies, you stopped." She uncorks her flask and gulps down water. While she is drinking, Yatin slips the ring away. She passes him the flask, and he draws a long pull. Rohan straggles closer, a few strides away.

"Rest up," I say, adjusting my pack. The straps dug bruising valleys into my shoulders while I was running. "I'm going ahead."

"Give us a minute, and we'll go with you." Natesa flaps a tired hand at the distance. Lights have appeared in the trees, visible in the twilight.

We have caught up to the army.

"Son of a scorpion." I drop behind a log. Yatin pulls Natesa down, and they kneel beside me. Rohan teeters up to us and slumps over, lounging on a leaf pile. I would lie down too, if I thought I could get up again. I drop my pack to lighten my load. "Yatin and Natesa, stay here. Rohan and I will go ahead and stake out the camp while it's dark."

"Why do I have to go?" Rohan gripes, his young voice breaking. "I'm starved!"

He has not complained once during our trek. I hesitate to push him further, but we are here to find Opal and Brac. And I need Rohan to do so. I grasp the back of his shirt and lift him. Fortunately, he is not fully grown or I would not have the strength. "I need your sharp hearing. Are any scouts nearby?"

Rohan listens to the breeze stirring the branches above. "No, but the soldiers setting up camp are loud, so I could be missing them over the ruckus."

Scouring the army's camp could take us all night. Rohan's exceptional hearing is the only chance we have of succeeding. "Expect our return by dawn," I tell Yatin. "Be on watch."

"Eat before you go," says Natesa, passing out rations.

I force down several bites of dried fish. The briny taste clings to my tongue like barnacles. I drain my water flask and give Rohan the rest of my fish. He shoves the chunk into his mouth, his cheeks bulging, and we set out.

The nearer we creep to the army, the wider the hole in my stomach expands. Torches extend so far into the distance I cannot make out the other end of camp.

Rohan and I carefully navigate the leaf-strewn forest, sneaking closer to the men, horses, and tents. We stop in the shadows and duck low in the brush. Torchlights illuminate the peaks of several buildings—barracks.

This is not just a camp. The army has stopped at a military outpost.

My mind spins to figure out which one. Yatin is the more proficient navigator, but if I remember right, the closest outpost to the location where Brac and Opal crashed was well within the Tarachand border. The army has traveled farther than I presumed. Should they continue their grueling pace, they will reach Vanhi a day ahead of schedule, and do so with swelling ranks. This outpost houses five hundred men, all of whom will be eager to join the imperial army under the direction of their returned rajah.

Their numbers are already large. They must have recruited while marching. When the army left Iresh, they could not have had more than two thousand men, both sworn-in soldiers and volunteer citizens. Now their ranks are vast. I estimate the army is composed of several infantry units, a light cavalry, and archers. But I am unable to accurately tally the army's head count in the dark. Perhaps it is better that I cannot discern how big their camp is, or else I might turn away.

Unbending from my crouch, I signal for Rohan to lead on. The trees shield us as we dart across an opening to the back side of a barrack. He listens for stray guards, then shakes his head. We have not been discovered. I peer around the corner.

Soldiers mill about between the pitched tents, cleaning their jackets and brushing off their boots. Many wear no military garb, but they fly the Tarachand colors, a black scorpion on a red backdrop. Though they are short on uniforms, they have plenty of weapons. Khandas, haladies, and machetes are propped against every tent. Wagons full of food and water are parked intermittently across camp. A massive wooden catapult rests off to the side. Wagons brimming with ammunition, bolts, and boulders outnumber those hauling food supplies.

I rejoin Rohan and whisper, "Any trace of Brac or your sister?"

"Nothing." Rohan's huge eyes are even wider than normal. He looks so young. "We should turn back. Something isn't right. When I reach for the wind, it doesn't come."

A breeze flows over us. "I don't know what you mean."

"Something is stopping the wind's whisperings."

A gong rings far off. I draw farther into the shadows. Rohan fits his thin back tighter against the wall, his chin lifted. The lump of his voice box protrudes from his elongated throat.

The barrack door slams, rattling the wall. I look around the corner again. The men inside the building have left. All the soldiers are moving to the center of camp.

"Let's go." I tug on Rohan's sleeve. "Stay close."

We slip into the empty tents. Rohan does as I ask, sticking to my side. I toss him a soldier's jacket that was left behind. I am still wearing mine. He slips it on, and the too-long sleeves hang past his knuckles. I hand him a machete and select a khanda for myself. The familiar military-grade sword feels right in my hand, but the wrongness of standing in the imperial army's camp as a traitor makes me restless.

If I do not belong here, where do I belong?

Gripping our blades, we tiptoe to the nearest barrack, and I open the heavy door. Bunks and cots and personal bags fill the one-room building. I back out, and we go to the next barrack, and then the next.

I assumed the demon rajah would hold captives in a more secure shelter than a tent, but none of the barracks we investigate house prisoners.

At my questioning glance, Rohan shakes his head. He has not heard our siblings. I consider returning to Yatin and Natesa, but our search has led us deep into the campsite. The soldiers congregate ahead. We work our way through them in search of another barrack, skimming the perimeter as much as possible. When we have no choice but to move within the throng, a voice cuts through the night.

"Welcome, troops!"

Rajah Tarek stands above the crowd on a platform that rings the outpost's water tower. His dark hair is trimmed short, like his tidy beard. His rather average physique is made regal by the finery of his tunic and trousers. His puffed-out chest and calculating gaze exude an inherent arrogance that demands esteem. Even when he stands on equal ground with others, he has a habit of looking down his nose at people. His charismatic, boyish smile and smooth voice counterbalance his majestic poise, trickeries that convince his subjects they can trust him. A deception I once fell for.

He's not Tarek, I remind myself. *Or his son.* Rohan tugs on my jacket, warning me to stay back, but I slip farther into the audience, so we'd better blend in.

"You are a marvelous sight!"

Criers repeat the demon rajah's pronouncement to the outer reaches of the audience. The soldiers cheer for their leader. But this counterfeit version of Tarek possesses a malevolence to his voice that the tyrant rajah was careful not to exhibit in public.

The demon rajah—Udug—lifts his arms. "Today, we welcomed five hundred men into our ranks! Many of them were run out of Vanhi and their comrades were beheaded by bhutas." Udug sneers on the word. "They tell me the bhutas' corrupt leader, the traitorous warlord, sits on my throne. But his rebellion will not prevail! With the gods behind us, we will unseat these vermin from our imperial city and send every last soulless demon back to the Void!"

The men applaud a liar. *He* is the vermin they need to eradicate.

Udug signals to guards waiting below. Up the ladder, they haul a man wearing a green uniform—a Janardanian soldier. His yellow armband distinguishes him as a bhuta. They throw him onto the platform at the demon rajah's feet. The prisoner's wrists bleed from where his captors let his blood.

"This abomination is a Galer," announces Udug. The spectators boo and spit, and Rohan sidles closer to my side. "This demon can read your thoughts. He can hear your inner fears, even from far away, and use them against you."

Rohan blanches. Galers can do no such thing.

"Our prisoner told me the warlord is aware of our approach. The rebels are fortifying Vanhi in preparation for our arrival. But the warlord does not know all." Udug's smugness drives fear into my gut. "We have contacted four more imperial outposts. All of them have employed their units to join us. By the time we reach Vanhi, we will be ten thousand men strong!"

A hard lump drops in my belly. The army will be more than double the size of the Lestarian Navy.

Rohan's voice trembles in my ear. "I don't know how the demon rajah is managing it, but he's directing sound away from camp."

"*He* is the source of the lull?"

"Bhuta powers don't exist in the evernight. It's as though the area around him is the Void."

A frightening deduction, yet Rohan may be onto something. Udug was unharmed by bhuta powers when he conquered Iresh. Even Kali's fire could not drive him back. Perhaps he wears his connection to the Void like armor. *Good Anu, please let us be mistaken.* If bhutas cannot harm Udug, no matter how big an army we amass, he will be unstoppable.

"We have allowed this atrocity to live long enough," the demon rajah calls. "The gods have granted me permission and bestowed upon me the authority to vanquish bhutas from our world. In honoring my duty, I cast this demon out on behalf of myself and all other faithful souls." He lowers his glowing blue hands to the Galer's head.

Instead of pouring his cold-fire into the man, he causes light to thread out of his victim. He parches the Janardanian soldier like a Burner can, except Udug does not stop sucking out the Galer's soul-fire as Kali or Brac would. He feeds off the Galer, gulping down his inner light. I turn Rohan away. He grasps my arm tightly as the Galer's agony-filled scream distills all sound. Then Udug finishes, and the bhuta crumples.

The demon rajah's fingers cast an eerie blue glow over the cheering soldiers. I tug on Rohan for us to leave, but someone I recognize climbs onto the platform.

Manas stands at Udug's right-hand side, dressed in a navy-blue military uniform and carrying a talwar, a single-edged curved sword. When I last saw Manas, I knocked him unconscious. He tried to kill Rohan, Opal, and me, and I thought to do the same to him, but before all that, we were friends. Before his hatred for bhutas warped him. Before he accused me of treason and tried to have me executed. Before he turned me in and I was lashed thirty times.

Manas steps over the dead Janardanian. Two soldiers roll the deceased off the platform. The corpse hits the ground and Rohan's shoulders jolt at the thud. Manas speaks privately with Udug. Even at a distance, I see the demon's eyes flash blue. Rohan tips up onto his toes to listen, but he still cannot hear what they are saying.

At last they finish, and the demon rajah makes another announcement to the troops. "General Manas has notified me that our scouts spotted rebel informants close to camp."

General? Udug entrusted Manas with the highest rank in the imperial army. *My* position . . . or the one I rejected.

"Our enemies are hiding in the forest not far from here. I will personally reward a bottle of apong and three hundred coins to the first soldiers who find them and bring them back, dead or alive."

Great skies. Natesa and Yatin.

Countless soldiers are motivated by the reward, which is four times their annual wage. The throng snatches up weapons and torches and sets off into the forest.

"What do we do now?" Rohan's last word pinches off in a squeak.

I pluck a torch from a post and start for the woodland. "We find Natesa and Yatin before they do."

11

Kalinda

I sway in the creaky rocking chair, the view before me dipping and rising. Out the casement, a sea of frosted evergreens dominates the lower mountain ridges. Above them, sharp slopes and craggy apexes thrust into the clouds. The mountains are so familiar they are like gazing at a friend's face.

The early cold almost dampens the scent of shedding pine needles. Beside me, the north tower beacon radiates warmth, shielding me from the night, and its light furthers my view across the forest. Bits of white lay along the shadowy landscape and lakeshore. Cupped in the mountain trenches, the lake is capped by a hard sheen of glittering ice. Even in the summer, the crystalline waters are too cold for swimming. Some say monsters lurk in the frigid depths, but I am more inclined to fear the Alpana Mountains' mighty summit, Wolf's Peak, the land-goddess's foremost monument to her domain.

Jaya believed Wolf's Peak was Ekur, the hallowed location where the mortals' realm intersects with the gods'. No one knows the actual whereabouts of their mountain house, except that it is somewhere in the Alpanas. Looking up at the pointed apex, I can easily trust that Wolf's Peak pierces the sky-god's vast realm. I am less comfortable with the notion that the gate to the Void, supposedly a cavern to the underground, is hidden in these knolls.

Snowflakes drift in through the open casement. I huddle deeper into the wool blanket that I borrowed from the infirmary, and I rock in the lookout chair. I came directly to the secluded tower upon leaving Healer Baka. The salve she rubbed into my knee eased the aching, but even though the beacon emanates warmth, the Voider's poison still gnaws into my bones.

A fire dragon crouches in the beacon's flame. I do not send the manifestation of my soul's reflection away, nor does it snap or hiss to gain my attention. The fire dragon waits patiently for my command, a pup sitting dutifully alongside its master.

A wolf howls in the far-off hills. The lonely call sends my gaze to the road. Hastin will arrive that way; it is the only thoroughfare in or out of Samiya. I will watch for him and meet him outside the temple gate. He will not come any closer to my home until we have an alliance.

As night dawdles on, the snow on the casement ledge deepens. I burrow into my blanket, and the folded parchment in my pocket rustles. While Healer Baka prepared the salve for my leg, I sketched a picture. Though it had been a while since I indulged in drawing, I labored over the details.

I open the drawing and examine Ashwin's face. In my rendition of the prince, shadows obscure half of his profile. Remorse and blame draw down his mouth, and in his eyes, sorrow coils. He has worn this precise expression every day since he unleashed Udug. Ashwin's self-blame troubles me. Every day Udug roams free and unchallenged, Ashwin's regret intensifies. The only good to come of it is that he looks less and less like his father.

Tarek never regretted any of his actions. My deepest, most painful memories originate from him—not only what he did to me but what I was led to do to him. I smothered and poisoned his soul-fire, just as

Udug is doing to me. Tarek deserved to die, not only for killing Jaya, but I loathe being his monster, just as he is mine.

A sudden wind sweeps through the tower. The strong gust extinguishes the beacon and my loyal fire dragon. Cast into the dark, I feel my neck hairs prickle.

"Your drawing flatters me, love."

I draw my daggers and jump up. My sketch of Ashwin falls to my feet. Tarek manifests in the darkness at the rear of the tower, away from the reflecting snow. More shadow than man, his grainy shape is like a pillar of sand.

Tarek evaluates the sketch, now ruined by the damp floor. "You've missed me."

"That isn't you."

"My son, then . . ." He tips his head back, thinking over that coupling. "You'll tire of him. Ashwin doesn't have the same fire inside him to mold the world with as we do."

I raise my blades higher. "How did you find me?" He must have traveled by shadows. The evernight exists beyond the light, confined to the dark. But that is little comfort at midnight.

"You summoned me, my wife." At my instant protest, he says, "You thought of me, did you not?" I did think of Tarek, though only in relation to his son. Then again, when Tarek visited me in the Pearl Palace, it was after I thought of the demon rajah disguised as him . . . "Put away your daggers. Your blades cannot harm me." He slides forward to the fringe of the shadows but comes no farther. "You were boorish that last time I visited. I could have chosen to ignore your summons, but as I said before, I must warn you."

"I need no warning from you."

"You do if you and Ashwin aim to locate the gate to the Void." Tarek smirks at my shocked withdrawal. "Ah, yes. You *are* searching for the gateway. I could tell you where it is, but you must come closer." He reaches for me, still circumventing the barest of light. "It's been so long since I've touched your hair."

My skin squirms. "You'll never touch me again."

"Then you will never find the gate, and without it, Udug will rove free. But I must warn you, Udug can find the gate. And should he be the one to open it . . ."

A leaden warning unfurls in my chest. Udug would only open the Void for an awful purpose. "What do you want in return?"

Satisfaction lightens his voice. "One small request, really. All I ask is that you summon me at the gate. Simply stand before the entry and call my name."

Nothing is ever simple or harmless with Tarek, but a greater threat roams the mortal realm. "Where's the gate?"

"Your pledge first, love."

"Not until you tell me where it is."

"Then you shall never know." Tarek's gaze strokes down my body. "You've always reminded me of Enlil's hundredth rani. Does it strike you as prophetic that we never learned her name? Of all the fire-god's wives, we learned only of her. Yet we only know of her in association to him. Her reputation lives on in infamy because she wed a powerful man. I, too, have blessed your life, Kalinda. Let me help you again."

I swipe my dagger at his murky chest, purposely missing. "Go back down the hole you crawled out of."

His eyes smolder, two sable pits. "Your temper will be your undoing. Udug will crush your world." Tarek glides backward, deeper into the shadows.

"Wait!" He pauses, his lips curling smugly. I edge forward, stopping before the toes of my boots touch the gloom he dwells in. "If you care anything for your son or me, you'll help us."

"Doesn't my coming here prove that I love you?" He beckons me nearer with his same vainglorious grin. The tips of my toes crest the darkness. The cold tingles, alive and crawling with tentacles. Tarek sidles up to me and grabs a handful of my hair. He lifts my locks to his nose and inhales. "Breathing you in is like drinking midnight."

"Where's the gate, Tarek?" His gritty hand brushes down my cheek. I force myself to remain still. "This could redeem you. Anu could forgive your indiscretions and invite you to the Beyond."

"The Beyond will never have me. I wish to return to the mortal realm." Tarek's grip tightens on my hair. "Udug stole my empire, but my name and power belong to *me*."

I try tugging away, but Tarek pulls harder, dragging me into the darkness. A blackout obscures me, a whirlwind of dust and grime. Rough lips slam down on my mouth. I cannot breathe or see past the filth. A rush of panic throttles me, and I drive my dagger into his chest. The blade sinks up to my knuckles into squirming quicksand.

Tarek chuckles into my ear. "Should you choose to behave and respect your husband, all you need to do is request my company, and I will come."

His dusty form disintegrates around me, vanishing to empty shadows. I draw in gasps of unsullied night air and search inside myself for my dying soul-fire. Finding my inner flame shrunken and weak, I tremble on the precipice of the evernight.

12

Deven

Torches bob around Rohan and me, like large fireflies illuminating the dark. We blend in with the other soldiers fanning out through the forest. Difficult as it is not to run ahead, we stay in the thick of the hunt. But as the troops disperse into smaller groups, we break out in front of the other search parties. Soon our torch is the only one for a hundred strides in every direction. We finally arrive at the place we last saw our comrades. The leafy covert is vacant.

"Where did they go?" Rohan asks, turning about.

"I don't know." They were not taken. No one from camp has searched farther out than this. The torchlights must have spooked them. I would suggest that Rohan send them a message on the wind, a whistle or birdcall, but torchlights close in on us. Too many men could become suspicious of our signal or any response our friends would send.

I sweep the torch over the ground and uncover a footprint of Yatin's boot. As a boy, he often hid from his five older sisters so they could not dress him up like a doll, or, when he grew older, saddle him with their chores. He would only leave a footprint if he intended for me to find it.

"This way." I hurtle over a fallen log and discover another footmark every few strides.

Rain begins to patter, dampening the fallen leaves to sticky mush and filling Yatin's tracks with puddles. The drizzle drenches my turban but does not deter the mob or hamper their determination. Torchlights press farther into the forest as the hunt goes on.

A shout comes from directly ahead. "A rebel!"

My insides vault up my throat. Rohan and I set into a run, along with dozens of other men. We come to a halt at the gathering of lights.

A man dressed in all black grasps an imperial soldier by the neck with both hands. Droplets of blood cry from the soldier's eyes and seep out of every pore of his exposed skin.

A soldier across the circle releases a bolt from his crossbow, striking the man in black in the spine. He arches in agony and collapses. The imperial soldier he strangled and bled falls with him, both landing in a heap. Another man checks them over.

The rebel and his assailant are dead.

The horde clambers over one another to claim the prize. Ultimately, the party with the soldier who shot the crossbow hoists the rebel and carries him back to camp. The rest of the hunters trickle after them, grumbling over the lost opportunity for coin. Bloodstains cover the fallen soldier's body. The rain dilutes the scarlet drops to streams of pink running across his skin.

"What did the rebel do to him?" I ask.

Rohan curls into himself, a statue of misery. "Aquifiers can leech the water out of someone's body little by little. Leeching is wrong. Bhutas should use their powers for good or we're no better than demons."

Opal once told me the same about winnowing when she explained a Galer can siphon air from another's lungs, asphyxiating them to death. Rohan cries silent tears, but I doubt they are for the rebel or the soldier. He must be thinking of the Galer the demon rajah executed—and his sister.

I pat his thin back. "Tonight has been difficult, but I need you to stay tough."

Rohan wipes his nose and nods glumly. The soldiers' torches drift farther away, leaving us suspiciously alone. I regret not pausing to bury or pray over the fallen soldier, but time is short.

"We need to return to camp to keep up appearances," I say. "After everyone turns in for the night, we'll sneak away and search for Natesa and Yatin."

Rohan falls in line with me, my feet dragging more with every stride. Two days of little food and even less rest hit me at once. It is all I can do not to keel over.

Halfway to camp, Rohan halts, and a sudden wind extinguishes our torch. The dark wicks away my exhaustion. I back up against a tree, my khanda ready.

Something hefty drops from above. Peering into the dimness, I distinguish Yatin's shape. A smaller shadow also leaps down.

"Almighty Anu," I whisper. "You could've warned me, Rohan." He heard our friends and blew out the torch to mask their presence.

"Where's the excitement in that?" Natesa thumps me on the chest.

Although meant as a playful jibe, the cuff hurts my tired body. "I found your tracks, Yatin."

"I tried to leave more," he answers, "but too many soldiers were around. Any trace of Brac or Opal?"

"No, but the demon rajah held a Galer prisoner, so he could have others." General of the imperial army or not, as the organizer of this mission, I cannot allow my friends to follow me any farther. "I'm going back to camp before everyone turns in for the night. The army is vast and growing. I'll blend in and search for Brac and Opal on the march to Vanhi. You three return to the wing flyer and meet with the Lestarian Navy."

"What about General Manas?" Rohan asks.

"Manas is here?" Natesa asks. "And he's the general?" She and Yatin scoff in reproach. Both are acquainted with Manas's and my history. "Deven, he'll kill you if he finds you."

"He won't." *Or he'll be sorry.* Regardless of our past friendship, my mercy for Manas is long spent. A gong resounds in the distance. "That's the call for curfew. I have to go."

Natesa grabs my arm, holding me in place. "Not without us, you don't. We took too long to find the army. We're supposed to meet with the navy day after tomorrow. Even if we run all night, we'll never make it in time."

"Then wait here, and I'll come back for you."

"No." Her grip tightens. "When my sister was claimed and taken from the temple, I never saw her again. The next I heard, she'd passed away." Rohan grimaces, and she tempers her tone. "I didn't get a chance to go after my sibling like you and Rohan have. Tomorrow morning, all of us will join the army and march to Vanhi."

Yatin crosses his arms over his chest. "The army will punish a female infiltrator differently than a man."

"Then I'll pretend to be a man," Natesa counters. "I'll wear a uniform and hide my hair. I won't get caught."

Yatin is right to worry. Neither of us would ever mistreat a female prisoner or abuse our rank to coerce a woman, but some soldiers take repulsive liberties. Natesa would be more at risk for certain acts of violence than us men. I can hardly guarantee my safety, let alone hers.

"Udug executed the Galer I mentioned," I inform her. "For your protection, you should all turn back."

"You can accept our help or not. Either way, we're coming with you." Natesa tromps into the woods.

"Where are you going?" Rohan whispers after her.

"To get the uniform."

Rohan makes a face. "The dead soldier's clothes?"

"Are you going to stop her?" I ask Yatin.

He leans against the tree. "There's no sense in it. Changing Natesa's mind is impossible."

Before long, she returns wearing the deceased soldier's jacket and trousers. Their roominess conceals her womanly shape. She ties her hair up and winds his turban around her head, hiding her long tresses. Although we do not wear turbans when we sleep, Natesa stares at me through the shadows, daring me to forbid her to come along. I have had loyal comrades in the past, men willing to fight for my life, but none of them has ever undressed a dead man and worn his clothes for me.

"Fine," I say. Off in the distance, camp has gone quiet. We will draw too much attention strolling in after curfew. "We'll sneak in when they break camp at dawn. Get some rest."

Through the dark, I hear Natesa's victorious accord and Yatin's lamenting exhalation. Rohan says nothing. I accept his silence as a bid of amenability.

The four of us bed down on the forest floor, sticking to the dry patches preserved by the thick branches overhead. Rohan curls up close to Natesa for warmth. She plucks a leaf from his hair and strokes the locks from his eyes. Kali told me Natesa has a dream of opening an inn someday. I can picture her with a place of her own, caring for weary travelers.

Watching her with Rohan drags up a memory. Once when I was ten and Brac was seven, he ran away from the palace nursery. Many hours later, I found him huddled beneath a lemon tree in the stoning courtyard. Bodies of dead bhutas were buried under bloody piles of stones, decaying in the desert sun. He had run off after I had railed at him for ruining my wooden sword. I can still recall the imprints of his small fingers seared in the hilt of my favorite toy.

That was when I knew Brac was special—and I had to protect him. I threw my wooden sword in the hearth, turning the evidence of what he could do to ash, and never spoke of his abilities. But after that, we both changed. Brac became calculating and distrustful, and I acted as though nothing was amiss. Pretending was the only way I knew how to save him from ending up in that courtyard.

I wish I could return to the days when I was his bigger, stronger brother, but we are not masking his birthright from a grudge-holding rajah. We are up against an enemy that not even his Burner powers can impair.

As the rain drums faintly, my concerns turn toward daybreak, when we will infiltrate the demon rajah's army.

13

Kalinda

Someone kicks my chair, bringing me upright. Indah stands before me, cradling a steaming teacup. "You sleep in the strangest places," she says.

"What time is it?"

"Midmorning." She shuffles in front of my chair and leans against the open casement. Sunlight falls in behind her. The snow clouds have passed, and the air is warmer. Icicles drip from the window. The tower beacon pushes warmth at my back, adding heat to the warming temperatures. I relit the flame last night after Tarek left. My memory of his visit is fuzzy in the light of day, pulling apart my confidence in what I saw.

Is it possible for souls to travel from the Void by shadows? Is there truth to *Inanna's Descent*?

"Ashwin sent me to find you," Indah says. "What are you doing up here? Have you been here all night?"

"I came to watch for Hastin." I slip my hands under the wool blanket. My inner chill is relentless.

"You don't have to do that. Pons is listening for his arrival."

"I know. I just . . ." Seeing Tarek reminded me of how Hastin manipulated me into trusting him. The longer I wait, the more Deven's warning weighs on me. But my apprehension may be for naught.

Whether Hastin comes or not, we must leave Samiya tomorrow morning to meet with the Lestarian Navy.

"Healer Baka sent this for you. She told me I could find you here." Indah passes me the teacup. I sip the hot drink, savoring its sweetness. She opens her cloak to the autumn air. Her cheeks have more color than yesterday.

"What were you doing in the infirmary?"

"I needed a remedy for my stomach. Healer Baka was very helpful. While she brewed anise tea for me, we discussed the temple's supply shortage. I wrote Datu Bulan and told him the sisters and daughters will perish if he does not send rations. The carrier dove left an hour ago. I anticipate he'll agree, but should he decline, we could petition the Paljorians."

The Paljor territory converges with Tarachand on the north side of Wolf's Peak. The tribe is closer than the Southern Isles, but reaching out to them is only a fallback. "Thank you. We'll wait and see—"

A thwack thwack of bamboo striking bamboo sounds below. I join Indah at the casement and look out. Pons moved the wing flyer from the courtyard, outside the gate near the road. Melting snow leaves puddles that dry in the afternoon sun. In the distance, a sheet of ice still shimmers on the lake, slower to melt, but the warmer autumn day has cleared away the frost from the temple courtyard. Wards wearing sky-blue saris train with staffs in the sparring ring. Their instructor, Sister Hetal, shouts commands.

"Their staffs are twice as tall as they are," Indah says.

"They're probably eight or nine." The age when the sisters start training the wards for battle. They believe Ki wishes for them to mold the wards into warriors, an honor and rite of passage.

Indah turns into the sun. She exudes the beauty of her homeland—pearly teeth, gilded eyes like the island sunset, and brown skin with undertones of sandy beaches. "Thank Enki the snow is melting."

"Isn't snow just frozen water?"

"Yes, but manipulating ice and snow aren't techniques practiced in the Southern Isles, for apparent reasons." Indah's attention slides to the stationary wing flyer. "I'll be glad to go home where it's warm."

Her eagerness to return to Lestari conflicts with her dislike of heights. "How did someone who doesn't like to fly fall in love with a Galer?"

Indah's gaze follows the girls sparring below while she answers. "Pons and I met during our Virtue Guard training. His father was a trader of rare treasures and often bartered with Datu Bulan. While he was traveling, he would leave Pons at the palace. His father died during one of his trips, and Bulan took him in."

"Why does your father disapprove of you and Pons?"

Frustration packs Indah's every word. "Pons is a Janardanian. My family lines trace back to the first families in the Southern Isles. My father wants me to wed a Lestarian and preserve our bloodline." She speaks the last in a gravelly voice, mimicking the admiral.

Parents. The one explanation I cannot relate to. However, I understand the obligation to uphold tradition. Never was I given a choice of which benefactor would claim me or for what purpose. I assumed women outside the temple had more freedom. Marriage proposals are often sorted out between families. But now I see that custom is also flawed.

Still, Indah was permitted to meet a man and fall in love. I was never given that option.

We lapse into a contemplative silence. As the wards take turns in the sparring ring, I grow fidgety.

"Indah, will you please fetch Ashwin and Pons? I have something for us to do."

She pushes away from the casement, keen to join me. She must be bored of waiting for Hastin too. "Ashwin may not come," she says. "He borrowed every book he could find on the Void from the library and was up all night reading. Last I checked, he hadn't found anything of use."

After what I learned from Tarek—if I did not in fact imagine his visit—I doubt the location to the gate will be cited in a text. "Tell him it's important. I'll meet you in the courtyard." I hurry off, leaving her to satisfy my request.

Outside, a pair of girls duels in the sparring circle. The rest of them wait their turn by the weapons rack. An eighteen-year-old ward I knew from my time here, Sarita, gives them instructions while Sister Hetal observes.

"Strike her knee and then—" Sarita cuts off. "Kindred Kalinda."

All the young wards whirl around and bow.

Sister Hetal scurries to the front of the group. "Kindred, Priestess Mita didn't inform me you need to use the courtyard."

"I don't. I came to watch the wards practice."

The girls whisper to each other, and Sarita scrutinizes my trousers. My former competitor in the sparring ring has not changed at all. Her shape is still soft yet firm, fit yet feminine. She and Natesa were good friends. From Sarita's glare, she has not forgotten the last time we sparred. I gave her a bloody lip.

Pons, Ashwin, and Indah come up the side stairway from the lower level. The girls' high voices pinch off at the sight of the Lestarian warrior with the partly shaved head, bare legs, and hairy chest. They are equally astonished by Ashwin's good looks, and most of them blush.

"Girls, protect your innocence." Sister Hetal covers the nearest girl's sight, and the others shut their eyes. Sarita hides her face but peeks out at Ashwin from between her fingers. "Kindred Kalinda, the wards mustn't see the men. Priestess Mita—"

"Would not presume to send away her prince." I tug him forward, and Pons and Indah follow arm in arm.

"I thought you were avoiding me," Ashwin says under his breath. I was, though at the moment I cannot remember why. His touch is like a sunrise on a frosty morning. "What are we doing here?"

"We're introducing these girls to their ruler," I answer and then raise my voice. "Prince Ashwin has come to view your sparring practice." Sister Hetal blathers on about propriety and innocence. I direct my next statement at Sarita, who has lowered her hands to gawk at Ashwin. "Would you like to demonstrate your skills first or should we draw lots?"

No one moves. The younger girls still have their sight shielded, though many steal glimpses of the men behind Sister Hetal's back.

"Kalinda, perhaps we should go," Ashwin says, shifting uncomfortably.

"These girls have been locked away long enough. There's a point when innocence becomes ignorance."

"I-I'm sorry, Your Majesty," Sister Hetal blusters. "Priestess Mita must hear of this."

She rushes off, and most of the wards lower their hands. Pons bows to them. His kind, wise eyes exude a surprising depth of vulnerability. He does not want them to fear him.

Ashwin chews his lower lip, still torn. "They're so young. I don't want to startle them."

The girls hang on his every word, his strange tenor transfixing them. None of them flee or hide. They are sister warriors in the making.

Remembering how awkward it felt to stand before a group of men as a lone woman, I push a smile of encouragement at Ashwin. "They have never seen a man before, but they're astute enough to recognize your handsomeness."

Ashwin's gaze slowly widens. "You've never told me I'm handsome."

"No?" My voice mellows. "I should have."

Sarita bows, a curt bend at her waist. "There's no need to draw lots. I'll demonstrate my skills for you, Your Majesty."

The last of the girls uncover their eyes and blink at Ashwin in wonder.

I select a staff from the weapon's rack and hand it to Sarita. "Go ahead. I'll be your sparring partner."

She laughs a little, not in derision but amusement. "You're still skinnier than a bamboo pole."

"I'm also a two-time tournament champion." She would probably flee if I told her I am also a Burner, but I do not want these girls to fear men or bhutas.

"This will be entertaining," Indah says, tugging Pons to the meditation pond. Some of the wards shuffle after them. They congregate near Indah, but do not shy away when Pons asks them questions about their training. More girls move closer to my friends, mesmerized by Indah's topaz eyes and Pons's gentleness. They even request to see his blowgun, and he shows them.

I grab another staff and square off with Sarita in the ring. Her entire focus is on me and not the men. She has recovered faster from meeting the opposite gender than I did. I was thunderstruck by Deven for days.

Sarita raises her staff to ready position. "Until first blood?" she asks, reciting the rules of the last time we sparred.

"Until first down," I correct. I have shed enough blood inside battle rings. Priestess Mita will return any moment, so I call the start and waste no time swinging.

Sarita blocks, and our bamboo poles connect. The clanging vibration shoots up my arms. She glances at Ashwin for approval. I slide closer and knock her in the side of the head with the end of my staff. She bends away and comes around, striking me in the hip. The impact throws me back a step.

"What's become of Natesa?" Sarita tries for neutrality, but I hear her concern for her friend.

"Natesa lives. She conceded the final rank tournament match to me."

Sarita swipes at my nose. I duck, but she gets me on the way back up, hitting me in the shoulder. "Natesa would never concede to you."

"She did." I pace away so Sarita can better view my earnestness. "We're friends now."

"They are," Ashwin confirms, standing at the rim of the ring.

Sarita adjusts her grip on her staff while considering this news. I check on Pons and Indah from my side vision. The little ones still crowd around them. One of the girls sits in Indah's lap, and another plays with Pons's tied-back hair.

"Where is she?" Sarita asks, jabbing.

I block her, locking our staffs together. "She's in love with a soldier. I think they'll wed someday."

Sarita drops her guard, her voice halting. "Natesa isn't a palace courtesan anymore?"

"No. She's been freed."

Sarita lowers her staff even more. Her incredulous stare goes right through me.

"Enough!" Priestess Mita bellows across the courtyard. She and Sister Hetal march for the sparring ring.

I lower my voice to Sarita. "Much has happened since I left. You don't have to stay here locked away, waiting for a benefactor to claim you. This is your life. Claim it."

Priestess Mita stomps up to me and yanks away my staff. She tosses it aside, and it lands with a clang, alarming the wards with Indah and Pons. "Daughters, leave us."

Sister Hetal herds the girls together and shoos them inside. After some prodding from the priestess, Sarita drags her feet after them.

Once the entry door is shut and all the girls are inside, Priestess Mita snarls, "You desecrate this sanctuary, Kalinda. Healer Baka told me you've invited the bhuta warlord here. How could you endanger these children? You're their rani, endowed with the power to protect them! You shame the Sisterhood and the land-goddess with your selfishness."

Ashwin steps to my side to defend me, but I wave him off. "You denied me the right to choose my fate," I say.

"The Claiming is Anu's will!"

"What about my will? What about Jaya's? The gods gave us the five virtues so we could *choose* to emulate them. They would never force us."

Color rises in her cheeks. "You ungrateful child. You're rani because of the Claiming! That rite gave you everything, and it will bless these daughters too."

My heartbeat roars in my ears. "I swear on my mother's grave that none of these girls will be claimed by any man. I'm doing away with the Claiming."

Ashwin's posture snaps straight.

"You wouldn't." Priestess Mita sizes up my unflinching glare and reels on Ashwin. "Your Majesty, what would become of these girls? They're orphans! They have no parents, no families to care for them. I cannot turn them out into the world of men unprotected."

Ashwin frowns, contemplating her protest.

"The Sisterhood temples save hundreds of orphans," the priestess continues. "With the war, even more children will need homes and assistance. These temples will be more essential than ever."

Ashwin smooths his hair back, choosing silence. His reluctance to pick a side only serves to strengthen my determination.

"This will be stopped," I say.

He raises his palm to quiet me. "I hear you, Kalinda, but doing away with the Claiming can wait." I fasten my teeth together to keep from screeching. Ashwin closes his eyes as though gathering patience. "We'll discuss this another time."

"Meet with Hastin on your own, then." I set off for the main entrance. My vision blurs from my tears, my chest pumping on each taut breath. I have been fighting for a future I thought Ashwin and I both wanted, a free empire for all. But he and Priestess Mita wish to press forward in tradition.

Swiping at my wet cheeks, I push inside the temple in search of the exact moment my freedom was ripped from me.

14

Deven

A bang in the distance wakes me. I go from lying propped against the tree trunk to standing in half a breath. Daylight rests upon the woodland, severing my drowsiness.

I groan. "We overslept."

Natesa opens her eyes from her place curled up against Yatin. I nudge him in the boot, and he jolts, thumping his head against their log. Rohan rouses, shedding sleep like the blanket of leaves that kept him dry last night. Sunup stole into the forest, and the day marched us well into morning, far past our planned departure at dawn.

Yatin scrubs the sleep from his eyes, and Natesa shoves strands of her fallen hair up underneath her turban. Tightness stretches all my sore, stiff muscles. I peer through the misty woods. The fallen leaves are saturated to a deep crimson from the passing rain. No tent peaks mark the army's camp. We were completely gone from this world not to have heard the army pack up and leave. I should have anticipated our exhaustion after our taxing days of travel.

"They're on the move." I brush dirt from my trousers and grab my sword. The others rise alongside me, wide awake.

We hustle to the outskirts of camp. The area around the nearest outpost barrack is deserted. I race across the trampled field, my friends right behind me. Up ahead, a group of soldiers and their team of horses pulling a catapult wagon were delayed. The back wheels of the wagon have sunk into the rain-soaked ground. A commander riding on horseback shouts at the four men to heave the catapult. They try to push the heavy artillery free, but it is mired deep.

The commander notices us from a distance, our scarlet jackets visible in the morning mists. "You there! Give us a hand!"

I run to the catapult and lean my shoulder into the board above a rear wheel. The rest of my group does the same. Mud loosens my footing. I hunker down for better leverage. On the commander's order, we push and the horse team pulls. The catapult wagon rocks forward, on the brim of escaping the muck, and then rolls back to its stuck position.

Stepping back, I search the area for something to wedge under the wheels. The commander continues to count, and the men push, but to no avail. I return with branches and lay them in front of the nearest wheel. The next time the men shove and the horses rally, the wheel rocks up onto the branches. But the other rear wheel drags the weight back into the mud.

"We need more branches," I say.

Natesa collects more with me. We return, our arms laden, and set them in front of the second rear wheel and resume our place behind the catapult wagon.

The commander, who has dismounted and joined the group of men pushing, leans into the back of the wagon and shouts, "Go!"

We rock one wheel up onto the dry branches. My footing slips. I switch places on the wagon, shouldering the weight of the lagging wheel, and we muscle it up onto the other branches.

"Forward!" the commander orders.

We impel the wagon onward until the burden of our load transfers to the horse team, and they plod along the trail. I bend over to collect my breath. Yatin pats me on the shoulder, his own rapid breathing loud. Rohan fastens his attention to the other soldiers, and Natesa lowers her chin and tugs at her turban.

Light rain lays a thin vapor over the forestland. We trek on, and the commander mounts his horse and paces us. I am certain I do not recognize him. He was not in the military encampment in the sultanate. But Yatin and I have served with many soldiers, and he could identify either of us. Or even Natesa if he frequented the rajah's courtesans' wing.

In short order, we unite with a lumbering ammunition wagon, and our horse team slows to a plodding walk in the long line of wagons and soldiers.

The commander rides up to my side. I pretend the rain bothers my eyes and fixate on the muddy ridges on the ground. "Where did you and your men hail from?" he says.

"South. We heard word of the imperial army marching and came to join you."

"The southern outpost was abandoned last moon," he replies, fists firm on his reins.

I correct my statement as smoothly as possible. "We rerouted to Iresh and followed the troops."

The commander rides alongside us for several tense steps, evaluating my group. His attention carries over to Natesa. She leaves her chin down. He looks past her to Rohan and then lingers on Yatin's sturdy bulk. "Do you have experience leading your men?" he asks me.

Out of the corner of my eye, I do not miss Natesa's lips twisting dryly. "Sir?"

"These other soldiers have been hauling the catapult since Iresh. You and your party will take over." He excuses the current team of soldiers, and they advance with the troops on foot. "You'll lead this horse team and catapult the rest of the way to Vanhi. Don't slow us down."

"Yes, sir," I say.

The commander taps his heels against his horse's flank and trots to the wagons ahead.

Natesa shifts to walk next to me. "That was unexpected."

"Not really," I answer. "The first rule of successful soldiering is to make yourself indispensable. No one will look twice at us so long as we follow orders."

"How will we look for Opal if we're stuck watching this big hunk of wood?" Rohan grumbles. Natesa had rolled up Rohan's sleeves so the ill fit of his jacket was not so apparent, but the imperial army uniform still drowns him.

"We'll search at night," I say. Rohan mutters, his strides short and agitated. "Trust me, Rohan. I know the army. We're safe so long as we keep our heads down and do our work."

Yatin grunts in agreement, but we both remain on guard and keep our weapons close. Our small unit fans out, Natesa and Rohan upfront. Yatin walks just ahead of me, patting his pocket every tenth or twelfth stride.

"Do you mean to give her that ring or go mad worrying that you've lost it?"

Yatin hikes up his trousers, which are roomier since he lost girth. "She wouldn't accept it."

I double-step nearer to his side. "What? Why?"

"She wants to meet my mother and sisters to make certain they approve of her first." He scratches his beard. "I told her it would be some time before they met, but she's decided."

Traditionally, Yatin would meet with Natesa's father to discuss the wedding, but her parents are deceased, so she can make the arrangements herself. A strong rapport with his family must be important to her, but I would wed Kali regardless of whether I had my mother's approval.

Our speed stays consistent as the day wears on, and we soon surpass clambering wagons and catapults. Once we reach the center of the ranks, I slow to uphold the pace of those around us. A mediocre position in the marching line will draw less notice our way. My feet already hurt and my back aches, but I ignore my protesting body and settle into the familiar monotony of military obedience.

15

Kalinda

The Claiming chamber is locked from the corridor, so I enter an adjoined room around the corner and close the door behind me. The cold, gray inspection chamber that is used for the first stage of the Claiming ritual is empty.

Circling the hollow area lit by wall lamps, I feel gooseflesh spread up my arms. Here in this very spot, the other recipients and I stood nude before Healer Baka for evaluation of our physical health, a practice to determine whether we were fit to be shown to the benefactor.

An inner door leads to the next chamber. Near it, on a table, is a pot of henna. The sisters used the henna to draw the mark of Enki down our spines. The single wave represented that we were in submission to the most fearsome benefactor who had ever visited our temple.

I am tempted to throw the pot and shatter the memory of Tarek's arrival, but I pick it up and cradle it close. I once carried the mark of the kindred, dyed in henna on the backs of my hands. The number one was a symbol to all that I was the rajah's first wife. Tarek may have avowed that I will only be remembered in association with him, but I earned my rank and nobility *despite* him.

And it all began in the next room.

On a whispered prayer for courage, I open the door to the Claiming chamber. The lamplit cave of a room is smaller than I recall but just as chilly. A mosaic of blue, white, yellow, and red swirls across the tile walls. A muslin veil hangs from ceiling to floor. In front of the veil, the red line on the ground is the same, chipped and worn. I set my toes on the painted mark. I stood here blindfolded while Tarek slunk out from behind the veil and first imposed his touch on me.

All at once, I am blind again. I crumple to the floor and hug the henna pot close. Gods alive, how many girls were claimed here? How many shook in terror and shed tears? The gods had a hand in my Claiming, but how many others can say the same?

Sobs wrench out of me. I cry for Jaya, Natesa, myself, and every other ward whose future was stolen in this chamber. For how long I weep, I do not know. But my inner winter emanates into the tile floor, muddying where my misery ends and the poison begins. Finally, spent, I lie in the dimness, too heartsick and frozen to leave this tomb of innocence.

Footfalls echo through the open door, compelling me to push myself up.

Ashwin fills the doorway. He takes in my swollen eyes and red nose. "Pons told me you were here." He enters the Claiming chamber and turns his attention to the room itself. He runs a fingertip across the colorful wall that is too cheerful for the terrible ritual held here. At the veil, he reaches for the cloth but withdraws before touching it. "I'm sorry I disagreed with you in front of the priestess. My deepest apologies for giving you the impression that I would retain the Claiming. But I wish you had discussed your motives with me before announcing your intentions. I would have approached the priestess with you, Kalinda. We could have told her we wish to do away with the Claiming as a united front." His levelheaded explanation negates my anger, for Ashwin is not the true source of my umbrage.

"I didn't think you'd understand."

He stares at the chipped red line on the floor. "I'd like to try."

I, too, want him to understand why he can never repeat his father's actions. "Tarek claimed me here." Devoid of tears, I am plain in my recounting. "I was blindfolded and naked. He . . . he touched me." Ashwin's gaze sharpens to daggers, and I amend. "My hair, mostly. The rite took only a minute, but it was the longest of my life."

"A minute is too long to be humiliated and terrified." Ashwin crosses the room and sits beside me, one knee against his chest. "The wards are safe. With the war, no benefactors will come to claim them." He leans his shoulder into mine. His touch is daylight in this miserable place. "I'll change whatever you wish about the temples. I depend on your judgment, especially now . . ." His voice collapses to a whisper. "I'm afraid my decision to unleash Udug will be our ruin."

I grip his knee. "You had to do it."

"I still brought this war upon us. Because of me, we may have no future. I need you . . ." He shakes his head and starts over. "I beg of you to trust me."

"I didn't mean to exclude you. I trust you. I do."

Ashwin toys with the gold cuff on my wrist, *his* gold cuff. He curls his fingers around my arm, and his thumb grazes my pulse. His caress smolders into me, lessening the constant cold, and I sink into his body. His mouth steadily lowers to mine and he says, "You came into my life like a star, the answer to all my wishes."

He rubs his lips lightly over my own. Heat sparks between us. I lift my chin, yearning for more. He clutches at my waist, and delicious warmth sears into me. My mind goes fuzzy, like I am stretching out in a pool of sunlight.

This feels so right.

No, more than right. Necessary.

I drag him closer. Ashwin inclines me back, lowering me to the floor, and presses his body against mine. I splay my hands across his shoulders, and a vision overwhelms me.

Ashwin and I live in the Turquoise Palace. We sleep in late and stay up into the night. We take our meals in his private atrium and rule our people from twin thrones. I bear him an heir, a son, a Burner who will someday rule the empire justly and with compassion for his people, an example set by his father. Ashwin loves his son as much as he loves me. He defers to me in all things and honors me before his court of wives and courtesans.

I am his singular favorite, his kindred and only love.

The strong image is irrefutable. But it is not mine. The palace looks different than I remember. A fine duplicate but missing details that authenticate the vision. The vivid picture transitions.

Ashwin and I are entangled in the sheets of an enormous bed. He wants more heirs. He wants me.

"Marry me," he whispers against my lips.

His hand slides up the back of my tunic. Before I can stop the vision from returning, we are in a bed once more in my mind's eye. Ashwin's hand creeps higher, tugging up my tunic, both in the Claiming chamber and in the palace. I want him to stop, but I am locked in two realities.

No.

I'm not in the palace, and this is not my dream. My dreams always include Jaya and Deven.

Always.

He kisses across my cheek, down my neck. "Marry me, Kalinda. Be my kindred. Fulfill my heart's wish." He nibbles at my throat. I push him away and leave my hands against his chest to prevent him from coming closer. His complexion is flushed and his lips damp. His hooded eyes still project the dream that played inside my head.

"What did you say?"

"Be my wife."

"No, the part about your heart's wish."

"You fulfill the wish of my heart." He leans in for a kiss.

I hold him back. My insides rattle apart. I twist from him, resting my forehead against the cool tile floor. "Oh, gods. I should have seen it before. Your heart's wish. *I'm* your heart's wish."

"Kali—"

I shove at him. "Get off me. Don't ever touch me again."

"I—I don't understand. What did I do?"

I adjust my tunic and rise on quaking knees. The wall patterns whirl around me. "You wished for me. When you unleashed Udug, you imagined me with you."

"I imagined ruling in the palace. You know that." Ashwin climbs to his knees, his hair disheveled from my hands stroking through the dark strands. My hunger for his warmth implores me to return to his arms, fasten my lips to his, and never ask another question.

"Did your heart's wish include me ruling beside you?"

Ashwin's eyes gleam his sincerity. "I've wished for you since we first met."

His answer hits me like a staff to my stomach. I bowl over, and the icy sickness inside me spreads fast now that we are apart. Indah said she sensed Ashwin lied when he told the datu we are not intended to marry. In Ashwin's heart, we are betrothed. When we touch, my pain eases because he wished for our union.

Ashwin wears a blank, slackened expression. "Kalinda, I told you how I felt about you before I unleashed Udug."

"But you *wished* for me." He returns my accusation with a series of rapid blinks. "This isn't real! I'm drawn to you because you wished it." The color in his cheeks drains away, and he presses his fist to his lips.

Another stone-cold thought strikes me.

Deven thinks I'm in love with Ashwin.

"If this is all an illusion, then why . . . ?" Ashwin waves at the floor and what just took place there.

"You wished that I'd rule the empire alongside you. Udug cannot defy your bidding." I grip my teeth together to ward off another round of shivers. "Udug's powers are still inside me. I'm safe from them when I'm near you."

"Then stay close." Ashwin steps forward to defend me from the cold, but I shuffle back and wrap my arms around myself. The violation of his imposed will crawls across my skin, stronger than my need for warmth. My teeth chatter involuntarily. I lock them down, but not before Ashwin sees. "You're in pain."

"Please keep away." Ashwin did not manipulate me intentionally, but I do not trust myself near him.

He balls a fist and strikes at the veil. "Why won't you let me help you?"

"Because I love Deven." I clutch at my aching chest. "He's my heart's wish."

Everything about Ashwin dims and sinks, his demeanor, his posture, his raised fist. Whatever light he shone for me extinguishes.

Why couldn't he be Deven? I demand of the gods. *Why did you tie me to a throne and a man my heart has not chosen?* If I thought I could fall in love with Ashwin, I could set aside Deven right now. In his considerate, honorable way, he knows the choice is mine and loves me enough to walk away. But I never wanted Ashwin. Even if I had, any possible future with him has been permanently skewed.

I slip off his gold cuff and hold it out. "This is yours."

Ashwin opens his mouth, but no words come. He reaches for his cuff, and his finger brushes my palm. My need for him hurts so badly tears spring into my vision. I pull back, and his chin falls to his chest.

"I'm sorry," I whisper.

The door opens. Sarita sees my watery eyes and averts her gaze. "Kindred, the Lestarian woman asked me to find you and the prince. She said for you to meet her and the baldish man in the courtyard."

Indah would only summon us for one purpose—the rebels must be close. Sarita watches us from the corner of her sight. Ashwin's hair is still mussed and his tunic offset. Sarita is too innocent to conclude what we have been doing here alone, but I have a clear memory and suffer the ensuing guilt. I should have guessed my connection with Ashwin was contrived.

"That will be all, Sarita," I say.

She hesitates in the doorway. "I'd like to go with you when you leave."

The complication of another person on our journey is too much to consider now. "I'll think on it. Thank you." She exits the way she came. "We should go."

The prince still will not look at me.

"Ashwin, please."

He tips up his head, his eyes frigid. I risk my willpower and edge closer. Tempting soul-fire wafts off him, physical solace within my reach, but I hold myself taut.

"I'm still with you, Ashwin. You have my loyalty through whatever comes next. I know you'll give the empire your all."

"Don't patronize me. I may be younger than you, but I'm not a child." He tugs down his tunic jacket, a meticulous gesture Tarek was known for. "You may still be kindred, but this is *my* empire, and the gods will hold *me* responsible for what comes next."

Ashwin storms out, his footsteps sounding like Tarek's the day he walked into my life and flipped my future upside down. Rajah Tarek was a vengeful man, turned hard-hearted after the woman he loved, my mother, jilted him for my father. But I am not my mother any more than Ashwin is his father.

I pick up the henna pot I left on the floor, dip my finger into the sticky paste, and paint the backs of my hands. Soon enough, the henna will dry and flake off to reveal the mark of the kindred. Then Ashwin will be reminded that my fate is also tied to what becomes of the empire, and he will see that I will continue to fight to make certain that the most important aspect of his heart's wish comes true.

Ashwin will be the next rajah. That is the only destiny I will accept.

16

Deven

Late into the afternoon, the plodding wagons spread out. The weariness of the day strings us apart and heavies our steps. Long trails of men wind from the woods and descend into the lowlands, where the air thickens with the dank scent of wet land. The sky opens to unstoppable stretches of blue over verdant grasslands. Men toil in the rice fields and the higher wheat fields, both crops recently planted for the coming winter.

Though I scrutinize every wagon and group of soldiers we pass, I have not seen or heard anything about Brac or Opal. The farther we walk, the more my premonition festers that they are in danger.

Ahead, our troops trudge through a village. Our catapult is one of the last to pass through the roadways lined with ramshackle huts. Yatin was raised not far from this area. His widowed mother and two eldest sisters worked long days in the fields while he and his other siblings kept house.

Women and children watch us roll through from their worn doorways. About a hundred strides in front of us, Manas, riding on horseback, stops at a hut. He and another soldier speak to the woman. All four members of my unit conceal our faces as we march toward them.

"Where's your husband?" Manas demands.

The middle-aged woman props a child on her hip, an older boy beside them. "The gods took him to the Beyond three years past." Her burr is rich and throaty, much like Yatin's accent.

"Any older children?"

"A fifteen-year-old son. He's in the rice fields."

"Send your son here to fetch him," Manas says and then calls to the other women shying away from the soldiers in their huts. "Rajah Tarek requires all able-bodied men ages fourteen and older to take up arms and join us."

Though Manas states no punishment for noncompliance, his talwar hangs off his hip. Most women shut their doors. Widows are common in the empire, and the life span of field workers is short. The young son of the woman Manas first addressed starts out for the fields, but Manas bends down from his saddle and snags him by the back of his tunic.

"How old are you?" Manas asks as we steadily march nearer.

"Twelve," he squeaks.

"I served the rajah as his boot-shine boy at your age. Fetch your older brother and return here to bid your mother good-bye. You'll work as a water servant."

My lip curls and I fist my sword.

The woman yanks her son from Manas's hold. "Please. I need my sons. Someone has to work in the fields and earn our keep."

We come up to them, the wagon nearly in line with Manas's horse. Every other door on the road is closed.

Manas regards the woman without a single yarn of compassion. "Send them both." He posts the soldier with him to stay and enforce his orders and then rides to the next road.

The woman sets her younger child down, a girl, and grabs her son to her chest in a double-arm hug. Her daughter cries at her knees. The sight of them, the mother and her two children, throws my mind back to my mother, brother, and me. The nursemaids had to drag us away from her after our weekly visiting hour in the courtesans' wing. Each time Mother had to return to entertaining the rajah or his men of court, our hearts were crushed. Brac took our partings especially hard. Afterward, I would hold him on our double cot in the nursery bunk room while he cried himself to sleep.

We roll up to a family's run-down hut. Our wagon is the only one in sight on the road. The soldier Manas left works to pry the mother and son apart, but the woman will not forfeit her child. The more the soldier wrenches, the more hysterical and desperate she becomes. Finally, he draws back and strikes her. She cries out and falls against the doorjamb.

The scene around me gives way to another.

Mother's hour with Brac and me has come to an end. She dallies for one last hug, surrounding us in the softest silk and sweetest jasmine. A man barges in and tells her he's tired of waiting. I stand between them, but he shoves me to the floor and hauls her off by the hair. Brac's hands start to glow in fury. I shield him from their view. His fingers singe my sleeve and nearly burn my skin. I hold him close, but I cannot cover both his eyes and my ears, which echo with Mother's fading scream.

The soldier scuffles with the twelve-year-old. I step away from the slow-moving catapult and pull my khanda. "Leave them be."

The soldier turns on me, and his eyes bulge. I recognize him as well. He and I were in the military encampment together in Iresh. He forgets the boy and draws his sword on me.

"General Manas!" he calls.

Manas has strolled around the bend in the road, out of sight. No other soldiers are near. I can scarcely hear my quick breaths over the woman's wailing.

The soldier shouts louder. "General! Cap—"

"Afternoon, soldier," Natesa purrs, pulling off her turban. Her dark-brown hair falls around her dirt-smudged face.

The soldier is so stunned by the sight of a woman—and a beautiful one at that—he does not see Yatin throw his haladie until it is too late.

The blade sinks deep into the soldier's chest, and he collapses before the family. The woman abruptly stops crying and picks up her young child. I shuffle forward to examine the fallen soldier. He is dead, or will be soon.

Yatin speaks from near the wagon. "Rohan, stay here and redirect all sound. Warn us when the general is coming. Natesa, put your turban back on."

Rohan kicks up a subtle wind, concentrating on Manas's whereabouts. One would not detect the mood in the skies unless already suspicious. Natesa quickly ties on her turban. Yatin strides past her to the family's hut. Adrenaline takes over, overriding my shock, and I help him lug the body inside.

Yatin retrieves his haladie and kicks dirt over the trail of blood on the ground. "Hide and don't come out until the army is gone," he tells the woman, who nods avidly. "Don't speak of this, and you'll be left alone."

She ushers her children inside, closes their door partway, then pauses. "Thank you, Yatin. Your sisters and mother will be overjoyed to know you're well."

I startle at his given name. She shuts the door, and Yatin and I hustle back to the wagon, into Rohan's winds. Two minutes, maybe three, have passed since Manas rode off. Natesa's turban again covers her hair. We lead the horses onward, and the next wagon comes around the bend. Rohan weakens his gusts, and we march on.

My heart beats two times faster than my feet.

"He's coming," says Rohan.

Manas rides nearer to us. At my prompt, Natesa tucks a loose strand of her hair down the collar of her jacket. Manas's horse canters past our wagon and slows. He looks back at the woman's door.

He remembers he left a soldier there.

Farther up the line, a commander calls for the general. Manas circles his mount and rides onward into the troops ahead. I release a quick breath, my heart flailing against my rib cage, and pray that no one pursues the disappearance of one soldier in this vast army.

Once we are clear of the village, I address Yatin. "Who was that woman?"

"A friend of my mother's. We can trust her."

We are not near Yatin's village; that *was* his village. "Where is your family's home?"

"Not far from here."

His sadness hushes me. Though this is the closest he has been to his family in many moons, he cannot stop to visit them. Had I been paying better attention, I would have suggested he and Natesa meet his mother and sisters and rejoin us later. If Natesa had not distracted the guard long enough for Yatin to throw his haladie, we would be finished.

"I'm sorry," I say. "You did the right thing."

Yatin slides an indirect glance at Natesa. "I'd do it again."

As would I, and that worries me. I once told Kali that sometimes the only solution for peace is war. But we are not here to fight these men or change their minds about their leader. We have come for Brac and Opal. And the sooner we find them, the sooner we can run far away from the demon rajah and his army.

17

Kalinda

I meet Indah and Pons in the temple courtyard. Night is falling, and with it, the clear sky leaves an opening for the cold winds pushing in from the north. Much of the snow has melted away, and ice forms on the puddles that remain. Ashwin arrived ahead of me. From his hard-set jaw, he is still simmering over our encounter in the Claiming chamber.

Pons hands Ashwin his machete and says, "The rebels are waiting near the lake. They wish to meet you and the kindred alone. I cannot tell how many there are. At least one of them is a Galer. I received her request to meet you but nothing since."

The rebel Galer must be redirecting the sounds of their movements to conceal their numbers, an uncomfortable beginning to our diplomatic engagement. I draw my dagger. "I'll throw up a flame if we need you."

Indah nods. Her powers will not be of much use to us in this cold, but she is still an adept healer.

Why am I thinking of needing a healer?

Because someone gets hurt every time we interact with the rebels.

Not this time. Tonight, we broker peace.

Ashwin and I exit through the gate. We turn away from our wing flyer by the road, into the chilly wind, and pass through the alpine forest. A figure waits outside the tree line, in front of the frozen lake. Even from a distance, I recognize Anjali, the warlord's Galer daughter. She wears black robes with a red belt cinched at her waist. Her ebony hair is tied back in a long, thick braid. Anjali was one of the rajah's top four favored women in his court, but she secretly worked for her father as a palace informant. Her winds swirl predatorily around her, a convex slithering of currents. We stop a fair distance away, and Anjali lulls her gusts. I sense within myself for my powers. My inner light is faint but accessible.

"Kindred. Your Majesty." Anjali bows, her welcoming discordant with her smirk.

"We were expecting the warlord," remarks Ashwin. Our exhalations shimmer in the air like silver plumes.

"My father is preoccupied with matters in Vanhi. As you're aware, the demon rajah's army is marching there." Anjali's intense dark eyes strike a balance against her oval chin, and her subtle curves are offset by a slim waist. "Our informants brought us disturbing news. Would you like to hear?"

"Tell us the message your father sent you to deliver," I reply, annoyed at her meandering discourse. Like a sidewinder snake, Anjali waits until her opponents are distracted by her indirect weaving and then strikes.

"The demon rajah is growing his powers."

"He doesn't need to grow his powers," I say. "He never tires."

"The longer he is out of the Void, the weaker he becomes . . . unless he feeds off bhuta soul-fire." Anjali wrinkles her nose. "You know that disgusting thing you Burners do? Parching? Udug does the same, only he parches his victim's whole soul."

The rebels have also learned the Voider's name, but Ashwin does not disclose if her knowledge about the Udug upholds his own findings.

"Creatures of the evernight thrive in the dark," Anjali explains. "They're the strongest in the shadows. Through feeding off bhuta soulfire, Udug is expanding the powers he brought into our realm. By the time he reaches Vanhi, he will be more powerful than the demon you battled. He will be unstoppable."

Ice radiates in my gut, stemming from the cold-fire strangling my inner light. Udug's powers work the same way on me as they do the rest of the world.

"The Lestarian Navy is on its way," says Ashwin, calm and focused. "With the rebels also on our side, we'll have sufficient bhutas to defeat Udug."

She wags her finger at him. "You unleashed the Voider, yet you need bhutas to vanquish him?"

"I don't share my father's hatred. An alliance with the rebels will ensure a place for bhuta Virtue Guards in the empire's future."

"An alliance is one answer," Anjali admits. "But we have another."

Ashwin boosts his chin. "And what's that?"

"For you to die." Anjali's smirk widens at his flinch. "Udug is tied to you through your heart's wish. If your heart stops beating . . ." She makes a *poof* motion. "He returns to the Void."

My powers hum just below my skin. "Your theory is unfounded."

"We won't know until we try. Your Majesty?" Anjali leers at his title. "You unleashed Udug. Do you have the courage to send him back?"

I step in front of Ashwin. "The prince won't forfeit his life."

"My father told me you'd say that, which is why for every hour the prince lives, one of the palace prisoners will die in his place. The warlord will start with your favorites. Your rani friends, Parisa and Eshana. Or maybe your servant, Asha. No, it will be Shyla, the one with the baby. She has a little girl, I believe."

Anjali's threat wrings me breathless. I raise my dagger to slice away her sneer, and she summons a wall of wind between us, halting my opening to strike her. Satisfied that I cannot touch her, she twirls a chakram—a circular throwing blade—around her wrist and switches her gaze to Ashwin.

"Decide quickly, Prince. My father will kill a rani every hour starting at sunup unless he hears that you're dead."

All warmth drains from Ashwin's pallor. He opens his mouth, his dry lips sticking together. "Are you certain this will stop Udug?"

I slice my blade in front of him. "You cannot consider this. Hastin is trying to frighten you into conceding your throne, and the only way to do that is through your death."

Anjali laughs lightly. "Oh, let the prince die. It's his right."

"Quiet," I snap. "Ashwin, we cannot believe anything she says. Hastin has the palace and he's afraid you'll win it back. This must be a trick."

"But if it isn't . . . ?" he asks.

"Then we'll find another way."

"Your friends will be killed," he whispers, holding the machete at his side. "My father's wives—my family—will die."

My throat aches, thinking of the ranis and Asha, my servant. Hastin could kill them no matter what Ashwin does or does not do. They are innocents, bystanders in this race for power. But they are more than prisoners. Every one of them is a sister warrior by heart and deed. As such, they would relinquish their lives to protect their families and their homeland's future.

"They aren't the rightful rajah. You are." I scrub away the flaking henna on the backs of my hands. "As the kindred, I'll stand at your right-hand side."

Ashwin sees my rank marks, and tears flood his eyes.

"Please give me the machete," I say. With my guidance, he gradually lowers the blade. "Now let it go." He does not, so I pry the weapon away.

He gasps for a saving breath, his chin quivering against more tears.

Anjali ejects a sigh and stops twirling her chakram. "You never know when to lose, Kalinda."

My instincts prickle. I back up for the trees. "Ashwin, get to the temple."

He pivots to run, but before he takes a single step, Anjali slings a chakram at him, boosted by one of her vicious gusts. I knock Ashwin down, away from its path. The chakram whirrs off into the forest and embeds itself in a tree trunk. We scramble up, and Anjali hurls a follow-up wind at us, flinging us back.

I land hard in the snow and drop the machete. Ashwin flies into a log, hitting his head, and lies in a daze. I throw up a flame, a signal to Indah and Pons, and draw my dagger. As I stand, I notice Anjali has disappeared.

The sun has sunk, and the dusky twilight rapidly fades to dark. I scan the shadowed landscape for her. The northern winds blast, each gust stronger than the last. I cannot discern which are Anjali's and which belong to the sky-god.

I back up toward Ashwin, and a wind whips at my ankles. I fall, dropping my dagger. Another squall lashes my back. The sting goes through my tunic to my skin. Then another strike belts me, followed by Anjali's laugh.

She whips me again with her slicing gusts. My tunic rips, exposing my back. Another few agonizing lashes come. Welts rise on my skin. I roll over and throw repeated heatwaves to make her stop. The color of my flames starts out a lime green and steadily intensifies to emerald.

Her flaying winds peter off, and nature's less punishing gales skim over me. Snow presses into my back and cools the pain. *Where are Indah and Pons?*

"Burners are supposed to be the most dangerous of us," Anjali says, standing over me.

I reach for my dagger, but a wind pushes my arm above my head. Anjali stomps on my other arm, pinning my fire powers against the frozen ground.

"Leave us be," I say. "Killing us will not stop Udug."

"My father has given me everything good in my life. I do as he asks." She leans over me and grabs my neck. "First you die and then the prince."

The wind on my raised arm has passed. I swing it down and seize her wrist. "I'll turn you into an ash heap first."

"I accept that challenge." Her powers dive inside me and squeeze my chest. She winnows my lungs, shriveling my breath and stealing my sky.

But our skin-to-skin connection goes both ways. I thread out her soul-fire, parching her. Her lips and skin dull to gray, yet she holds on.

The loss of air weakens my grip.

I. Must. Breathe.

A streak darts across my vision. Ashwin shoves Anjali off me and swings his machete at her. She lobs a wind at his weaponized arm, and it involuntarily goes over his head. While his blade is restrained, she captures his throat with her hands. Ashwin stills and shudders.

I funnel my powers into a burning ball and toss my emerald fire, now blue at the edges. Anjali's free hand summons a wind that casts my sphere of flames into the trees.

My odd, sickly fire devours the underbrush. The northern wind picks up the embers and showers the forest with them. Sparks grow to flames that spread despite the cold.

Ashwin shoves and kicks at Anjali. He breaks free, panting, and she grabs him again. I hurl my dagger at her, burying the blade into her leg. She screams but does not release him.

I pull my second dagger, and a huge chunk of ice smashes into me. Pain bursts down my spine. I fall forward, dropping my dagger, hands deep in frost. I reach for my weapon, but flying icicles impede my path.

Behind me, Indira, a rebel Aquifier, throws her icy blades. I roll away from them, farther from my weapon. And then Indira is on me, her cold hands wrapped around my wrists. Her powers flow inside me and sing a song to my blood that entrances the rivers of my veins. She pulls, and like a tide following the moon, droplets bleed from my body.

Her powers lock me in place, like a leaf caught in a whirlpool. From the corner of my eye, I see Anjali still winnowing Ashwin. His arms turn limp, and his struggles lessen. My blood cries tears across my skin. Its irony wetness seeps into my mouth and nose. My heartbeat slows to muted thuds, and my vision dims.

Ashwin's eyes roll back into his head. Mine start to do the same.

My inner star pierces my haze.

Indira is draining my lifeblood but also depleting the cold inside me.

I pulse my dwindling soul-fire at her, sending forth a burst of scorching heat. She tumbles off me shrieking, her robes on fire. Behind her, the forest is ablaze. Indira rolls around on the ground into the flames. The fire sweeps over her, and her shrieks and frantic movements stop.

Winded and dizzy, I climb to my knees. Flecks of blood cover my exposed skin. Dark stars sweep across my vision, blending into the sky. *What did Indira do to me?*

Anjali releases Ashwin, and he sags in a lifeless heap. *No, Anu. No.* She jerks my dagger from her thigh and tosses it, then rides a swift wind and lands in front of me. Anjali snatches my throat, and her powers crush my lungs. Having spent all my fire on Indira, I clutch the Galer's arms with a weak, useless grip.

"I burned your father's journals. Used them as kindling." Anjali's winnowing powers unfold into my limbs, siphoning out every last bit of breath. "Consider it payback for betraying my father."

I weep inwardly for the loss of my father's journals. I will never read his thoughts, never see my mother through his eyes. Never know them for myself.

The forest fire blazes, lighting up Anjali's silhouette. My powers that sparked the inferno have grown wild, into nature-fire. Serpents slither in the flames.

Come to me, friends.

None heed me.

Please, I need you.

They continue their crazed overtaking of the forest. Ashwin has not moved. I will be next. Where are Indah and Pons?

I latch on to the only weapon within my reach—Udug's cold-fire. I summon it as I would my powers. Sapphire sparks shoot from my fingers.

Anjali releases me with a shriek. I land on all fours, coughing in loose chunks of air.

Pons and Indah charge into the clearing. Both bleed from cuts on their faces. Pons aims with his blowgun and shoots three darts at Anjali in swift succession. She diverts them into the fire with well-timed gusts.

Anjali stumbles away, favoring her wounded leg. Indah stays back, the cold frustrating her powers, but Pons stalks closer. The forest fire hedges Anjali in. Pons fastens his winds into a whip and lashes at her. While I stay low, she rallies her own drafts against him.

Across the way, Ashwin has not stirred. *He's too still.*

Pons and Anjali fling their powers at each other. The sky crackles. Their airstreams clash, and a clap blasts above me. Lying on the cold ground, I cover my ears. Anjali falters a step. Pons's winds push her back to the wall of fire. Anjali emits a guttural cry and ducks. His airstream blows past her into the trees, picking up flames and pitching them into the distance.

Anjali commandeers the northern wind and flies over me. She heaves a chakram at Pons. He dodges the spinning blade, and she soars over him and Indah. He chases her with lancing airstreams. Anjali dashes into the smoke, out of sight.

Indah runs to me, scrapes across her forehead and cheeks. "We tried to get here sooner. The northern Aquifier iced the courtyard gate shut and attacked us with icicles."

"Help Ashwin," I croak, rubbing my hoarse throat.

She hurries to the prince. Pons comes over, collecting my daggers along the way, and helps me to the lake. Slashes from Indira's attack run up his forearms. I rest near the icy shore, and he returns to assist Indah with Ashwin. Pons lugs him over his shoulder. As they cross back to me, a streak of white zips into the sky. Anjali takes off aboard our wing flyer, vanishing into the night.

She will return to her father and report that she winnowed the prince to death.

Anu, spare him.

Pons lays Ashwin down on the rocky lakeshore. Though he does not wake, his chest rises and falls. I send up a prayer of thanks, but we are not out of harm's way. We have to put out the fire.

Indah reaches for the lake, but the water is trapped under the ice. My own powers are spent, and I cannot wait for them to recover. Teeth clacking, I look down at Ashwin. Stealing another's soul-fire to increase my own is wrong, but I need my powers to stop the fire from reaching the temple.

Gods, forgive me. I touch Ashwin and tug in his white-hot light. Warmth pours into my chest and fills up my heart.

Not too much. You'll hurt him.

But his soul-fire is so warm . . .

"Kalinda!" Indah wrenches my hand from him. After a horrified look at me, she checks him over. Ashwin is still breathing.

I have what I need.

Favoring my knee, I dash off. Heat rolls off the nature-fire, roaring with fiery serpents.

Shh, my friends. Sleep.

They rage onward to the temple, the unrelenting northern winds pushing them to and fro.

Pons runs up alongside me, diverting the smoke with his winds. "You need to send the nature-fire away."

"I'm trying," I say, and then cry at the flames, "I am fire, and fire is me!" I reach out with my powers, but my hands glow a cold, pale sapphire. None of my soul-fire is visible within me, only this cruel blue.

The fire is beyond my control.

"Pons, we have to get everyone out!"

We sprint through the gate, past chunks of ice from when Pons and Indah hacked their way free. Priestess Mita ushers girls out the main entry into the courtyard. Several of the younger ones know Pons, and they rush to his side. He scoops the littlest up in his arms. Healer Baka comes with more wards. A stream of girls and sisters races for the lake.

Everyone has gotten out. Priestess Mita would not leave a single girl behind.

The fire snaps closer and closer. I attempt to quell it one last time. Priestess Mita gasps at my glowing blue hands. *Please, Anu. Please.* I concentrate so hard my head aches. But the nature-fire will not obey.

Priestess Mita and I dart outside the gate. She rounds on me. "You're an abomination! You brought this destruction upon our heads!"

Her beliefs about bhutas are wrong, but I have no justification. My powers did this. I started this firestorm.

Smoke stings my watery eyes. Hungry flames chew onward, the wildfire feasting without restraint. All my years with Jaya are slowly leveling to ash. Are the gods punishing me for going against the Claiming? I only wanted men, especially men like Tarek, to lose their right to these girls. I never wanted this.

A shadowy figure appears nearby on the road. Tarek has come to witness the desecration of the gods' sanctuary. The back of my throat cramps as the fire climbs to the north tower and devours the beacon in its cinder teeth.

Anu, send him away. If you have any mercy, you won't let him revel in my pain.

But Tarek delights in the cruelty of the night, smiling not at the fire but at me.

18

Deven

The soldiers who earned the coin and bottle of apong sing rowdily across the way. My unit rests on the ground against the catapult wheels. I am dirty, sweaty, and so tired the campfire embers look like lanterns floating off into the sky. I could do with a long pull from that apong bottle, but I settle for the dirty cup of water and charred flatbread a meal server brought around.

Yatin sits alone and stares into the rocky plain while flexing his hand into a fist over and over. He and Natesa have not spoken since we left the village. Rohan eats quietly, his gaze jumping around so often my own nerves crackle. No one has come looking for the missing soldier, but that could still change.

A mild western wind swirls through camp, flowing from the barren region ahead. At our pressing pace, we will reach the Bhavya Desert the day after tomorrow, a full day ahead of schedule.

Natesa itches her neck. "How do you wear these?"

"We take our turbans off at night," I say.

"How fortunate for you." She scratches harder. "I'm not used to sleeping with something on my head. You'll have to make sure I don't rip it off and throw it into the fire."

The group of drunkards across camp bursts into laughter. Rohan jogs his knee. His hunger to search for his sister will not be satiated tonight.

"When it gets late, I'll take a stroll around camp alone," I tell him.

Rohan sits taller. "I should go with you and keep an ear out."

I can determine how upset he is by how often his voice breaks. That was three times. "It would be suspicious for us to wander around together. After today, we have to be selective about our risks."

"You mean after you nearly got us caught?" Rohan grumbles.

"I won't repeat my mistake," I promise. "Have you heard anything?"

"No." Rohan crosses arms, his frown understandable.

I lower my voice between us. "If Brac and Opal are indeed in camp, we'll find them. Please wait here while I'm gone."

"Is that an order?" Rohan's voice pitched only once, but it was so apparent Yatin glances over.

"I'm asking for your trust."

After my prolonged stare, Rohan concedes with a begrudging mumble.

Natesa stretches out her legs. "I'm fine right here." She sneaks a tentative glance at Yatin seated at the end of the wagon. His aloofness bothers her, but she leaves him be.

I stride over to him. "How are you faring?"

Yatin glowers at his fist, his sight in line with my boots. "Natesa shouldn't have taken her turban off today. She risked too much."

I purse my lips in thought. "I doubt she sees it that way. Natesa's a sister warrior. She was trained to stand up for herself and those she loves." Yatin unclenches his fist, and I spot the lotus ring in his palm. Holding on to it must be adding to his unrest. "You should propose to her again. She may give you a different answer."

"She's stubborn."

"Be more stubborn."

Yatin grunts noncommittally and slips the ring into his pocket. The noises around camp have lessened. The men are turning in for the night. I pat his shoulder and then walk back to the others. Natesa is by herself.

"Where did Rohan go?" I ask.

She picks dirt out from under her nails. "He needed the latrine."

"Keep an eye on him and Yatin while I'm gone."

"Are you assigning me to watch duty, General?"

Why does everyone take what I say as an order? "You can call it that if you prefer." I thumb at Yatin. "He's worried about you."

"No, he's mad that I took off my turban, but we would have been caught. At the very least, you would have. Kali will burn us alive if anything happens to you."

"I'm not so certain she cares," I admit.

"Don't be a dolt. Of course she does." Natesa thumps my shin, a friendly bump. I return her badgering with a nudge of my toe. She does not smile. "Yatin wants to marry me."

"Oh?"

"You're an awful liar, Deven. I know Yatin told you. He doesn't understand why I want to meet his family first, because he has a family. But it matters to me." Natesa hugs her knees to her chest and tries unsuccessfully not to glance at him.

"He wants you for his wife," I reply. "He already considers you part of his family."

She loosens some. "You better go before Rohan comes back and talks you into taking him along. Be careful."

"You too." I pick up my empty water cup, salute her in farewell, and head off.

I maneuver through the sleepy camp, careful not to draw much attention. The soldiers have settled in tents or lain out under wagons. To keep up the appearance that I am out for a drink, I stop at the watering hole. No one pays me any mind as I down a cup of stale water and head off in a direction opposite to the one I came from. Since we have not found any sign of prisoners, the demon rajah must be keeping them close by, so I set out in search of his tent.

Near the front of camp, the covered wagons multiply. At the end of a long row, the demon rajah's grand silk tent is pitched. Manas ducks out the tent's entry. I flatten against a wagon, and he strides to the far end of the nearest row.

I start after Manas. Heaviness burdens my approach, and a high signal drones in my ears, as though I am standing too close to a ringing gong. I close in on the tent, and a thick, cloying darkness permeates the night. Even the torchlights do not shine as far.

A blue light flashes from inside the tent, and a sudden tremor shakes the ground. Then stunning quiet.

Cold fingers pry at my chest. That quake came from a Trembler.

Ignoring the fear simmering in my gut, I tiptoe down the row of wagons, navigating the gloom to my advantage.

A shadow moves in front of me. Someone else sneaks to the wagon at the end of the second row. I recognize the person's small, slight shape and whisper his name.

Rohan pauses, the only indication that he heard me, and carries on. I hiss for him to come back, but he tiptoes closer to the last covered wagon.

Skies above. I should have ordered him to remain with Natesa and Yatin.

I dart to the line of wagons and nestle in the shadows. A swift, suspicious gust ruffles the draped opening of the demon rajah's tent and knocks over a lamp within. Two guards and Manas dash inside to stomp out the fire.

Rohan must have caused the sudden wind. He hurries for the wagon nearest the tent. I stop at the front of the wagon, by the coachman's bench, and peer around the corner. Rohan hovers at the corner of the covered wagon's rear door.

"Opal?" he whispers.

I strain my ears but hear nothing. Manas will have weakened the bhuta prisoners by poisoning them with white baneberry and snakeroot or by bleeding out their powers.

A muffled voice comes from inside the wagon. "Rohan?"

Opal. I listen for Brac, but another voice calls out.

"General," says the demon Udug in Tarek's stolen timbre, "we have a visitor."

Manas and two soldiers armed with crossbows race out of the tent. Rohan summons a raging gust, and the opulent tent starts to lift off the ground. Furniture tips over, and lamplight flickers. Both soldiers release bolts. Rohan's wind diverts the first one, but the second strikes him in the shoulder.

Rohan falls, and his winds dwindle.

"Bind him," says Manas.

The soldiers tie Rohan's wrists behind him with a vine of toxic snakeroot, and the last of his powers recede. In the stillness, the demon rajah strides out of his tent.

"You're audacious, boy." Udug's snide voice rings with amusement. "Are you alone?"

Rohan bends over, in pain from the bolt in his shoulder. "You have my sister."

"You mean Opal." Udug elongates the *o* and snaps the *p*. *Ooo-pal.* "Your sister has proven to be very valuable."

Manas speaks up. "This boy served as a guard for Kindred Kalinda and Prince Ashwin."

"Oh?" Udug looms over Rohan as he would a drooping flower. "How are my son and first wife? Have they run into any further trouble?"

My stomach plunges. He must mean the sea raiders. Did they follow the navy or Kali and the prince?

Rohan groans through firm-set teeth. "Release Opal. Take me."

"I have no need for two abominations." The demon rajah grabs Rohan's head as he did when he executed the Galer.

Anu, don't let this be happening.

Rohan also recognizes the fatal grip and toughens to someone sager than his fourteen years. "Prince Ashwin is our true ruler. He and Kindred Kalinda will stop you."

His boldness tugs at my pride. His voice did not break once.

"You will not live to see how wrong you are." Udug's fingers glow an eerie azure as his fingertips dig into Rohan's head. "I cast you out, demon."

Rohan's expression fixes in a silent scream. White light, his soul-fire, filters out of him and into the demon's grasp.

Pounding sounds from inside the wagon. Opal bangs against the door, her shouts indistinct. I have to get to Rohan. Perhaps I could dispatch Manas and one of the guards before the other releases a bolt at me, but could I cut down all three? And then how do I stop Udug?

All my muscles strain for me to step forward—to protect Rohan, to stop Udug, to do *something*—but Opal's wailing holds me back. I promised Rohan I would save his sister. Revealing my presence would jeopardize my chance of keeping my word. Any attempt to save Rohan would put Opal, Natesa, and Yatin in danger, and by all reason would be suicide. I cannot do anything for Rohan, but I *can* still help Opal.

Dropping my head against the side of the wagon, I fight the need to act. *Why couldn't Rohan have listened to me and stayed behind? Why didn't he trust me?* I should have known he lied to Natesa about needing the latrine. I should have stayed at the wagon until he returned. I failed him. I failed us all.

The night transforms around Udug, thickening to a suffocating depth of nothing. Rohan's soul-fire fades like a dying day. I grasp my sword so tightly my palm aches. Finally, Udug steals the last of Rohan's essence and lets him go.

Rohan folds in a heap like a husk, limbs and head angled wrongly.

Opal's frantic thuds and cries lessen. Udug stares up at the sky and scowls at the stars that defy his darkness. Then he strides into his tent.

Manas wrenches the bolt from Rohan's shoulder. I cringe from the grisly sound of blade ripping flesh. "Get rid of it."

The soldiers pick up Rohan and lug him away. Opal's weeps reverberate into my bones.

Manas raps his fist against the wagon. "You in there. Shut it." He mutters to himself and ducks inside Udug's tent.

I wait two breaths. Then five. Then twelve. No one returns.

Opal's cries continue. Brac must not be with her or I would have heard him by now. *Perhaps Udug stole his soul-fire too.*

The pair of soldiers returns and stands guard at the end of the prisoner's wagon.

I press my lips against the wall and whisper so only the wind can hear me. "I'll get you out, Opal. I swear it."

Trusting the wind to deliver my message, I slip away to the end of camp. The moon and stars reveal two sets of footprints leading into the rocky field. I follow their trail to the body.

The soldiers dumped Rohan in the grass. They did not even lay him so he looks to the heavens. I roll him onto his back and sniffle away my tears. *He was so young.*

Without a tool to dig a grave with, I will lay him to rest another way. I set to work gathering rocks. Taking off my jacket to use as a bindle, I load and carry four or five rocks at a time. I stack them around Rohan, burying his feet and legs first.

A rustle in the grass draws me up short. Scavengers must have caught the scent of the body. Before long, they will circle in. I double my speed, gathering and stacking until Rohan is encased in stones.

I kneel back, sweat dripping down my forehead, and try to center myself. My anger against Udug drove me to labor through most of the night, but I must let go of my hard feelings long enough to pray.

"Gods, bless Rohan's soul so that he may find the gate that leads to peace and everlasting light." I recite the Prayer of Rest more often than feels fair, but the blessing always instills harmony in my heart.

I sit with Rohan until sunrise stirs on the horizon. Then I leave him to his rest and trudge back to our catapult wagon. Yatin and Natesa are wide awake, sitting upright beside each other.

"Rohan didn't return," Natesa says. Her lower lip is red from gnawing it.

Tears I thought I left at the grave site burn my eyes. "He found Opal locked in a wagon. The demon rajah . . . got to him first."

Natesa's expression crashes in as she succumbs to shock and sorrow. I slide down to the ground and drop my head in my hands.

"And Brac?" Yatin asks.

My shoulders curve over my hollow chest. "No sign of him."

Yatin and Natesa fall quiet. We alone cannot stop Udug. We are three mortals against an immortal demon. We could sneak off now, as though we were never here. We could steal horses and run for Vanhi ahead of the army, or backtrack and seek out the Lestarian Navy along the river. But my vow to Opal stops me, and despite my better instincts, I muster the fortitude not to flee.

"I'm staying," I say. "You two can leave."

Natesa draws short breaths, working up the nerve to run or hide or both. Yatin wraps his arm around her, and she leans into his side.

"We need to stay together," he says.

My heart fills until it may burst. They still trust me, even after my terrible mistake. I thought Rohan would regard my plea for him to stay with the others. I should have commanded him not to leave, but I refused to take full responsibility for his life, and now I am partly responsible for his death. I will not repeat my error.

"If you stay, you stay on as my troops." I leave no quarrel about my authority. "You'll do everything I order. No questions. No debates. You follow me."

Yatin does not so much as blink. "Yes, sir."

"Yes, General Naik," Natesa amends.

Her use of my rank rubs at an old sore, but I let it alone and rest against the wagon for what is left of the night.

Daybreak gradually pours across the grassland, stinging my tired eyes and waking the troops. I could sleep through the ruckus, but sunup pushes us to get underway.

My unit packs up. The loss of our fourth member is stark as we divide the work to ready our horses and wagon. I would like to visit Rohan's grave site before we leave, bring Natesa and Yatin along, and allow myself another moment to rage about his death. But the wagons ahead of us roll out, so we set off for another grueling day of marching.

19

Kalinda

I stare bleary-eyed at the smoking rubble. Snowflakes drift down upon the smoldering piles of stone and melt to steam. The fire flattened the structure in the night, dancing like cackling demons around a pyre. This charred wreckage is all that remains of the Samiya temple.

A low, whitewashed sky has long since lightened to the bleakest gray, casting an abysmal glare over the scene. The hundred or so temple wards huddle as one in the crisp cold. In their rush to escape the fire, few sisters and wards brought cloaks. Flakes of ash entwine with the snowflakes and tarnish the sisters' humble blue robes.

Frightened and saddened tears clean trails down the wards' sooty faces. The older girls comfort the younger ones, and the sisters comfort the older girls. The wards are too distraught to do little more than steal astonished glances at the men, and the sisters do not stop them. In the wake of this devastation, they do not fear the loss of innocence. *I* am the enemy they dread.

Priestess Mita huddles with the sisters to discuss what they should do next. Our situation is beyond desolate. By the time Indah and Pons chipped a hole in the icy lake and she sent streams of water at the temple, the inferno was ravenous.

My fault.

Shifting off my bad leg, I shiver against the wind. The ache in my knee has returned, digging in with frozen claws. Pons and Indah wait down shore, the Aquifier having healed their cuts and the welts on my back. Ashwin broods by the lake, holding a chunk of ice to the back of his head. We have yet to speak, and I can hardly look at him. Does he remember I stole his soul-fire? The remnants of his parched warmth lasted until a few hours ago, and Udug's cold poison took charge once more. But for a few merciful hours, I felt whole.

I cram my chilly fingers under my arms, but I have little body heat left to share. *Take some soul-fire from one of the wards. Just enough to drive back the cold.*

No. Living off another's essence is a base, disgusting kind of survival.

Healer Baka separates from the group of sisters and comes to me. "Are you feeling better, Kalinda?"

"I'm fine. How is everyone else?"

"A few bruises from our evacuation, but as a whole, well." Snowflakes melt on Healer Baka's spectacles, but the droplets do not interrupt her avid stare. "The prince blames himself for this."

I huff a dry laugh. "He doesn't deserve that right. The glory of this is all mine."

"This was an accident, Kalinda." Baka rotates me away from the other sisters' direct view. "They've voted for the prince, your friends, and you to leave."

"But our wing flyer was taken," I say, planting my heels. "And Indah sent for aid. The Lestarians will come with rations. We should wait here for them together."

Healer Baka wraps one arm around me. "Priestess Mita wants you and your companions to start down the mountain. We'll send the Lestarians for you after they arrive."

I jerk from her hold. "The sisters and wards should know the truth. Bhutas are *good*. Don't send us away or they'll always fear my kind."

Priestess Mita speaks from behind us. "They *should* fear you." Healer Baka and I whirl around. The priestess's glare ties my thoughts into a jumble of apologies, rendering me speechless. "You're no sister warrior, and you're not my kindred. Leave this place and take the Lestarian abominations with you."

I am unsurprised that she would cast aside bhutas, but her disrespect for Ashwin unknots my tongue. "What of the prince? He's your ruler."

"My ruler is Rajah Tarek," Priestess Mita corrects. "He leads the empire, not the prince."

I reel on Baka "You told her?"

She extends an apologetic grimace. "As you said, they deserve to know the truth."

"Anu sent Rajah Tarek back to save us," Priestess Mita rails on. "He will preserve our sacred rites and finish exterminating your kind."

Her gullibility floors me. "The gods never send souls back. They send them forward, to their next life. The rajah isn't Tarek; he's a demon in disguise."

She screws her lips up like I am a piece of filth on her tongue. "You have no place to brand anyone a demon, slag."

Baka gasps at the priestess's use of the derogatory term for a Burner. I am flabbergasted they even know it.

Priestess Mita lifts her voice louder, unashamed of her contempt. "Go from here before the gods strike you down for the ruin you have brought upon these faithful sisters and wards."

I tense my body to ward off my shaking. "These wards should know who they're following. Rajah Tarek is a—"

"Go!" bellows the priestess. "Go and take your lies and corruption with you!"

Healer Baka speaks. "Mita—"

"Hush, Baka!" The priestess directs the full force of her animosity at her instead. "Either you side with us or you leave."

The healer deflates. "I'm sorry, Kali. The wards need me."

I need you too. I bite off the admission and seek a softening of heart from the sisters behind them. But they are united in their dismissal.

Sarita steps forward, little ones at her side. "Kalinda, take me with you."

"You're needed here," I rasp, my emotions clogging my throat. The girls with Sarita stare up at me. I bend down to speak to them. Despite the priestess's claim that I am demonic, they abide my presence. "Stay with Sarita and Healer Baka. They'll keep you safe." After I muster an encouraging smile for Sarita, I trudge across the snow to Ashwin. "We've been asked to leave, but they cannot make us."

"No more contention," Ashwin replies, rubbing at a headache. "We'll go."

He starts for the road, and Pons and Indah follow. I lock in a shout. *Why is Ashwin listening to the sisters? He's their rightful leader!* I squeeze my fists at my sides and trail him down the road. Pons wraps his arm around Indah, and she leans against him. I cannot tell if she is sick again or simply exhausted from our horrible night. Whatever the case may be, she needs to rest. She should not be trekking down a snowy mountain.

My anger pushes like a blade into my gut. I stomp up to Ashwin. "Are you giving in?"

"Does it appear that way?"

"You're feeling sorry for yourself. You should be thinking of our people."

He addresses me, his walk swift. "A ruler doesn't force himself upon his people. He cannot demand that they love or respect him. Besides, the priestess is right to send us away. We invited rebel deceivers here and they destroyed the temple."

"So that's it? You're going to let them think the demon masquerading as your father is a better leader than you?"

Ashwin comes to an abrupt halt. "Who are you angry at, Kalinda? The priestess for sending you away? Me for not caring? Yourself for burning down your childhood home—"

I throw a small flame into the air between us, and he jumps back. "You're Tarek's son with or without me. Accept your fate and claim your throne. Stop pitying yourself."

"I am my father's son, but that doesn't entitle you to speak to me so."

"You've never been the exact image of your father until just now."

His gaze flattens to a wall. "And you're his murderess."

Indah wedges in between us. "Stop it. You're like dragons, snapping at each other's gullets." She clutches her stomach, and my temper dissolves to concern. Indah covers her mouth. Heaving into her hand, she runs for a shrub alongside the road.

Pons strides over to her. I fire a glare at Ashwin for letting the priestess bully us into leaving. Indah's condition is his fault. She finishes retching and wipes her mouth on her sleeve.

"Why didn't you tell me you're ill?" Ashwin asks.

"I'm not ill. I'm . . . I'm with child," Indah replies. Ashwin and I stare openly. "Pons and I have known for a while. I'm more than five moons along."

Her explanation adds to my amazement. She was with child when she traveled to Iresh to fight in the trial tournament. "Why didn't you say anything?"

"My father will be angry," she whispers.

Pons tugs her in close. "Perhaps at first," he says, "but he'll praise Enki once he's a grandfather. He loves you, and he will love our child."

Ashwin fidgets with his gold cuff. Our gazes meet, and once again, I can envision his dream for us. The dream I stomped all over. His dejection is still too fresh, too visible. I have to look away.

A sudden northern wind arises, twirling down the road the way we came. Pons tilts his ear to the sky, and his eyes progressively widen.

"What is it?" I ask.

"Come along." He leads Indah back the direction we came.

Ashwin and I hustle after them, following the smoke spiraling into the sky, around the bend in the road to Samiya. A mahati falcon, feathers rich red with orange undertones and yellow tips, circles the site of the fire. Its master rides the giant bird on a woven saddle. Her silvery hair flies behind her, striking as lightning against her sepia skin. The falcon screeches as it dives. The sisters and wards scatter and hide in the unburned section of forest. The great bird, its body large as a wagon and its wingspan three wagons wide, lands near the ice-covered lake.

Tinley, the daughter of Chief Naresh of Paljor, dismounts her falcon. Her crossbow, her favored weapon while she competed against Indah and me in the trial tournament, is strapped to her back. Tinley was eliminated during the first trial, but I believe we parted on amiable terms. At least that is how I recall our time together.

The Galer surveys the woods for the frightened women and wards. Tinley still wears a sarong, and a high slit emphasizes her long, slim legs. A single strip of cloth is wound around her chest. The only change in her appearance is her bearskin cloak.

Tinley taps her talonlike nail against her bottom lip and considers me. "I saw the smoke trail while I was patrolling the border. You wouldn't have anything to do with this disaster, would you, Kalinda?" I try not to take offense at her teasing, but her humor is too close to the mark. She evaluates my downturned mouth and dips her head sideways at Ashwin, her usual reluctant bow. "Your Majesty, gods' grace to you and your kindred. When is your wedding?"

"We're not getting married," I say, ignoring Ashwin's grimace.

"Are you planning another trial tournament?" Tinley demands. "Because I'm not competing. No disrespect, Your Majesty, but I'm content patrolling the skies. Marriage would only bind my wings."

"We aren't arranging another tournament," Ashwin assures her. "As you can see, we're in no state for such designs. We need your help."

Tinley strokes her mahati falcon's side. "I sent out a message for the nearest patrol vessel when I first smelled the smoke. They should arrive shortly." Her milky eyes, like two moons, turn to the clouds. "And here they come."

A huge shadow pushes through the overcast sky. The vessel, larger than those in the Lestarian Navy, floats on a tremendous wind and boasts three masts decorated with countless sails, a patchwork of varying shades of blue. The quilted sails are not confined to the top of the ship but also extend as wings. The stern is elongated, like a bird's tail, and sports even more sails, akin to tail feathers. The Paljorians have mimicked their revered mahati falcons for the vessel's design, with a bird figurehead fronting a sleek hull and high prow. Galers on deck direct gusts into the bulging sails, propelling the craft forward. More Galers maneuver airstreams under the hull, suspending the ship high above ground.

Winds disperse the smoke plumes and toss my hair. The airship flies over us, tucking its wings close to the hull, and lands in the clearing near the lake. Its crew lower four clamp-like feet to stabilize the rounded hull on the ground. A plank drops from the port side, in front of the wing, and a man disembarks.

Though his long, straight hair is white as a new star, his physique is strapping. His arms protrude beneath a loose tunic and the russet bearskin draped over his shoulders. His low-cut collar shows a sliver of his deeply tan chest. A short skirt hangs above his thighs, which rise and dip like valleys and mountains.

Ashwin greets the older man. "Chief Naresh, I recognize you from a portrait I saw years past. You haven't aged a day."

"You must be referring to the rendition in the history text. I had that portrait commissioned before you could walk, Prince Ashwin." The chief's eyes twinkle. His language drags a little and he drops his long vowels. Tinley's accent is the same, but her father's is more pronounced.

The chief's light-brown eyes dart to me. "Kalinda Zacharias." Beaming, he hauls me into a breath-stealing hug. Chief Naresh leans away, and his gaze roves over me as though seeing a long-lost friend.

"You have your mother's hair and your father's sure-footed stature. Kishan was a great man, and Yasmin was the bravest sister warrior of her time. Their love was a bridge between bhutas and mankind. I mourned their passing."

This demonstrative, complimentary man is not what I expected, considering his daughter is more frigid than a midwinter wind. His affection for my parents eases my envy that he knew them, while I will never have that privilege.

Chief Naresh greets Pons and Indah with more hearty embraces, then says, "Come aboard where it's warmer." He raises his voice to the women and girls in the woods. "All are welcome!"

Priestess Mita, well within hearing range, can judge for herself that the chief's invitation is genuine, but she does not budge. The sisters and wards loiter too, wary of the mahati falcon ruffling its fiery feathers in the numbing cold.

"They're afraid of bhutas," I explain.

Chief Naresh winks at me and speaks louder. "Then they must decide which they fear more—bhutas or freezing to death." With that ominous choice, he ascends the ship's plank with great, hefty strides. Indah and Pons go after him.

Priestess Mita waves insistently at Ashwin. "Don't go, Your Majesty. They're Paljorians! They let their birds live with them, and their women betroth themselves to men when they're just little children."

"Our women aren't locked away in a henhouse," Tinley drawls. "We let them strut about the yard with any rooster they like."

Color flares across Priestess Mita's collarbone. "Your Majesty!"

Ashwin bats a finger at Tinley, requesting her forbearance. She growls through bared teeth and stalks aboard the ship. "I ask that you not use my formal title, Priestess," Ashwin says. "From you, it's a mockery."

She pulls back in offense, and Ashwin marches up the plank.

I signal the girls in the forest to come forward. Sarita picks up a child and steps out, undeterred by the giant falcon peering at her with glassy eyes.

"Sarita!" the priestess calls. "Get back here!"

She remains on course. "I'm going to get warm and, hopefully, find something to eat."

At the prospect of shelter *and* food, more wards dash after her for the airship. Healer Baka leads two little girls out, her head high. After a tense stare-off with the priestess, even Sister Hetal quits the woods. Their parting prompts an exodus. The rest of the wards and sisters rush for the airship, leaving the priestess behind.

Sarita starts up the plank. "Do you think Priestess Mita will realize she's excessively pigheaded?"

"Gods as my witness, I don't care." I whisk ahead, climbing aboard in search of elusive warmth.

20

Deven

Our horse team stumbles up another dune, spraying sand in my eyes. We ascend the slippery rise halfway, and then the catapult mires in the sand and jerks to a halt. From the time we set out this morning, we have intermittently charged across the hot sand and spun our wheels. Like the gods, the desert is no respecter of man.

I urge the horse team up the dune while Yatin and Natesa push the catapult from behind. Our sleepless night slows our ascent, but we trudge onward.

"Come on, come on." My half plea, half prayer encourages the horses to conquer the sand dune.

Overlooking the landscape, I squint at the sunburnt dunes rolling into the distance. Our troops trek up and down them like organized lines of red ants. I collect my breath and guide our horses and wagon over the ridge to descend the other side.

Sweat trickles into my eyes. I swipe the stream away with my arm, also slick from perspiration, and smear grit across my brow. Soldiers trudge alongside us, their headscarves shielding their mouths and noses from the sun and sand. I pinned my headscarf across the lower half of my face, as did Yatin and Natesa. She was elated to discard the turban this morning and pick up a headscarf in the last village before the desert. There, we united with a legion of imperial soldiers waiting to join our march on Vanhi.

With them, our ranks have swelled to ten thousand men, maybe a few hundred more. Our growing numbers have allayed some of my anxiousness about being discovered, but I am still on edge. The soldier Yatin dispatched with his haladie was reported missing. A gossipy water server alluded to suspicions that the man deserted. But Manas may not be so quick to dismiss his disappearance.

My unit rallies and starts the climb over the next sand dune. On a parallel rise, another wagon becomes stuck. I spot Manas on his horse coaching a team of men to dislodge the wagon. Eager to get ahead of them, I yank harder on the harness. My arms quiver from urging on the horses, but soon we exceed the elevation of the other wagon.

Nearer to the steep ridge, our wheels sink into the sand. The wagon slides sideways down the incline and the top-heavy catapult tips. The horses stumble backward with the heavy wagon, snorting and braying. I dig my heels and skid with them.

Shouts ring out, and soldiers rush over to stabilize us. Hands and backs wedge against the leaning side. Yatin props himself under the shadow of the tilting artillery. Natesa relieves me of the reins so I can join him. My feet slip, but more soldiers help to steady the catapult.

Frozen at an angle, the wagon continues to drift. The men at the back push up and stop the wagon's descent, but it is still tipping. The catapult will land on them and take out the soldiers in its path downhill.

"We need weight!" I say. "Yatin, jump on the high side!"

He goes around the wagon and climbs onto the catapult. His weight lowers the raised wheels some. Another three men leap on, and the wagon drops onto the sand. The men jump off, and our unit finishes hauling the catapult up and over the dune.

Down in the trench, Yatin, Natesa, and I collapse against the wagon, breathless and sun worn. The same commander that assigned us to man the catapult trots up on his horse.

"Well done, soldiers."

I wipe my clammy brow with my headscarf, cleaning the grit from my eyes. "Just doing our duty, sir."

He calls for a water server. Natesa pets the horses, her gaze downcast. She cannot drink without removing her headscarf, so she waves the server off. I down half my cup.

"May I keep this?" I ask the commander. We usually return our cups for reuse, but I want to reserve the rest of my drink for Natesa.

"You've earned it," the commander says, then looks to an officer riding to us.

Gods, almighty. Manas.

Natesa maneuvers around the horses, tending to their bridles. Yatin hovers at the fringe of my vision, his broad shoulders bunching. I let the brim of my headscarf fall to my eyebrows, the cloth still pinned across my lower face.

"Commander," Manas says by way of greeting, "well done saving the catapult."

"This is the soldier you should thank." The commander motions at me.

I bow. Manas's stare bores into me with the severity of the afternoon sun.

"You've crossed this desert before," Manas remarks. I nod, my head still lowered to conceal my eyes. "What's your name?"

I need a name. Any name. I blurt out the first one my mind latches on to. "Chitt."

"We're missing an officer, Chitt. You seem to be the vigilant sort. Did you see an officer depart from the troops yesterday?"

The soldier was an officer. Gods alive. No wonder Manas put out a report for him. I coarsen my voice so he will not recognize it. "No, sir."

His horse paws at the sand, digging trenches that I feel in my chest. Soldiers continue to advance past, many slowing to get around us.

"I could use another man to replace the missing officer," Manas says. "I admire your dedication, Chitt. I'm promoting you to captain. Come with me."

I mangle a guffaw, cramming it inside me. Manas is promoting *me* to captain. I was *his* captain and commander. For him to advance me—or in all actuality, demote me—scalds. Regardless of his arrogance, at any moment he will discover who I am. Natesa and Yatin need time to vanish into the troops.

"No, thank you, sir." I lift my chin.

Our gazes meet, and Manas's eyes fly wide open. He leans down and pulls off my headscarf. While he bends over me, I drop my water cup and slug him in the nose.

He swings away, cradling his injury. His fingers come away bloody. Manas crushes my headscarf in his fist. "Seize him!"

Soldiers rush in around me. I do not struggle as they apprehend my sword, wrench my arms behind my back, and bind my wrists. Natesa and Yatin are gone.

Run and don't look back.

"Commander," Manas snipes, grasping his talwar, "this is Captain Deven Naik, a conspirator for Prince Ashwin and Kindred Kalinda. This man is a traitor."

The commander falls all over his words. "He—he said he was from the south. He was wearing a uniform—"

"Enough!" Manas rides to his side, both astride their horses. "Did he have any companions?"

"Two men, one large and one small."

"Is that all?"

"Yes, General."

"Good." Manas draws his talwar and plunges the curved blade into the commander's belly. His whole body twitches, blood blooming around the wound. Manas wrenches out his weapon, and the commander keels over, plummeting off his horse to the sand.

Manas sheathes his talwar and points to the closest unit of soldiers. "Find Captain Naik's accomplices!" They obey in haste. Manas leans over me, his head impeding the sun. "I should've known you were skulking around when we caught the Galer boy. That filthy vermin begged for his worthless life."

Rohan did no such thing, but I bottle a retort. Manas will not bait me.

Soldiers haul Yatin over to us. Also robbed of his headscarf, my friend walks with his shoulders back. His size must have given him away . . . or maybe not. I interpret his stubborn, set jaw. Yatin was caught intentionally. He let the soldiers find him to give Natesa more time to escape.

"Where's the third man?" Manas demands.

"No sign of him, sir," answers a soldier. I do not miss Yatin's fleeting smile.

"Keep looking!"

The men dash off to search, but Natesa is clever. And with the extra time Yatin's capture provided her, she will not be found.

Manas smirks down at me. "You should have killed me when you had the chance, Deven." I close my mouth, unwilling to grant him the satisfaction of agreeing. "Bring them."

The soldiers tether our bindings to the commander's horse and shove Yatin and me after their general. We slog up and down sand dunes, grime blowing in our eyes and mouths. I stumble to my knees, and the horse drags me until I find my footing again.

Ahead, far past the furthermost soldier and wagon, a haze distorts the sweltering horizon. The smoggy film marks the beginning of a mirage, the gods' presumed doorway to paradise. But not even the illusion of a fictional haven can close the pit in my stomach.

As we near the front of the troops, the air holds a leaden tang that bleeds on my tongue. The heaviness accompanies, or originates from, Udug. I can feel him near. His presence sticks to me like cobwebs, snagging on everything and itching my skin. We gain on a large unit of soldiers hoisting an elaborate litter. The draperies are closed, sealing its rider in the dark, but pungent bitterness pours from it, tangible as smoke.

Manas calls for a covered wagon to halt and opens the rear door. Opal shelters her eyes from the sunlight. Dried blood covers her bound wrists. Manas could have restrained her with snakeroot or fed her neutralizing tonic to dim her powers, but cutting her is crueler. Her shoulder is wrapped with a bandage, and burn marks the size of fingerprints dot her arms. Yatin and I are impelled inside with her. Manas slams the door and casts us into darkness.

"Opal, are you all right?" I ask.

"Tell me I'm wrong," she whispers. "Tell me it isn't true."

My eyes adapt to the dimness and distinguish her slight shape. She is shorter than Kali but nearly as thin. "I'm sorry," I say. A whimper ruptures from her lips. The wagon starts to rock, bouncing us around. "We came looking for you and Brac."

"We were separated when the wing flyer crashed. I haven't seen him since."

This should be good news. Brac was probably never with the army. Rohan never heard him nearby, and we did not discover a second prison wagon. Then where is he?

"I almost got away." Opal sniffles. "But the demon rajah struck me with his blue fire." That explains the bandage on her shoulder. "Manas recognized me and put me in here with other bhuta captives. The demon rajah . . . he . . . he fed off the others' soul-fire. I'm the only one left."

Yatin shifts uneasily. We are both grateful Opal survived, but why her? "The demon rajah told Rohan you've been of use to him," I start, selecting my words carefully.

"He invites me to supper every night and asks me questions."

"What about?" Yatin inquires.

"He asked me about Vanhi. I didn't know the answers, so he . . . he burned me. I made things up, but when I couldn't tell him about the rebels, his frustration grew." Tears clog Opal's voice. "I would have said anything to save Rohan."

Yatin slides closer to her, and she rests against him, crying.

Thank Anu that Natesa got away. We have a friend outside the wagon who knows we are here, but Udug is out there too. And he has no incentive to let mortals such as Yatin and me live.

Little quills of gooseflesh bristle up my arms. *He feeds off bhuta soul-fire . . .*

Udug is growing more powerful. Try as I might, I cannot strategize our next move. When battling an opponent bigger or stronger than I am, I was trained to go for his feet, knock him down, and disarm him. Udug set his footing on unstable ground—his borrowed identity—but no one will believe me over him. Even if I could knock him off his imposter throne, I cannot disarm him of his powers. Never have I fought an enemy more entrenched in the dark.

The wagon rocks headlong across the desert, bringing us closer to Vanhi. Closer to the start of the war.

21

Kalinda

The airship's hull provides ample room for all the sisters and wards. Ashwin, Indah, and Pons stay on deck while I help the little ones descend the ladder to below.

Straw carpets the floor, and several yaks penned in the corner account for the stench of manure. I overhear a crewman say the airship was en route to deliver the herd to the clan in the arctic tundra but switched course when they received Tinley's urgent message about the fire.

We rest on bales of grass and escape the freezing temperature huddled beneath wool blankets the crew passes out. I try to repress my shivering, but the blanket merely insulates my cold. The wards, however, are resilient. One of them begins a game of Fly-Fly Crane, and soon a group of them are darting between the bales with their arms spread like wings.

The sisters let them play, the semblance of normality welcome. After some time, Priestess Mita wanders down the ladder, each of her steps more unenthusiastic than the last. Even after the Paljorians pass out dried apricots, she maintains her scowl.

Sarita shares the bale beside mine with two girls, all chewing fruit. Their soul-fires glow dimly. Need flares at the back of my throat.

I could take a little. Just enough to muffle the cold screaming inside me. If they could feel my deadening heart, they would offer up their light.

I slide my hand under the blanket, reaching for the closest girl's arm.

"Hungry?" Sarita holds out the dried fruit for me.

"No, thank you." I jam my quaking fingers between my thighs. I nearly stole soul-fire to stoke my own. This is wrong, yet the craving burns so strongly my eyes sting. I curl into myself. *It's so cold.*

Sarita rests her hand on my arm. "Kalinda, are you all right?"

Parch her. Take her light—

I twitch away and rise. "I cannot stand the priestess's ingratitude any longer."

A partial truth. Priestess Mita has not given thanks to our hosts, but her disrespect is also an excuse to leave. Shedding the blanket, I climb the ladder to the open deck. The tidy area is stained mahogany and coated with a glossy veneer, and rigging and rope ladders are strung all over. Chilly air encases me like a snowy tomb. I hug myself to find my elusive inner warmth.

Tinley crosses the deck to me. "There you are. My father and Prince Ashwin are waiting for you." She drapes a bearskin over my shoulders and directs me to the chief's private quarters.

I draw the pelt closer. "Are you coming in?"

"I need to see to my falcon, Chare." Tinley points at the mahati she left near the woods. Her prior falcon, Bya, died during our trial tournament. Tinley was devastated. Mahati falcons imprint on their handlers as hatchlings. The pair became more than master and bird; they were best friends.

"How did you find and train Chare so quickly?"

"A trader was selling her for her feathers. She fell into a depression after her handler died. She wouldn't let me ride her at first. Now all she wants to do is soar."

Chare squawks at the airship.

"She's hungry." Tinley opens her satchel to show me a dead hare and then disembarks. I watch her feed Chare and scratch her feathery breast. I wonder if Chare learned to trust Tinley because she sensed she was brokenhearted too.

After a brief knock on the chief's door, I enter. Lanterns brighten the modest cabin. Animal teeth of all sizes are strung across the wall behind the chief's desk where he and Ashwin are seated. Indah and Pons sit off to the side.

"Kalinda," says the chief, "please join us. Prince Ashwin was explaining your circumstances."

I occupy a chair near Indah and Pons, and Ashwin resumes.

"After the demon rajah fulfills my wish, I believe he intends to assist Kur in avenging Anu for usurping the mortal realm from the primeval gods. My study of the Samiya temple's texts reinforced the grudge between Kur and Anu. I'm even more convinced the demon rajah plans to release his master. The only way to vanquish him is to cast him through the gate to the Void, but nothing I read has cited where the gate is located."

Chief Naresh lays his hands over his broad chest. "We don't know where it is either. Only demons or fallen souls can find the gate."

"I know of a way," I say. We have failed to unite with the rebels, but we can still accomplish one task before we leave the mountains. "Rajah Tarek visited me. He said my thoughts summoned him from the Void." My gaze bounces from Indah, to Pons, and then to the chief. They stare at me in confusion.

Ashwin pales. "You saw him again?"

"On our first night at the temple. He came to me in the north tower."

"He's done this before?" Indah asks.

"I understand it sounds . . . odd, but I'm not imagining it."

"We believe you," she replies, and Pons nods. "Our people have tales of souls traveling by shadows."

"As do ours," the chief adds.

"Tarek knows where the gate is," I say. "He said he would show me. In return, he asked that I stand before the gate and speak his name."

Ashwin pushes to his feet. "No. You summoned Tarek just by thinking of him. Consider what power it would give him if you *spoke* his name at the gate."

"The prince is right," says Chief Naresh. "Names hold power."

"But what if this is the only way?" I ask.

Chief Naresh exhales, building a long pause. "The mortal realm is closely intertwined with the Beyond and the Void. We cannot tamper with that balance."

Ashwin paces in front of the desk. "We cannot bargain with Tarek. We'll find another way to find the gate." He anticipates my protest and raises a palm. "Don't think of him, Kalinda. Don't invoke the evernight. We'll turn to the light for help."

"Like we turned to the rebels?" I rejoin.

Ashwin stops pacing and looks up, dodging our gazes. "That was my fault. I shouldn't have trusted Hastin."

His admission drops a pause over us. I am just as to blame as he is. I wish I could take back the cruel things I said to him this morning.

Chief Naresh breeches the silence. "Prince Ashwin told me the warlord thinks ending him will also end Udug."

"I believe the opposite," Indah says, quiet but definitive. "Ashwin should have died from Anjali's winnowing, but he healed rapidly. Not even bruises remain. I can only presume that Ashwin's heart's wish ties him to Udug in other unseen ways."

My mind races to reach her logic. "You think Udug's immortality extends to Ashwin so long as he is bound by his heart's wish?"

"Yes."

Indah knows nothing of my strife with Ashwin, but could her theory also extend to me? Ashwin's bargain with Udug may explain why the icy poisons have not consumed me. The heart's wish of the prince could be prolonging my life.

"Our Galers are storing up strength for the flight back to Paljor," says the chief. Indah whitens at the mention of the airship flying. "We'll provide temporary refuge to you, as well as the sisters and temple wards."

"Thank you, but I cannot go." I smile to ease my refusal. "I'm needed in Vanhi."

"You'll never make it in time to join the navy," says Pons.

"I will if Tinley flies me on her falcon."

"My daughter isn't going near the war front," Chief Naresh answers.

"We understand," Ashwin replies. I arch a brow at his use of "we." He intends to come with me? "She can take us as far as you're comfortable."

I add one last entreaty. "Please, Chief Naresh. We have to help our people."

He sits up from his reclined position. "I'll permit this out of respect for your parents, Kalinda. Let's speak with Tinley." He and Ashwin rise to find his daughter.

"I'll be there in a moment," I say, staying with Indah and Pons. "Will you two be all right going to Paljor?"

"We'll be fine." Pons rests his big hand over Indah's small belly. They must be glad to miss the war front.

Indah pats Pons's knee. "Would you leave us a moment, please?" He kisses her cheek and goes. I presume Indah wants to speak about her father or her pregnancy, but she focuses her serious gaze on me. "I'm concerned about you, Kalinda. I saw what you did to Prince Ashwin last night. Parching may seem like a reasonable remedy for your pain, but too much parching is dangerous."

I bristle in defense. People are not afraid of Burners merely because they fear fire. They fear the violation of someone parching their soul. "I only borrowed Ashwin's soul-fire because I was trying to stop the wildfire from spreading."

"You didn't borrow anything—you robbed it. Parched soul-fire cannot be returned."

I snap my mouth shut. The opposite of parching is scorching, wherein a Burner pushes their powers into another and scorches them to ash. So, no. I cannot return the soul-fire I take.

"Parching too often is addictive. You could become dependent on others' soul-fire to replenish your powers." Indah places her hand on mine. "What are demons most known for?"

"Frightening people."

"They frighten us because they thrive off destroying all that shines. Demons spite the stars, curse the moon, and abhor the sun. I know Udug's cold-fire is still within you, but the cost is too great for you to give in. You'll sacrifice your inner radiance for a moment in the sun—then it will fade, leaving *you* parched for light."

I tell Indah what I dare not admit to Ashwin. "I don't know if we can defeat him."

"You can. Fight him, Kalinda. Hold on to your inner star and don't let go." Indah seals her encouragement with a kiss on my cheek. Being with child has opened her to all sorts of affection. "I'll go see where Pons got to."

She leaves the chief's quarters, but her caution acerbates my worries. Will Udug's cold-fire forever change me? I know of only one way to find out.

I exhale and close my eyes.

A tiny light glows in my mind. My inner star's color has changed from a clear light to brilliant sapphire. The longer I search for purity in the blue light, the icier I feel. The star grows razor-sharp points that spike into my skull. Behind my eyes, it burns like frostbite. I open them, and tears pour out. The stinging inside my head stays, a rising pressure of cold.

Indah and Pons come back in to find me doubled over and clutching my head.

"Kalinda, what happened?" Indah asks, hurrying to my side. I wait for the flash of cold to thaw, but the icicles impale deeper. She presses her warm palm to my forehead. "You're freezing."

Her warmth is like a cool drink in the desert. I react as a starving soul and draw in her heat. Her soul-fire flows into me, trickling down my body. Indah gasps, locked against me, as I parch more and more—

Pons wrenches her away. She teeters, and passes out. He catches her limp body and jostles her. Indah does not wake. His terror-filled gaze darts to me. I have devoured Indah's soul-fire, chewed it up and swallowed it down.

Backing away, I have no words. No justification.

I flee the chief's quarters and run down the plank. A brisk wind slaps my cheeks, but I am warm. So wonderfully warm and bright.

Demons steal the light.

Is that what I am becoming? Udug's cold powers are strangling the mortal and bhuta sides of me. Without them, just one part of my heritage will be left—the ancestry line that traces back to the fire-god's natural father, the demon Kur.

Clutching the bearskin at my throat, I slow near the mahati falcon. Tinley and her father ready the great bird for our journey. While they pass heated words back and forth, Ashwin waits a respectful distance away. He also wears a bearskin for our flight.

After a reticent glance at me, he explains, "Tinley wants to stay in Vanhi and fight, but her father forbids it."

"I'm sorry I was angry with you. It was unfair of me."

His attention jumps to me. "I'm sorry my heart's wish hurt you. I wasn't aware I had . . . that it tied us together."

Behind the squabbling father and daughter, strings of smoke rise from the temple wreckage. Standing before the ruins of my home, my own heart's wish comes to mind with painful clarity. "For years, my dream was to live here in peace with Jaya."

"And now?"

"I still wish for peace." I bury my chin in the bearskin, imagining Indah's disappointment in me when she wakes. Though I could try to rationalize my actions, I endangered her and her unborn child. I stole her peace of mind and possibly ruined her trust.

Chief Naresh's voice breaks through my thoughts. "I'd like you to come home when you return from Vanhi, Tinley. Your mother and I miss you."

"I cannot," she says in a frustrated growl. "Chare didn't hatch from one of our nests. The flock will view her as an intruder. She's so small, she could get hurt."

Ashwin and I size up the falcon. Bya was massive, but Chare is still large. How big do mahati falcons grow?

Chief Naresh briefly closes his eyes, seeking restraint, and strides to us. "Tinley will take you now. Kindred, it's been a joy." He envelops me in a hug. Deven holds me like this, until my heart may burst from his goodness. "The gods will watch over you. Go on your way now. You're losing daylight."

The chief hands his bearskin cape to his daughter. She accepts it, kisses him hastily on the cheek, and leaps astride her great bird. Ashwin helps me up and hoists himself behind me. The hems of my trousers ride up, and the bird's sleek feathers skim against my ankles.

Chare extends her swooping wings and leaps into the air. Tinley summons an elevating gust, and I momentarily lose my breath. The abrupt climb is like taking off in a wing flyer.

From above, the temple rubble is more visible. Is this what Anu sees when he looks down upon us? Did he see the fire was an accident?

Wolf's Peak juts into the slate sky. I comb its cliffs and impenetrable vertexes for Ekur, desperate for a glimpse of the gods' mountain home. *Show me, Anu. Show me you forgive me.* But Chare banks south, putting the pinnacle of the mountain behind us.

22

Deven

Soon after the wagon stops for the night, Manas returns.

"Get out, Deven. The rajah has asked for you."

I am hardly surprised. Opal dissatisfied Udug with her lack of knowledge about Vanhi. Who better to inquire of the palace and rebels than the former captain of the guard?

Opal starts to get out too, but Manas throws out his arm. "Stay here, filth. The rajah is finished suffering your repulsive presence."

"Yet he surrounds himself with you," I say, climbing out of the wagon.

Manas smacks the back of my head. I stumble forward to my knees, my hands still tethered behind me. As I rise, the scene beyond camp emerges. The Turquoise Palace shines upon the hill, and Vanhi stretches out below it. To those who love Vanhi, it is known as the City of Gems, a sparkling oasis for all. But the mines beneath the palace that once harvested rich veins of turquoise were boarded up long ago. Like those dried-up veins, Vanhi's shutters are closed and dim.

Men rush around us, situating the catapults and unloading the ammunition. Preparations have begun for the army to break through the city wall.

Manas shuts the wagon door and nudges me across the sand toward Udug's tent. "Who did you bring with you, Deven? The commander saw a third man."

"I don't know who you mean."

Manas pushes me, nearly tripping me again. I already have sand in places I would rather not think about. "The missing soldier was your fault, wasn't it?" he asks.

"You're missing a soldier?"

Another push. "Rajah Tarek will end your life."

The night thickens as we approach the tent. "I told you in Iresh: he isn't Rajah Tarek."

"Quit your lies." Manas cuts my bindings free and shoves me inside but does not follow.

Lamplight glows upon the lavish gold, purple, and red carpets laid out on the floor. An unnatural coldness dulls the air. A table full of rich dishes of food wafts of decadence. My mouth waters at the spicy scents. Silk cushions are set around the table, and Udug occupies the head.

"You know who I am," he says, tearing off a chunk of flatbread.

I rub my wrists, bruised from my bindings. "You're the Voider."

He smirks as he chews. "My master calls me Udug."

"Your master is the demon Kur?"

He bites off more bread. "I know him as Kur, God of the Evernight."

Kur's name with the descriptor "god" rankles. The Parijana faith teaches that Kur, the First-Ever Dragon, was created by a primeval goddess to combat her son, Anu. But Anu prevailed and usurped his mother. Kur, belonging neither to the skies nor the land, claimed the evernight as home for himself and his depraved followers.

Udug speaks with his mouth full. "I have missed this ritual of eating. You mortals, especially your rulers, bask in self-indulgence." He smacks his lips. A bread knife rests near the center of the table. If I lunge, I may reach it before he does. "Why are you here, Captain? Why aren't you with the kindred? Has the prince claimed her?"

"Kali cannot be claimed," I say shortly. "Tarek is proof of that."

"Tarek is guilty of selfishness and conceit, but never overreach. He took what he lusted after, claimed what he desired, and ruled what he could seize. *He* was never complacent." Udug says the last as though accusing me of such. "You're here because you're not that sort of man." Again, phrased as an insult. "Prince Ashwin, however, has the potential to rival his father. I saw his heart's wish. He lusts after it all—the empire, the imperial army, the kindred. His desire to rule with Kalinda is why I have not taken her life."

My joints lock down. "But you wounded her."

"Not wounded, restored. Within her Burner soul is great potential. I provided her a push toward a better state. Alas, you are utterly forgettable." His conversational tone contrasts his pitying expression. "Dutiful men are all the same—martyrs. You want for everything but take nothing for yourself. You sacrifice your own happiness for others and validate your ensuing misery with your magnanimous loyalty."

I lick my lips, my mouth dry and sticky. "I deserted the army."

"By word perhaps, but not by deed. You blended in with my troops without difficulty. You tricked a commander and went so far as to risk revealing your identity to stop a catapult from landing on a group of comrades. You will always be a soldier."

His statement reverberates too deeply. My godly duty is to serve the rajah, and whenever I go against my purpose, awful consequences follow.

"You hide behind the will of someone stronger than you and call it honor," says Udug.

I must point out the irony. "You're hiding behind Tarek."

Udug concedes with a twitch of his head. "Tarek's physical form is required for my bargain with the prince. When I am free, I will reveal my true self." He drinks his entire glass of wine, gluttonous in his feasting.

I anticipate he will inquire about the city's fortifications or how best to infiltrate the palace, but he asks me nothing. I shuffle closer to Udug and the bread knife. "What part do I play in your scheme?"

"Mankind has no part," he says, refilling his wine chalice. "You will all disappear when the evernight devours the lights in the sky."

"And the bhutas?"

A blue flame flashes in Udug's pupils. "Only Burners will be offered the choice to serve Kur or perish. His ancestry flows through them. They were born of fire and venom."

A breath of his foul cold skulks over me. Opal thinks Brac got away from the army. *But what if he didn't?* "My brother is a Burner. He's missing."

Udug's lips pull upward patronizingly, an exact replica of Tarek's condescending expression. "Is that why you've come? To find your brother? This is tragic. You came all this way, got that boy Galer *killed*, and yet your brother isn't here."

I lunge for the knife. My fingers brush the handle when a blue flame hits the plate. Cold bites into my hand. I rear back, clenching my teeth down on a howl. My struck fingertips turn white like hoarfrost. I puff out quick breaths to drive away the pain.

Udug pings the wine bottle against his chalice, a summons, and Manas appears. "I'm finished."

"Yes, Your Majesty." Manas jerks me from the tent.

I clutch my injured hand. Why are they keeping us prisoner? The army holds captives for few purposes: to await execution, exploit them for labor, or use them as ransom. None of those options are pleasant. "Manas, you have to listen to me. That isn't Tarek. He—"

His fist drives into my gut, and I bowl over. He grabs my hair and yanks my head back. "You're alive because of Kalinda. When the rajah realizes you're worth nothing to her, I'll finish this."

"You can hit me all you want. The truth is still the truth."

"The truth is you lost." Manas grabs my tunic and hauls me to the wagon.

The ammunition is nearly unloaded. Soldiers position the last of the catapults in a line facing the wall. The army is hours away from launching its attack, yet no torchlights flicker in the city watchtowers. Where are the rebels?

Two soldiers guard the wagon. One unlocks the door, and Manas pushes me inside. I will have bruises from his handling, but they will hurt less than my frostbitten hand.

"Time for your appointment with my dagger, filth." Manas leans inside and reaches for Opal. He means to let her blood and weaken her powers.

I slam my foot down on his hand, jamming it into the floor. He groans and tries to pull free, but I knee him in the jaw.

The two guards draw their swords. One stabs at me. I twist away, grasp his wrist with my unwounded hand, and pull down. The man tumbles inside the wagon on top of Manas. Yatin whams his elbow into the side of his head. The soldier goes limp.

The second guard attempts to run, but Yatin catches his neck with his bound hands and slams him into the door. Another guard is out.

I pin Manas to the floor, digging my knee into his throat.

"You'll suffer for treason," he rasps. "Rajah Tarek will drop you in a den of scorpions. You will feel the sting of a thousand—"

Someone outside the wagon whacks Manas over the head with the hilt of a dagger. I twist to see a soldier with a headscarf draped over the lower half of his—no, *her*—face.

Natesa lifts the headscarf. "He was irritating me." She cuts Opal's and Yatin's bindings. He scoops Natesa up and kisses her. She tugs fondly at his beard. "We have to go *right now*."

An explosion goes off across camp. Fire and embers brighten the night.

I climb out beside Natesa. "You've been busy," I remark.

"Someone had to get us out of here." She passes me her second dagger and notices my burns. "What happened?"

"It's nothing. Let's go."

Opal slides out, and Yatin helps her stay upright. We follow Natesa through camp. Soldiers rush about, preoccupied with the fire. A catapult blazes in the distance.

"Is that the catapult we pushed here?" I ask.

"I couldn't let our hard work go to waste." Natesa glances over her shoulder at her handiwork. "A little bit of lamp oil, and look at it glow."

We skirt around a group of soldiers. I pick up a bucket, as though to gather water for the fire, and we leave camp. Opal starts to slow from her injuries, so Yatin carries her. I guide us across the sand dunes to the River Nammu that runs through the city. I toss aside the bucket and hurry down the bank. Natesa and I wade into the river.

The cool, shallow water mitigates my stinging burns. Opal hangs on to Yatin's neck, and we swim upstream. Guards on the outer wall regularly monitor the river for intruders, but no one calls for us to halt.

We reach the culvert and pass through one at a time, fighting the current into Vanhi. I slog out of the water on the other side of the city wall. A stone walking path rims the riverbank. Past it lies a courtyard, and beyond that, the roadways are cramped with huts. I detect no signs, noises, or smells of the living. Everyone has long fled the warlord.

"Where to now?" Yatin asks.

My sight drifts up to the palace. Whether the rebels are with us or against us depends on the outcome of Kali's meeting with Hastin. I still do not trust the warlord, but we have a better chance of allying with him than surviving another encounter with Udug. "We'll use the old mine tunnels to sneak into the palace."

"Do you think the rebels are on our side?" Natesa asks, squeezing water from her braid.

"We'll find out tomorrow. We'll need torches or lanterns to navigate the tunnels. Let's find somewhere close by to stay the night."

We cross the pathway near the river and venture into the courtyard. Piles of stones litter the clearing. I pass a heap, and my belly clenches. Bits of scarlet from an imperial soldier's uniform are buried within. The rebels must have stoned the soldiers who were taken captive when they seized the palace. We hasten between the stoning piles, across the courtyard to the tightly packed rows of huts.

The gods take pity on us. The first hut I investigate is vacant except for the rats that flee when I open the door. I enter the one-room domicile and pick up an overturned chair. Sand covers the floor and furniture. I refill an oil lamp and light it. Natesa shades the windows with blankets to seal in the glow. Yatin ducks through the low door with Opal and lays her on a straw mattress. She rolls onto the sandy linens and shuts her eyes.

While Yatin scrounges through the worn kitchen cupboards for food, Natesa brings a dry rag for my hand. She winds the cloth around my fingers and ties it tight. Yatin finds a couple of shriveled limes and cuts them up. The tangy smell carries to me, but I pass on my portion. Natesa and Yatin dine on the citrus, savoring the juice like it's honey.

I prop the chair against the door and sit with Natesa's dagger in my lap. We should be safe here until morning, but I trust nothing in this hollow shell of the city I once knew.

Leaning my head against the doorjamb, I fall into old habits, listening for potential dangers. My desertion from the army did not fool anyone. Even Udug recognized my passion. I rely on the orderliness and discipline of the army. The only reason I would leave for good is for Kali. Yet every time I try to force our paths together and turn my back on my oath to serve the empire, disaster befalls me and those I care about. I wish I could say what that means for us, but all I know is that I am needed here to defend what is left of my home.

23

Kalinda

We fly into the night, the mahati falcon undaunted by the dark. Glittering stars chase us, so close they promise the warmth of a thousand wishes but mock me with their unreachable light. The soul-fire I parched from Indah has long since receded, and as she cautioned me, I am colder than before.

My jaw aches from clamping my chattering teeth. Ashwin holds on to me, a rock against my tide of shivers. I thirst for soul-fire. The temptation to parch him or Tinley presses into my chest. *If I move my hand to Tinley's arm—*

No. Remember Indah. I will not violate another friend's trust.

Midway through the night, I drift off into delirium. When I wake later, night still stretches to infinity, and my shivers have stopped. I am not cold; nor am I warm.

I feel . . . I feel . . . nothing. Even the ache in my knee has gone.

Freedom from pain would be a gift, but the sudden emptiness unsettles me. My heart beats slow, a sluggish thump. I shut my eyes and search for the star in my private night. My soul-fire is so tiny, shrunken to a sapphire pinpoint, I nearly miss it.

Dreading what I will find, I hold one hand between Tinley and myself and call upon my abilities. My fingers glow blue. I wait for a shiver, but none arrives. I let the light fade. Udug's powers have usurped my own, yet my soul-fire must still be there, buried far down inside me, or I would have perished. Or the prince's heart's wish is the only thing left keeping me alive . . .

I seek out the crescent moon, its silver illumination my only protection against the persistent night. I expect tears to come, to rise from a well of panic, but they, too, are frozen within me.

Gods, preserve me through the night. I repeat the plea until the sky lightens to dusky blue hues, and I utter a myriad of thanks.

The sunrise reveals grassy fields and a winding river. Chare is quick, even quicker than Tinley implied. We soar over the valley, trailing the River Nammu. Up ahead, a long line of vessels sail the waterway. My outlook brightens. We have found the Lestarian Navy. Deven and the others should be with them.

Ashwin yells for Tinley to pursue the vessels. She directs the falcon lower. Chare's reflection zips over the river like a stream of fire. As we soar nearer to the last boat, a conch shell sounds. The sailors dash to their water cannons.

They don't know who we are.

Tinley guides the mahati higher while Ashwin and I wave. Admiral Rimba stands atop the lookout platform on the lead vessel. He recognizes us and signals his crews to stand down. Seeing Indah's father presses more guilt upon me. My hunger for soul-fire has passed, dulled by the numbness, but not my memory of what I did.

Chare lands along the riverbank. Tinley jumps down, and the falcon hunts for hares in the grass. I slide off and brace against the bird on rickety legs. Ashwin dismounts and rubs his sore thighs. He leaves his bearskin on to fend off the cool of the morning. The brisk dawn does not bother my already frigid fingers and toes.

The navy moors along the riverbank. Admiral Rimba comes ashore in his all-white uniform, Princess Gemi with him. She studies the large mahati falcon and her wild-looking rider with keen interest.

I scan the boat decks. "Where's Deven?"

"His party wasn't at the meet point," Admiral Rimba replies, a lump of mint stuffed in his cheek.

A weight hammers down on me. Deven does not break his word. His search for Brac must have gone awry. Then why not send Natesa or Yatin?

Admiral Rimba chews the wad of mint in his mouth faster. "Where's Indah?"

"She and Pons have gone to Paljor," Ashwin replies.

"Paljor?" the admiral demands.

Tinley stiffens but keeps her back turned to us, giving her attention to her falcon.

"They're safe," I say, the last word sticking in my throat. I hope Indah is all right, but what if I hurt her more than I thought?

"Pons will look after Indah," Ashwin says. He is so impatient to explain what happened, he misses the admiral's granite stare. "Our meeting with the warlord was a farce. Hastin sent rebels to attack us, and the Samiya temple was destroyed. Chief Naresh saw the smoke and came to investigate. His daughter Tinley graciously agreed to fly us here. Indah and Pons have gone to Paljor to await word from Datu Bulan."

"The rebels are still against us," Admiral Rimba summarizes. "But you're unhurt?" He has graciously extended his concern for his daughter to us, but I do not deserve his kindness.

"We are," Ashwin replies, then answers more of the admiral's questions. As he recounts our battle against Anjali and Indira, Princess Gemi interrupts him.

"*You* stood up to bhutas?"

"I defended myself and Kalinda," Ashwin answers modestly. Princess Gemi considers him anew, raking her gaze over him. He clears his throat and resumes speaking to the admiral. "Any word about the imperial army?"

"Last we heard, they were nearing the desert. That was yesterday."

I am pinned to my spot by panic. The army is ahead of schedule. They may already have reached Vanhi.

"We'll arrive tomorrow," the admiral says. "You may come with us, but I suggest you continue to travel by sky. The sea raiders are following a few leagues behind us." Ashwin and I peer downriver but see no trace of Captain Loc or his vessel. "They thought you were aboard one of our ships. We've maintained a wall of silence to deflect their listening Galers, but they won't have missed the mahati falcon. They'll figure out you were never with us."

"What . . . what will they do?" I ask.

"They have no means of flying, so they'll probably continue to pursue us. Captain Loc isn't one who gives up easily."

Princess Gemi ventures up to the mahati and strokes her vibrant feathers. Chare peers at the princess and tolerates her touch.

Eluding the sea raiders is motive enough to fly, but Chare will also be faster than the navy. After a nod from Ashwin, I answer, "We'll go with Tinley and meet you there."

"I'd like to fly with you," says the princess.

Admiral Rimba nearly spits out his mint. "Your father would disapprove."

"I'm headed for the war front regardless." Gemi strokes the falcon, undeterred. I look closer at her hand and see she has dyed the moon phases on her fingers. The henna marks match the patterns on her feet. "Can your falcon carry another rider?"

Tinley squints at her in distrust. "Chare can handle you, but it's up to His Majesty."

Gemi squares off with Ashwin. "You could use another bhuta." Her tone lacks the confidence of her posture. It matters that Ashwin thinks enough of her to let her come along.

I would rather she not. We do not know what we will find in Vanhi. I cannot worry about protecting two royals. I have not performed a full test of my powers since the numbness has set in. My blue glowing fingers from last night have left me unsettled about what else has changed.

"We're losing time," Gemi presses.

"You may accompany us," Ashwin says slowly, as though uncertain about his decision.

Gemi dips into a regal bow. "Thank you, Your Majesty."

I cannot decide whether to hit Ashwin in the arm or pat his back. He finally understands that Gemi has the right to make her own decisions, but I am impatient to find Deven. Having missed the meeting point, he would go to Vanhi, the next location where he is assured Ashwin and I will be. The princess had better not slow us down.

24

Deven

The explosions start just after dawn.

Our unit is already packed and hiking the path along the river. Quakes from the army's assault on the city wall vibrate up from the ground. We all removed our disguises, leaving our scarlet uniform jackets and headscarves in the hut. When I woke, my fingertips were healed. I cannot figure out why my burns are gone while Opal's are still healing, but it is a mercy I have no time to question.

I increase our pace uphill in the bare morning light. Natesa and Yatin keep pace with me. Opal lags some, but her pallor and posture have improved from yesterday. Her Galer powers are returning, so she listens for rebels.

The stone pathway ends at a low tunnel. The entrance to the mines lies in the shadow of the Turquoise Palace. I pause to light a lamp we took from the hut, and a chakram flies past me, nearly slicing my nose. The blade embeds itself in the wall.

All of us reel around, and the path beneath our feet drags us backward on a rockslide. Our backs hit the wall. Bands of hard dirt shackle our arms and legs.

The bhuta warlord strides down the steps to the river. Hastin's deeply tan complexion is distinguished by patches of white hair at his temples. His gray eyes are hard as stones. Anjali accompanies her father, chakram in hand. Two more rebels in all-black uniforms trail them.

"Captain Naik, you insult me." Hastin's voice is gravelly, like pebbles roll in his gullet. "Did you really think you could sneak past us?"

I slant a glance at Opal. "I had hoped."

"I'm sorry," she whispers. "My powers are returning slowly."

"A bhuta?" Hastin asks, tipping back on his heels. "The demon rajah sent one of my own to spy on me?"

"We aren't with the army," Natesa says. "We serve Prince Ashwin."

Hastin trembles the ground beneath us. "The demon rajah and the prince are the same. Both are out to destroy our world."

A warning echoes in my mind, and my old suspicions manifest. "We were told you wished to unite with the empire."

Hastin manipulates the stones around just me, pressing me into the wall. "I'll never ally with Tarek's heir or his kindred."

"Are they alive?" I squeeze out.

"Concern yourself with your own inevitable death," Anjali drawls.

Hastin releases us from our dirt confines. Opal falls forward onto her knees, residual grime in her bloodletting scars. Natesa helps her up.

"Take them to the wives' wing," Hastin tells his daughter and then points menacingly at Opal. "Don't cause any trouble, or I'll throw you in the dungeons."

The palace dungeons are laced with poisons that dampen bhuta powers. Hastin's reluctance to strip a fellow bhuta of her defenses is a courtesy he does not offer us mortals. His soldiers disarm the rest of us.

The warlord marches up to the palace. He must be holding us hostage for the same purpose he captured Tarek's ranis and courtesans—leverage. Hastin hungers for the whole of the empire, and he intends to manipulate Kali and Prince Ashwin, or entrap them, into getting what he desires. We are alive so long as they are, which is comforting in a sense. If Kali and the prince were dead, we would be too.

Anjali yanks her chakram from the wall and pushes the rounded blade so close I can see my reflection in it. "Misbehave and you'll lose your nose." Yatin puffs out his chest, an instinctual reaction to protect me. Anjali's blade comes even closer. My breath fogs the steel. "Keep your troops in line, Captain."

She and her comrades herd us up the stairway to the palace wall. This section has no gate, yet one of Anjali's men opens a passageway in the clay bricks with his powers. We pass through the temporary door into the palace grounds, and the Trembler closes it behind us.

The rebels prod us down a pathway through the garden. The untended flower beds are overrun with weeds. Palm trees molt dead fronds, and the topiaries need a trim, but the grounds are still verdant and smell of sweet citrus and flowers.

We enter the palace through a side door. Familiar jewel-toned draperies sweep across terrace doorways. Cool marble-tiled floors, white with rivers of nickel, echo our footsteps. Aromatic scents waft in from the high-arched open corridors: desert sand, budding neem trees, and coconut oil. The corridors that once bustled with servants, court officials, and guards are lonely. Only a flamboyant peacock struts down the hall, dragging its brilliant tail feathers behind as it searches for sand fleas to dine on.

Silence pours out of the courtesans' main entertaining hall. No music plays or jade glass bottles clink. No hint of hookah smoke hazes the entry or scent of women's perfume lingers. The absence of life startles me. Natesa slows and then quickens her gait away from the deserted wing. Her servitude as one of Rajah Tarek's courtesans is a time she would rather forget.

The doors to Tarek's chamber and atrium have been torn off. Within his private quarters, furniture and cushions lie about haphazardly, as though swept up by the wind and dumped in a jumble. Glass shards sparkle like frozen teardrops across the tile floor. Torn draperies hang lopsided, and piles of sand gather in the corners. The destruction of the rajah's quarters makes Hastin's rule more tangible.

We are guided to the top floor of the wives' wing. Arched casements open to a view over the garden, palace wall, and forsaken city. Past them, dunes ripple into the horizon. Streaks of red, soldiers in their uniforms, swarm the main city gate and launch boulders from catapults. A gut-shaking boom resounds in the distance.

"The army will break in," I say, mostly to myself. "It's inevitable."

"They'll enter the city only when we're ready." Anjali's cryptic reply tests my assumption that the rebels pulled back to protect the palace.

"How?" I ask.

She scoffs. "Think, Captain. What's the city wall made of?"

All at once, their strategy becomes clear. "Clay bricks."

"And where does clay come from?"

She is patronizing me, but I answer all the same. "The land."

"My father stationed Tremblers around the city to uphold the wall. As I said, your army won't enter unless we allow them."

"As *I* said, we aren't with the army."

"If my father suspected you were, you'd be dead." Anjali stops at the doorway to the Tigress Pavilion. "Hold your breath."

"What—?"

A wind barrels at us, smacking my breath away and pushing us back. My unit skids across the floor and through the pavilion threshold. A final gust slams the door shut after us.

In the sudden stillness, I blink dust from my eyes. The Tigress Pavilion, the ranis' main social area, comes into focus. I never spent much time here, but it, too, looks different. The black-and-white tiled fountain has run dry, the water basin slimy and stagnant. Barren weapon racks line the far portico wall. Gone are the countless blades and staffs that the rajah's wives trained with.

"General Naik," Opal says, her stance alert. "We aren't alone."

Brac steps out from behind a low wall. My whole body locks with shock.

"*General* Naik?" Brac strides to me. "We *have* been apart a while." He hauls me into a hug, my arms pressed at my sides. My brother's golden eyes gleam. I am struck by how alike they are to Chitt's.

"What are you doing here?" Natesa thumps him in the shoulder. "We've been searching for you, you dolt. You scared the sky out of Deven!"

"I only scared Deven?" he teases, and Natesa hits him again.

Yatin grabs Brac up in a wholehearted embrace. My brother's voice squeaks out. "Missed you too, big man." Yatin puts Brac down and rubs his head, mussing his coppery hair. Brac scans Opal up and down. "You look worse off than I do. Where are Rohan and Mother?"

Opal turns away, teary. I let Yatin explain. His gentle burr cushions everything he says.

"Mathura is well, but Rohan . . . won't be joining us."

Brac's eyes spread in understanding. He lightly touches Opal's arm. "My sympathies."

Across the pavilion, behind low walls and lattice screens, shuffling noises and whispers sneak out from the wives' divided dining patio.

Brac whistles. "You can come out! It's just my brother."

Just his brother?

"Gods alive, Brac," I say. "I thought you'd been captured!"

He glances from me to Opal and back again. "Didn't Opal tell you I got away?"

"That was days after I followed the imperial army looking for you!"

A flood of women pours into the main pavilion from the dining patio. The assembly is made up of ranis, courtesans, and palace servants, each group differentiated by their hair and attire. Ranis wear their long hair loose down their backs, and their saris are elegant and intricate, while the courtesans tie their hair back in braids, their apparel more garish in design and color. Servants wear plain robes that are boxy in shape. Children of all ages accompany them, holding hands with and carried by nursemaids. The stunning ranis and courtesans, all scarred in one way or another from their days competing for rank in the arena tournaments, file into the pavilion until it is full.

Brac explains in a hushed voice. "I was thrown from the wing flyer when we were struck in the sky. I fell into the Morass and the crash knocked me out. The army probably thought I was dead or would be soon. When I came to, I found the crash site, but Opal and the army were gone. I didn't know how to get to you and Mother in Lestari, so I went to the nearest village, borrowed a horse, and rode here. I walked up to the palace gates and surrendered to Hastin. He gave me the option of rejoining the rebels or staying with the women. After what he did to you and Kali, I couldn't stomach serving him again."

"You've been here, with these women, all this time?"

"Good idea, eh?" Brac winks at a pair of very pretty ranis, and they giggle. At my short sigh, he sobers. "I knew Kali and you would eventually return for the ranis. Coming here was the surest way I could think of to find you."

I grip the back of his neck and drag him against me. "I'm glad you're all right."

"You too." He pats my back and lets me go. "We should probably address the women. They don't have much patience these days."

Our audience's stares pull me back. A few courtesans whisper to each other. I hear one slur Natesa's name like an obscenity. She holds herself with an air of aloofness, but stays close to Yatin's intimidating bulk.

A servant steps forward. Long-healed red scars run down her cheek and over one eye. "Where is Kindred Kalinda?"

The whispers cease, and Yatin sets his mouth in a grim line.

"I don't know." My voice falls off, dragged away by worry.

"I'm certain the gods are watching over the kindred," says a young rani, a baby propped on her hip. "I'm Shyla." She motions to the pair of ranis who tittered at Brac earlier. "That's Eshana and Parisa. And the woman there"—she gestures at the scarred servant with downcast eyes—"is Asha, Kalinda's servant."

I recognize them now. Eshana was one of Tarek's favored four. Asha, the servant, once wore a heavy veil that hid her facial scars. She took good care of Kali.

Shyla moves in closer. "We're the kindred's friends, but some of the women are upset that she ran when the rebels invaded."

From the women's accusatory glares, they consider Natesa and Kalinda's actions cowardly. But Kali has been fighting for her people since she left, and Natesa is here now. The truth of their efforts scalds my tongue.

Brac tugs my arm, turning us away from the crowd. "They don't know what's happening outside these walls. Hastin believes they're too beneath him to tell them anything, and I didn't want to upset them even more. We should speak in private." He revolves and tosses the women a charming grin. "We apologize for interrupting your breakfast. Please, return to your meal with your children. We'll gather again shortly."

He escorts a rani to the dining patio. She smiles at him as they go, and they pick up more women and children along the way. *Skies above. Brac hasn't told them he's a Burner.* Gradually, everyone returns to their meal, except Shyla, Parisa, and Eshana, and the servant Asha, whom he invites to stay.

We gather around the fountain. Brac returns and motions for me to start. I do not waste time on pleasantries. These women are all battle survivors. They can handle the truth.

"The imperial army, ten thousand men strong, has gathered outside the city wall."

"That's good, isn't it?" Parisa asks.

"No. The army is being led by a demon who escaped from the Void." I wait for my explanation to permeate. "The demon is disguised as Rajah Tarek."

Eshana and Parisa gasp. Shyla covers her open mouth.

"But Rajah Tarek is dead." Frown marks indent Asha's scarred brow. "We saw his body. Before he burned it, Hastin threw it on a refuse cart and carried it around the city for all to see."

"Rajah Tarek *is* dead," I affirm. "The demon has convinced the army that the gods sent him back to this life to avenge the empire against the warlord."

"This demon rajah . . ." Shyla glances at her child, one of Tarek's heirs. "He's headed for the palace?"

"Yes. His freedom relies on his success. The imperial army is trying to break through the city wall right now."

Eshana blanches. "But we have no way to defend ourselves. The rebels took our weapons."

Parisa frowns at her fingers. "They even confiscated my favorite nail file."

"The Lestarian Navy is on its way here," I say. "Kalinda and Prince Ashwin might be with them."

"Might?" Brac asks. Some of this information is news to him as well.

"Hastin was supposed to meet them and discuss allying, but it was a ruse. I believe they're alive, but I have no idea where they are."

Opal clutches my arm. A second later, an earsplitting explosion goes off and a cloud of dirt stains the skyline. Everyone quiets across the pavilion and in the dining patio. The palace walls and floors rumble.

The Galer releases me, her hand shaking. "The army has broken through the city wall."

Curse Hastin for his arrogance. Despite Anjali's assertions about the rebels' superiority, Udug bludgeoned his way through.

Shyla bounces her baby on her hip nervously. "We need to warn the others."

"We can do better than that," counters Parisa. "We can fight."

The rajah's wives and courtesans have ample experience contending for their lives, and the scars from their rank tournaments prove it. A piece of Parisa's earlobe was hacked off, and scars run widthwise across Eshana's torso. Shyla is missing two fingers on her left hand. These women are dedicated daughters of the land-goddess Ki and have the right to defend themselves, their homes, and their families. They are not standard soldiers—they are better. They are sister warriors.

But even they cannot stand against the demon rajah and triumph. I should warn them of our remote chance of victory, though I doubt that would discourage them. It did not change my mind. I, too, am willing to fight against Udug for all that I love. The ranis and courtesans deserve that same choice, and perhaps together, we can make a difference.

"Brac," I say. "How fast can you find their weapons?" No one knows the palace passageways better than he does.

"Could take a while. Galers are monitoring the corridors."

"I can help," Asha offers, her voice shy. "I was there when they stashed them. They're in an antechamber off the throne room."

"That's in the center of the palace," Natesa grumbles.

Asha nods. "I can lead us through the servants' passageways. One connects to the antechamber, but the door is locked on the outside and I don't have a key. We'd have to go through the throne room to the antechamber and unlock the door from the inside. We can use the passageway to carry the weapons out."

I make a split-second decision. "Asha and I will go."

"Won't the rebels be guarding the main entrance?" Natesa asks. "You'll have to pass by it to enter the throne room."

Brac hops slightly on his feet, eager to help. "I'll take care of the guards at the main entrance."

"Good," I reply. "Yatin and Natesa, stay here with Opal. Defend the entryways. Hastin may do something rash if he feels threatened or suspects we're organizing our troops."

Opal speaks up, wearing a mask of intensity. "I'll cover everyone's movements the best I can."

I hearten her with a quick, one-armed embrace, and she tucks into my side to lengthen our connection. Her need for comfort is so great I regret not consoling her sooner.

"We'll help too," Eshana offers. "Parisa, Shyla, and I will tell the other women what's happening."

"Yatin and I will help answer their questions," says Natesa. The ranis assess her, a lower-ranking courtesan in their strict hierarchy.

"Good idea," Shyla says, slipping her arm through Natesa's. She leads her ahead of Yatin and the others to the dining patio.

"Did you hear him?" Parisa whispers to Eshana as they go. "Deven called us his troops."

"I wouldn't mind being under his command," Eshana replies. Their giggles drift away, and Yatin lumbers after them.

Asha goes to the doorway of the servants' passageway and waits. I hesitate to leave my brother so soon after finding him. I still need to have a word with him about Chitt. But a new worry stops me. What if Brac is excited to hear about his father? He, Mother, and Chitt will be a family, and I do not know how I will fit in. Our conversation can wait.

"Look after yourself," I say.

Brac grasps me by the shoulder. "Stop worrying about me, Deven. I've been sneaking around the palace since I learned to walk."

"We'll meet back here shortly," I promise. My words are partly snatched away by rising winds. The rebels are gathering their defenses against the army. Time to move.

I join Asha at the doorway and pause to look back. Wind lashes at the silk draperies. Brac's hair dances about his brassy eyes. I wave farewell and duck into the passageway.

25

Kalinda

Hot wind guides the mahati falcon over the waves of ginger sand dunes. Ashwin and Gemi stoop forward in apprehension as dust builds on their skin. I search the blurry horizon, sepia fading to azure heavens, for the City of Gems.

A shadow deepens on the skyline, materializing into view. Civilization rests upon an old, rounded mountain. The Turquoise Palace appears first, its gold-domed roofs a burnished reflection of the desert sun. White-walled towers gleam like ivory teeth above the drab city kneeling at the palace's feet.

Red-coated soldiers flying Tarachand banners with black scorpions swarm the outer wall. They crowd a blown-out hole and fling huge rocks to smash the gap wider. The imperial army is only minutes from breeching the city.

Deven and the others would have found a safer, quicker route past the wall to await the navy. He will expect our arrival, so Rohan should be listening for us. *Please hear us coming.*

Tinley clucks her tongue, and Chare dips lower. The falcon circles a soft-mounded dune and lands. Gemi slips off and then Ashwin. He extends his arms to me. My feet hit the sand, and my knees crumple. I clutch his shoulders and wait for feeling to return to my lower half.

"I've been stationary too long," I explain.

The corners of his mouth crease. He stays close a moment until I can transfer my weight to my feet. Numbness runs down my legs, but my knees adjust to standing and hold strong.

"I must be off," Tinley says from upon her saddle. The mahati falcon digs her hook-like beak under a scrub bush and comes up with a scorpion to chomp on.

"Will you go to Paljor?" Ashwin asks.

"I wish I . . ." Tinley halts herself. "My father says wishes are for dreamers, not doers."

"Your father may be the biggest dreamer of all," Ashwin returns. Chief Naresh is a pacifist, a rare visionary and advocate for peace. "You only have one home, Tinley."

I sigh inaudibly, or so I thought. Ashwin brushes his hand against mine. Neither of us has been blessed with a family praying for our safety. Tinley's devotion to her falcon is admirable, but she may be avoiding Paljor for another reason. Perhaps she is not ready to confront her memories of Bya and replace them with Chare. But I hope she finds the strength to go home.

"Thank you, Tinley." I stroke Chare's feathers. "Let the sky lead you, the land ground you, the fire cleanse you, and the water feed you."

"And you." Tinley yanks on the reins, and the falcon launches into the air. They soar away from the late-afternoon sun, back over the hungry, brutal desert.

Ashwin stares in the opposite direction, at the gleaming palace domes. I slip my hand into his. He has not seen his palace, his legacy, as an adult. It must be odd to return to a place that belongs to him but is vacant of memories.

Gemi frowns at our linked hands. "Should we go?"

I release Ashwin to pull my dagger. Gemi brought a trident from her homeland, wielding it with poise. We ascend the rise and go down the other side. As we climb another dune, I slip and fall forward. The parts of me that are not yet numb radiate iciness.

Gemi crawls to the crest and lies on her belly, batting sand fleas away. Ashwin edges up beside her. I force myself to crawl the incline to them and peer over the ridge. We are about a thousand strides away from the rearmost ranks of the army.

The hole in the wall is finished. Hundreds of soldiers push catapults and wagons through the passage. My anxiety mounts as more troops disappear into the city. The protection of the palace relies upon the rebel army. They must uphold the palace's outer wall until the navy arrives. By morning, they will be begging for our aid.

"We'll wait here until the entire army is through, and then we'll follow," Ashwin says.

Gemi grabs his forearm. "Did you feel that?"

"Feel what?"

She shushes him and then launches to her feet. "Run!"

Gemi takes off across the dune, in clear sight of the army. I gape at her. What is she—?

A fearsome tremble rises from the ground. Ashwin and I scramble up. The quaking grows to a knee-buckling roar like a slumbering dragon has awoken. Gemi does not slow for us but sprints directly east, to the river. Ashwin and I clamber after her across shifting sand.

My leaden legs and feet, weighed down by numbness, impede my speed. Ashwin grabs me and helps me along. Out in the open, our view of the army is unhindered. They see us too. But as we run, an infantry drops and vanishes into the desert floor.

A stronger tremor jolts up my legs. I weave, and Ashwin catches my balance. Jagged cracks snake across the ground, spreading wider and wider. Gemi is carried away on the far side of one rift, and we are stranded on the opposite half. Ashwin and I go right up to the ledge. The chasm between us is wider than a catapult wagon.

Gemi summons a bridge of compact sand to span the gap. "Hurry!"

Ashwin pushes for me to go first. I stumble across the temporary conduit, Ashwin right behind me. I reach Gemi on the other side. Just before Ashwin meets us, another tremor opens the crevice broader, and the bridge disintegrates.

Ashwin leaps but misses my outstretched hand. Gemi throws up a burst of sand, blasting him in an arc above our heads. He falls and lands in a roll beside us, dusty and coughing. The ledge beneath us shakes. The two halves of the gulch are closing.

Gemi yanks Ashwin to his feet. We lurch down the shifting dune to the river, side-foot into the muddy bank, and splash into the cool water. Behind us, the quakes in the desert cease. The troops surrounding the city wall have disappeared.

I scan the sandy plain. "Where . . . where did they go?"

Gemi's chest heaves, her trousers wet up to her knees and her chin quivering. "A powerful Trembler split the desert floor open. The soldiers fell into the cracks, and the Trembler closed them again."

The warlord did this. Hastin is the most powerful Trembler known. Horses, wagons, catapults, hundreds of men—all devoured in sandy crevices and entombed.

Those soldiers were not our enemy; they were our *people*.

"Gods save them," I pray.

Ashwin sloshes out of the river, his strides hasty. We backtrack to the army's burial site. Gemi closes her eyes in anguish. I listen for the screams of survivors, but death prevails.

Lonely winds swirl sand tunnels across the barren war front. *Please let Deven be in the city. Let him be anywhere but here.*

The surviving troops have marched beyond the wall. Blue flames and eerie blue-gray smoke mark their progression up the winding roads to the palace. Udug leads the campaign, clearing their path with his destructive cold-fire. Given the number of casualties, his escape must be more than chance. Anjali said he was growing more powerful. He could have burned through the wall, but he relished knocking it down and forcing the rebels to retaliate. In one act, the demon rajah proved that he is beyond Hastin's abilities.

Ashwin picks up a stray khanda, the only object left of the men who stood here, and steals through the opening. Gemi and I traverse the wrecked clay bricks, my blade drawn and her trident in hand.

Under the shadow of the breeched city wall, Ashwin's and my gazes are guided to the Turquoise Palace looming above.

"Welcome home," I tell him.

26

Deven

I stand straight as a pole against the corridor wall. Asha waits beside me, listening alertly. My muscles are stiff from hours of skulking down from the upper floor of the outer wing to the center of the palace. The door to the throne room is around the corner, but we can go no farther without the rebel guards at the main entrance seeing us.

Where in gods' name is Brac? He should have caused his distraction by now.

A quake rattles up from the ground, extending in huge, terrible waves. Tapestries fall, and glass orbs shatter against the floor. Furniture skids across the tiles. I peer around the corner at the main entry. No rebels. I do not know how Brac managed it, but this must be his distraction.

I dart out to check the entry and double stairways. Both are empty. I gesture to Asha, and we slip into the throne room.

Daylight shines down from the high casements. Gone are the tidy rows of floor cushions for the rajah's court to kneel upon. Tables have replaced them, set up in stations around the room. Upon the dais, the rajah's throne is tipped over. One leg is broken, as though kicked free.

Asha hurries to the antechamber while I guard the entry. She tugs on the handle, but the door is stuck. "Someone jammed the hinges with stones." She uses her nails to try to pick the hinges clean.

Noises sound in the entry hall. I snatch up a floor cushion as a defense and lean against the doorframe. The patter comes closer. I hold the cushion like a shield. *I should've searched for a proper weapon.*

A peacock struts by. I lower the cushion on an exhalation. The next intruder could be a rebel, so I leave my post to help Asha unseal the antechamber door.

"We need something to pry it open with," I say, searching the tables for a makeshift tool.

An errant wind ruffles the swooping draperies, and a voice speaks.

"I thought I heard a couple of rats." Anjali struts into the throne room. Asha goes stock-still. "Annoying little vermin, aren't you?"

"We share the same enemy," I reply, my gaze snug on her weapon. Gusts spin about her, coils of sky poised to strike. "We should help each other."

"Help us? You'll only ever be in our way." Anjali hurls one of her squalls at Asha, slamming the servant into the wall. Then she sweeps a gale at me and tosses me off my feet. I hit the hard floor, pain exploding up my side, and roll over. Anjali crouches down and presses her chakram to my throat. "Don't move or I'll take your head off."

"The demon rajah is coming," I say. "Give the ranis and courtesans back their weapons and let us fight him with you."

She scrapes the blade across my throat, almost breaking skin. "Which would upset Kalinda more? Taking your limbs off one by one or winnowing you so slowly you'll wish I'd decapitated you?"

I hit her hands straight up and lunge for her chakram. Anjali knees me in the mouth. Stars shoot across my vision, and she seizes my throat. Our skin-to-skin connection is all she needs. Her powers dive inside me and suffocate the sky from my lungs.

"Your kind are worthless scarabs."

Her asphyxiation process is torture. She squeezes out every puff of air, first from my muscles to weaken me, and then my organs. My pulse thuds slower, each beat a hollow echo, and my vision distorts.

I hear a whack, and Anjali slumps over.

I gasp for saving breaths. Drawing in the precious air reawakens my senses. Asha stands above me, clutching the broken leg of the rajah's throne. Still wheezing, I push Anjali off me and take her chakram. Asha tosses aside her makeshift club, her pale face stark against her red scars.

"Come on," I pant.

Using the chakram, I pry out the rocks jamming the door and force it open. The antechamber is full of hand wagons stacked with the ranis' weapons. Opposite our entry is the exit to the servants' passageway Asha spoke of.

Anjali is still passed out in the throne room, but voices echo in from the entry hall. I pile more daggers, haladies, and swords on top of two hand wagons. Asha and I both grab handles. She checks the servants' passageway and waves me forward.

Shouts erupt behind us. I only distinguish Hastin's voice.

"Let them have their measly steel. We haven't time for this. Return to the palace wall!"

We steer the hand wagons through the dim passageways and lug them one at a time up steep stairwells. Finally, Asha wedges open a low door, and we enter the Tigress Pavilion. Asha and I wheel the weapons out and stop to gather our breaths.

Natesa rushes over, Yatin stalking close behind her. The ranis, courtesans, and servants have congregated on the floor cushions. Opal stares up at the darkening sky, her eyes blank and ears listening.

Natesa lifts a khanda off the top of the pile. "Oh, how I've missed you. Good work, Deven."

"I couldn't have done it without Asha," I wheeze. The timid servant blushes. "Where's Brac?"

Yatin also chooses a khanda. "He isn't back yet. He mentioned something about going beyond the palace wall and then left right after you."

I bank down a rush of unease. This does not mean something went wrong. Returning from beyond the palace wall would take him longer. But how exactly did Brac cause the tremor that distracted the guards? I turn to Opal for her report.

"I'm sorry," she says. "My range of hearing is lessening as the army approaches. Udug's powers are dwarfing mine. I cannot hear anything outside the palace walls."

Explosions go off in the city. Some of the women shriek and duck. The winds kick up, and storm clouds steamroll across the sky, blotting out the sunset. Thunderheads crash, chased by flashes of lightning. The rebel army is deploying, and we must too.

"Will the women fight with us?" I ask.

"They're confused," answers Natesa. "We told them Rajah Tarek is dead, but some of them only gleaned that he's coming to release them and their children. We need to rally them."

We will start by returning their control.

I select my old friend, a military-grade khanda, and pick up a second. I carry both khandas to the women and lift my voice. "The imperial army has been deceived by a demon. Their counterfeit commander does not care for us or our empire. The true ruler of the Tarachand Empire is Prince Ashwin, and Kalinda Zacharias is your kindred. She has not forsaken you. She fled here to find and protect the prince. She knows that to save the empire she must preserve its heir."

Natesa comes to my side. "Tell them you trust the prince," she whispers.

I bristle. She wants me to lie?

Natesa huffs impatiently and addresses her peers. "Prince Ashwin gave Kindred Kalinda the choice to wed him or go free. He has never spoken of retaining me as his courtesan, and he won't force any of you to stay in wedlock or servitude to his inherited throne." The women murmur to each other in astonishment. "Prince Ashwin is a fair and noble ruler. He cares for his people and the fate of our empire."

A clatter of thunder foreshadows crooked bolts of lightning flashing overhead. The women cry out and stoop down. A baby wails, and mothers cradle their little ones nearer. I cannot bring myself to preach to these frightened women about the prince's virtues, but I can warn them about Udug.

"The demon rajah doesn't care for your well-being," I shout. "He hungers to wipe out our world." I hand my spare khanda to a rani with thick white scars on her arm. "You're free to decide your own fate. You can fight for your homeland—or stand by and watch it fall."

Parisa and Eshana rise and come forward to choose a weapon. Shyla passes her baby to a nursemaid and selects a sword. Asha would have received less training than most of the women here, yet she picks up two haladies. They and my friends join me, each armed, and we start for the doorway.

"Where are you going?" a rani calls.

"To fight," I reply. "If you wish for your children to live through the night, you'll pick up a weapon and come with us."

Outside the Tigress Pavilion, through the corridor casements, I see rebel soldiers stationed in the garden. Tremblers fortify the perimeter wall, and Galers conduct the thunderstorm. Repeated lightning strikes glint above. Farther out in the city, Udug's spooky blue flames flicker closer.

"Hastin knows we're coming," Opal says. "Deven, he's waiting for you in the entry hall."

Only the sister warriors who collected weapons stand with me. I do not wait for the other ranis and courtesans to come. I leave the wives' wing for the central palace.

At the landing of the curved stairway in the rotunda entry, Hastin shouts orders. Out the open main door, I see Tremblers erect a thick barrier of clay bricks to protect the front gate, and Aquifiers roll heavy water barrels into the grounds and set them on end. Anjali sits on a lower step of the opposite staircase, pressing a compress to the back of her head.

Hastin's gray eyes bore into mine. "Tell me why I shouldn't smash your bones to pieces for accosting my daughter."

"We're here to fight with you."

He leers, all surliness. "We don't need you interfering, Captain."

"General," I correct. "Prince Ashwin appointed me as head of the imperial army." Hastin sniffs in dismissal and starts to go. I call after him. "We deserve to go to battle too."

He revolves on his heels. "Were your people hunted and slaughtered?" he asks, then waits for my reply.

"No."

"I was away from home when the soldiers came to my village. They broke down my door and executed my wife and sons. I found Anjali, a newborn, bundled in a blanket. My wife had hidden her in a pot so the soldiers wouldn't find her."

"I'm sorry."

"I don't want your apology," he growls, trembling the floor. "I want you to stop wasting my time. Retreat to the wives' wing and take these women with you."

I follow his gaze to the lines of armed ranis and courtesans packing the curved staircases. Shyla and Asha lead the troops, Parisa and Eshana beside them. I do a swift head count. Nearly all the women have come.

I inflate my chest, my pride uncontainable. "These sister warriors can hold their ground in battle. Udug's army is ten thousand strong. You'd be a fool to refuse their aid."

The warlord balls his hands into fists, like two sledgehammers. He could grind my bones to dust. I have suffered a Trembler's grinding once before, but I do not let my remembrance of the agony move me. "You could never understand," he says. "You're not a father. All of this, unseating Tarek, seizing his palace, facing a demon, is to make a better world for my daughter." He points at Anjali on the staircase. "She is the reason I will not let you stand in my way."

"Many of these ranis and courtesans are mothers. They want their children to survive the night, just like you."

"I let their children live!" Hastin bellows, stamping so hard he dents the marble title. "I could have slaughtered Tarek's wives and sons like he slaughtered mine, but I showed them mercy! These women should drop to their knees and thank Anu they do not know true heartache."

In the wake of his echoed anger through the rotunda, I reply, "If our people do not come together, we will all know that sorrow. None of us will have a future."

Warning shouts reach us from outside the main entry. Then the palace walls shudder. The sister warriors clutch the staircase railing. I widen my stance, bracing until the shaking passes.

A rebel races in and reports. "They've armed their catapults!"

Hastin marches out, the ground vibrating with his every step. Anjali and I hurry after him. Night has fallen, driven away by the thunderheads. Booms ricochet from catapults at a distance, and several boulders sling toward the palace in an arch.

"Redirect!" shouts the warlord.

Winds propel the boulders back over the wall, into the city. A lightning bolt strikes one, breaking the boulder apart. Rocks the size of my fist shower the courtyard. Before they pelt us, Anjali blasts them away with a gust.

Aquifiers unleash a downpour from the storm clouds, drenching my turban and dripping into my eyes. The thick sheet of rain will hinder the army's view and slick the catapults' inner workings, but that will only slow them. Udug and his soldiers will reach the wall, and the bhutas will need more than winds and rain and quakes to defeat them. Bhuta powers are limited, and even with their combined strength, the rebels will tire against an army this size. We all pray the rebels can overpower Udug, but he has already breeched the city when they thought he could not. Every single warrior, bhuta or not, must stand against him.

"Hastin," I plead. "You need us."

The warlord taps his index finger agitatedly against his thigh, his gaze darting over the finished clay wall blocking the palace gate. "Very well. Fight at your own peril. Station your troops on the ramparts. They'll intercept the soldiers. The rebels will combat Udug."

"Father!" Anjali objects.

Hastin shushes her with a low growl and transfers his stony stare to me. "Move your sister warriors into position, General."

My troops will be the first line of defense up on the wall, but I have faith in our ability to hold the line against the soldiers. I return to the sister warriors waiting in the entry hall and scan their solemn countenances. "The rebels have accepted our aid. It is my great honor to lead you into battle. On your life, do not let the demon rajah pass through this gate. Defend your family and homeland. Make Ki proud."

The sister warriors hoist their weapons. Yatin, Natesa, and Opal do the same. Have I done wrong by them? Am I leading them to their doom? I plow through my fear before they detect my uncertainty. We need only hold out until Kali and the navy arrive.

Bowing my head, I offer up an earnest prayer. "Great Anu, preserve the Tarachand Empire and guide us to victory."

My troops repeat the prayer, a solemn echo of our united devotion. Then I pivot and lead them out under the war-strewn sky.

27

Kalinda

The cold cripples me halfway up the hill. I sway forward and land on all fours in the road. Between the rain and the deadness in my muscles, I cannot feel my feet. If the rebels' intent is to drive the invaders back with a storm, their strategy is working on at least one person.

Ashwin notices I have fallen behind and jogs back to fetch me. "Do you need to rest?"

"Just for a minute." I collapse against him. His soul-fire glows like a beacon, but I am so frozen not even his warmth appeals to me.

Gemi backtracks to us. "Is she hurt?"

"She just needs to get warm." Even to me, Ashwin's assurance sounds feeble. He lifts me into his arms and hefts me up the hill.

A catapult snaps nearby, flinging a boulder at the palace. Ashwin freezes and then sidesteps out of the middle of the road. Just when the threat is gone, a mighty gust redirects the boulder at the city. The projectile soars overhead and smashes into several huts on the neighboring road.

"Keep going," Gemi says, watching for more flying boulders.

She and Ashwin speed up, but everything within me turns sluggish, as though I am sinking in quicksand. Ashwin beelines for a large structure on the next higher road, the Brotherhood temple.

Gemi pries the front door open with the prongs of her trident. The temple corridors and chambers are fixed in shadows. She lights a lamp, and Ashwin pursues her into the chapel. The lamp's sparse glow reveals murals of the sky-god and his consort, Ki. They remind me of the mural in the Samiya temple chapel I grew up admiring.

"I've always wanted to learn to paint," I slur. Even my tongue is lethargic. "Jaya loved my sketches. Did you know I sketched you, Ashwin? Tarek thought I drew him, but he should've known better."

Ashwin lays me on the altar and touches my forehead. "Sweet Enlil, you're frozen."

"Am I?" I try to wiggle my fingers or toes but feel nothing.

Gemi tests my temperature for herself. She draws back, as though my skin burns. "I'll look for a blanket and dry clothes for her."

Ashwin expels a breath, his gratitude immense. "I'll start here. You check the other rooms."

Gemi lights another lamp and heads off.

Ashwin skims my cheek, though I hardly feel the gesture. "I'll be right back. I won't go far." He takes the lamp across the chapel to search the baskets along the far wall.

Shadows plunge into the gap of light, dropping around me. My muddled thoughts pull me back and forth between now and my childhood when I was confined to my sickbed. More than once, Healer Baka blanketed me in snow to reduce my fevers and calm the fire within me. Unlike Indah, I love the snow. But I would trade never seeing it again for the cure to this poison.

Perhaps this coldness *is* a feeling. For this gradual decay of my senses and faculties, this loss of control—this is how it must feel to die.

The realization comes at me as a piercing whisper. The end of my path does not lie far ahead. Death is here. In this sanctuary. Upon this hallowed altar.

A splinter of fear embeds itself inside me. I cannot leave this world now, not like this, with the godly part of me smothered. I watch the mural of Anu and Ki, brightened by Ashwin's faraway light, and wait for the gods to intervene.

Something else comes.

Tarek's smoky figure separates from the gloom that grips me. "Hello, love. I've always wished to have you laid before me on an altar."

I pry apart my chapped lips, my whisper tattered. "How did you find me?"

"I traveled the roadways of shadows. They led to every cover of darkness in the mortal realm." He sits beside me on the altar and fiddles with my wet hair. "I've come to be with you while you pass on from this life."

"Why?"

"You know why. You must believe me when I say I love you. I had high regard for my other wives. Even your mother, Yasmin. How I worshiped her. But you challenged me in a way no other woman did." He leans his mouth over my ear. "Do you know what will happen when the cold-fire inside you takes over? Your soul-fire will go out, and you will consist solely of the dark lineage within you. You will no longer belong to this world. You will belong in the Void with me."

My tears freeze to icy drops. I have made poor choices and done wrong, but I cannot bear an eternity in the dark with Tarek. That is my worst fate imaginable. "Please don't let that happen. Please help me."

He shifts his lips to my forehead. "Shh, love. Give in to the evernight, and you will be free from sorrow and strife."

Ashwin's lamp bobs, still across the chapel.

"Ashwin," I rasp.

Tarek strokes my chin. I manage to flinch, but his demanding touch pursues me, relentlessly taking, taking, taking. "He cannot see me. Only you. Our love binds us, Kalinda."

He traces my lips and caresses my hair. I try to scream or sob, but the numbness grips me. The cold is winning. *He* is winning.

My heart slows to a lurching plod. All physical awareness falls away, and stillness settles over me. The lack of feeling in my body hones the clarity of my mind.

Our bond is not of love but of hatred. I am anchoring Tarek to this world. I am giving him power and permission to enter my life.

Healer Baka once told me that peace is a choice. A decision not to be at odds with the world. I have been at odds with Tarek for so long, I know no other way. But we are not the same. I have to make a better choice than he did. I must let go, or I will earn a place with him.

Words swell up my throat, hurting everywhere. "I forgive you." He tilts closer to hear. I repeat myself, strongly. "I forgive you for claiming me. I only married you to end your life. I've loathed you since we met, but I cannot hold on to my hatred any longer. I forgive you for taking me from my home and ruining my dream of peace."

He unleashes an animalistic growl. "Kalinda, this is nonsense. You love me. You're my wife."

"I forgive you for murdering all those innocent bhutas and destroying their families. I forgive you for being a poor father to Ashwin and for your unkindness toward your wives and courtesans." My voice snags, but I push onward. "I . . . I even forgive you for taking away my best friend. I forgive you . . . for killing Jaya."

Tarek's itchy darkness weakens. He wrenches at my chin. "You owe me your life. I did as the gods willed by claiming you. I made you my kindred. Without me, you are no one. History will only remember you because of *me*."

More frozen tears cling to my eyelashes, blurring my view. "I forgive you because you brought Deven to me, you introduced me to Ashwin, and you united Natesa and me in friendship." His darkness recedes to smoke. He tries to silence me with his hand over my mouth, but I speak through him. "I forgive you, Tarek. For everything. Do not come to me anymore. Do not follow me in my shadow. I'll never summon you again."

"Kalinda!" Tarek's clawlike fingers snatch at my hair but pass right through. His haziness tremors in rage. "I am your husband! You'll never be rid of me. Never!"

Within me, a heaviness I am so accustomed to carrying falls away, and peace warms me enough to melt my icicle tears. "Good-bye, Tarek. I will pray for your soul."

He lunges for me, but like smoke dispersing into the sky, the last of Rajah Tarek fades.

Shaky breaths tumble in and out of me. Though I am still numb, lightness fills the emptiness of his parting. I have sought freedom and peace all my life. I thought I had to fight for them, earn them, or wait until the gods saw fit to grant me both. But peace of mind was always within reach.

Ashwin returns, his arms full of cloth. "I found this hung over a doorway." He drapes the heavy material over me. I recognize the tapestry as the one that conceals the tunnel leading to the palace. I saw it when I came here to raze many moons ago . . .

"Ashwin, pick up my dagger."

"What? Why?"

"Please. Just do it." He takes one of my mother's daggers by its turquoise hilt. "I need your help. I am too frozen to do this on my own. I want you to cut me." With great effort, I indicate the places on my wrists.

"You want me to *cut* you?"

"We need to let my blood. The healer in Lestari said it will help." For a time. Then the poison would return twofold, but I will reap those consequences later.

Ashwin backs up. "I cannot hurt you."

A blast discharges outside the chapel, shuddering the rafters. Ashwin comes behind me and hauls me into his lap. I recline into him, too wilted to move unassisted. From the explosions growing louder and nearer, we have no time to waste.

"You won't hurt me," I say. "I would do it myself if I could."

Ashwin lowers the blade to my arm but pulls away. "I cannot do this."

I drop my head against him, my breaths slow to strenuous draws. "I wouldn't ask if there were another way."

"The last time I was forced to act in desperation I unleashed a demon!" His heart charges against my back. "I did this to you, Kalinda. I released Udug. Deven has been right all along. I was selfish. I wanted . . . I wanted my heart's wish. I dreamed of the palace, the army, the people—and you."

"I've never blamed you for releasing Udug," I slur. The full agony of the frost returns. The numbness will debilitate me soon. "I've always wanted you to retain your throne. I need you to return my help." I roll my wrists up for him. "I'm dying, Ashwin. If you don't do this . . ."

He shoves at his tears. "Here and here?" He traces my skin with the blade.

"Yes." I speak between gasps. "I don't know what will emerge . . . when you break the skin . . . so stay behind me." The first time I razed, heat burst out so hot my tears puffed to steam.

He trembles the dagger over my wrist. He can do this, but he must trust me. Trust himself. Ashwin rests his blade against the smooth skin.

I inhale a tiny breath. "Go."

Ashwin cuts just deep enough to draw blood. Pain greets my demand, and a rush of freezing air flows out. The cold slaps me like a frigid wind. Ashwin suffers the onslaught and shifts the tip of the blade to my other arm, slices a little deeper, and even more winter rushes out.

He drops the blade and holds my bleeding wrists. I slouch against him, beads of sweat collecting at my temples. I close my eyes and search inside myself. My soul-fire burns in my inner sky. As I bleed into Ashwin's grip, the starlight becomes purer and more intense. I am still weak, far from my strongest self, but less disarrayed.

Gemi returns with her arms full of clothes and drops them with a gasp.

"Don't be alarmed," I say. "Ashwin helped me raze—"

An explosion above us drowns me out. Gemi covers her head, and Ashwin bends over me. Dust and clay fall from the ceiling, spattering the altar. The roof holds, but I no longer trust our security here.

Ashwin lets my wrists go and pales at the sight of his bloody hands.

Gemi passes him a cloth, covering them. "Clean up. I'll help Kalinda."

He puts some distance between us while Gemi binds my wrists with more cloth. They hurt, but the pain is more manageable than the cold and less terrifying than the numbness. The inner chill persists, ever lurking. I push my powers into my fingers. They glow blue instead of white, but my bleeding wrists bank the worst of Udug's cold-fire, for now.

She ties off my bandage. "I've never seen a Burner raze without an Aquifier present. It's too dangerous. Ashwin must care for you very much." Gemi's wistful tone is almost envious.

"He's a good man." The return of my senses brings with them sharpened worries. We have not come upon Deven in the city. I can scarcely consider the possible dangers he and my friends could be in. Too much could have gone awry.

Ashwin rejoins us. "We have to leave here."

"Let's find Hastin," I say. "He may be more open to an alliance now." I stand with Gemi's help and take a lamp to the corner where Ashwin unpinned the tapestry. Gemi and Ashwin come to view the opening, the princess carrying her trident. "This tunnel leads to the palace."

Ashwin squints down the stairwell. "Is this the only way?"

"It's better than running into the army in the city."

A blast rocks the temple. The ceiling sags and then crumbles, caving in. We dart down the stairs, debris tumbling after us. At the bottom, Gemi halts the landslide of rubble with her powers, sealing off the city above.

Ashwin swivels toward the open end of the passageway. "Well, that settles that." He extends the lamp in front of him, and we navigate into the city's underground.

28

Deven

The sister warriors line up on the ramparts. Yatin, Natesa, Opal, and I are in the center of the troops, on the wall near the gate. Everyone is silent, like the flashes of lightning overhead, while we watch the army steadily approach.

Galers conduct the storm from the palace balconies. Aquifiers are stationed beside open water barrels set around the grounds. Hastin and his Tremblers reinforce the outer wall from the courtyard and garden. The rebel army is small, about two hundred bhutas according to my estimate, approximately the same number of sister warriors.

Brac has not returned, a concern I have no time at the moment to resolve. I cannot leave my troops, so I hope and pray he finds us.

The torches of the army break through the roads. The infantry and archers fan out in front of the wall, men marching and artillery wagons creaking. They are as loud and mobile as we are motionless. Manas rides with the light cavalry and raises his hand for a halt. Hastin calls for the same. The rain and thunder stop, but the dark clouds still swirl, interspersed by bolts of lightning.

Udug rides up to Manas's side, identifiable by his glowing blue hands, and he dismounts. His ranks have diminished to nearly half the size, but we are still outnumbered by thousands. The disguised demon strides to the barricaded gate. The torches reveal his appearance. The sister warriors inhale in unison.

He directs his speech at the shaken women. "My wives, I have come to free you. Lay down your weapons and let me into our home."

"Hold your ground," I command. "Don't believe his lies."

Shyla answers, her tone hushed, "We know our husband. That isn't him."

"He isn't Tarek," Parisa and Eshana agree in tandem.

More ranis and courtesans murmur the same proclamation down the line. *He isn't Tarek.* I should not have doubted them or their conviction.

"Captain Naik," Udug calls out, "what falsehoods have you told my family?"

"I told them the truth. You don't belong in our world."

Udug scoffs and waves at Manas, who dismounts and starts for an ammunitions wagon. "I have no interest in destroying my palace in my effort to return to my home. Perhaps you and I can work out an exchange. You let me through the gate, and I won't execute your brother."

Manas drags Brac out of the wagon and throws him to the ground. Brac lands on his side, motionless. His wrists are bound with snakeroot. My heart dips so low I feel nothing but its quickening thrum.

"My scouts found him outside the palace wall. He was trying to light a palm tree on fire. Amusing, isn't it? You thought I held him captive when I didn't, and this is a surprise to you now." I grind my teeth down on a response. "Open the gate and you can have him."

Hastin climbs the ladder to the top of the wall and glowers at Udug. "General Naik is in no position to negotiate."

Manas sneers at the warlord's mention of my rank. I would relish his fuming if not for Brac, bound and unconscious at his feet.

"You want bloodshed?" Udug pushes his eerie blue fire into his hands. "You will lose this battle." He signals his men. "Archers ready!"

Hastin instructs his rebels. "Galers ready the sky! Tremblers hold the ground!"

Brac is so close, yet I cannot get to him. *How do I get to him?* The archers light their arrows aflame and aim toward the churning storm clouds.

"Get low!" I shout to my troops.

Manas calls, "Fire!"

Arrows whirl at us. I loop my arm over Asha and pull her down with me. Galers summon a gust that throws some of the fiery arrows back. The loose ones strike stone and bounce away. Natesa and Yatin crouch near us. An arrow barely misses Yatin's leg. Two sister warriors are struck.

The whizzing arrows stop, and I peer over the rampart. Brac has not moved. Soldiers heft ramps and prop them along the wall. Galer winds sweep the ramps into the clouds. But more soldiers bring additional ramps, pressing with them into the storm.

Udug heaves his blue fire at the barricaded gate. Hastin and several Tremblers fortify the clay bricks from their side, but on the outside, the blue fire melts a hole. I need to go now, while the Voider is distracted.

"Natesa," I say, and her attention snaps to me, "you're in charge. Remember, do not engage Udug, only the soldiers."

I leap over the wall onto a ramp. My knees jar, and I roll down the incline to the ground. I push up, and a talwar blade jabs at my middle. I reel away and draw my khanda on Manas.

"You're the general of who?" he demands. "Those women?"

"Sister warriors," I correct, parrying his thrust. Lightning touches down behind us, and the air crackles. Men scream. A catapult burns from the lightning strike. "You're serving the wrong master. Walk away, Manas."

"So you can save your dirty bhuta brother?" He elbows me in the side, and I spin away. Our blades stretch between us. "As soon as the rajah wins back his palace, I will keep your brother prisoner and let his blood every day. I will cut him over and over again." Manas swings his talwar, and our weapons clang. "He will beg for me to finish him."

"You're done hurting bhutas." I slam down, striking his bent knee, and then rotate and bury my khanda in his chest. "May Anu have mercy on your soul."

Manas jerks once and keels over. I wrench my sword from his chest. Behind me, soldiers brace ramps against the wall and scale them. A quake rattles them, and the ramps fall, slamming into the ground.

Hail the size of my fist pummels down and bashes the forefront of the troops. Men dive under wagons or catapults for shelter. The beating hail dents the catapult buckets and mangles the springs, rendering them unusable.

I run for Brac and cut away the snakeroot binding his wrists. His eyes snap open the second the poison is gone, and he moans. The last of the archers release more whirring, burning arrows. Sudden rains and winds redirect most of them back over the wall at us. Brac throws up a heatwave, singeing them. Ash drifts down and washes to silt in the downpour.

My brother clutches his chest. "Gods, burning something felt good."

I clap his shoulder and hoist him up. "A palm tree on fire?"

"It was a good idea. Would have worked too, if those scouts hadn't caught me."

Behind us, a quake opens a crater in the ground. Several rows of archers drop into the sinkhole. Past them, the road beneath the light cavalry warps and heaves. The spooked horses scatter and buck, throwing their riders. Many are trampled in the animals' retreat.

Brac scoops up a dropped shield. "Time to get out of the way."

We dash to the shelter of the wall. Sister warriors battle above us on the ramparts, but the wind and hail obscure my sight. Udug has burned a tunnel through the reinforced brick and hurls his unnatural fire at the last defense, the gate. The bars warp and melt. He opens his arms wide in triumph and passes through the huge, smoking hole. He need only step foot in the palace, and he will be free from Ashwin and his heart's wish.

Aquifiers wait for him on the other side. They draw streams of water from the prepositioned barrels and shoot. When the water suspends itself over the Voider's head, the streams harden to jagged icicles and rain down. The daggered ice impales Udug's back and the ground around him.

He yanks an icicle from his arm and throws it aside. His cold-fire burns the last of them away. His puncture wounds seep tarlike blood. But one after another, they seal up and heal.

"Your powers cannot harm me," Udug says. "The bhuta soul-fire I consumed protects me against your defenses."

Gods' mercy.

Another cloudburst unleashes directly over us. Brac and I slip through the palace gate to flee the onslaught of ricocheting hail.

The rebels are wreaking havoc inside the gate. Aquifiers shoot streams of water from the barrels at soldiers, drowning them by flooding their mouth and nose. Men are flung over the wall, blown into the night by Galers. I spot Opal among them, winnowing a soldier who gets too close. Tremblers use bricks and rocks to smash their opponents' skull. Despite the gruesome casualties, imperial soldiers continue to pour into the palace grounds.

The last of the light cavalry charges in, and a rider snaps a whip at Brac. The corded weapon, weighted by a trio of balls at the end, swings around his legs and trips him.

Though his arms and hands are free, Brac lies limp on his side. I slice through the cord, disconnecting him from the rider. While the soldier reaches for his khanda, I arch my blade overhead and cut him down.

I go to Brac and disentangle him. Up close, I see the whip is not made of leather but interconnected cords of a poisonous vine—snakeroot. The soldiers fashioned a weapon that can neutralize bhuta powers. All the riders have them.

"Son of a scorpion," Brac says, shaking out of the last of the weighted cord.

I help him stand. "Stay clear of those."

"You don't have to tell me." Brac pushes fire into his fingers. His abilities returned, he throws a curry-colored heatwave at another rider.

The sister warriors hold the line atop the wall, but I do not pick out Yatin or Natesa in the fray. Bodies are strung about, as many imperial soldiers as ranis. None I recognize, but the loss of life sickens me.

The ground trembles beneath us. Brac and I hunker down to withstand the tidal wave of quakes. Across the courtyard, a crevice opens in the ground between Hastin and Udug. A handful of unlucky soldiers fall in, their screams dying off. The warlord pulls the palace away from the demon, and a divide grows between them. We are stranded on the side the warlord pushed away, the chasm between us.

Udug treads up to the gulch. "You bhutas think you're such masters of nature." He manifests two burning balls and throws one to his left, one to his right. They blast through the rebel lines, clearing a path.

His soldiers march through the gate with ramps. Galers turn squalls on them, propelling them back. Some of the gusts pluck up the ramps and whirl the men off into the sky. But there are too many soldiers and ramps to stop them all. One unit reaches the gap, drops its ramp, and fashions a bridge to the other side.

Udug rushes across the ravine, and then a quake shakes the temporary bridge loose, and it falls out of sight.

"We have to get across!" Brac says.

The Galers tossing soldiers around gives me an idea. I grab a ramp and drag it to Opal. "Use your winds to throw me to the other side."

"Deven, that's dangerous!"

"Udug is already there. Do it!"

Brac throws a heatwave at a soldier behind me, and the man runs away screaming and covered in flames. "Send me too," Brac says.

Opal sees Udug on the palace side and gives in to our lunacy. "All right. Turn around and hold your breath."

Brac and I overlook the chasm and lift the ramp in front of us.

"I hope you know what you're doing," he says.

"I do." *I think.*

"On three," Opal says. Brac and I hold our breath. "One, two . . . !"

Gusts barrel at us. The ramp we are holding serves as a sail, lifting us over the chasm. I make the mistake of looking down into the ravine, but we soar over the expanse and drop the ramp, so we land and roll.

Brac rises beside me. He held on to his shield, and I kept my sword.

The rebels hold their ground in front of the palace, fighting the imperial troops that had attacked before the chasm opened. Soldiers howl as rebels winnow, leech, and grind their opponents. We join the fight, Brac with his fire and I with my sword.

Hastin and Anjali defend the entrance. Udug cuts at them with his powers. His flames burn Anjali's arm, and she falls back. Hastin roots himself in front of his daughter and throws bricks and pavers at the demon, who burns the debris to cinders.

Udug gains on Hastin until they are toe to toe. Hastin grabs Udug's throat to grind his bones. Their skin-to-skin connection backfires. Udug pushes his powers into him, and the warlord ruptures into blue light. Anjali cries out in rage but is too injured to confront the Voider.

The palace entry lies ahead, wide open.

I knock out a soldier and shout at Brac. He whirls around, sees Udug nearing the palace, and lobs a heatwave at his back.

Udug bunches his shoulders to absorb the hit, pivots, and returns fire. Brac ducks behind his shield, but the blast flings him over the gully. Opal cushions his fall with a well-timed gust. His shield protected him, but he is on the wrong side of the trench again.

Less than fifty strides, and Udug will be inside the palace.

I dash into his path, blocking the entry. My knees lock as I raise my khanda. I should run, hide, cower. I should apologize for my foolishness and beg for all our lives. But I have never been more certain that this is my path.

Udug strides up to me, hands blazing. "You're no champion, General. You're forgettable. A side dish. An afterthought." Blue flames flicker in his pupils. "You're ash in the wind."

His fire wallops me. I fly back into the palace, slide across the marble floor, and thump into the bottom step of the staircase. Pain slices across my skin and burns through my veins.

Prince Ashwin kneels at my side. Behind him, radiating astral light, Kali enters the main hall. And then everything shutters to black.

29

Kalinda

Deven's head slumps to the side. Smoke rises off his chest, the foul scent of scorched flesh stomach curdling. Udug's fire burned through his tunic, down to his skin. His flesh is charred and seared. The need to go to him claws at me, but Udug nears the threshold. *Anu, don't let Deven die,* I pray and cross to the palace door, leaving Ashwin to care for Deven.

"Don't come any farther," I shout to Udug.

"Dearest Kalinda," he purrs, "how are you enjoying the cold-fire I gifted you?"

"I don't care for your poison. Take it back."

His taunting laugh knocks against my tender spots. "I heard about the Samiya temple. I admire your nerve. Few mortals would dare burn down one of the gods' sanctuaries. You must admit now that you belong to the dark."

"No, Udug. I belong right here."

Behind him, across a gulley in the palace grounds, Yatin clobbers a soldier. Sister warriors combat more imperial troops, the onslaught contained on the far side of the ravine. Our side is strewn with the dead.

Udug paces sideways, his arrogant smile needling into my skin. He means to unnerve me with his resemblance to Tarek, but my heart is free. "You could have only survived this long by feasting upon another's soul-fire," he says. "Was it delicious? Did you savor their warmth?"

"I'm not like you." I ready my powers, my hands glowing greener by the second.

He glares at the blood dripping from my wrists. "You cannot carve out your true self. The demon part of you is too strong."

Udug strikes me with a torrent of cold-fire. I defend myself with my blue burning hands. His powers propel me back, my feet skidding across the ground. The flames disperse, and I stop. Udug is directly before me. He grabs my chin, fingers biting like icicles, and breathes his powers into my mouth and nose. The freezing poison slithers inside me, reawakening the toxins my bloodletting banked.

"Nothing strengthens a demon more than bhuta soul-fire," Udug croons. "Stepping into the palace is merely a formality. I have stored up enough powers to outlast every army in the world. Nothing in your realm can hurt me. The evernight is coming, Kalinda. You cannot stop us, but you can join us."

Udug lets go. I land sprawled at his feet. His powers return two-fold, insatiable in their greed. The flames frost my heart, digging icy shards into my muscles and weakening my bones to brittle. I spasm and writhe, bathing in a bitter sea.

He steps over me. Once he enters the palace, the heart's wish of the prince will be satisfied, and the blue flames inside me will prevail. My soul-fire will collapse, a broken star, and wherever Udug goes, I will go with him.

Perhaps I belong with him. His poison could not survive in me were I not part monster. Perhaps I should let him have me so he will leave this place.

I grip my teeth against the agony. "Bring me with you. Just stop the pain."

Udug watches me thrash around. "You wish to serve the God of the Evernight?"

"Yes," I pant. "Please, take your powers from me and I'll go with you."

He strides back slowly, prolonging my suffering, and bends over me. "I will collect my powers from you, but first you must swear fealty to the evernight. Do you vow to obey Kur in all things?"

I gaze across the room at Deven. Going with Udug would mean never seeing him again. Deven is too good for the Void. After this life, Anu will send him to the Beyond. I understand why we call it that now. The Beyond is outside mankind's reach—and beyond the reach of the Void. Darkness cannot dwell in the light. I can ultimately only belong to one or the other. And I know which god I serve.

"No." I reach for the vile cold-fire inside me, push it into my hands—and shoot it at him. My sapphire flames strike Udug's upper torso. He stumbles back, his shoulder scorched.

Nothing in *our* realm can hurt him.

I hurl more sapphire fire at him. He slings his own at me, but I roll out of its path. Mine slams him squarely in the middle. He flies backward through the palace door and lands in the entry, grasping at his charred chest.

The blue light in his hands dims. I stand over him, my fingers glowing sapphire.

"Darkness, return to me," he commands.

His powers within me abruptly still and disintegrate, as though dismantling my skeleton bone by bone. I stagger to my knees, my head washed with dizziness. Udug's cold poison pours out my nose and mouth and evaporates like fog. The plumes retreat until every last cold flame has left me.

I hunch over, trembling and faint, as though I have fallen from the sky. Udug lifts his hand to blast his muted powers at me, but he waivers and slackens. Tarek's empty gaze stares into nothing. Sulfur-scented smoke curls from his parted lips.

Udug recalled his powers from me to save himself, but he was already too injured to survive.

Warmth floods me, relighting my soul-fire and restocking my bhuta powers. I need not close my eyes and search for my inner star. I have lived so long in the dark, I recognize the light.

Across the entry, Ashwin kneels beside Deven. I start to drag myself over to them, but halfway there, Ashwin points behind me and whispers my name.

Blue light emanates from Tarek's corpse. The saturation of the azure brightness increases until it stings my eyes. I shield my sight, and when I look again, Tarek's body crumbles apart.

A scabby, pale demon with grotesque veins, bat-like fangs, and buggy eyes wriggles out of the carcass. The demon's skin is so translucent I can see its thumping heart. Its spiny, transparent wings unfurl, slimy with mucus and riddled with veins of tar.

Udug's true form grows larger until he stands taller than any man I know. Burns from our battle damaged one of his wings.

He arches his head and discharges a high-pitched screech. A chill breaks out over me. His otherworldly cry reaches the battlefield, and both sides pause. Udug bares his yellow-stained fangs and flaps his spiky wings. He rises in the rotunda, his wounded wing causing him to fly off-kilter. Finally, he swoops down and shoots out the door. The soldiers and sister warriors scream and dive from his path. The demon flies higher, soaring over the wall and city.

Gemi comes in from the corridor. Ashwin convinced her to take shelter after we arrived. "The demon can *fly*?" she says.

Deven groans. "Kali?"

I crawl to him and touch his chest. His burns have healed. His clothes are scorched, yet his skin is smooth and unblemished. "How?" I breathe.

"I don't know." Deven opens an arm to me. I lie down beside him and stroke his bearded chin.

Ashwin looks away from us. "Don't question a mercy from the gods."

Brac strides in, burn patches covering his trousers. "I lost sight of Udug over the desert."

"I thought he was dead," Gemi says.

"He cannot be killed," Ashwin replies bleakly, "only vanquished."

Out the open entryway, the bloodshed has ceased. When Udug flew away, the false rajah was unmasked. I hear Natesa calling for the imperial army to lay down their weapons and the rebels to rein in their powers. But peace arrives too late. Bodies litter the courtyard. Losses were sustained only on our side. Mankind's.

"What now?" I ask, laying my cheek against Deven's shoulder.

"Udug is injured. You saw him. He could barely fly out of here. Tomorrow, we'll figure out how best to pursue him. For right now, we get off this hard floor."

"In a minute." I nuzzle into the crook of his neck, and for the first time in a long while, I am warm.

My open balcony door teems with morning light. I stretch my toes to the end of my canopy bed, reaching for sunshine. Noises of working men rise from the garden. Last night, Gemi closed the gulch in the palace grounds, and Brac led the surrendered rebels to the dungeons. Most had exhausted their powers during battle, preventing them from fighting or fleeing. Including Anjali, just over half survived.

Ashwin sent Deven and me to rest and then took charge, sorting through the dead and overseeing aid for the wounded. Though I wanted to visit with the ranis and courtesans, I was glad to leave the battle site. Until yesterday, none of my palace friends were aware that I am a Burner. We have much work to do to reeducate our people about bhutas.

Deven rubs his foot up my insole, tickling me. I prod him with my toe to stop.

"We should get up," I say, a suggestion born of guilt more than desire.

Deven hooks me with his arm and drags me against him. "Not yet," he mutters sleepily.

After peeling ourselves off the marble floor, we stumbled to my old bedchamber and passed out from exhaustion. I hardly remember pushing the ridiculously huge pile of satin pillows from the bed and falling asleep beside Deven.

In thinking over last night, I remember the initial death toll—twenty-one ranis and forty-nine courtesans. We have yet to tally the soldiers, though the total missing and deceased is anticipated to be in the thousands. Deven also informed me of Rohan's demise. In turn, I told him of the destruction of the Samiya temple. My sorrow returns for all those who gave their lives, but some aspects of yesterday remain murky.

"How did you convince Hastin to unite with the sister warriors?"

Deven traces swirls across my arm. "I realized you were right and told him we needed to work together. I even gave a speech to the ranis and courtesans about your devotion to them."

I splay my fingers across his chest, cherishing the low flicker of his soul-fire. "You did?"

"I was very complimentary."

"Care to share what you said?"

He chuckles, a deep, rich sound. "Where's your humility?"

"I have none when it comes to your praise." I tuck my head beneath his chin and swing my leg over his, my knee high on his thigh. His sandalwood musk permeates my clothes and bedcovers.

"I told them you'll do what's right for the empire," he says, his voice husky.

I slide my fingers under his tunic neckline to erase more distance between us. "Ashwin will do what's right for them. Our people need to look to him for guidance."

Deven stops drawing on my arm. "Are you and he still . . . close?"

"No, at least not that way. What you saw between us wasn't real. Ashwin included me in his heart's wish. In his ideal empire, he imagined me at his side. His vision protected me from harm but also drew me to him."

Deven's voice pitches to a dissatisfied grumble. "He manipulated you to get close to him?"

I'm not explaining this well. "Neither of us knew his heart's wish had that much power. I figured it out in Samiya, and Ashwin had no idea. I would have told you if I knew." I make myself ask the question I have been dreading since our argument in Lestari. "Did you—or do you—really believe I'd choose Ashwin over you?"

"I prefer not to think that your choice is between him and me, but me and your throne."

I wrinkle my nose. "I never wished for my throne."

"But you need it to accomplish the change you wish to see in the empire." His answer is too smooth to convince me of his dispassion. Deven pretends not to care when he cares the most.

I rest my chin on his chest and gaze up at him. "I'm sorry I hurt you. I didn't think you'd leave angry."

"I didn't think you wouldn't say good-bye."

"I tried."

His composure cracks a little. "You did?"

"You were already in the air. Then Mathura came to see me . . ." *I did not intend to discuss his mother.* I rest my cheek on his chest again, but Deven is curious.

"Kali, what did my mother say?"

I decide against telling him that Mathura disapproves of our closeness, and instead, I summarize her opinion of me. "She thinks I'm foolish for not wanting to be a rani for the rest of my life."

"My mother had a different experience in the palace than you. She wasn't . . . valued as you and the other ranis were. To her, becoming a rani was the best life any courtesan could dream of. But she believes in you, Kali. And she's right. You're the rani the people need." Deven brings the back of my hand to his lips, kissing the symbol of the kindred. "But you aren't foolish for wishing for more. You have a right to your own dreams. That's why I left without saying good-bye. I was angry, but I also wanted you to make up your own mind." His heartbeat pounds against our chests. "Truthfully, I thought you'd choose Ashwin—er, your throne."

"I care for Ashwin like family, but I fell in love with you before I was a rani." I lay my hand upon his flat stomach. "The day will come when Ashwin will take his own wives, and I'll step down as the empire's kindred."

Deven smooths my hair from my shoulder. "And then?"

"And then . . . I want a future with you. A future of our own making."

He slides down the bed until we are eye level and strokes my hip. My nerves stir and tingle, hypersensitive to every glancing touch. His beard grazes my chin, his lips a head tilt away. "We have the same dream."

He throws the sun-scented blanket over our heads. I stretch out against him, and he kisses me until my limbs quiver and my skin burns for more. Silky sheets, wet lips, and needy hands overrun my senses. We explore each other in ways we were never allowed to and never dared. No fears temper our desires. We set our dreams free, soaring to limitless heights of fulfilled wishes.

Deven tries to shift away, but I pull him closer. "Don't go yet," I whisper.

He kisses me long and slow, melting me into my pillow, and then sits up and tugs on his trousers and white tunic. The baggy sleeves hang off his arms, and the low neckline reveals the hard cuts of his chest.

He looks back at me. "It's difficult to leave you."

I grab the hair at the back of his head and drag his lips over mine. When I let go, hunger shines from his eyes, and I know I can coax him to slide back under the covers with me.

My door to the corridor swings opens. Giggles move across the room, and then Shyla, Eshana, and Parisa pile on the mattress with us. Asha strolls in behind them carrying a meal tray, a bandage wound around one hand. The ranis are covered in various scrapes and bruises. Parisa's broken ribs are the worst injury. Bandages wrap around her torso beneath her sari. I do not miss what a mercy it is that we all survived.

"Morning, ladies," Deven says too brightly for my taste.

Parisa assesses the flattering fit of Deven's loose tunic. "Don't you mean good afternoon? The kindred has kept you preoccupied."

"Other way around, actually." Deven galls me by adding a wink.

Eshana fans herself at his suggestive tone. "The prince is looking for you, and we need to ask Kalinda a few questions." Her pointed stare is a push for Deven to leave.

"General Naik forgot to tell us how handsome the prince is," Parisa adds.

"Or how kind," says Shyla. Her baby girl, Rehan, sits on her lap and sucks one of her mother's few fingers on her maimed left hand. "He kissed Rehan on the head when he met her."

"My apologies." Deven taps my nose in farewell. "I'll leave you ladies to chat."

I sit up, clutching the blanket around me. "Do you want me to come with you and find out what the prince needs?" I am not dressed, but I can be in a moment. These women have just learned I am a Burner. I am nervous about what they will say.

Deven tosses one of the fallen bed pillows at me, and I catch it. "Stay and enjoy your friends." His eyes twinkle, knowing I would rather go with him, but Eshana and Parisa start to natter about Ashwin's dashing chin, and Deven slips out.

"The prince is even more attractive than Tarek, and—Oh, Kindred." Parisa picks up my hand and clucks her tongue. "Your nails are ghastly!"

Eshana runs her fingers down my tresses. "But she still has the comeliest hair."

"Perhaps the kindred wants to get out of bed," suggests Asha, folding her arms over her chest.

"Doesn't Asha look pretty?" Shyla notes of my servant. "We had a lot of free time while we were trapped in the Tigress Pavilion. It took some persuading, but Asha finally removed that hideous veil and let us do her nails. Even her toenails are painted!"

"Asha has always been beautiful," I reply, and her color turns as red as her nails.

"You could have told us you're a Burner," Shyla says, altering the tone of the mood.

I grip Rehan's little hand in mine to avoid meeting their gazes. "I was afraid you'd hate me."

Eshana throws her arms around me, followed by a more careful Parisa protecting her sore ribs. "We could never hate you, Kalinda," Eshana says "Your rank tournament brought peace to the palace." I jolt, certain I had done the opposite. "Your victory brought the courtesans and ranis together. We're sister warriors fighting alongside each other now instead of against one another."

"You're our kindred," Parisa adds. "We were so worried when you left."

I never imagined they would miss me. "I worried about you too."

Shyla cuddles Rehan closer. "Asha kept saying you'd return. None of us doubted you."

Asha holds herself removed from us. Eshana extends her arm to her, and Asha adds her hug to our collection. Seeing them treat her as an equal gives me hope that change can come to Tarachand.

"Um, Kalinda," Eshana says, letting me go, "I do believe you're nude."

Parisa smacks her side lightly. "As if you didn't know!"

"I didn't! I thought she and the general were . . ." Eshana flushes a flattering pink. "Oh my. Does this mean you have no claim on Prince Ashwin?"

Parisa tosses a pillow at her. "I was going to ask her!"

Their petty arguing draw laughs from the rest of us.

"You're free to pursue the prince." In fact, I look forward to witnessing how Ashwin fares against the vivacious Parisa and flirtatious Eshana.

A streak of red-orange zips past my open balcony. I slip into my robe and go outside. Tinley and Chare land in the garden. The other women rush out to view the mahati falcon. As they marvel over Chare, I dress, strapping on my mother's daggers as always, and rush downstairs.

The garden smells of ripe lemons dangling from their trees. I duck under one and walk up to Tinley. "I thought you left Tarachand."

"I did." She drinks from her water flask and continues. "We were returning to Paljor when the wind told me Udug escaped. Chare and I tracked him across the desert. He stopped there at dawn to tend to his injured wing. He'll rest during the day and travel at night."

All cheerfulness filters out of my good mood. "Is Udug headed for the gate?"

"He must be." Tinley turns her milky eyes to the clear sky. "The sun was full when I woke this morning."

At first, I do not understand her meaning, but as I shade my eyes and focus on the sun, I notice a slice of it is missing.

A shadow is eclipsing the sun's supernal light.

The eclipse is slight, but even as I stand here, the veil falls further and my dread deepens. Demon powers are stronger in the dark. Stopping Udug from opening the gate when the sun is fully eclipsed will be impossible.

Ashwin must have seen this and sought out Deven. The two are probably strategizing a plan right now. Ashwin will want to avoid hysteria, and Deven will employ our resources to stop Udug. The other sovereigns will see the sun disappearing and send help, but rallying our allies will take time. The darker the sky becomes, the less likely we are to stop Udug.

I eye the falcon munching on a mouse that she frightened out from behind a bush. "Could Chare fly fast enough to outpace Udug to Samiya?"

"He has a head start, so it'll be close. You'll make better time without me." Tinley pets her falcon's side with her long, sharp nails. "Chare is quicker than any wind I can summon, and my added weight would slow her."

"You were headed home," I say, remembering what she told me.

"I thought I'd try." Tinley tosses her silver hair behind her, a nonchalant gesture undone by the ache in her voice. "Truth be told, I miss it."

My gaze lifts to the battle-worn palace. Holes pockmark the walls and roofs, but the structure held. The palace is my home now. So many people I love are here, and they are finally free. I have to force Udug through the gate and vanquish him.

"Everything you need is in the saddlebag." Tinley hoists me into the woven saddle. Chare turns her head and blinks at me.

I grab a fistful of her neck feathers as I have observed her rider do. "Thank you, Tinley. Please tell General Naik and Prince Ashwin I said good-bye."

"I'm sure that'll pacify them," she says dryly. Tinley steps back and whistles through her teeth. "Chare, take Kalinda to Samiya. Show her what it is to outrun the wind."

The falcon opens her wings and launches into the sky. My stomach dives as we ascend over Vanhi. I steal one last glimpse of the palace, then we level off and zoom over the desert, racing the vanishing sun.

30

Deven

I come upon Brac in the upper corridor off the main entry. He is dazzling a pair of ranis with a single flame dancing over his palm. I clap him on the back. "I need you to come along and speak to Prince Ashwin with me."

Brac extinguishes the flame and sends a parting grin at the women. "I'll show you how I put out fire later," he says. They are all swoons and big eyes as my brother and I start down the staircase together.

"Those women know you're a Burner, and they aren't afraid of you?" I ask.

Brac pushes out a raw laugh. "Odd, isn't it? I spent my whole life hiding that I'm the most dangerous type of bhuta in the world. But now that the kindred saved the empire with her Burner powers, my rarity makes me desirable."

His buoyant voice holds an undercurrent of resentment. Brac may not need to conceal his powers any longer, but this sudden acceptance from society does not expunge the years he spent hiding in fear.

Natesa and Yatin sit on the opposite curved staircase. Yatin sports a black eye, and Natesa wears a sling for her dislocated shoulder.

"Deven! Brac!" Natesa waves us over . . . and keeps waving until we reach them. She fans out her hand to show me the lotus ring on her finger. "Yatin and I are intended to wed!"

Brac envelops her in a gentle hug. His enthusiasm may be fresher than mine, but I mean it wholeheartedly when I congratulate them.

"Yatin is inviting his mother and sisters to visit," Natesa says, stroking my friend's ropy beard. "He thinks they may move here to be near us."

I envy the straightness of their path. Although Kali and I found a temporary resolution for our rani and soldier dilemma, my position in the imperial army is uncertain, as is how I healed from Udug's fire blast. Kali accepted my miraculous recovery as a mercy from the gods, but I suspect something else shielded me from harm.

Natesa spots a courtesan up the stairway, then drags Yatin after her to show off her lotus ring to the next person.

I pause with Brac outside the throne room. "Brac, before we go in, I have something to tell you."

"Is it how you became general? Because Yatin already told me."

"No, it's about Mother." Brac rocks back on his heels, and his brow lifts in question. I hesitate to go on, but I started this conversation, and I must finish it. "I met a man in Lestari. Have you heard of Ambassador Chitt?"

"I have." Brac brushes ash from his tunic while I mull over the best phrasing. *I met your father.* Or, *Your father is alive.* Or maybe, *Mother is with your father. He looks like you. Rather, you look like him, only taller . . .*

Brac barks a laugh. "Deven, just say it."

"Ambassador Chitt is your father," I blurt out. Brac closes off his expression, cold as burned-out charcoal. Skies, I am fouling this up. "Mother confirmed it. They met here in Vanhi. He tried to acquire her from Rajah Tarek, but he refused his offers." When Brac still does not respond, I add, "You have his eyes."

Brac retains his straight-faced stare—and shrugs. "Is that all?"

"Yes, I— *What?*"

He grabs my stiff shoulder and jostles me. "Relax, Deven. I know Ambassador Chitt is my father. Hastin helped me piece it together a long time ago. It wasn't too difficult. Not many Burners visited Vanhi the year I was born, and Mother couldn't leave the palace, so that narrowed down the possibilities to one man."

"Skies alive, Brac." I scrub the tightness from the corners of my mouth. "You could have told me. Have you seen or spoken to Chitt?"

"I didn't feel the need to travel all the way to Lestari to meet a stranger. You and Mother are all the family I need." He frowns at my attempt to regain my composure. "What did you think would come of it?"

"I thought now that you have Mother and Chitt . . ."

Brac grabs my shoulder again softer and gives me a companionable shake. "We've been brothers our whole lives. No one can change that." He bumps his forehead into mine and grasps my neck, pressing me against him. "You're a good brother, Deven, but you worry more than you should."

I pat his back. "You haven't exactly made it easy on me. The sneaking off, the women . . ."

Brac pulls away, grinning slyly. "Speaking of women, that Princess Gemi is quite a lady."

"She likes to think she's persuasive."

Brac slings his arm around my neck and hauls me toward the throne room. "She seems to be working her charms on Ashwin."

Gemi and the boy prince? The princess has better taste than that.

We stroll into the throne room. Prince Ashwin stands before the dais, hands deep in his pockets, as he stares at his father's overturned throne. The rest of the room is in disarray, tables overturned and floor cushions in heaps. Princess Gemi waits off to the side. She sees our approach, but her attention is fixed on Ashwin.

Or maybe she isn't choosy.

My brother and I pause behind the prince. I leave Brac near Gemi and go to him.

"Prince Ashwin," I say, bowing.

He revolves while leaving his hands in his pockets. Exhaustion darkens the skin under his red-rimmed eyes. "General Naik. Oh, pardon me, Captain Naik . . . or is it just Deven?"

I lower my voice to extend only between us. "We should discuss that. I've been contemplating how I survived Udug's attack, and all I can settle upon is that someone with power protected me." Ashwin rakes a hand through his disheveled hair, on end from him ruffling it all night. "Kali told me the details of your heart's wish. She said it protected her, which I can understand given your, ah, closeness. What I don't understand is *why*. Why did you include *me* in your heart's wish?"

Ashwin reaches up to muss his hair again, stops, and shoves his hand back into his pockets. "I envisioned you as my general. The Turquoise Palace is your home. While I . . . this place is a stranger to me. I felt I couldn't succeed without both you and Kali. You're unerringly faithful in your devotion to the empire." He rests his foot on the bottom step of the dais, adjacent to the toppled throne. "Tarachand's future would be incomplete without you."

I believe him, and not just because I cannot think of another explanation for how I healed when Udug burned me, twice. I survived Udug's powers the same way Kalinda did—through Ashwin's love for the empire. I am humbled that I am included in his vision for the future. Me, a man who has struck him down, defied him, distrusted him, and generally disliked him. A man who Kalinda, the woman we both love, has repeatedly chosen over him. He may be an idealist, but his intent is pure.

"I owe you my life."

Ashwin sighs a little. "Consider it thanks for your years of service."

His swiftness to forgive my mistakes shames me. "I must apologize for my unruliness." Ashwin's gaze bounds to mine. "If you'll still have me, it would be my honor to serve as your general, Your Majesty." I bow as low as I would for the rajah. When I rise, Ashwin holds himself perfectly still except for his mouth, which ticks upward a tad.

"Thank you, General. I'm afraid I know little about leading our troops. They're confused by the bhutas among us. The commanders are keeping the men in line, but I fear a revolt. What would you—?"

A wind sweeps into the throne room, startling Princess Gemi, and then Opal charges in. "Deven, Kalinda has left. She flew away on Tinley's mahati falcon."

"Tinley?" I ask, recognizing the name from the trial tournament in the sultanate.

"Chief Naresh's daughter has been helping us," Ashwin explains.

"Kalinda has gone to Samiya." Opal flourishes her hand, and wind pushes the high draperies away, uncovering the upper windows. "Udug has crossed the desert. He's on his way up the mountains to open the gate to the Void." She points out the windows, and we squint up.

A piece of the sun has been shaved off.

"The celestial lights are dimming," Ashwin murmurs.

"Pardon?" Brac asks, his head jerking back in alarm.

"The dimming of the sun and stars is the definitive sign that the evernight is entering into our world." Ashwin rubs his forehead with his thumb. "We don't have long. The eclipse takes a day to complete . . . or was it two? I don't remember."

"What book did you read this in?" I ask.

"The text was lost in the Samiya temple fire." Ashwin grips his chin in contemplation. "I need a full report on our troops, General."

"The imperial army isn't fit to defeat Udug alone. The Lestarian Navy should arrive shortly, but we need a strategy to transport as many bhutas to Samiya as fast as possible." Fear leaves my voice jagged and torn. *Gods, Kali. Why did you go without us?* I gesture Brac forward. "This is my brother, Brac. He's a Burner and a soldier. He'll serve as my second-in-command."

"I'm grateful to have you, Commander," Ashwin says, accepting my hasty appointment.

Brac bows. "An honor, Your Majesty."

Opal's concentration goes out the doorway. "Deven, the Lestarian Navy has arrived."

All at once, we run for the door. Breaking ahead of everyone, I sprint to the main courtyard in front of the palace. Navy vessels pack the river that weaves to the city wall. Far past the last navy ship, another vessel plods up the river. I recognize the ship's yellow paint and curse under my breath. The sea raiders are relentless.

A commanding, statuesque girl with hair like lightning saunters up to my side. "You must be General Naik. I'm Tinley, Chief Naresh's daughter."

"*You* let Kali fly away on your falcon," I say.

"Kalinda asked me to tell you she's sorry she didn't say good-bye. I told her an apology wouldn't appease you."

Her honesty robs most of my annoyance. "You're right. It doesn't."

"Is that the Lestarian Navy?" Tinley asks, then sniffs, unimpressed. "A little late, aren't they?"

"They did their best."

"I'm sure," she says dryly. "My father has a fleet of airships piloted by Galers, not unlike the navy you see there. Only our fleet doesn't have to squeeze down a waterway to get where we need."

I do not respond to her blunt arrogance. Her opinion of the navy is moot, considering the Paljorian air fleet opted not to ally with us at all. I wander nearer to the contorted gate and step over a crack, all that remains of the crevice the warlord made.

Tinley keeps pace with me. "If you intend to help the kindred, I suggest you leave for Samiya right away."

I pinch the bridge of my nose. Just how I am supposed to do that? My mind whirls to take everything in.

Kali gone to Samiya. The navy's arrival. The sea raiders. Chief Naresh's daughter. Airships . . .

I spin toward Tinley. "How many Galers does it take to fly an airship?"

"Depends on the weight of the cargo." She leans her upper half away and crosses her arms over her chest. "Why?"

Ashwin and Gemi catch up, followed by Brac and Opal.

"Can you fly any vessel, or must it be one of your airships?" I ask Tinley, continuing our conversation without pause.

"With enough Galers and sails, we could fly this entire palace."

I gaze hard at the navy ships. "I know how to get to Vanhi, but I need more Galers. A lot of them."

"There's only me," Opal says. "The navy will have a couple dozen, but that's all."

"Princess Gemi," I say, "don't the sea raiders have Galers?"

Gemi wags a finger at me. "No, General. The sea raiders are profiteers. Captain Loc won't help us."

I gesture at the sun, becoming more eclipsed by the moment. "We show them that, and they will. We'll offer them the same bounty they would have gotten for capturing Prince Ashwin and Kali. Commander Brac, you and the princess meet with Captain Loc. The prince and I will speak to Admiral Rimba." My gaze slides to the long line of navy vessels, and I try to picture what they will look like airborne. "I have a feeling we're both in for a difficult conversation."

I head back inside to prepare my proposal for the admiral. The prince falls into step behind me.

"General," he starts, "I know what you have planned, but what will it cost me?"

"We need to prevent the sun from dying, and you're concerned about the fee?"

Ashwin stays with me, his strides clipped. "I'm afraid for Kali, and for us all, but I must consider every consequence and outcome."

We pass through the palace threshold, the gilded elephant door handles gleaming. I respect Ashwin's determination to place his people first, but he has missed the most vital part of his desired success—Kali is the heart of the new Tarachand.

Lose her, and the future is meaningless.

Irritation seeps into my voice. "The only certain outcome right now is Kali's death. You'd let her fall to keep your fortune?"

"I am rajah now," he answers, a sort of resigned acceptance of his mantle. "I cannot compromise for anyone."

We enter the throne room, our daylight dimming. "Your Majesty, we're far past compromised. We're nearly out of time."

31

Kalinda

I dismount Chare and set foot on snowy ground. The falcon immediately spreads her massive wings and launches off. She soars west, her fiery feathers blending in with the sunset. After almost an entire day of flying, the sun is more than three-quarters eclipsed. By dawn tomorrow, a mere crescent will rise. If the sun rises at all . . .

Before Chare landed, I relied upon a bird's-eye view of the area to search thoroughly for Udug within the frozen landscape. I did not see him. Tugging the bearskin closer, I hike over the hill, away from the frozen lake, past the burned forest, to the remains of the Sisterhood temple. The smoldering heat has gone. Ash and snow blanket the debris of what was the north tower. Part of the blackened piles of stone crumbled down the cliff to the gully below. I hold in tears. The tragic end of my home will never cease to devastate me.

Darkness falls, a crisp curtain of raw winter. My banked soul-fire simmers, sending heat to my extremities. I consumed all the food and water Tinley had in her saddlebag to stockpile my powers, and my inner star hums.

I traverse back to the skeletal woods and hunker down in my bearskin to wait for the stars. None come out to join me. Neither is the moon much company. Its weakening paleness provides no solace from the shadows. Anchored in the dark, I wait anxiously for the night to peel back its lips and bear fangs dripping of fate.

The sound of rocks sliding breaks the silence. I grip the cold handle of my mother's dagger and whisper my full name, *"Kalinda Zacharias."* Firmly grounded to my father's ancient line of Burners and my mother's sister warrior courage, I seek the scent of scorched sulfur.

Claws appear at the ledge of the cliff. A whitish demon with deformed features and hideous veined wings clambers up onto the ruins. I lower myself within the charred tree stumps. Udug extends his wings. The sharp bones stick up behind his head like a single set of antlers on a stag. He is jagged ice and splintering bones.

Udug jets into the sky and flies over the dead forest. I push through the trees, pursuing the flapping of his ugly wings. He lands near the shore of the frozen lake, its surface lit by the starving moon. I creep closer, quiet as my weight and caution can bear. Udug snaps his head up, revolves, and peers at me.

"Come to meet your master?" he sneers.

"We serve different gods."

"Where are your gods now?" Udug spreads his arms and wings to the lost stars and fading moonlight, which is frailer than when night fell.

I leave the dead forest, dagger firmly grasped. "They're watching over me."

"They've abandoned you," he counters. "Kur is the only god left here, and he has been restrained for too long." Udug steps backward to the lake with his clawed feet. I pace him, questioning his route. *Where is he going?* "He will be your almighty master. With his return, conviction in things believed but never seen will be obsolete. You will have your god hereto and forever to rule over all flesh, *in* the flesh."

"Mankind is not here to fulfill Kur's bidding."

"Do you not already live per your godly purpose? How will serving Kur be any different than living up to Anu's demands? Unlike Anu,

Kur will have no virtues for you to adhere to. Your purpose will be his." Udug steps onto the ice. Not trusting the thickness or stability of it, I pursue him but remain close to shore. He edges out to the center of the lake. "I have no regrets or sorrow." He throws out his wings and inhales the dark. "Through Kur, all will be free."

Something hits the ice under my feet. I jolt and nearly slip and fall. Craggy rifts spear across the lake. I scramble back to land. Shadows dart under the breaking surface. Udug tarries on the lake, leering with snaggy teeth. Great fissures tear open the frozen sheet to the water below. Figures jump out in an explosion. I shield myself against raining shards of ice.

A trio of demons wades out of the waters of the craterous lake. The largest demon's physique bulges of rocks. His giant frame is hardpacked and rigid as a mountain. His mouth is a slash, a grimace, and his eye sockets are crevices of nothing, like caverns. The demon lumbers closer, the ground trembling with each step.

The second biggest demon has a sinuous face like a dragon cobra, her scaly skin reminding me of a jungle crocodile's. A thick, rough tail drags behind her, as long as she is tall. Her three-forked tongue flicks in the air. Its trio of sharp tips resemble an urumi, an advanced warrior weapon with whiplike blades.

The demon third in line comes ashore chomping on a snow trout. Her razor teeth rip through the fish's flesh and bone. She bears resemblance to her aquatic prey: glassy, circular eyes, gills down her neck, finlike hands and feet, and iridescent scales. She swallows the trout's head whole in one bite.

Good gods, the *lake* is the gate to the Void.

Udug floats over the broken ice to shore and points at the rock man. "Meet Asag." Then the crocodile snake. "Edimmu." Lastly, fish eyes. "Lilu."

I push my powers into my hand, illuminating my quivering fingers, and carefully backtrack to the shadowed woods. Coming alone was a noble thought when I was up against a solitary demon. Confronting four demons by myself is lunacy.

Udug's siblings glare at the night sky.

"The moon issss too bright," Edimmu hisses, flicking her multi-forked tongue.

"The celestial powers are failing," Udug assures her.

Out of spite, Asag heaves a stone the size of my head at the moon, as though to knock it from its velvet curtain. His throw falls short, and he grumbles. I am less than ten paces from the cover of the forest when Edimmu tastes the air with her tongues.

"What'sss thisssss?" she asks.

Lilu sniffs, her neck gills flaring like nostrils. Her fish eyes roam to me. "It smells like . . . like us. Only is rotten."

"She's an offspring of Enlil," Udug explains. "Kur wants her preserved."

Asag answers, his voice a cavernous rumble. "You were supposed to bleed the light out of her before master arrives."

Blue flames ignite in Udug's hands. "We have time."

Asag picks up a hefty rock along the shore and hurls it at me. I leap out of its way and blast a heatwave at him. *It feels good to have my abilities back.* My fire strikes his chest and disperses. He sustains a small scorch mark.

I rise from my crouch. *Uh-oh.*

Edimmu unrolls her long tongues and flicks the air between us like a whip. A powerful gust throws me backward into the trees. I hit a log hard. When I look up, unblinking fish eyes stare down at me. Lilu grabs me with slimy hands. My veins lurch, tangling and knotting painfully.

"I'll leech the rotten light out of you," Lilu says, her voice a watery gurgle.

I buck in agony as she coaxes out my blood. Droplets bead from my pores, draining my strength. *I suffered this once. Never again.*

I scorch my fire at her, through her scaly skin. Lilu shrieks and scuffles away. I lob another heatwave after her, but Asag blocks it with a huge rock.

Udug flies into me, slamming me into the ground. I try to burn the demon with my hands, but my fire does not harm him. "I will cleanse you of your conscience, dear sister."

He starts to pour his cold-fire powers into me, but mighty gusts rip him off. Lying on my back, I clutch at the pain ebbing from my chest. Two Lestarian Navy vessels hover above, their multiplied ivory sails brimming in the high winds. I urge my mind to comprehend what I am seeing. The sea ship is *flying*.

Udug and his demon siblings retreat to the lakeshore. The vessels land near the road, and armed sailors shimmy down rope ladders. Several run to meet me. Deven and Ashwin lead the charge, Natesa and Yatin after them. Brac and Gemi take up the rear.

What in the skies . . . ? Captain Loc is a passenger of one of the vessels lowering itself to the ground. His crew of raiders, Opal, and Lestarian sailors navigates the navy ship, suspending it on their winds.

Udug and his demon siblings guard the lake, surveying the array of forces. They will not surrender their post unless we compel them.

"You brought the raiders?" I ask my friends, watching the ships land.

Deven looks me over with a troubled frown. I have stopped bleeding from every pore, but I must look a mess. He, however, is imposing in the strict lines of his navy-blue general's jacket. "We needed Galers, so His Majesty bought their loyalty."

"Temporarily," Ashwin adds.

Admiral Rimba joins us, leading his trident-wielding men. Captain Loc and his raiders, a mishmash of rogue bhutas, also boost our ranks.

"Kalinda, what are those hideous things?" Natesa asks, as though the demons' unsightliness were the worst side effect of their release.

"They're Udug's kin, here to guard the gate—the *lake*," I emphasize and then explain what they are, in haste. "We have to vanquish them before the celestial lights go out."

Deven eyes the failing moon. "Take your positions!" And then to Ashwin: "Your Majesty, stay at my right."

Ashwin grips his sword too low on the hilt. He has little practice or skill with a khanda. The world has never been drearier, but my loved ones remind me the gods are on our side.

Deven raises his sword. "All forward!"

We have marched halfway to the lakeshore when visibility reduces to graininess and our enemies wane to murky shadows. The ground shakes, an ongoing quake that rattles my knees, and the center of the lake boils.

Udug and his siblings howl gleefully at the darkening sky. The lake simmers faster, sending rippling waves that spill onto the shore. I grip the sleeve of Deven's wool jacket, fastening us together, as the moon and stars go under, drowned by the evernight.

32

Deven

My breath snags on nettles of terror. Every soldier experiences setbacks in battle, but never have I felt more vulnerable. Surrounded by my family, I have more to lose than my life. I could lose the people who make my life worth living.

Udug's and his siblings' jubilant screeches abruptly stop. Splashing fills the darkness, and then deep, resonant thuds vibrate up from the ground.

Something has risen out of the water. And it is *big*.

"Gods, Deven." Kali strangles my forearm, but I am grateful for our connection. More whispers of shock and horror resound around us in the impenetrable dark.

"What . . . what's out there?" Natesa whispers.

Booms approach our front line. The trembling ground knocks Kali and me back a step.

"I don't think you want to know," replies Opal. Her amplified hearing can detect what is coming our way through the obsidian night.

Brac tosses a heatwave at the forest across the way. His fire ignites the stubby alpine evergreens and strips back the darkness.

The biggest dragon mankind has ever beheld towers over us. Taller than what was once the north tower of the temple, the dragon's blue-black serpentine body glistens and drips icy water. His front feet and talons curl into the wet lakeshore. He drags his thick shape out of the water and roars, a gut-shaking bellow. Kali covers her ears, and I shrink down in my general's jacket. The dragon twists his neck, turning his long snout with pointed, wiry whiskers away from the firelight.

Kali lowers her hands and whispers, "I saw this war once in a mural in Ki's ancient underground temple. Kur was battling an army of men in the mountaintops."

"How did it look for us?" I ask.

"He burned the army to ashy silhouettes with his fiery breath."

Brac's fire gradually extinguishes. The snowy trees are poor kindling, so Opal feeds the flames with her winds. Fire brightens the area once more.

Kur hisses and narrows his gold eyes at the blaze. "I do not like the light." His guttural voice rumbles through me. I lock down my courage before it wriggles away.

"Kur!" Kali shouts. The dragon turns his head toward our troops. "Return to the Void and take your underlings with you!"

"Do you know what happened to the last mortal who threatened the First-Ever Dragon?" His talons claw ditches into the wet dirt. "I disemboweled him, splattered his entrails all over his friends, and picked my teeth with his spine." The god of the demons leans down so we can see our reflections in his gold eye. "I existed before these mountains were a pile of pebbles, before mankind was a grouping of stars Anu pilfered from the heavens for his gain. I am born of Tiamat, the saltwater-goddess, filled with fiery venom to avenge her and destroy all who worship her traitorous son Anu."

"Anu left this world to mankind and bhutas," Ashwin calls out.

Kur blinks at him. "You reek of fear, boy."

Ashwin raises his sword. Of all the times he could exhibit courage, this is not it. I edge in front of him, garnering Kur's notice.

He sniffs the air and his throaty voice hardens. "You . . . you smell of *sacrifice*. Your saccharine scent curdles my stomach." Kur sniffs again, and his glowing eye focuses on Kali. "You are mine. And another," he says of Brac. "Why do you stand with weaklings, children of the evernight?"

"My fate is my own," Kali says, boosting her chin.

Brac points to Udug and the other demons. "And who wants to look like them?"

The demon Kur hisses a breath that smells of decaying bodies. "I could drag you into the Void and teach you the way of the shadows." Kali hoists her dagger to him, gripping it crosswise in front of her, and Brac readies his axes. "No? Then you are finished."

Kur lifts his massive head, stretching until his whole height looms over us. Smoke billows from his nostrils.

"General," Admiral Rimba says, "your order?"

"Hold to the plan. Keep your ranks tight and push them back toward the gate."

"Delightful." Brac widens his stance and grips his axes.

Kur crooks one of his talons, and his underlings charge. The demons run at us, but Kur crouches like a snow leopard, opens his jaw wide, and blows a ribbon of fire at our ranks. I dive away from the heat, and Kali goes the opposite direction. She lands with Brac on the other side of the inferno. Ashwin lies beside me, his shirt on fire. He bats at it helplessly. I strip off my jacket and use it to beat out the flames.

Ashwin droops in relief. "Thank you."

"Don't thank me yet."

I haul him up. Across the way, Kali dashes into the fray, headed for Kur. I try to keep sight of her, but she disappears behind a line of Aquifiers, who draw water from the lake and shoot it at Lilu. The fishlike demon duels back, spraying her own streams of frigid water at them. Yatin and Natesa intercept Edimmu, the reptilian one, and Princess Gemi and Captain Loc go after the lumbering rock demon, Asag.

Suddenly I see Opal, opposing Udug on her own. Her brother's killer has trapped her against a high embankment over the ice-riddled lake.

I run to help her, dragging Ashwin after me, and push him behind a boulder. "Stay here!"

Opal is backed over the edge of the embankment, her heels meeting the drop-off. Udug gathers blue fire in his clawed hands. I sprint, khanda raised over my shoulder, and slice through his wing.

Udug yowls high and loud. Opal slides between his legs and jams her machete up through his thin-skinned belly. Black sludge oozes out. He retaliates with a burning sphere of cold-fire, blasting her.

She wrenches back and crumples.

Udug flies off with one fully functioning wing, cradling his injury.

The stench of charred flesh and seared muscle accosts me as I lean over the Galer. Burns cover more than half of her body, her skin completely gone along one arm and part of her neck.

I hold her unwounded hand. Her return grip loosens, her breaths wrenching gasps. Her suffering drags up my sorrow over Rohan's death. Once again, I can do nothing.

"Opal," I scratch out. "I'm sorry."

Her pained whimpers lessen, and her focus turns inward with startling intensity. The battlefield drifts off to another world. "I can hear them calling."

"Who?"

"My mother and Rohan. They're waiting for me."

I press her hand over my heart. "You should go to them."

"Yes . . ." Opal's torso jolts wildly, one final protest of her physical anguish, and her gaze empties of life.

My chin drops to my chest. *Anu, let her family receive her.* I grant myself a moment of grief and let her go.

The battle continues at my back, but my hearing still rings with Opal's final breaths. I will not leave her out in the open for our enemies to revel over. I carry her to Ashwin and set her behind the boulder. He lays my jacket over her middle, covering her wound.

Flashing flames draw my attention to the front line. Kali and Brac exchange fire blasts with Kur. The First-Ever Dragon will wear them out. Bhuta powers are limited. His are eternal.

A rock crashes into our boulder. I crouch over Ashwin as rubble pelts our backs. Asag pummels us with more splintering rocks. The boulder shielding us cracks from his repeated hits.

"Can you swim?" I ask Ashwin.

"Yes. Why?"

I grab a stone and toss it at Asag. It pings off the brute's chest. He extends his huge chest and growls.

"I don't think he likes that," Ashwin says.

"Run for the lake!"

We take off for the shore. I stay right behind the prince as a buffer between him and the demon. We pull ahead of the lumbering Asag, and I am knocked off my feet by a flying rock.

I fall forward, my bones jarring, and roll onto my back. Asag stomps on my chest and leaves his foot there. Something snaps inside me and releases pain. My spine presses into the ground and seals off my breath.

Ashwin runs into my side vision and swings his khanda at Asag. The blade clangs against the rock giant. Asag shoves the prince away, then removes his foot from my chest, only to aim his next stomp at my head.

A hand shoots through the demon's thick middle.

Princess Gemi yanks out a fistful of rocks. Asag tips backward in a slow-motion fall. Gemi sweeps him up in a wave of summoned dirt and heaves him into the lake. He smacks the surface and sinks underwater.

"So that's how you vanquish a demon," Princess Gemi pants, hands on her hips.

"Evidently," I croak, clutching my torso. Asag broke at least one of my ribs.

Gemi lifts Ashwin and hangs on to him. He will be safe with her. We need to vanquish three more demons, and I am not losing another soldier tonight.

"Stay together," I tell them as I fetch my sword and take off for the main battleground.

33

Kalinda

Kur will not be moved. No matter where Brac and I throw our fire, the demon god steps farther from the lake. The evernight will prevail if he gains more ground. I feel it in my gut.

Brac discharges another heatwave at the serpentine dragon, his unique orangey flame weaker than his last. Our powers do not penetrate Kur's scaly shell. We will soon lose the convenience of our soul-fire with this useless strategy.

Nature-fire feeds off the trees, lighting the battlefield. Serpents dance in the flames, swirling and twirling happily. Their flickering eyes trail me, worshipful and adoring in our mutual love of the light. I stretch my fingers to them.

My friends, I have missed you.

Fiery tendrils shoot out and encircle my body, hot and heady. I call them to action.

Create me a helpmate.

The nature-fire hisses, and more flames zip from the wildfire. They whirl and fasten together, combining ferocity. A monster forms between Kur and me, a serpentine beast that rises to the demon god's great height. The nature-fire mimics the First-Ever Dragon's proportions and builds a blazing dragon of his girth and stature with short legs; a sleek, proud neck; and a snappish snout. The fire dragon glows every color of Burners' powers—vivid white, sun yellow, scarlet—and inside the sweltering beast flickers a heart of sapphire.

I marvel at how rapidly and seamlessly the nature-fire melds into a tangible creature of one mind and purpose—to obey my command.

Brac lists back on his heels. "When did you learn to . . . ?"

"Guard my flank." My dragon lowers, and I mount it, absorbing the heat without suffering any injury. For I am fire, and fire is me.

Riding atop the immense dragon, I am eye to eye with Kur. His gaze flashes. "You think you can use fire against me? I am born of fire *and* venom."

I lean into my dragon, preparing to ride. "I am born of the stars, and I will see them shine again."

Push him to the lake. Let's take back the heavens.

My fire dragon drives its head into Kur's chest and muscles him back. Kur sidesteps and breathes flames. I duck behind my mount's head. The column blows past me, but his venomous fire rips small holes through my dragon.

Brac throws heatwaves at Kur's front feet. He bats Brac away with his talons, flinging him into the dark.

Fly!

My dragon launches into the sky. Kur chases us with a blast of white-blue cold-fire. We evade him by flying higher.

Kur lunges at my dragon's neck, clamps down with his jaws, and throws us to the ground. Everything jostles and trembles as we roll. I struggle to hang on until we are upright again. My dragon crouches, the path we rolled over scorched. Kur ejects more cold-fire at us, tearing new gaps in my dragon. The solidity of the flames beneath me begins to disperse.

As Kur gathers a finishing blast, an astounding sight appears.

Elephants? In the Alpanas?

Green-clad Janardanian warriors ride them, boasting their green-and-white dragon cobra flag. Mathura and Chitt ride together atop an elephant with ivory tusks. The herd stampedes onto the battleground. Land barges—large slabs of stone over rock wheels—roll to a halt. More elephant warriors charge off the barges into the front line, machetes raised.

They shake the ground, loosing the dirt at Kur's feet and hauling him toward the gate. Kur's tail crests the cold water. He vents a gut-rolling roar and blows fire at the forward row of elephant warriors. I watch in horror as his venomous cold-fire consumes rider and beast alike.

I hunch into my mount, fury boiling through me. *Get him!*

We take off. Kur releases a stream of flames. We swerve, but it hits the center of my dragon. The solid fire beneath me dissolves to spindles of smoke and steam. The world washes to red—orange—yellow—blue. I am falling. Fire tunnels around me in a whirlwind of shrieks and snaps.

I smack into the ground, my fire dragon fading above me, just like stars. The quakes continue with the stampeding elephants, the Tremblers relentless. They force Udug and his sister demons to the lake, but Kur is too big and heavy for tremors to topple him.

The First-Ever Dragon slams his front claw over me, locking me down. He pushes one pointed talon into my thigh. Something pops and tears. He digs in farther, puncturing through skin, meat, bone. My ears echo with screams. Only until I find my breath do I realize *I* am the one screaming.

Trembles carry off from the elephant warriors—distant booms in the ground. Kur's snout comes over me. One breath and he will burn me to a heap of ash.

"It's not too late to send you to the Void, my child. You will never suffer pain or regret again."

I push up against his talons. Nothing but venom burns within him to parch, cold and unyielding. Falling back on my powers, I send my scorching soul-fire into him.

Kur's brimstone breath cascades over me. "Your powers are insignificant. But another power dwells within you that can never fade. Come into the evernight." He squeezes, crushing my sides. His whiskers brush over my face, stinging like tentacles. "I can free you from your weak mortal chains. I can make you magnificent."

I reply through gritted teeth, "I already am."

Screeches fill the mountaintop, a clarion call to fight. A flock of mahati falcons, the birds of prey larger than any I have seen, dive at Kur, tearing furiously at the demon. He rears up, wrenching his claw out of my limb and releasing me from his clutches. I roll to my side, gasping and cradling my bleeding leg.

Tinley leads a unit of Paljorian warriors who ride the birds. As natural enemies to serpents, the mahatis fight on instinct. They circle Kur's crown in expert formation. Their talons scratch, and sharp beaks peck at his scaly hide. Indah and Pons ride in tandem upon a falcon with burgundy feathers and release crossbow bolts into Kur's breast. He chases the circling flock and breathes fire. They scatter, fast and agile, but he strikes one falcon, and it plummets into the lake.

"Kali!" Deven drops to his knees beside me.

"Deven, my leg—"

He strips off his tunic and ties it around my thigh. "It's all right. Don't think of it. You can outlast this."

I groan, a guttural wrench of pain, as he finishes tying the cloth. His white tunic is quickly stained crimson.

The mahati flock's harassment drives Kur into the lake up to his hind legs, but he knocks another two falcons from the sky with his venomous fire.

A sudden wind stirs, and in the distance, lit by lanterns, a fleet of Paljorian airships speeds into view. Chief Naresh directs his crew at the bow of the lead ship. The Galers on board summon the northern wind and propel gusts at Udug and his sisters.

The ground vibrates around Deven and me, stones hopping and jumping. Whitecaps cover the surface of the lake, whipped into a frenzy by the wind. Aquifiers stake their tridents through Lilu. She flies back into the waves, and they smother her. A Trembler traps Edimmu's flicking tongue with a boulder, and a landslide pitches her into the lake.

Udug, wounded, shoots blue fire at elephant warriors. Tinley dives at him with Chare. The falcon plucks him up, her talons ripping through his wings. Udug flails, but the falcon lowers to the water and drops him in. A swell sweeps him under.

We're winning. We're going to resurrect the morning. Anu is watching over us from Ekur on high. He will not let us fail.

The falcon warriors combating Kur take their leave to give room for the airships. Kur sends fire at the sky, striking one. The patchwork of sails ignites. The ship tips, the flames overtaking it, and careens into the land.

The other Paljorian airships harness the northern wind and converge on the demon dragon. Their gusts slide Deven and me into the knee-high frigid water. Deven stabs his sword through the cloth of my tunic, embedding the blade in the lakeshore and anchoring me to it. He grips the hilt, and I hold on to him.

The airships fly nearer, intensifying their winds. The Lestarian Navy pushes Kur with waves, adding to the impetus. The onslaught impels him farther into the choppy water.

Deven's hand slips. I catch his wrist before he flies away. I hang on to the sword, but his wet grip slides from mine. He spins off into the lake.

"No!"

I lose sight of him, foam and dirt in my eyes. He reappears swimming helplessly against the powerful currents and crosswinds.

"Someone help him!"

Indah and Pons's mahati dives, claws outstretched to pluck Deven up, but the gales knock them back, and they pinwheel out of range.

Kur sinks up to his breast. Deafening winds howl at me. My tunic rips free from the sword, but my hand holds me in place. Behind me, the lakeshore has been cleared for this attack. Even the Aquifiers conduct the waves from afar. I am the closest person to Deven.

I inhale a deep breath and let go.

Gusts pitch me across the water. I land among the chunks of ice, up to my neck in freezing waves. The cold bites, the water like teeth dragging me to Kur. Deven is caught in a tide pool near him, dipping in and out of sight.

A surge pushes me under. Another heaves me up and whirls me about. Kur's claws rake at the air. Our forces are sending all they have at him, but his head remains above water.

He needs a reason to go under.

I ride an incoming swell to him and latch on to his scaly side. With one hand, I reach inside him and pull, parching him. His venom powers flow into my burning palm. My fingers blister and boil. My skin melts, but I hold fast. I can stand his cold-fire. I can embrace the night.

Kur tries shaking me free. I hold on and bring the evernight into my bones. Agony screams up my arm, begging for me to stop. The pain spreads everywhere, excruciating to the point of near blindness.

Unable to draw in anymore, I let go, and a whitecap drags me from him. My fingers continue to shrivel, eaten by the cold venom I welcomed inside me.

"Kur!" I bellow.

He lowers his head to me, and I throw the cold-fire I parched back at him. The sapphire flames burn across his snout and ignite his whiskers. He tosses his head to extinguish them, but the venomous fire blazes across scales, indiscriminate in its destruction.

A wave pushes me under and up again. Kur is eye level. He lowers his snout to the water to put out the flames. I reach for the last of the cold-fire within me and send the blue-white flames at his eye. He roars and thrashes as it burns and burns.

"Kali!" Deven calls.

He is trapped in Kur's wake. Our gazes connect, both rife with terror. Kur is still on fire. Unable to withstand the pain, the demon god submerges to extinguish the flames.

The strength of his descent whips up a massive tow of crosscurrents. A maelstrom spins me around its outer radius. Closer to the center of the violent whirlpool, Deven is sucked under.

"No!"

I dive for him. Shadows writhe below, grasping and pulling like hooks. I push my powers into my uninjured hand, but the muted glow does not reveal Deven or Kur. The blackness is all-consuming. My lungs pang for air. But the darkness tugs at me, tying itself to my ankles like millstones.

I descend into the cold nothing, closer to the gate.

A sudden upsurge drills into my side. The current launches me into the air. I gasp, sputtering, as I am wrenched on a wave across the surface to shore. I land on the wet rocks, wilted and panting.

Cold chatters my teeth. My leg bleeds freely, lying limp and frozen before me. My injured hand—my *drawing* hand—is so mangled it is unrecognizable. Its flesh has been nearly eaten away, the remnants of the fiery venom still burning. I cradle my hand close and scan the waves between the chunks of ice for Deven.

Ashwin races up to me in the dying winds. "Kali, where's Deven?"

I concentrate, pushing against my draining consciousness. "Kur took him." Ashwin considers the roiling lake, his jaw hard-set. "He went under—"

"I'll find him, Kalinda." Ashwin tears off his jacket, splashes in, and dives underwater.

Just as he goes, Natesa and Yatin reach my side. She blanches at my disfigured hand and bloody thigh, and calls for Indah. The quivers within me rise to uncontrollable quakes.

"Where did the prince go, Kalinda?" Yatin says.

"Kur grabbed Deven. Ashwin dove in to find him."

Yatin pales and shouts to the troops behind us, "The prince is in the lake! Find him! Get him out before he's dragged through the gate!"

Aquifiers splash into the water up to their knees. The rest of the troops crowd along the shore and call their god by name.

"Anu, God of Storms . . . Ki, Mother of the Mountains . . . Enlil, Keeper of the Flame . . . Enki, Bearer of the Seas . . ."

Why are they praying? They should be jumping into the lake. They should be looking for Deven!

The stars blink into brightness, and the moon reveals its haunting eye. But their reappearance brings no joy. How dare the stars shine without him! How can they return when he is gone? How can the world be saved when my heart is destroyed?

The mournful praying continues, and so does my raging at the heavens. *Anu, you cannot! Deven is good. Kur cannot have him!*

A wave crashes nearby.

"I have him!" Admiral Rimba shouts.

Which one?

I compel my eyes to open. A man lies on the ground, soldiers crowded around him. I try to sit up, but the abrupt movement rips my strength away. Numbness steals over me.

Is it Deven?

Please, Anu. For all that is good in the world, you must bring him back.

A voice calls my name. I cannot tell whose. My spirit succumbs to the venom, and I float off into the night, seething at the stars.

34

Kalinda

The Tigress Pavilion is warm today. Spring awakens heat from the afternoon, and a breeze ushers in a sweetness scented of blooming irises and sun-warmed citrus. None of the women or girls complain, of course. We are content with the sunshine, remembering vividly a world under a broken sky.

I have finished my art lesson and dismissed my class. Sarita, my co-instructor, will come by later to pack up my supplies and return them to my chamber. She has an aptitude for painting, and as I may never sketch like I used to, she is a fine asset.

In the center of the pavilion, Parisa and Eshana demonstrate sparring strategies. Their class of temple wards sits cross-legged in front of the full weapon racks, their attention rapt on the ranis wielding staffs. Near the black-and-white-tiled fountain, Shyla shushes three girls for whispering instead of listening and then lectures them on the importance of honoring the land-goddess Ki and her sister warriors. Rehan toddles at her feet, her little hands clinging to her mother's knees.

Priestess Mita, Healer Baka, Sister Hetal, and all the other sisters kneel on floor cushions in the shade of a ruby-red canopy. They sip on chilled mint-and-lemon tea and select ice chips from a bucket to suck on or wipe across their brows. Natesa suggested the wards and sisters stay at the palace until another temple could be built. Construction may not begin for a long while, though, as benefactors are reluctant to contribute to our collection now that we have altered the terms of the Claiming. Some of them like the challenge of winning over a sister warrior, while others believe it is improper for women to select their occupation and, should they desire, a husband. Regardless, the land-goddess Ki always intended for women to have a choice, and so they will. Eventually we will collect enough funds to erect the first Sisterhood temple in Vanhi, but I already lament the day when these girls will leave us. They have been a pleasant distraction.

Parisa's voice carries across the pavilion. "We should always be kind to our sisters," she advises her pupils.

"Unless we're sparring," Eshana replies, bopping Parisa on the hip with her staff.

Their class giggles as the pair exchange a series of light, playful whacks. I slink by the row of girls, waving good-bye to the few who also attend my art course, and slip out.

In the corridor, I maneuver past men working high above on scaffolding. They spread white plaster across the wall and ceiling, patching holes and cracks in the ivory facade. Repairs on the palace began as soon as we returned to Vanhi.

Well, almost immediately. First, we banished the rebels to the arctic tundra. Anjali and the rest of Hastin's followers were commanded never to set foot in Tarachand again. Given their gross offenses, their punishment was a mercy. Then we helped our refugees relocate to their homes in Vanhi. The city is still partly empty, but more and more people return every day.

I stride through to the center of the palace. The gate to the rajah's private atrium hangs open. I start down the path of the well-tended garden, alive with leafy trees and brightly colored flowers, and pause before I step on a fallen lime. I pick up the ripe citrus with my left hand, my only hand. Indah had to amputate my other one. She told me afterward that demon venom is deadlier than a dragon cobra's, which can kill a man in fifteen minutes and an elephant in a few hours. Pons crafted me a prosthesis out of wood and leather, but I returned it to him so he could improve the cuff and strap. It fell off while I was teaching my art study. None of my students laughed—they have more respect for me than that—but I will not wear that hand again until it fits right.

Through the shady trees, Natesa and Yatin bustle about. Brac, Mathura, and Chitt help them set up for tonight's feast in celebration of the arrival of Princess Gemi and Datu Bulan, as well as Chief Naresh and Tinley. The lot of them flew in this morning. This is our first reunion since we left Samiya.

I was in terrible shape that day. I spent the entire flight back to Vanhi holed up in my cabin on the chief's airship, refusing to see anyone except Indah for my healing sessions.

Somedays I wish I had never left that cabin.

Setting down the lime, I back out of the atrium before my friends see me and invite me in. I ascend the staircase down to the main entry hall. Before I make it out the main palace door, Indah calls to me. She and Pons catch up, their bundled newborn cradled in his big arms.

"How was your visit with your father yesterday?" I ask Indah. Admiral Rimba and his wife came ahead of the datu and princess to spend more time with their daughter and grandchild.

"Better," Indah says, leading us into an alcove off the entry. "Whenever he's grumpy, I pass him the baby. Little by little, he'll accept our new family."

I heard the admiral's fit of temper while aboard the airship. He was none too happy about his daughter expecting a child out of wedlock, which evidently was more shameful to him than what Pons would experience from most Janardanians. Natesa told me later that he tried to wed Indah and Pons right then, in the air somewhere over northern

Tarachand. But Indah would not allow her father to pressure her into a life-changing commitment like marriage before she was ready.

The three of us, or four, including the baby, enter the hushed chapel. Burnt offerings lie in ash on the stone altar, the scent of sandalwood in the air. The chapel has rarely been empty since our return. Natesa and I burn sacrifices every day for those who perished on the mountaintop. I spend more time here than I do my bedchamber.

Pons holds their swaddled infant out for me to see.

I peer down at her. "She's already growing."

"She's twelve days old, and you haven't held her yet," Indah replies.

"Oh, I don't think—" Indah extracts her daughter from Pons's arms and places her in mine, and then pauses to see how I do with just one hand. I cuddle the sleeping baby snugly. "Have you decided on a name yet?"

"We chose Pons's mother's name, Jala." For a moment, I thought Indah said Jaya. "Pons and I discussed it. We'd like you to be Jala's godmother. I never told you, but when I was carrying Jala, I felt at peace around you. Perhaps that's why I took to you, despite our being competitors. Odd as it may be, my feelings strengthened as Jala grew. Even seeing her with you now feels right. Look how happy she is. It's as though she recognizes you."

Tears burn behind my nose. I cannot say if this little soul is Jaya come to her next life, or her contentment with me is Indah's imagination, but holding Jala does feel right. Nothing remains of the Samiya temple, but this little girl . . . she feels like home.

"Will you accept?" Pons asks.

"Of course." Although they both forgave me for parching Indah, I have still wondered if such a violation could or should ever be forgiven. Their entrusting me with Jala's welfare rids the last of my doubts, and I promise myself never to question them again.

The supper gong rings. Indah reaches for Jala, and I pass her to her mother. I will not wait another twelve days before I hold her again.

After I slip an incense stick into my pocket, I trail them out of the chapel.

"Are you coming to the feast?" Indah asks.

"I have something I need to do." I pretend not to notice her and Pons's frowns.

Indah gentles her tone. "Kalinda, you need to try to move on."

At some point, all my friends have given me this advice. But they do not tell me what I should move on *to*. They just want to push me over a cliff and see where I land.

"Thank you for letting me hold Jala," I say, and then resume my path out the front entry.

Palm fronds rustle beneath a quiet dusk. The palace gardens, recently restored to their prewar grandeur, are empty. Everyone is gathering for the feast. Natesa will spoil our guests with decadent dishes and desserts. She even arranged for dancers with bells on their ankles and wrists. My absence will disappoint them, but this is a happy occasion, and I cannot bring myself to fake a smile tonight.

My mother's tomb lies between the two eucalyptus trees on a pathway lined with sweet- and fruity-scented marigolds. My fingers tremble as I trace the newly carved names on the door beneath hers.

KISHAN ZACHARIAS.
GENERAL DEVEN NAIK.

I skim the rough imprint of Deven's name but feel only emptiness, as if the tomb were made of his body. When I awoke on the airship on the flight home from Samiya, my first question was: *Who? Who washed ashore?* Indah told me the Aquifiers brought back Ashwin, and then ice reformed over the lake, sealing off the gate. But I cannot accept that Deven is gone.

Pressing my palm over his name, I loiter on the threshold of the dead. The shadows around me deepen from dusky hues to inky velvet.

I inhale their dewy scent. Nighttime has become my haven. I can be myself in the dark.

An awareness prickles up my arms. Someone is watching me. Maybe it is wishful thinking, yet I strain to see through the shadows.

"I like that you still wear trousers," Ashwin says from behind me.

The sensation of being watched passes as I turn toward him. "You're late to the feast."

"As are you." He shoves his hands in his trouser pockets. He is dressed in his finery for supper, a gold embroidered scarlet tunic jacket with a stand-up collar and matching turban. "Everyone is having a grand time. Chitt offered to train Brac for his position. I want him for my bhuta ambassador."

"He'll be perfect," I say. Brac will ensure that all bhutas feel welcome in Tarachand, but also keep them in line. Recent squabbles have raised questions about how to enforce laws for those who misuse their powers. Bhuta children, especially, need proper rearing and training. I am certain that Brac's first assignment will be to create a fair solution.

Ashwin swings his shoulders casually, searching for something else to say. "Natesa and Yatin asked to hold their wedding here."

I do not believe his nonchalance. "They asked or you offered?"

"I may have suggested it. They don't have much means, what with their inn opening soon." Ashwin plucks a bloom from the neem tree and twirls it in his hand. "It's odd to plan a wedding that isn't mine. I've chosen four Virtue Guards but cannot commit to a single bride. The ranis and courtesans are growing restless waiting. I told them they can all stay . . . but there's only one name I wish to announce as my kindred."

"Ashwin," I say tiredly, "it's time that I step aside and let there be another."

"If the role of the kindred is unappealing, be my second or third wife."

"You know I cannot." My duty to the throne ended when I vanquished Kur. "I'll serve as your Burner Virtue Guard, though you really should choose one with two hands."

He sobers some. "How is your sketching coming along?"

"Slowly." I have sketched every day since returning to the palace, and have shown improvement, but my poor drawings are not much to boast about. "Ask Gemi to marry you, Ashwin. She'll be a good wife, and your union will strengthen foreign ties."

And as an heir, Gemi will understand Ashwin's need to place the empire first, above even her.

"You've thought through all the advantages," he says, tossing the flower aside.

"You know I'm right," I reply in kind. "It's time for you to marry. The empire needs ranis, and you're ready."

Ashwin skims his finger across my cheek. "I wish it could be you."

"You'll always place the empire first. That's how it should be. But I . . . I have a different dream for myself."

My attention strays to the shadows, to the sandalwood incense in my pocket, to the sketch in my bedchamber that I have been working on for a fortnight.

Ashwin takes my hand in his. "If you ever change your mind . . ."

"Thank you." I squeeze his fingers lightly.

He releases me without any more provocation. "Are you certain you won't join us? Yatin's older sisters are going to recite tales of the gods."

"That does sound divine, but I really am tired." This is my customary excuse to reduce his disappointment in my absence or lack of interest about the happenings in the palace. "Please send our guests my regards."

"I will." Ashwin tucks his hands in his trouser pockets and strolls off.

I pick up the bloom he dropped and lay it in front of the tomb. "Good night, Mother and Father."

By the time I return inside, the lamps are lit, and the aroma of rich spices from the feast permeates the corridors. The balcony doors in my bedchamber are closed, the room stifling. Asha has been busy as of late. She is apprenticing to become a healer under Baka. I kick off my sandals and open the exterior doors. A wind ripples the draperies. I remember a time when Deven and I cocooned inside them, tangled up and—

I stop myself before I cannot breathe, and I return to my bedchamber.

Parchment and charcoal sketches are spread out across my table. I light the lamp, casting a glow over the sketch on top. An intriguing portrayal, mostly finished, stares up at me. His angular jaw that I have grazed, sweeping cheekbones that I have cupped, full lips that I have kissed, and kind, resolute eyes.

His nose still is not straight. My left hand struggles with the evenness of the charcoal strokes that my right hand could once perform so deftly. It took me nearly three days to replicate the thickness of his eyelashes. But the effort must be put in.

The sketch will be of no use until his nose is correct.

I sit and try once more. Tiny trembles shake my left hand. The first line is wrong. I rub it clean and try once more. Then again . . . and again . . .

The oil lamp burns low. The moon rises high, and the far-off noises from the feast quiet. Charcoal stains my fingers and nails, and my back aches from hunching over. When I am certain I will never draw a perfect line again, I finally do it. I draw the straight slope of his nose, and there he is, in all his perfection.

My nerves spark, revitalizing my purpose. I have done it. I am ready.

I take out the sandalwood incense I pocketed from the chapel. My fingertip glows with fire, and I ignite the end. A steady flow of smoke rises, hazing the chamber, and treating my senses to a smell I have missed.

The sketch I toiled over for many days is laid on the table. Several moons' worth of preparation and practice to regain a level of artistry with my weaker hand waits for me. Is it good enough? Does it look like him? Or have I forgotten any details? The thought sets me ill at ease. I pick up the sketch and examine it, racking my memory. Each detail required painstaking care.

No, I haven't missed anything. This is him.

But if I am wrong. If I fail . . .

My nerves cannot handle another moment of wavering. I blow out the lantern, and shadows fall in around me. Pressing the sketch over my thudding heart, I survey the darkest corner of my chamber. Inhaling the sandalwood scent, I welcome the shadows, for they are the door to the evernight.

Anu, please let this be . . .

Closing my eyes, I go deep into my mind and unlock my chest of treasures. Memories of Deven Naik, alive and whole, fill me. His deep chuckle, satiny kiss, and soft beard. I continue the trail of memories, going back to the first time I saw him atop his horse, riding toward the temple. I hone my senses, seeking for a change in the dark, and open my eyes.

No one is here. I expand my sense of awareness, seeking a presence in my dim room, but grasp on to nothing.

Names hold power.

I call to him, first with my mind and heart, and then with my lips. "Deven Naik."

The shadows do not stir. I am speaking to myself, to a ghost, to a lost dream.

The tears come, though I scarcely feel them. They are so prevalent as of late, especially at night when I am alone. I set down the sketch and put out the incense.

Moonlight frosts my balcony. I shut the doors, deepening the shadows in my chamber, and trudge to my bed. Tears fill up my nose and throat. I always think they will drown me, but they never do. I drop onto the mound of frivolous pillows, though I have found one use for them. Selecting a square one, I press it over my face and release a sob. Natesa sometimes checks on me at night, and I do not want her to hear me.

I weep into the satin cloth until my head swims with a headache. Tossing it aside, I wipe at my soggy nose, and a sudden awareness passes over me.

Someone is here.

I capture my breath and slowly sit up.

A shadow of a man stands near the empty hearth. I gasp, my lips trembling. I can hardly exhale as he crosses to me. At the side of my bed, I push up and lift my fingers to his profile, the one I sketched this evening and dream of each night.

"Kali," Deven says at the same moment I touch his cheek.

He is real, not a pillar of dark. He pulses soul-fire.

"You came. You found me." I leap at him, and his arms lock around me, solid and strong. He is a real man. I grab him close as can be, terrified that if I let go he will disappear. "I knew you were alive. I looked for you in the shadows."

He buries his face in my hair. "I tried to come before, but the dark made it difficult. There are so many pathways to take. I felt you stronger tonight. You were like a beacon."

I lean back and cup his bearded chin. His serious eyes are the same rich brown. Though his hair is longer, the shaggy length frames and softens his stern jaw. He smells of his normal sandalwood, tagged on by a hint of mist. "You're trapped in the evernight?"

"Yes."

I run my hand down to his chest. His heart thuds regularly against my palm. "Does it hurt? Are you in pain?"

He strokes my hair. "It's dark, but I'm all right."

"I have to get you out of there. I know of a tale. Inanna's . . . *Inanna's Descent.* She saved her intended from death. She went down into the Void and found him. I can use my powers to come for you." I push a glow into my hand, and he starts to fade from view. I pull back on my soul-fire, and a frustrated groan lodges in my throat.

He is confined to shadows, unable to come into the light.

Do not cry. He doesn't need your weeping. But as I gaze at Deven once more, his soul-fire feels wrong, like a flame trapped behind glass.

"I'm so sorry. I should have done more, gone back in the lake after you or made the others onshore search harder and longer." My tears squeeze past my restraint. "I tried. I did."

He rests his forehead against mine. "When I went through the gate, I thought . . . I thought I was dead. I thought all light was gone from existence, and I . . . I wanted it to be. But each night I could feel you dreaming of me, wishing for me. You kept me from fading away. I couldn't have navigated through the shadows without you, Kali."

I run my hand up and down his arm.

He's alive. He's here.

"We'll find a way to bring you back," I promise. "I'm just grateful you're here now."

Deven presses his cheek to mine. "Now that I know the path, I'll come to you every night. Nothing will keep me away."

Hunger for life that I have not felt since he was taken quivers inside me. I throw my arms around him, and his kisses sprinkle my forehead. I swear on every star in the heavens, I will find a way to descend into the depths of the Void and bring him home. But for this moment, and in this time, I rest against him and revel in the bliss of the midnight hour.

CHARACTER GLOSSARY

Kalinda: orphan turned first queen, a Burner
Deven: general of the imperial army
Prince Ashwin: heir to the Tarachand Empire
Natesa: former imperial courtesan
Yatin: soldier, Deven's best friend
Brother Shaan: member of the Brotherhood
Indah: southern Aquifier, Virtue Guard
Pons: Galer, Virtue Guard
Brac: former rebel, Burner
Mathura: Deven's and Brac's mother, former imperial courtesan
Admiral Rimba: Indah's father, southern Aquifier
Captain Loc: captain of the raiders
Princess Gemi: heir to the Southern Isles, Trembler
Datu Bulan: ruler of the Southern Isles
Rohan: brother to Opal, Galer
Opal: sister to Rohan, Galer
Rajah Tarek: deceased ruler of the Tarachand Empire
The Voider (aka the demon rajah, Udug): demon unleashed from the Void
The demon Kur: ruler of the Void
Manas: general of the imperial army
Priestess Mita: leader of the Samiya temple

Jaya: Kalinda's deceased best friend
Healer Baka and Sister Hetal: sisters at the Samiya temple
Tinley: daughter of Chief Naresh, Galer
Chief Naresh: ruler of Paljor, Galer
Shyla, Parisa, and Eshana: ranis
Asha: palace servant
Hastin: the bhuta warlord and leader of the rebels, Trembler
Anjali: Hastin's daughter, Galer
Indira: rebel, northern Aquifier
Edimmu, Lilu, and Asag: demon siblings to Udug
Yasmin: Kalinda's deceased mother
Kishan: Kalinda's deceased father, Burner

ACKNOWLEDGMENTS

Sending praise and salutations to these fine individuals:

Jason Kirk, my commander in chief. Not an e-mail passes between us that I don't utter appreciation for you as my editor. You've made my publishing journey a true joy.

Clarence Haynes, the depth of your insightfulness and soulful questions knows no bounds. Without you, this book would be a shell. As you often say, excelsior and peace.

Kim Cowser, Brittany Jackson, and Kristin King, for your cheerleading from afar and your buzz-building efforts. You're my sister warrior street team.

My ever-supportive agent, Marlene Stringer. I fulfilled my vision for this world and story because of your unfailing support. Thank you for loving Kalinda.

Kate Coursey, we are bosom buddies for eternity. You're never getting rid of me.

Fellow sister warriors: Veeda Bybee, Kathryn Purdie, Breeana Shields, Kate Watson, Tricia Levenseller, Charlie Holmberg, Caitlyn McFarland, Lauri Schoenfeld, Angie Cothran, Erin Summerill, Sierra Abrams, Brekke Felt, Shaila Patel, Leah Henderson, Jessie Farr, Catherine Dowse, Michal Cameron, Mikki Kells, and Wendy Jessen. You are all kindreds in my eyes.

Fellow warrior book lovers: Krysti Meyer, Sarah Cleverley, Beth Edwards, Benjamin Alderson, Jaime Arnold, Gabrielle Saunders, and Rachel Piper.

Michael Bacera, for picking up the phone and answering my weird questions.

Jessica Springer, for cheering me on. Got that book written yet? (A promise is a promise.)

My parents, Debby and Keith, for teaching me how to dream big and for cheering me on as I do. Eve and Chris, for your sensitivity for all things cultural. Sarah and Stacey, for GIF texts and political rants.

Joseph, Julian, Danielle, and Ryan, for tolerating a year of go, go, go. You are the most amazing kids. You must be. Otherwise I would still be drafting.

John, my best friend and sweetheart. You step into my shoes and never complain when I ask for five more minutes to finish the sentence I'm on. Someday that may be true . . .

My readers, for your e-mails, tweets, and instant messages. Your kind words bring me joy. And to every other reader who took time out of their busy life to read my words. You're pretty awesome.

Lastly, but most importantly, my father in heaven. Three whispered words on a night when I felt hopelessly lost gave me direction for years to come. Thank you for the inspiration and fortitude to see this through.

ABOUT THE AUTHOR

Photo © 2015 Erin Summerill

Emily R. King is a writer of fantasy and the author of The Hundredth Queen Series. Born in Canada and raised in the United States, she is a shark advocate, a consumer of gummy bears, and an islander at heart, but her greatest interests are her four children. Emily is a member of the Society of Children's Book Writers and Illustrators and an active participant in her local writers' community. She lives in Northern Utah with her family and their cantankerous cat. Visit her at www.emilyrking.com.